WHEN MAPLES TURN RED

Growing Up in the Adirondacks

A Novel by

RICHARD KING

outskirtspress
DENVER, COLORADO

When Maples Turn Red
Growing Up in the Adirondacks

v2.0

Author Information: papatya@gmail.com

Outskirts Press, Inc.
http://www.outskirtspress.com

Paperback ISBN: 978-1-4787-1228-2
Hardback ISBN: 978-1-4787-0601-4

PRINTED IN THE UNITED STATES OF AMERICA

Also by Richard King

Imaginators

Adventures of Harry Sasquatch

Snorty the Moose

Sensory Approach to Creative Writing

Acknowledgements

So many people have offered me encouragement that I can't remember them all. Certainly I must single out my wife, Maggie, for helping me persevere. Also, the editing, typing, and encouragement by Jane Ehlers were instrumental in psyching me up for the final push.

Introduction

The ironical part of this story is that even though I am now an octogenarian, the main character is a teenager. A person can't help but ask himself if an eighty-year old remembers what it was like being young.

The reason for the age spread is that the story was started long ago. First it kept running through my mind, and finally the words seemed to pour out as if I had become the character. It became a passion and demanded a written life.

At first the writing went rapidly, but then numerous health problems arose, one after another. As each issue presented itself to me, the story was pushed aside yet again, awaiting a return to health. There were times when I despaired, thinking that I would never complete the manuscript. Now, finally, here it is.

Several people who read a few chapters asked me if it was autobiographical. The answer is no. The setting, nevertheless, is borrowed from my youth. Any similarities to persons living or dead are purely incidental.

Part One

Chapter 1

In the early spring of 1832, a few months before Guillaume Coulbron was born, his father and mother sold their small dairy farm on the north shore of the Saint Lawrence River near the town of Beauharnois, Quebec, and purchased a larger farm farther south. This was located barely inside the border of New York State in a remote region which was only then being developed into agricultural land. The tiny village closest to the farm was called Churubusco, and it was in his parents' new farmhouse that little Guy drew his first breath of fresh air.

Guy grew up as a farm boy with four brothers and three sisters, learning many skills and developing exuberance for life and family living. He worked hard, played hard, and became a strong, handsome young man. His parents died shortly before his nineteenth birthday, and from then on he was on his own.

Although his parents had been born in Canada and continued to speak Quebecois-French throughout their lives, he was happy to be an American. This, he knew, was a land where a person who made good plans and had the determination to succeed could make a reputation for himself and be able to take good care of his family.

Being the middle son in a family where there were five male offspring meant that Guillaume received no more than a meager inheritance. This consisted of his father's bootmaking tools, his youngest mare, and his farm wagon. Guy's sisters had already married, and his two youngest brothers stayed on to run the farm. The two older men had already taken jobs farther south in Plattsburgh, New York.

Guillaume decided to use what he had been given and became a leather worker. He perfected his craftsmanship while working as an itinerant boot and harness maker in the northern fringes of upstate

New York. For five years Guillaume moved from one family to the next, teaching farmers how to tan their animal hides and then using their prepared skins to make leather goods for them. At the end of this time he was an expert craftsman. He could make a two-horse set of harnesses in one day or, if a client preferred, two first-class pairs of boots.

He travelled by horse and wagon from farm to farm making boots and harnesses wherever his expertise was needed. He was single in those days, but he did not intend to remain a bachelor forever. Being lodged a week or two at a time with one family before moving on to the next gave him ample opportunity to meet and live in relative proximity to quite a number of eligible daughters.

At the age of twenty-four Guillaume Coulbron had no intention of founding a dynasty. He did, however, feel that it was high time to make his move in life. That year he met and courted the curly-haired daughter of one of his clients. While making shoes for the Bissette family near Chateauguay, he slept in their house and ate hearty meals with them at their dining table. Their oldest daughter Marguerite volunteered to wash and mend his clothing and, when the occasion offered itself, she practiced her female wiles and let it be known to him that she was interested in knowing him even better. A month later when Guillaume returned to the farm to repair some of her father's harnesses, Marguerite invited him to a box social, followed by a square dance, which she just happened to have arranged for the enjoyment of everyone who wished to participate.

Guy accepted the invitation willingly and with no small amount of expectation. The day before the scheduled event, Guy and several other men gathered at the school house to stack some of the school desks in the woodshed in order to make room for the dancing. They decorated the room with farm implements, and created a straw cow held together with twine. To complete their bogus bovine the men painted a cowbell in vivid pink and attached this to the straw creature's neck with a matching ribbon. They also braided a rope tail for Bossy so that it could be used for a game of pin the tail on the heifer. The ladies, meanwhile, were preparing and decorating their box lunches, as well as primping themselves for the social.

The next evening, seated in desks that were too small for them, Marguerite and Guy gazed longingly at one another while eating slices of the wild blueberry pie which she had baked especially for him. Then they whirled through the country dances until they were dizzy. When the fiddler finally released the tension on his bow, signaling the end of the dance, the young couple disappeared for a few minutes and stood clinging to one another inside the woodshed where the aroma of the freshly split maple wood helped Mother Nature practice her magic spell. This rapid courtship evolved into a happy and stable marriage.

The young couple was very much in love. They rented a room from one of Marguerite's sisters, but Guy's job kept them apart for weeks at a time, and they felt this separation to be too great a hardship. As a *célibataire*, Guillaume had been saving his money for five years but, now as a family man, he had growing responsibilities and needed a greater income.

His leather work brought him one day to the iron-mining village of Rock Mountain in the northern Adirondacks. This town was located some miles south of the region where he had previously been working. Here, on the western slope of the mountain, a mine, whose veins produced shiny black crystals of magnetite ore, had been operating sporadically since well before the civil war, depending on the needs of small forges and local blacksmiths.

Now, as the nation's population was growing and industrial needs expanding, the demand for iron was increasing in like proportion. A consortium of iron and coal interests in Pennsylvania purchased the mining property on Rock Mountain and built a railroad to the mine so that blooms from the adjacent forge could be shipped to the steel mills which they owned. During the mine expansion many kinds of workers other than miners were hired. Guillaume Coulbron saw this as an opportunity and went there to make harnesses for the mules which the miners used to haul ore cars from deep underground.

Guillaume and Marguerite rented a two-room log house in the mining village of Rock Mountain next to a pile of dusty ore tailings and here their son Wilfrid was born. Neither parent liked living in this gritty little town filled with brawling, immigrant miners. They talked the situation over one night while the infant Wilfrid slept in his hand-carved cradle and agreed that a farm would be a better place to live out the lives that God had granted them. They agreed, likewise, that a farm would be the best place to raise their children.

They were content, nevertheless, that most of Guy's harness work so far had been accomplished above ground since cave-ins at the mine and blasting accidents were becoming increasingly common. In addition, some miners were known to contract a chronic disease called silicosis. Although mining officials disputed the doctors' findings, miners knew that the disease was the result of the inhalation of silicon dust that was raised by drilling and blasting with explosives in the narrow confines of mining shafts. Only rarely was Guillaume obliged to enter the big steel cage with the hard-rock miners and descend a thousand feet or more into the bowels of the earth with a carbide lamp strapped to his helmet. After an occasional underground shift which he spent mending mule harnesses, he was more than happy to return home to the comfort and security of his family. Underground mining was not to his liking, so he continued to save his money, hoping that the right opportunity might present itself.

The mules were even less lucky than the miners. Once these animals entered the mine, few of them were ever allowed to see sunlight again. In time they would become blind due to their long hours in the darkness, and when a mule died, its corpse was stripped of its hide, which Guillaume then tanned and used in making more leather harnesses. Miners disposed of the beasts' carcasses by dumping them down an abandoned ore shaft and burying them under heaps of rubble.

The Crystal Penn Mining Company had managed to acquire a huge acreage of forested land to fill its need for mine timbers and charcoal to fuel the Catalan forge. When Guillaume learned that the company was offering a portion of its land for sale, he was excited and rushed to the local company office to find out the details of the proposed sale and investigate the possibility of starting a farm on a piece of it.

A company official laid out a map on his desk, and when Guillaume noted the availability of land in a lake valley that stretched out on the east slope of Rock Mountain several miles away from the mining village, he was determined to check it out. This, he hoped, would become the place where he and his wife Marguerite might fulfill their dream.

One April morning while he could still see drifts of crunchy snow hiding in spots which resisted the spring thaw, Guillaume got up early on his day off. The air was clear and crisp. He kissed his wife and child, and armed with a packet of maps, set out to find their land. As he walked to the livery stable that morning, he was glad that he had not sold his horse and wagon when a drayman had offered to buy them. Not only did he need them now to explore for farm land, but he would most certainly need them for developing his farm.

Guillaume Coulbron turned east from the mining village and headed for Echo Lake. The dirt road was barely passable because of recent thawing, and the wagon wheels made deep ruts which oozed rivulets of melting water. The road was fairly wide, however, and some parts of it had even been gravelled. Guillaume noticed that where the route was marshy, workmen had laid logs across in corduroy fashion. He knew this road was used frequently for hauling charcoal from the kilns to the mining company's forge.

He first spotted the lake when he reached the crest of Teamster Hill. He gazed out at the blue expanse of water that reminded him of the Saint Lawrence River which he had seen several times in his travels. He rested his horse and stepped to the ground to stretch his legs. He patted the horse's flank and talked to it kindly.

"You see that land on the north side, Nell? Somewhere over there you and I are going to build a farm. And you are going to drop me some strong, healthy foals because I'll be needing more horses soon."

The man and the horse had already crossed the narrow gauge railroad twice that morning, and now they crossed it a third time before reaching the shore of Echo Lake. When they came to a brook which drained into the lake, Guillaume relaxed his grip on the reins and said, "Whoa, Girl."

The horse dipped her head and drank deeply from the stream. Guillaume looked in the direction of the lake and was startled to notice a bearded man rowing a skiff toward the mouth of the brook. He tied Nell's reins to a bush and hurried toward the shore, wanting to meet his first new neighbor.

The boatmen beached his vessel and stepped ashore next to Guillaume. Guillaume started the conversation in English, but when the other man responded in French, Guy switched languages effortlessly, and the two of them spoke rapidly in the *patois* Guy had learned as a child. The neighbor was wearing a red Mackinaw which he had repaired repeatedly with fish line. He announced proudly that he was the first white person to ever live at Echo Lake. He said that, except for his dog Abe, he lived alone in a dugout cabin on the other side of the lake. He seemed proud of the fact that he had lived there for over thirty-five years, and that even though he was past seventy, he still made his living by catching lake trout and selling his catch to people who worked at the state prison farther to the east.

Sangimaux pointed to the pile of trout lying in his boat and, still speaking in French, announced, "The ice, her, she just went out yesterday. This is one of the best time of year to catch the big trout. You want to buy some? I sell you what you want. Look! You see there is still a little bit of ice on the edge of the shore. You wrap your big fishes in that, and they stay fresh like they just been caught."

"That's good!" said Guillaume. "I'll take those two fat ones right there."

Old Sangimaux picked the fish up one at a time and slit each of them open from anus to gills with one slice of this thickened thumb nail. He eviscerated the trout and handed them to Guillaume who placed the fish in a gunny sack with ice.

"You don't come here only to buy the fish," said Sangimaux. "Why is it you come to this place?"

Guillaume pointed toward the northeast. "There's land for sale here," he said. "I think it would be a good place to start a farm."

He pulled a map out of his pack and spread it open for Sangimaux to examine. Together they poured over the document. Sangimaux spat a brown stream of tobacco juice and said, "I take you to those places, *M'sieu*. Me, I know this country better than anybody. Me, I hunt all those mountains many times."

The cost of the four hundred acres Guillaume was about to purchase seemed like an exorbitant sum that would consume most of the money he had been able to accumulate. Yet, later that afternoon after he had had the opportunity to survey the region with Sangimaux and stand in awe, dwarfed by the hemlock and spruce which towered above him, he knew that he could capitalize on this resource and turn a profit. He noted, also, that the soil was thin and heavily scattered with flat rocks. Still, he knew that with proper management thin soil would produce suitable crops of hay and oats. Even rocks are valuable when used as the foundations of buildings or to build fences.

Guillaume liked what he saw that day and returned home well after dark. He hurried inside to tell his wife about the tall trees and the swift brook which he could dam up to supply water for a sawmill. Marguerite asked if he had located a sunny place to build a house and if their child would have a safe place to play out of doors. She was excited at the prospect of having their own home and suggested that they place some wooden hoops and canvas over their wagon so they could live in it while they built a log cabin. Guy shrugged his shoulders, grinned broadly, and asked, "Why not?"

That night they uncovered their hoard of coins and recounted them. In the morning Guillaume and Marguerite became landowners on the shore of Echo Lake.

In the years to come Guillaume and Sangimaux remained good friends. When Sangimaux was not feeling too lame, he would come to work with Guillaume, clearing land to create meadows and cutting timber to be sawn into lumber for a house and barn. A few years later, following a bad storm, Guillaume discovered Sangimaux' body washed up on shore. He buried the old fisherman next to his dugout home and brought the man's dog to live with them.

When Guillaume and Marguerite first arrived at Echo Lake, there was only one other farm family living within several miles of them. Edouard Lavoy was a Union Army veteran, and had been granted land as payment for his military service. Guillaume and his wife were glad to have a neighbor living only a mile away. When it came time for barn-raising or other difficult tasks, Guillaume could count on Edouard and his sons being there to help. And when Marguerite was ready to give birth, Emilie Lavoy was there to assist her.

Within a few years' time Guillaume had finished his barn and begun to stock it with animals. Actually, the sawmill was the first thing finished because the lumber it produced was needed in the construction of the other buildings. From then on, however, Guillaume had lumber to sell to the other families who were settling in the valley. He converted the log cabin into a chicken coop. He had not yet completely finished the interior of their new woodframe house, but it was habitable.

A half dozen more families had moved into the valley during that time, and since the Coulbron's own children were growing, it became apparent to Guillaume and his wife that soon they would need a school. The school house was built of flat rocks, and the scholars sat on long benches. They used individual slates with chalk for writing words and calculating sums. All four of Guillaume's sons and his three daughters attended this school, and on cold mornings the children appreciated the fact that the school was only two hundred feet away from the back door of their house.

Over the years Guillaume sold small parcels of lakeshore to city people seeking summer solitude, and he used the money from these sales for building projects or for the purchase of more modern farming equipment.

Chapter 2

Guillaume and Marguerite aged gracefully, and when their health began to fail, they went to live with their married daughter near Albany. One son, Wilfrid, stayed on to manage the farm while the other three moved away and got jobs elsewhere.

After Guillaume died at the age of eighty-two, his land was parceled out among his children to do with as they wished. Although the other brothers and sisters each sold the property which they inherited, Wilfrid decided to keep his one hundred acres which consisted of a mixture of tillable land, rocky pasture, and second-growth forest west of the home place. Wilfrid added to this by leasing more land from the mining company so that he could start his own farm and logging operation. He called his place Cold Spring Farm because of the sparkling water that bubbled forth at the base of the foothills. He used this spring water for drinking and for cooling the milk his cows provided before it was carried off for sale.

Wilfrid soon realized that the dairy farming and logging would not provide enough income to care for a family properly. He supplemented the income from his dairy farm by selling milk and cream directly to the miners' families and by working as a carpenter. During this time Wilfrid obtained plans from the New York State Education Department in Albany and used them to help build a more modern wood frame school building.

Wilfrid liked to hunt deer. The only weapon he owned, however, was an old scattergun. He was pleased when one of the Lavoy sons, who lived nearby, offered to trade him his father's Union Army carbine for a load of cedar fence posts. The next afternoon Wilfrid returned after a hunt carrying the carbine over his shoulder. He walked into the barn and harnessed one of his horses. His twelve-year old son David came running out of the house.

"As-tu tué un grand bouc, mon père?" ("Did you shoot a big buck, my father?")

"Non, mon fils. Pas un bouc, mais un très grand ours! Viens avec moi." ("No, my son. Not a buck, but a great big bear! Come with me.")

"Oui, Papa! Où l'as-tu tiré?" ("Yes, Dad! Where did you shoot it?")

"La-bas, sur la cote de la montagne." ("Over there, on the side of the mountain.")

Wilfrid and the other members of his family used French and English interchangeably but often reverted to the language of their forbearers when they were excited. Now he returned to English.

"David, go get the singletree and hook it on the traces."

When the boy returned with the oak swiveling device, his father motioned for him to mount the horse and handed his son the singletree to hold in his lap while Wilfrid walked behind to guide the horse.

The boy was excited as they headed up the side of the mountain, and as soon as he sighted the bear, David called out, *"Un monstre, Papa! Tu as tiré un monstre!"* ("A monster, Papa! You shot a monster!")

The man smiled and asked, *"Tu est certain, mon fils, que ce n'est pas un loupgarou?"* ("Are you sure, my son, that it is not a werewolf?")

The boy leaped to the ground and ran his fingers through the animal's fur and pulled back its lips in order to examine the teeth. Wilfrid looped a rope around the bear's neck and attached it to the center link of the singletree.

"Combien est-ce-que la bête pèse, Papa?" ("How much does the animal weigh, Papa?")

"Je dirais à peu près de quatre cent livres." ("I'd say nearly four hundred pounds.")

"Ouais! C'est beaucoup!" ("Yeah, that's a lot!")

"I'm starting to get tired out," said the father, "and we've still got work to do skinning the bear tonight. You ride in front and hold the reins. I'll ride behind you. Old Maude will have to support both of us and drag the bear."

"Papa, are you going to tan the hide? Can you make me something out of it?"

"Of course, my son. How would you like some warm mittens or a vest?"

"Mittens, Papa! And then I can wear them to school."

That winter the family ate the meat of the bear and used the fat to waterproof their leather boots. David was proud of his bearskin mittens whenever he wore them to school, and the other boys envied him. At suppertime Wilfrid felt more than a tinge of pride as he watched his youngest son gnaw on the bones of the great animal as though he were a healthy, young wolf.

Many of the largest evergreen trees in the area were gone by the time Wilfrid was farming his land, and recurring forest fires reduced the amount of saleable timber even further. Still, in some areas Wilfrid could find large enough stands of aspen so that he and his sons could harvest the bolts for pulpwood. Wilfrid and his older sons felled the trees with axes and cut them into four-foot lengths with a crosscut saw.

David's two main jobs in the family's logging operation were to peel the green bark from the aspen logs with a steel spud and use Maude to skid the logs to a collection point where they were sawn to length and stacked. So certain was the boy of the mare's gentleness that he often worked around her barefooted. He appreciated not only her gentleness but also her intelligence. He would hold on to the mare's halter with one hand and lead her to the butt end of an adjacent fallen log. Then he would attach a steel choker chain, which was connected to the singletree, snugly around the log. Again he would grasp the animal's halter, make a clicking sound with his mouth, and lead her to the collection spot. The boy soon realized the he only had to lead her into position twice before she knew exactly where to go. She would skid a log directly parallel to the last one, stop, and back slightly so that the boy could more easily unhook the chain. They worked day after day at this task. Neither ever tiring of it, nor did they have any accidents.

Wilfrid cut the aspen in the spring and summer because it was easier to debark the logs then. By fall the bolts of pulpwood would be drier and lighter, making them easier to handle. Then they hauled the pulpwood using a team of horses and a wagon to a railroad siding only a mile and a half away. There they loaded them by hand onto open rail cars for shipment downstate.

During the Great War Wilfrid's two oldest sons went off to fight the Kaiser. Only one of them returned. The boom times of the twenties were good times financially for the Coulbrons. Wilfrid and his two remaining sons built a new house and barn to replace the log ones which he had built first. They modernized the farm further by installing an electric system using a wind charger with a diesel-powered engine as a back-up. They worked with the other farmers who had come into the valley to install their own telephone lines and connected them to other systems.

David grew into a strong young man and enjoyed working on his father's equipment. Other farmers often called upon him to repair truck engines or any other mechanical apparatus that had malfunctioned. When Wilfrid purchased a farm tractor, his son David maintained it and taught his father how to operate it. David purchased a used motorcycle with a sidecar and took his friends and sisters for rides. A number of the young women in the region admired him, but he was so bashful in their presence that he remained unattached.

When the Great Depression hit in 1929, many iron ore miners lost their jobs in Rock Mountain and moved away. In the near-by prison town of Dannemora, the guards' wages were cut in half. Wilfrid, not yet sixty-five years old, struggled through the first few months of bad times. His wife succumbed to pneumonia, and he, too, fell gravely ill.

Chapter 3

While Wilfrid Coulbron and his wife were both still alive, they had hired an eighteen-year-old woman named Lillian Gonyea from Rock Mountain to cook meals and do housework. She had dropped out of school the year before after becoming pregnant as the result of being an accessory and coach to her fifteen-year-old neighbor as he made practice attempts at learning the facts of life.

Immediately after her delivery Lillian gave her twin girls up for adoption, went home, and argued incessantly with her mother. She hired out at the first job she could get so that she could be independent.

The youngest Coulbron son, David, still lived at home. Lillian was the prettiest girl David had ever seen and, although when he was younger he often experienced painful embarrassment when he was in the company of girls, he now would frequently find himself staring at Lillian as she did the housework.

Several years earlier David had resigned himself to the belief that he would remain a bachelor farmer all of his life. He was deceiving himself, however, by assuming that the furtive glances he continued to make toward the hired girl were strictly on the order of curiosity rather than the result of a budding passion. He believed that his only source of excitement came when he delved into the intricate mysteries of cold, hard mechanical objects, and certainly not into the delicate curves of women with their unfathomable emotions.

Lillian was a vivacious, libidinous woman who had no intention of spending the rest of her life cooking and cleaning for someone else. She was aroused by the existence of this potential cohabiter who slept alone upstairs in a loft above the kitchen. Moreover, she found him to be attractive even though he was several years older than she was.

One night David lay in his bed wondering how he might repair the shattered blade of the electric wind charger. The solution eluded him, and he dozed off. During the night his mind flickered with the fractured images of dreams. He rolled onto his side and uttered several unintelligible sounds. Some unusual but enticing sensation disturbed him, and he began to regain consciousness. The perception came that there might be someone else lying behind him in bed, intimately cuddling his back. He was uncertain whether it might be phantom or reality. He thought that it might be another of those bothersome deliriums that invade a person's mind when he is half asleep. Yet somehow, this one was different. Tentatively he groped his hand behind him and was shocked when he realized that the incubus was nude. Startled and confused, he sought to run from the room, but something gripped him. It felt as though a mink-covered body was encircling him and pressing him down. Again he sought to flee, but he had not the will to resist this new sensation that flooded his loins.

Lillian Gonyea knew from experience how to cure male shyness in ways that were both direct in their approach and remarkable in their effectiveness. Her voice was soothing and seductive while her actions evoked instant desire in him. His site of manhood swelled until he thought it might burst, and his whole body shivered in excitement. Something wonderful was about to happen, and his thrusting body sought to hasten it.

Fulfilled as never before, David knew that he had been snared, but the taste of this sweet ambush had been delicious. In succeeding days David and Lillian still rarely spoke to one another, but the evenings were alive with moans and sighs. He came to anticipate these clandestine encounters and enjoyed the fact that they occurred in increasing frequency.

Lillian cared for David's father during his illness, spooning soup into his mouth and bathing the perspiration from his body. Wilfrid's lungs were filling with fluid and his heart would race out of control.

Nursing an invalid was more than Lillian had bargained for so she decided to speed up what she considered to be inevitable. She reasoned that David was too good a catch to let go, and she wanted to be able to spend more time with him. One morning before breakfast she eased into the father's bedroom and watched his labored breathing. She closed the bedroom door and approached the man's bedside. She placed a pillow over his face and pressed down forcefully. His struggles were feeble and short-lived. She removed the pillow, fluffed it, and checked to see if Wilfrid had a pulse. Satisfied that there was none, she returned to the kitchen to eat her breakfast and wait until David came inside after completing his milking.

Lillian would never win an award for her acting ability; yet she did a credible job feigning sadness when she announced to David that his father had died in his sleep. After the funeral Lillian stayed on, ostensibly as a housekeeper and cook for David. She became pregnant right away, and David asked the Rock Mountain priest to arrange a quick marriage ceremony. When the child was born, they named him Philip David Coulbron.

At first the new couple enjoyed some happiness, but during the sixth month of Lillian's pregnancy, David began to notice changes in his wife's behavior. She accused him of unfaithfulness. Her clothing and hair were becoming increasingly unkempt, and she would not rise until noon. She allowed dirty dishes to pile up in the sink and stopped doing the laundry. She ate sparingly or not at all. David set aside some of his outdoor work and took over the household tasks without complaint. He tried to encourage, to praise, to coax, to wheedle, but nothing worked. Lillian seemed to have lost all sense of order, and her accusations became increasingly absurd. She insisted on sleeping alone, and she denied David his marital privileges.

At the same time that Lillian was slipping into this state of incoherence, the country's economy was continuing its decline. Milk prices plummeted, and David was obliged to sell most of his livestock because his feed costs were greater than the return he received from selling milk. He kept one of his better cows, a few pigs, and enough chickens for their own needs.

David looked everywhere for work, but there was none. He and his family survived on a subsistence basis, neither better nor worse than other families in the valley. A few of them accepted charity, but David was too proud to even consider it.

An official from an electric company came to David's house one day to ask that he call a town meeting in the schoolhouse. David was now the school trustee, and he complied with the request by distributing notices in the grocery store and in the barbershop. During the meeting the official explained the company's proposal to buy up all of the land surrounding the lake and construct a dam in order to have sufficient water flow year 'round to operate a hydro-electric plant downstream. David was reluctant to sell any of his land, but when he realized that the project would create many jobs locally and that they all could have inexpensive electricity, he acquiesced. The landowners approved the plan, and David was able to hire out as a truck driver hauling sand and gravel for the dam construction.

The dam project came to an end after two years, and David was out of work again. He read that the federal government was trying a variety of programs to create jobs and improve the economy. One of these was the Works Project Administration. David's farm was divided by an unpaved state highway. When he read another announcement that their highway was scheduled to be paved with concrete soon, David applied with the contractor for a mechanic's job and was accepted. By any standards, the pay was dismal. David worked full time on this job, and by working overtime several hours each evening, he was paid the sum of thirty dollars a month. Without the food they obtained from their home-grown produce and farm animals, they would not have been able to make ends meet.

Lillian started to take bus trips alone to visit her sister in Malone, and David thought that she seemed to be snapping out of her problems. She became somewhat more responsible around the house, gave herself a permanent wave, and sewed a new dress. One Saturday afternoon she announced breezily that she had joined a church congregation in Malone and would need the use of their car every Sunday morning from then on. She stated that Malone was merely thirty miles away and added that she would no longer be accompanying David to Mass at St. Matthew's church in Rock Mountain.

David was upset with her decision for several reasons, but he knew that she was headstrong and that there was little he could do to change her mind. He told her that the car tires were worn down and that he could not afford to buy new ones, nor could he afford the cost of the gasoline. When he hid the car keys from her on Sunday morning, she retaliated by hitchhiking to Malone and did not return.

At first David was not too concerned about his wife's disappearance because he thought that she was staying with her sister. On Monday morning when his wife had not yet returned home, David brought his young son Philip to stay at a neighbor's house and then went to his construction job.

Lillian, meanwhile, was not visiting her sister. She was occupied elsewhere. She yawned and rubbed her eyes. "Where are we, Sweetheart?" she asked of the man lying next to her in bed.

The Reverend Cecil Dodgson was still tired and didn't want to be awakened. His head throbbed from the whiskey the two of them had consumed in a speakeasy the previous evening. He had noticed her one Sunday morning while he was delivering a rousing sermon on the evils of sin. After the service had finished and everyone else had left, she introduced herself. He was single and lonely. She was pretty, was not wearing a wedding ring, and Preacher Dodgson thought, "Oh, what the hell!"

Cecil Dodgson was not an ordained minister, although as an orphaned Indian boy he had lived several years with the family of a fundamentalist preacher. He had been born not far away in the Mohawk reservation near Hogansburg and had been abandoned by his mother while very young. He had been raised by his grandmother who died when he was still a young teenager. He walked away from the reservation on the day of her funeral and had wandered around in search of the man he thought might be his father. Eventually, he was taken in by Mrs. Pierce, the preacher's wife.

Later, after he got kicked out of the house, he decided to get in the preaching racket himself. Years passed, and he found himself running a mission in Malone.

The Sunday night of Lillian Coulbron's disappearance, the man called Cecil Dodgson impregnated her as they lay in a rented room, in an old-fashioned white iron bed with spindly spokes and a lumpy mattress. She conceived a male child whose name was destined to become James Guillaume Coulbron.

Lillian's sister Sharon was a registered nurse who lived with her husband in Malone. She worked in the psychiatric ward at a state hospital in nearby Ogdensburg. Other than having shared the same parents, Lillian and Sharon had little in common. Neither did they have much love for one another. Still, Sharon would give her younger sister a bed for the night whenever she asked for it.

When David telephoned Sharon after work on Monday, he felt embarrassed to ask if his wife might be at her house. Sharon informed him that she had not seen her sister in nearly a month, but, if he were to come to her house, the two of them could go looking for Lillian.

David had been getting increasingly concerned with his wife's behavior for some time. It was not that she was always incapable of being a responsible wife and mother, it was just that she seemed to fly out of control on occasion and become totally irresponsible. He wasn't really sure if he had ever actually loved her or not but, after all, she was the mother of his child, and he felt that he owed her the best that he could offer.

David was feeling apprehensive as he drove to his sister-in-law's house. He kept thinking that his wife should have called him if she were staying away. He met Sharon and the two of them went in search of Lillian. They checked with all of the ministers of the mainline churches first, and not finding anyone who recognized the photograph of Lillian, David and Sharon eventually met the Reverend Mr. Dodgson sweeping the floor in his store-front church. He seemed pleasant enough and appeared to be genuinely worried to learn that Lillian Coulbron was missing. Understandably, he refrained from revealing his rendezvous with her. For their part, David and Sharon were somewhat surprised to see an Indian man running a church mission in Malone.

After David and Sharon left, Mr. Dodgson drove off on a search of his own. He found Lillian lying in a booth in a country roadhouse. She had passed out as a result of having consumed too many gin sours. He brought her back to the mission and tried to sober her up. It took him several hours to locate David and Sharon by telephone. When they arrived, they discovered that Lillian had locked herself inside the mission's restroom.

David and Mr. Dodgson forced open the door with a crowbar and found Lillian unconscious and lying naked in a pool of her own blood. One hand still grasped a pair of bloody scissors, and sticky red fluid oozed from her wrist. She had sheared off most of her hair, and judging by the amount of it in her mouth, David and Sharon knew that she had been attempting to eat it.

David called for an ambulance and waited in the Malone Hospital while doctors tried to save his wife's life. He spoke several times with Sharon.

"What in Heaven's name am I going to do?" he asked in desperation. "What in the world am I going to do?"

Sharon patted his hand. "You have got to face facts, David. You have got to have her committed in an asylum.

David was distraught. Tears flooded his eyes. "I couldn't do that, Sharon. Little Philip needs her."

"You are only fooling yourself, David. I've seen this coming for a long time, and I'll bet that you have, too. The next time she might succeed in killing herself, or she might hurt Philip. This may sound strange because I'm her sister, but I think that the best thing for you would be to divorce Lillian and get yourself a new wife."

"No, Sharon. I'll never remarry while she is still alive. You know all about mental hospitals. What will they do to her there?"

"First of all, she'll probably be sedated. Then when she is feeling better, the staff will evaluate her to try to determine the seriousness of her problem. Later on, after she receives treatment, they might allow her to go home on furlough. If not—who knows? But for sure, things can't stay the way they are now. That would be too dangerous for everyone. She is very sick and needs help."

Reluctantly, David committed his wife to the mental hospital and, as Sharon had predicted, Lillian was allowed to return home. The staff taught David how to watch for signs of recurring symptoms while she was at home, and Sharon would stop in occasionally to check up on her sister.

Within a few months of Lillian's first furlough she again attempted suicide - this time with an overdose of her prescription medicines. During her second stay in the hospital, Lillian's pregnancy came to term. The hospital had no birthing room, so there in the emergency room of the psychiatric ward, Lillian Coulbron delivered her second child.

A doctor called David aside and suggested two things – first that he consent to having his wife sterilized and secondly that he give up his child for adoption. "Have you looked at the baby?" he asked. "Are you sure that you are his father? Also, the baby may have been permanently damaged by overdose of the drugs she took."

David nodded affirmatively to the doctor's first suggestion, but denied the possibility of allowing the second. Both David and Sharon had guessed as much about the baby's parentage. Sharon was overwhelmed by the beauty of the infant and pleaded to take the child to raise as her own. David however, was not willing to give up his wife's baby and had already made up his mind to bring the tiny infant James home in a few days and have him baptized.

Chapter 4

On his way home from the hospital David Coulbron stopped at the Rock Mountain grocery store. Waiting in line next to the cash register, he heard news that the mine was soon going to re-open. He paid for his purchases and drove directly up the hill to the main office to apply for a job. He joined a line of men waiting to be interviewed and, when it was his turn, he explained the mechanical experiences he had had working on his father's farm and his current job repairing road building equipment. He was surprised when the personnel chief told him to report to work in the morning for a physical and, if he passed that, to report for work in the concentrator the next morning.

Much like his grandfather Guillaume, more than a half century earlier, he had no desire to become an underground miner. Yet, he would have taken the job, even drilling and blasting through the rock wall with explosives. The thought of maintenance work on heavy equipment above ground, however, did interest him a great deal.

A few days later on a warm August morning, David arrived back at the hospital to carry James home with him. He was glad that he had been hired to work at Rock Mountain on a job that paid reasonably well. He was sad, however, when he checked in on his wife and found her heavily sedated and unable to speak. He walked over to a telephone in the lobby and called his sister-in-law, Sharon.

David listened on the receiver as the telephone rang. "Hello, hello," said a hollow voice.

David recognized this as the voice of Sharon's mentally disabled husband. "Hello, Alphie, is Sharon there?"

"Hello, hello", said the voice on the other end of the line.

"Alphie, this is David Coulbron. Please call your wife to the phone."

Then David heard Sharon's voice coming from a distance. "No! Don't hang up. Give me the phone and go sit down. Here, Alphie, drink your milk. Yes? Who is it please?"

"It's David, Sharon. I just checked in on Lil."

"How is Lillian?"

"It's hard to say. It looks like they knocked her out with drugs."

"Sometimes that's the kindest way. If she doesn't settle down with medications, they may have to strap her in a straightjacket."

"Oh, Lord, Sharon, I'd hate to see that happen."

"You've got to face facts, David. It's going to get worse before it gets any better – if it gets better. Believe me. I've worked in the mental ward in Malone and sometimes in Ogdensburg for quite a while now. I suppose you are going to bring little Jimmy home with you today."

"Yes, and that's not all of the good news. I've got a job in Rock Mountain for Crystal Penn Mining. Now I'll be earning more in a week than I was getting for a month with the WPA."

"That's great news, David. Will I see you before you leave?"

"I'm afraid not. I told Mrs. Lavoy that I'd be home by three."

After speaking with Sharon, David walked back to the room where the infant was kept. A nurse had just finished feeding him and wrapped him with a lightweight flannel blanket. She repeated to David her instructions for preparing the infant's formula and handed the baby to him.

Having helped care for his first son, Philip, diapers and baby formula held no surprises for David. He cradled the baby in his arms and headed toward the exit. He was surprised to see his sister-in-law, Sharon, waiting for him outside the door. She was carrying a bag filled with baby supplies, and her eyes were moist with tears.

"David," she said gently, "I brought these for little Jimmy. I thought you could use them."

"Oh! Well, thank you. What's in the bag, Sharon?"

"Just some baby bottles and diapers that I bought." Her voice was trembling as she spoke. "David...David, could I keep him for you... for just a little while, please?"

"Gosh, Sharon, I don't know. You're pretty busy taking care of Alphie, aren't you?"

"Actually, he's been quite good lately."

"Didn't he start a fire in your house last month?"

"That wasn't too bad. It was just his chair that burned. He fell asleep and dropped a lit cigarette down the crease next to his cushion. I take his cigarettes away when I'm gone now."

David knew the story of Alphie's problems. In fact, he had gone to high school with the man before the First World War. Sharon and Alphie had married in 1917, just a few days before he boarded a troop-ship and headed for France.

On days when his mind was clear, Alphie would tell about huddling in the trenches while German artillery shells containing mustard gas and chlorine fumes exploded near him. He would tell how shrapnel ripped his body and tore his mask away. He had returned home less of a man. His lungs were rotted out, and his mind was altered forever.

Sharon cared for him and took the nursing job in Ogdensburg so she could be near him when he had to be readmitted for flare ups of his mental condition. Much of the time, however, he was able to live at home. Sharon had wanted very much to have children, but her husband's service wounds precluded that. Even now, fifteen years since her husband's return from the war, Sharon longed to have a child – to hold it, to smother it with love.

"You will be so busy with your new job, David, and Philip is still so little. I'd love to help by keeping Jimmy."

David knew that Sharon's intentions were genuine, but he wasn't ready to relinquish his wife's baby.

"Mrs. Lavoy babysits Philip for me, and she is willing to care for Jimmy, too. I'm hoping that Lillian will get better soon and can come home."

"We all hope that, David, but for now, at least, let me care for Jimmy. You can see him when you visit Lillian."

David thought it over for a moment and handed the baby to Sharon. This arrangement worked well. In time, Lillian responded to treatment and was released from Ogdensburg. Sharon was reluctant to let Jimmy go, but her husband was failing again and was demanding more and more of her time. The little boy called Jimmy Coulbron went to live in Echo Lake with his family.

Upon her return, Lillian behaved as though nothing unusual had happened and resumed her position as wife and mother. Philip was delighted to play the role of big brother and helped his mother care for the baby. In time the two boys became inseparable friends.

On his first day of work at Rock Mountain, David was given the job of operating a crane which was used to hoist steel bowl liners for rock crushers. He liked the job, and he enjoyed the camaraderie of working with a group of men. David was well liked by his co-workers because he dove into any task and worked hard until it was finished. He appreciated the fact that these men liked to work and that there was little disagreement among them. His foreman and his superintendent, likewise, took notice of David.

The next year when the mine expanded operations, David was made millwright and put in charge of repairing crushers and conveyors. Two years later, he was asked if he would like to become foreman. He accepted the promotion. Finally, he had achieved a measure of financial security for himself and his family.

When Jimmy was four years old, his mother had another nervous breakdown, and David was obliged to bring her back to the state mental institution in Ogdensburg. He felt guilt each time he had her committed, but he knew also that her combination of paranoia and delusions could lead to suicide. He had no other choice.

Whenever Lillian's condition worsened, David would confer with his sister-in-law and together they would decide whether or not his wife needed treatment. Usually after a few months of therapy, Lillian would be ready to return home and resume her life.

For whatever reason, the father sheltered the boys from the full realization of their mother's problem and asked Sharon not to discuss it with them. Whenever their mother had to be recommitted, he simply told them, "Mother's gone away for a while." The boys grew up accepting this type of hiatus in their relationship with her. It was something that was, then suddenly, it wasn't.

This created a ping-pong existence for the boys. One moment they had a mother who was caring; the next moment she was aloof or, on some occasions, even abusive. Jimmy and Phil had grown up accepting these trips as well as her irrational behavior and unpredictable mood swings. They could sense, even at their immature level, that she was emotionally weak. Fortunately, they learned to take strength from their father.

There were other times when Lillian was away from home. If her preacher friend was unavailable, she would strike up an acquaintance with any other man who might want her. On these occasions either David or Sharon would go looking for her in the Malone bars and roadhouses. These escapades were often a prelude to another breakdown.

David had been born just after the turn of the century, so that when the war was started in 1941 he was considered too old for conscription into military service. Having a wife and dependents would not have exempted him. Even the fact that his iron-mining job was rated as a national priority would not have protected him from the draft. Actually, he would have served willingly, as had his two older brothers in the Great War. If the government had felt that he was needed, he would have gone. The only reservation being that he knew he was sorely needed at home.

The demand for iron and steel during the war years was great and, because of this, the mine at Rock Mountain operated at full capacity.

Men were frequently called upon to work overtime and double shifts of sixteen hours became routine.

David Coulbron was caught up in this with a certain level of willingness, partly because he felt it was a matter of duty but also to better provide for the needs of his family.

Chapter 5

The fourth time his wife required hospitalization, David was working long hours of rotating shifts at the mine. He realized that he must hire a woman as a housekeeper and to care for his children while he was away.

Although there were several young women nearby who were willing to do housework and care for children, David wished to avoid any possible complications to his life. He looked for an older woman and found just such a helper in the person of Mrs. Yvette Papineau. She was a short woman of considerable girth. Bumpy fat globules, attached to the inner surface of her massive arms, hung like bags of marbles from her armpits to her elbows.

For house dresses she favored a flower-print fabric from the feed store. Oftentimes, the wives accompanied their husbands to the feed store, and they were the ones who chose the brand of pig feed that their husbands bought by the attractiveness of the sturdy cotton sacks.

The animal feed companies knew this and, in their effort to compete, learned to disdain burlap in favor of good quality cotton cloth manufactured in colorful print designs. Moreover, cotton was a patriotic American product whereas the hemp used in burlap was imported from who knows where.

Yvette sewed her own dresses and created her own patterns, partly out of economic need and partly because the Montgomery Ward catalog did not list any sizes large enough for her.

After the good woman's husband Cletus died, leaving her with a son, she took on housekeeping jobs in the neighborhood. She no longer ran the farm at the same level as previously but did keep enough livestock for her own use and to sell some milk. The raw material for her clothing as well as some for her offspring came from the grain she purchased at the Purina feed store. By measuring the cloth carefully and not being overly generous with the hem length and the superfluous bodice covering, she was able to create a passable house dress with the material from only three one-hundred pound sacks of hog chow.

Yvette's stripling son was an invaluable aid in her endeavor. For measuring purposes, she would lay out lengths of reddish-brown building paper that Cletus had stored in the barn for use in eliminating drafts in the hen house. After unrolling and overlapping a double layer of the building paper, she would roll her body onto it. Then, with pencil in hand, her son would trace an outline of his mother's body. With this knowledge on file, she became adept enough to meet her immediate needs as a seamstress.

Her only attempt at style, other than color and print pattern, was to attach a smart little collar in white around the neck of each dress so that it extended down past the front of her waist and continued to her knees where it intersected the hemline. This would be a front-buttoning garment, of course, to facilitate dressing and undressing.

Upon meeting Mrs. Papineau on summer days for the first time, shopkeepers and country peddlers alike would stare in awe, their mouths open, at the initial viewing of her considerable cleavage.

David Coulbron didn't have time to ask for references. He had heard that the woman was available and drove over to pick her up. He waited while she loaded up three suitcases and her thirteen-year-old son, Lawrence, aptly named after the great river which flowed alongside the place where his life was conceived one June evening in the back of a pick-up truck.

Yvette comfortably ensconced herself and the river boy in the Coulbron household as maid, cook, and baby sitter, with the lad being given the task of completing the farm chores. Working double shifts six days a week left David little time to care for his boys, and so Mrs. Papineau took over complete control.

Not known for her culinary skills, Mrs. Papineau prepared pea soup and Johnny cake as the most frequent evening meal. The inevitable effect of their digestive juices acting upon this excess of legumes made themselves sulfurously known to the inhabitants of the house so that numerous windows were always open.

This woman undertook each household task on a prearranged schedule that best suited her. Nothing could interfere with her enjoyment of Ma Perkins on the radio. Whether or not the boys had dressed themselves yet and eaten their oatmeal porridge was immaterial to her. Her routine demanded that every Tuesday at precisely eight A.M. it was time to dust mop the upstairs bedroom floors.

One morning Phil had already gone down for breakfast, but little Jimmy was dawdling. He climbed out of bed, used the potty, and shed his pajamas. Suddenly, without warning, he heard the thudding steps of Mrs. Papineau as she huffed up the stairs. The boy had always been intimidated by her size and didn't want her to see him naked. He dove under the bed and hid among the cookie crumbs and dust balls.

From his place of refuge, he watched wide-eyed as the housekeeper swished her dust mop in long sweeps. Since it was time for her once-a-week swish under the bed, she squatted wide-legged, slid the cleaning tool underneath, and soundly thumped the boy in the face with it. He withstood the blow stoically and remained mouse like, hoping she would go away.

Mrs. Papineau, however, knew that she had hit something that wasn't there last week and was determined to discover what was hindering her task. She attempted several more pokes, each more violent than the previous one as she tried to dislodge the bothersome object. In desperation, Jimmy grabbed the mop and pulled it in with him. Her ire aroused, the woman knelt down and peered sideways under the bed. She cackled loudly and swooped one hand underneath in order to drag a tan body out by the heels.

She snatched the boy to her bosom, and in consolation, hugged him until he thought he might smother. In spite of her somewhat coarse behavior, she did possess a nurturing soul and genuine love for children.

As usual, she was without a brassiere and a bit disheveled from bending. Fearing the monster might attack again, Jimmy sank his teeth into her right nipple. She emitted a curdling scream and dropped him with a thud. He recovered quickly and dashed outside to hide in the woodshed. His brother discovered him there, naked and shivering, and brought him some clothing.

That evening when the boy's father returned home from work, Mrs. Papineau, no worse for the wear, retold the story three times, once in English and twice in French, laughing louder with each retelling. Until bedtime, Jimmy stayed glued to his father's side and chewed his fingernails.

Because of her size, it was difficult for the housekeeper to complete all of her work without assistance. Each of the boys, Jimmy, Phil, and Lawrence, were assigned definite tasks which they could not escape without a punitive result. Being the oldest, her own son carried the responsibility for the care of both her farm animals and the Coulbron's. The Coulbron boys learned to wash dishes, set the table, and hang the laundry outside to dry. She tolerated no shirkers. She frequently emphasized her commands with statements such as, "If you don't work, you don't eat!" She tempered this with copious praise whenever it was deserved.

The only curse words ever known to emanate from Yvette's mouth were reserved for use on the gasoline-powered washing machine which lay in wait for her in the basement of David's house. This mechanical contraption worked well enough for washing and wringing clothing once the operator had its engine started and running smoothly. Although David never had any problem starting it, it caused Yvette considerable consternation.

Because the machine was mounted on castors, Yvette would call upon the boys to push it close to the rear door of the basement. Then

Lawrence would push one end of a flexible steel hose through a hole in the door and attach the other end to the exhaust pipe of the engine. Phil would check to see that the fuel tank contained gasoline. Jimmy would cringe behind his brother, close his eyes, and cover his ears with his hands. These tasks complete, Yvette would order the boys to the far end of the room, all the while admonishing them in French, "If she go boom, we all be the dead body."

When all appeared to be ready, Yvette would approach the *"maudit monstre"* gingerly. Placing her left hand on her left thigh and leaning in that direction so as to direct thrust with her right foot against the kick starter of the engine, she would bellow out an incantation in French which fortunately the boys did not understand.

On rare occasions, the engine would start on the first kick, in which case the boys would cheer. More often, however, it would totally ignore the kick or merely issue a weak 'pop'. This would be cause for a new and more forceful expression. Eventually, after repeated curses and kicks, the engine would run more or less flawlessly until it ran out of gas. Yvette always accepted this problem because it was one she could understand. "Zat machine, her, she tired and 'ongry. We let her rest now. Lawrence, you, you give her ze gas when she cool down. Now we all go up the stair to eat ze molasses cookie and drink ze milk." Seated inside the confessional on Sunday mornings prior to mass, Yvette would never fail to disclose her Monday morning sin.

Jimmy's and Phil's association with Lawrence, who was several years older than Phil, brought with it mixed results. In one way, the younger boys appreciated having what amounted to a big brother. On the other hand, he shared with them the girly magazines he had acquired through trades with still older boys. He also introduced them to the art of self-pleasuring, although at their age neither activity seemed important.

Lawrence's other vice involved peeping through the hole he had bored through the wall from his bedroom into the adjacent bathroom.

Once he permitted the boys to each take a look as his mother took a sponge bath. To them, peeping seemed meaningless. At their age, a body was just a body whether it was clothed or not.

Mrs. Papineau's son, Lawrence, developed a great affinity for the contents of David's wooden cask of cider. In the evening, just before bedtime, he would sneak down into the basement and chug down two or three glassfuls of the amber liquid. This, together with his tendency to be a perpetual bed wetter, created extra laundry for his mother and upset her routine. To counter this, during what came to be known as 'the wee hours of the night', Yvette would bellow out, "Low-rentz! Get up and piss!"

Unless the boy was heard to jump out of bed immediately, she would repeat the command more forcefully, *"Low-rentz! Tu petit, son-a-bitch, va pisser!"* It was as though using a combination of French and English she could cause the great river to start and stop its flow at her command.

The first time Jimmy and Phil heard this, they bolted upright in bed and clung to one another, but they soon became accustomed to the outbursts and learned to ignore them.

Within a few months, Lillian recovered enough so that David could bring her home. The boys hugged her, and all seemed well. Mrs. Papineau and her son were discharged. Yvette repacked her bags and returned home leaving behind the descendants of some little things she had brought into the house with her. Lillian nearly had a relapse when she discovered bedbug bites on the boys and, soon, on her own body as well. She boiled all of the clothing and rugs. She sprinkled powders on the mattresses and put the boys to work washing all of the woodwork in the house with kerosene. In time they managed to eliminate the unwelcomed guests.

Mrs. Papineau's services were required several more times over the years. After that initial encounter in his bedroom, Jimmy grew to accept and finally enjoy having her in the house. She did make passable cookies, and she knew how to comfort small wounds with kisses and hugs.

Chapter 6

Morning dew was still beaded on the grass as Jimmy Coulbron climbed the foothills of Topless Mountain in upstate New York. The sky was nearly cloudless and the effect of the sun striking obliquely on his left shoulder together with the physical effort caused perspiration to trickle down the boy's back. It formed droplets on his forehead and on his newly sprouted dark moustache. So much had happened lately that he felt he had to be alone to sort things out.

He turned and faced the sun, searching far below for any sign of the little farm where he had grown up. Some maple trees, gnarled with age, interrupted his view. He climbed higher now, picking his route carefully among the tumbled boulders. This was one of a thousand Adirondack peaks that had been smoothed by ancient ice sheets. It had no special significance except to Jimmy and to those who lived near it. It was inhabited by no one except wildlife and occasional schoolboys on an outing.

The Coulbron's called it Bear Mountain because Jimmy's grandfather had shot a bear on it years earlier. The rural neighbors referred to it as Coulbron's Mountain since it was closest to their farm. A certain cartographer must have had a different idea when he labeled it Topless – perhaps as a whim. The name didn't matter to the boy; it was the view he was seeking. On top of this mountain he could see his whole world.

Alternate freezing and thawing had caused a rockslide to form thousands of years ago, and this had created a jagged cliff on the granite forehead of the mountain's face. The boy had been here several times before, and once had even tried unsuccessfully to scale the cliff without a rope. He glanced up and knew that now he could climb it if he chose to. Still, that would have to wait until another time. He circled around the cliff and came out on top of the mountain.

He had no inkling of what drove him that morning because nothing seemed to make sense anymore. The fact is he needed a ritual of baptism into adulthood, but no organized rite of passage existed for him. Instinctively he knew that the world must be made aware of his impending manhood. Puberty had started more than three years earlier for him, and the evidence had become clear. Although he was not as tall as his brother Phil, he was broader and more muscular. He had already shaved the circlet of black hair that surrounded his chin. More out of curiosity than vanity he had allowed the meager lip hairs to grow.

Today the boy's mind was a jumble of thoughts and strange new feelings. He had read about primitive tribesmen whose elders perform a ritual to initiate their youth into adulthood, but there was no ceremony for him. He felt as though he were being pushed by forces he did not understand and, deprived of direction, he realized that he was obliged to create his own passage.

Once his life had meaning. He and Phil had played together and had cared for the few farm animals their parents raised. They had walked together to the one-room rural schoolhouse and later had ridden together to the village high school in Rock Mountain. This transition had been easy for Jimmy. His smile and genuine friendliness had helped him to be popular. Today, however, he needed no one. This was his day and nothing could change that.

Jimmy gazed across the expanse between two mountains and the triangular peak of Whiteface that peeped up between them. Even though that mountain was thirty miles away, it stood out sharply in the clear air. Jimmy knew that there were ski resorts on the mountain and planned some day to visit them. Jimmy's father had promised that he would take the boys to Whiteface the first day he had a chance. Some years earlier their father had driven the road that snakes its way to the summit. He had said that from there he could see not only Lake Champlain but also part of Vermont and even Mt. Mansfield in New Hampshire. He had said that when the air was clear, you could see the St. Lawrence River and into Canada.

Jimmy had never travelled as far south as Whiteface, but he felt that he knew it through the Movietone News clips he had seen of Olympic trials held at Lake Placid. He hoped that some day he would be able to watch, and perhaps even participate in bobsled races held on Mt. Van Hoevenburg, which was close to Whiteface.

To the youth's right was Teamster Hill. Jimmy knew it well because on school days his bus driver would always have to shift to a lower gear as she drove up the slope. The kids would groan each time the bus slowed and would tease the driver, but she always would take this in stride and would smile as she told them that someday they might have to get out and push. After a few more miles on the highway, Jimmy and a handful of teenagers from Echo Lake would join other students and attend classes in Rock Mountain High School.

Behind him stood another mountain, and beyond that the St. Lawrence River. The river was as far north as Jimmy had ever travelled, except for one visit to the Canadian city of Montreal.

To the east rose Dannemora Mountain. At the base of that alp stretched the village of Dannemora, whose entire north side was dominated by the gray concrete walls of the state prison. From there the highway tilted downward until it reached the city of Plattsburg on the shore of Lake Champlain.

Yesterday Phil had gone to Plattsburg, having been chased out of the house by their mother. "Don't worry about me, Jimmy," he had said as he left. "I'm going to join the Army. I'll write to you soon."

Jimmy turned his attention away from the mountains and sought the location of his farm home. The glare from the metal roof of the barn showed up best, but the house and fields were also clearly defined. The boy followed with his eyes the routes they had taken to Plattsburg yesterday in Phil's favorite possession, a '34 Pontiac.

Jimmy's eyes misted over and welled tears as he surveyed the farmstead. He began to relive the past few days as though they were part of a movie...

"You drive," Phil said. "It's your car now. I won't be needing it."

"But I don't have a license," the younger boy protested.

"Nobody will catch you this one time. When you get it back home, park it under the shed. You'll have your license soon enough."

"I'll take care of it, Phil. You can have it when you come home."

"I won't be coming home – not for a long, long time. Maybe for your graduation. Then we'll have a time."

"I'm keeping you to that promise. Remember that. Oh, God, Phil, how can I do this without you?"

"You'll do it because you have to, and because I say you can. I'm eighteen. I don't really want to go into the Army, but anything will be better than staying near her."

The boys shared a Coke in the depot, waiting for the Trailways bus to arrive. When the time came, Phil grabbed his packsack and gave his brother a friendly punch on the arm. "You'll be all right, Jimmy. You've got what it takes."

Then the boy was alone.

He drove Phil's car home and parked it in the barn, hiding the keys behind a beam. Then he walked purposefully behind the house to the spot where he had found his father's body lying face down in the gravel four days earlier. His hand trembled as he felt the earth, his mind wondering if the ground might still be warm.

He recalled, now, how his hands shook that dreadful day when he rushed to his father and rolled him over to feel for a pulse on his neck. There was none. As usual, his mother was gone, so the boy called for an ambulance and ran into the woodlot to locate his brother. They were too stunned to speak to one another as they followed the ambulance to the hospital in Phil's car.

The next few days passed slowly, and the nights seemed to drag endlessly. Even the funeral arrangements could not be peaceful. The boys' mother insisted that her preacher conduct the funeral service in his church in Malone.

Jimmy remembered that several years earlier when his mother still had some influence on them, she tried to force the boys to attend church services with her. They went with her at first, and they enjoyed the singing, but were frightened and confused by the rantings of the preacher and the parishioners' coarse behavior and shabby clothing. The boys talked it over at night in the bed they shared and agreed to oppose her. She glared spitefully at them when on Sunday mornings they accompanied their father to Mass at Saint Matthew's.

It was Phil who telephoned Father Orgebin to explain the situation with his mother and the funeral. Interceding on the boys' behalf, the priest saw to it that the father was given a catholic funeral.

A neighbor drove the boys and their mother to Rock Mountain for the funeral, but Lillian Coulbron refused to speak a word to anyone.

Jimmy felt numb during the funeral Mass and also during the placing of the casket in the ground. He was unaware of the fragrance of the incense and the sprinkling of holy water on the casket. He did not listen as Father Orgebin mumbled in Latin. He would be unable to recall the color of the clergyman's sacerdotal gown. Nor would he be able to remember the names of the hymns the choir sang. Lillian Coulbron left with Jimmy and Phil immediately after the internment on the hill behind the church. After they returned home, the boys' mother continued to ignore them. Instead of grieving together she drove off alone in the family automobile. Having been confused by their mother's behavior, the boys wandered down to the lake shore where they spent time skipping rocks and remembering good times with their father.

Now, sitting on the crest of the mountain, Jimmy's memory of the events sharpened, and he could feel even more strongly the emotional impact of the preceding days.

Jimmy and Phil returned to the house and noted that although their mother had returned, she had shut herself up in her bedroom. They wondered how she had gotten home since their father's Studebaker was nowhere to be seen.

Jimmy knocked on the door. "God Damn it," she screamed, "Can't you kids ever leave me alone?"

The boy winced upon hearing her words and rolled his eyes toward his brother. They retreated to the kitchen and ate some of the casserole a neighbor had dropped off the day before.

The shades of night crept into the mourning household, and along with it, there came her preacher. Late that night Phil awakened when he heard noises, and he became suspicious. Normally he was a gentle person, but this time he was enraged. He stared for a few seconds into his mother's bedroom, then pounced inside, and physically dragged the naked preacher off his mother's body, and beat the man with his fists.

Jimmy stood aghast at the bedroom doorway as the Reverend Mr. Dodgson cowered on the floor. He saw Phil kneeling on the man's chest as he pummeled his face. Their mother, equally bare, cursed obscenities the boys had never before heard, then she attacked her eldest son with a brass lamp. Seeing the crimson fluid ooze from his brother's temple, Jimmy pushed his mother aside and dragged Phil from the room.

Phil recovered quickly and rushed out of the house to the attached wood shed. He grasped the splitting axe, and attacked the preacher's car, splintering the headlights first, then the windshield. Jimmy grabbed the two quilts from their bedroom and led his brother, who was shuddering with rage, to the barn where they could talk.

They lay side by side in the sweet-smelling hay, which they and their father had only recently packed into the mow. A wan moon sent slivers of light through the cracks between the vertical boards.

"Get away from her as soon as you can," seethed Phil. "She's no good. She never was."

Leaning over, Jimmy stared at his brother's face, attempting to draw greater meaning from Phil's words, then asked, "What do you mean, Phil? Do you know something I don't know?"

The older boy eased his arm under his brother's neck and grasped his shoulder on the far side, creating for him a human pillow. "Please forgive me for telling you this, Jimmy...but...dad isn't your real father."

"What? What do you mean?"

There was a measured silence before Phil responded. "A long time ago I overheard them talking about you. She doesn't even know for sure who your real father is. I'm sorry, but you had to find out sometime." Having sheltered his brother from this knowledge for so long, he now felt the hot flush of pain and guilt invading his face.

Jimmy scuffed his feet into the hay and clenched his fists.

"How about you? Was Dad your real father?"

"Who knows for sure? Even our slut of a mother probably can't answer that. At least I look a little like him. Look at us. Nobody would picture us as brothers because we're not full brothers. We're only half brothers."

"As far as I'm concerned, you'll always be my full brother, and Dad will always be my real dad because he was good to me. He never let on for one second."

"You know why he stayed with her, don't you, Jimmy?"

I suppose it was for us, wasn't it?"

"That's the only way I can figure it."

"He was the best, Phil. Do you remember the fun we used to have working together, the three of us; how we'd be scything hay or sawing wood. No matter what it was, he'd make it seem like fun."

"Yeah, Jimmy, I remember. How could I ever forget? I looked forward to those jobs. How about staying up all night to boil down the maple sap, throwing chunks of wood in the fire and skimming off the foam? Remember how the orange sparks would wave back and forth as they came out of the stove pipe? They'd rise real high and then they would wink and go out. Then we'd tell stories, and dad would play his mouth organ."

"We'd try to harmonize while singing 'Red Wings' and my voice would crack when I tried to hit the high notes."

'There were lots of good times, Jimmy, and there'll be lots more for both of us. As for her, she's got what she wants." The older boy paused then and sighed.

He spoke slowly. "Jimmy, did she ever do anything to you that she shouldn't have?"

"What do you mean?"

"You know. Did she ever touch your body wrong? She did it to me for a while when I was little."

"Yeah, she did…I was pretty little then, too, and I thought that all mothers did that to their kids. It made me feel real funny though, like somehow I knew it was wrong."

"How did she do it with you? Or don't you want to talk about it?"

"It's all right, Phil, I can tell you. It always happened when Dad was working nights. After supper she'd start calling me her little man. Then she'd give me a bath in the tub. She would wash me all over – I mean all over. She'd touch my little bug so much it would stick straight out, and she would kiss it. Then she would tell me that I should sleep with her because she was lonesome. At first I liked to sleep with her because it was warm and cozy, but then she would play with my thing a lot and pull me on top of her. She'd keep pushing up and down on my seat. She told me never to tell anyone or God would punish me, and I'd go straight to hell. I guess I wasn't doing her much good because finally she would push me off and tell me to go to bed. Is that what she did with you, Phil?"

"Just about, but it didn't go quite that far. Don't worry about it though. It won't make any difference. Nobody will ever know. Someday you'll meet a girl you really like. You'll get married and do it the right way."

"What do you mean by the right way?"

"Well, you know – you've seen cows and bulls doing it. People are supposed to do it too – but only with the person they're married to."

"I wonder what it's like – doing it when you're a man. Have you ever done it with a girl, Phil?"

"Almost, but not really. I suppose it's a lot like when you play with yourself but only better."

"I had a crazy dream last night that I was in a room alone with Shirley Morrison. She's that redhead who was in my class but moved away."

"Oh, yeah? I remember her all right."

"Well, anyhow, nothing really happened in the dream. We didn't do it or anything. It's just that she kept looking at me and I kept looking at her, and I felt so doggone good all over."

"Then did you wake up?"

"Yeah, and the funniest thing was I had slippery stuff smeared around in my pajama. At first I thought I had wet the bed, but the stuff smelled different and felt different."

"Join the club, little brother, that's how you know you're becoming a man. That juice you shot out when you had the horny dream is what guys need to make babies with. Besides, now you know you're not queer."

"Why's that?"

"If you were, you would have dreamed about a guy. I have to go to sleep now, Hotshot. I've got lots to do tomorrow."

"Good night, Phil."

Jimmy rolled over and faced the blackness of the interior partition, but sleep did not come easily for either of them.

Chapter 7

Jimmy could see almost all of Echo Lake from his vantage point on the mountain. The wind had been picking up from the northwest, and he could see where gusts of it were stirring the lake's surface. Large arcs of darker blue with reflecting glints of silver marked its path. At Deep Inlet it was relatively calm, because there the air currents could not hit unless they came from the south.

He stared at the spot where two fishermen had drowned a few years ago. The wind had been from the south that day, causing huge swells to roil the water. The boys had been working outside when they first heard two men yelling, "Help! Help! For God's sake, help!"

Now, as Jimmy stood on the edge of the cliff, looking down toward the lake, the memory of that tragedy became so vivid that it seemed as though it had happened that very morning.

The men's cries sounded muffled and faint, but the few words the boys could understand frightened them so that they kept trying to comprehend the situation. Then they could only hear the voice of one man. As soon as they realized what was happening, the boys called to their mother and then rushed to the boathouse. Standing on the dock, Phil spotted the head and arms of one of the men floundering in the swells. Jimmy heard the sound of an outboard motor, and then saw a boat headed toward the swimmer, but it was a long way off.

Jimmy and Phil dragged their rowboat down the wooden poles which formed a slide over the rocks and started rowing toward the drowning man.

From a distance their mother called, "Come back you fools, there's nothing you can do."

The boys' craft was a sturdy, flat bottomed skiff that their father had helped them build from pine boards. The boys were proud of it and had painted it bright yellow, then had christened it 'Thud' because of its weight.

When the boat dipped into a trough, the boys were surrounded by walls of water and could scarcely see the top of the mountains. At the crest of each wave neither the bow nor the stern of their boat was supported, and water would slop over the gunwales. Frantically, they rowed using a single set of oars, one pulling, one pushing.

Phil's back was to the bow so that he could not see the drowning man, but Jimmy faced the bow and directed their efforts by pointing. He cringed when he saw the man raise his arms as high as he could and gulp air before slipping beneath the waves. Finally, they reached the other boat, a small outboard powered runabout with two older men in it.

One of the men cupped his hands over his mouth and shouted, "Can you still see them?"

Jimmy shouted back, "A couple of minutes ago, one of them was right here. Now I can't see either of them."

"We're too late," the other man said. "You kids go back right now. You've got six inches of water in that tub."

A feeling of hopelessness overtook Jimmy when he saw his brother take a long look across the horizon before shaking his head negatively and sweeping the oars so that they were headed back to shore. The men in the other boat circled and re-circled the area. On land the boys hurried to the telephone, but their mother had already called in the emergency.

Word spread fast and soon crews of men were dragging the lake bottom for the rest of that day and part of the next before both bodies were found. Their homemade metal boat was never located. David Coulbron helped in the search but sent the boys into the house when the bodies were carried ashore.

Jimmy's eyes wandered next to the highest of the mountains that encircled the lake. The prominent feature on the southwest slope of the mountain was a bowl-shaped depression, or, rather a half bowl so that it formed a natural amphitheatre from which sounds were magnified when the wind was right. Without this, the boys would never have heard the dying men's shouts. What they did hear was their echo.

He fantasized skiing all the way down from the fire tower right into the lake's edge, and then being able to zoom back up again for another run. He knew this mountainside would make a terrific ski resort, and he wished that some day it would be developed into one.

By now the sun had warmed the wind enough to make it comfortable even though it whipped the sparse sumacs and stunted spruces that struggled to survive in cracks in the bare rock.

Jimmy turned to face the wind. He still wanted to prove and punish himself at the same time, but wasn't sure why. He felt guilty about not having been able to row any faster, for then he and Phil might have been able to save those men. He wondered if God wanted to punish him for letting his mother touch him indecently. He felt that surely God must hate him, and that it was his fault his mother behaved the way she did. Then, too, perhaps it was his fault that David had died.

Stronger than ever now, he was consumed by the need to escape from the restrictions of childhood, to initiate himself, to prove to the world that he was rapidly becoming a man – a good man – a man like David Coulbron. And, just as importantly, he needed to resolve the feelings of guilt that tortured him.

Deliberately, he stripped off his clothing and piled a rock on them so they would not blow away. Standing naked, he raised his arms as high as he could, then faced each direction of the compass in turn and shouted, "Here I am world! This is the real me. My name is Jimmy. Jimmy...the nature boy. Do with me as you will."

He inhaled as deeply as he could and enjoyed the sensation he felt as his lungs expanded to their fullest. He exhaled slowly and sat down on a large flat boulder facing the lake. He glanced down at his world, knowing that soon that world would fall completely apart.

Yesterday his mother had told him that she was donating their farm to the church. Mr. Dodgson would sell it to help finance the sect's move to Montana. She had said that her preacher was really an American Indian prophet who would lead all of his believers to a new life. Jimmy had no more room left for panic. He had simply told her, "I won't go with you…Mother."

He pictured the two of them sitting across from one another at the kitchen table, and his eyes seemed to burn as he saw her lighting a new Lucky Strike from the glowing stub of her old one, sucking in the fumes, and blowing a dense cloud of smoke directly at him.

"What makes you think you're welcome to come?"

The remark felt like a lash against his face; yet he did not respond to the taunt. He merely stared through her until she turned her head to avert his gaze. He remembered feeling that to answer her would have been an admission that he was still a child.

He stood up alongside the boulder and squinted, searching for the one-room schoolhouse that he had attended for six years. His grandfather Wilfrid had built the school just prior to World War One. The wooden shingles had weathered gray making the structure hard to spot. Jimmy distinguished the two outhouses first because they were painted white. Then he could make out the woodshed, and finally, the schoolhouse itself.

For the most part Jimmy had good memories of the little school. During his first few years there Jimmy and Phil were both in attendance often sitting side by side in the double desks. Later Phil attended high school in Rock Mountain.

As he stood looking at the school, Jimmy wondered why, during all the time he attended this school, the picture of George Washington was on his right and that of Abraham Lincoln was on his left. He felt an urge to go down right now, and switch the pictures around simply to shake everyone out of his or her complacency.

His first bad memory was that of being kicked by Cecile Dufour when he was a skinny first grader. Even now he cringed at the recollection. She was an obese eighth grader who couldn't waddle fast enough to escape being tagged during recess. Wisely, he only made that mistake once.

Sometimes on Friday afternoons, the priest from Rock Mountain would come to give religious instructions. With Christmas approaching, he was questioning the whole group, first through eighth grade, about Christ's life. He asked, "Where was Christ born?"

At the time, Jimmy was upset because no one answered the priest's question. After all, it was so easy. He stared at the ten year olds. Surely, they must know the answer. He stared at the eighth graders sitting there like blocks of concrete. Finally, six-year-old Jimmy could not contain himself any longer and piped out, "Bethlehem!" The priest raised his eyebrows, nodded his head, and said, "Very good, my son. I'm glad someone is paying attention."

Next, Jimmy recalled with amusement how, for one of their contributions to the Christmas program when he was twelve, he, along with Petey and Victor, sang, "Praise the Lord and Pass the Ammunition" while wearing their leather aviators' helmets and goggles. Now, he wondered why no one at that time, not even the adults, had thought that their song was incongruous, perhaps even sacrilegious.

He remembered arguing with his friends about the relative merits of the British Spitfire and the German Messershmitt 109, and whether or not bi-planes would ever make a comeback for use in combat.

He frowned for a second as he recalled a fight he had engaged in against Billy Ducharme when he was in the sixth grade. Billy was two years older than he but was mentally slow and had been retained in school. Most of the kids had learned to avoid Billy because he was a bully whose favorite trick was to trip other children when they were running in the yard. He delighted in pushing smaller children around. Finally, after a third-grade girl had been tripped by Billy and bloodied by falling on a rock, Jimmy was fed up and told the older boy to knock it off or else suffer the consequences.

Jimmy recalled the way the kids of all sizes had gathered around as a fight threatened to break out inside the woodshed where the teacher could not see.

Jimmy could feel adrenalin pumping through his body. The skin on his face prickled. He tensed himself and waited for the roaring in his ears to subside. He didn't want to be involved in a messy kid fight with more name calling than action. He wanted it over quickly and for good. He had seen Billy fight before and knew how clumsy he was. Still, the older boy won fights by sheer weight and size.

For a brief moment Jimmy recalled some of the boxing lessons his father had taught him and Phil. He remembered the sparring sessions with his older brother as his father gave advice. Then he thought how his dad used to admonish him, saying, "Keep your cool, Jimmy. Use your head."

Billy glowered at him and raised his fists in front of his face almost comically. The older boy was pudgy but strong. Jimmy sensed that if Billy got on top of him he might not be able to wrestle him off. Jimmy enjoyed the feeling of power that came when his adrenalin rush eased, and along with it the sensation of knowing that he was gaining control of his body.

He grimaced and folded his arms across his chest. He walked slowly around Billy saying in mock arrogance, "Okay you big bag of cow shit, make your first move!"

The insulting remark stung the older boy, and he lashed out with his fists. Jimmy grabbed the pudgy boy's arm and used his opponent's momentum to cause him to stumble against a rack of stove wood. Billy started to pull himself up and cursed savagely as he grasped a stick of beech wood that he flung in Jimmy's face. The chunk of wood cracked against the younger boy's cheek and blood began to flow. Then Billy lunged with his whole body, but Jimmy responded by raising his half-open palm smartly. This blow caught the bigger boy under his chin causing him to bite his tongue. Stung by the sudden pain, Billy raised both of his hands to his mouth. Jimmy responded by landing his final blow into Billy's midsection and then, suddenly, it was all over except the writhing on the floor.

The audience of kids laughed to relieve the tension and rushed outside to play while Jimmy stayed behind and sat down beside Billy. He took out his handkerchief and wiped the blood from Billy's mouth and from his own cheek. Then they grinned at one another and shook hands.

"I'm sorry, Billy. I didn't want to do that, but you've got to learn not to push other people around."

The Ducharme family moved away a few months later, but for a time there was harmony in the school yard.

Jimmy's eyes swept back toward the water of Deep Inlet, and he winced upon recalling the time he had nearly drowned in the far end of the lake. He and Phil had decided to set up a fishing buoy. To do this, they had needed a cedar fence post for a float, a heavy anchor, and a long piece of rope or wire. The first item had been easy to come by. There always seemed to be a pile of old fence posts lying next to the barn.

The boy's recollection seemed to merge into reality, and he could see himself and Phil selecting a two-hundred pound slab of quartzite for an anchor. This was much too large, but the boys thought they could handle the stone slab. Good rope was hard to come by, so they decided to use abandoned telephone wire even though it was stiff and formed tight coils.

The boys were twelve and fifteen years old at the time. Together they tumbled the rock end over end onto the dock, floated their skiff next to it, and slid the anchor aboard. Using heavy pliers from the barn, they fastened one end of the wire to the rock. Phil rowed out to what they assumed must be the deepest part of the lake. Jimmy used a lead sinker attached to a fish line to test the depth. He remembered the old timers claim that the lake was ninety feet deep. They found only seventy feet where they were but they thought it would suffice.

They strained to ease the rock toward the gunwale of the boat and tried to slow its descent into the lake with the wire. The wire got hot from friction as it slipped through the palms of their hands and fingers. One coil suddenly swirled around Jimmy's arm and snatched him overboard. The skiff tilted sideways and nearly overturned, but Phil shifted his weight to counter the angle of the craft. Jimmy could feel the pinching of the wire as it cut into his forearm. He held tenaciously to the boat's edge with his other hand. Phil braced his feet on one side of the boat and slowly pulled the rock anchor up high enough so that his brother could free himself. Jimmy scampered aboard and flopped into the bilge water. He looked up and grinned an appreciative thanks to Phil.

Jimmy was proud that instead of abandoning the project, they finished the task by securing the top end of the wire to one end of the post so that the other end stuck out of the water and could be seen from a distance.

The following day they returned and baited the spot with meaty bones and cooked macaroni, hoping this would attract bait fish which, in turn, would entice lake trout. In succeeding days they would row out to the buoy and tie the bow of their boat to the post an hour or so before dusk. Then they would fish until dark and tell stories. The few small trout they managed to catch might not seem worthwhile to adults, but to the boys it was a great adventure. Neither one ever revealed the close call to anyone.

Jimmy continued his introspective gaze, and wherever there was a meadow, he could see the highway. Where it was wooded, however, the road seemed to disappear. He could see the spot where they had rolled their father's car over the previous year. They had planned to go into town to get their hair cuts, but Phil's car wouldn't start. Their dad had been working the night shift at the mine and was asleep. Not wanting to awaken him, they borrowed his car.

It was mid April, and a late spring snowstorm had dumped a few inches of slushy snow. Phil was a good driver, but this day the conditions had made the driving surface treacherous.

They were hardly out of sight of the house when the car started to skid. Phil wrestled with the steering wheel, but the vehicle veered across a shallow ditch and climbed the bank diagonally. It rolled once and sparks flew as its roof screeched to a halt on the centerline of the pavement. The boys were conscious but wedged upside down between the instrument panel and the seat which had been wrenched loose. They wriggled their bodies around and tried to open the front doors, but these were so distorted by the impact that they would not budge. Phil lifted up the seat and squirmed his way into the back of the vehicle where he tried to kick those doors open.

Neither boy panicked. Jimmy sensed something in his mouth, and rolled his tongue across the chipped cusps of his molars. He felt the roughness on them and spat out pieces of enamel.

"What if it catches on fire, Phil? What'll we do?"

"I don't think it will. But I'm worried that a car coming up the hill might not see us in time. Keep trying every door and window." Finally Phil kicked out a shattered window and the boys crawled free.

"Dad, Dad. We wrecked the car!"

David Coulbron sat up suddenly. "Is anyone hurt?"

"No, Dad."

"Well, let's go take a look." Although there was no scolding or recriminations, Jimmy refrained from telling his father about the pieces of tooth he continued to spit out.

From the mountain top Jimmy could not see the small stream where he used to fish brook trout with Phil. He could, however, approximate where it lay and could glimpse a sliver of the beaver pond upstream and the path of the Delaware and Hudson Railroad that curved its way around the hills beyond.

Jimmy loved this world – the world his great-grandfather had helped pioneer so many years earlier. Like many other French-Canadians, Guillaume Coulbron's family had filtered its way south from Quebec. The boy knew the family history well – how his great-grandfather Guy had been an itinerant boot and harness maker – how, later, he had made harnesses for the mules that pulled iron ore cars deep inside the mine at Rock Mountain – how some of the mules were born and died there, never having seen sunlight. Jimmy knew that Guy had purchased land from the mining company and had started farming and logging. He knew the story of the bear hunt as well and of the fur mittens. Jimmy's grandfather, Wilfrid, had died before Jimmy was born, but his father had told him about his life.

Jimmy's eyes were focused on the small pond which had once held back water to power Guillaume's sawmill.

Then the boy trembled as he realized that it really wasn't his great-grandfather who had bought the saw mill, nor was it his grandfather who had built the school. Suddenly, he became aware that in reality he did not belong here at all. At first his throat seemed to squeeze so hard he was unable to utter one word. Then the tension eased and he shouted, "None of this is my world, and it never was. I'm nothing but a dirty bastard...a mistake...my mother's dirty, nasty, bastardly mistake!"

Chapter 8

By now the sun and the wind on the mountaintop had dried the perspiration on the boy's body and goose bumps began to form. He glanced down at his naked genitals and marveled at how these private parts had doubled in size during the last two years. He grinned slightly and yanked on a tuft of the kinky black hair that was growing around them as if he wanted to test its reality. As he watched, he noticed his penis begin to swell, and he desired to pleasure himself but resisted the temptation, preferring denial as a form of needed punishment.

A flush of androgens caused an urgent sense of power to emanate from Jimmy's thighs and engulf his whole body. This sudden new mystery frightened him momentarily until he recalled the ceremony he had just performed. He felt assured that the ceremony worked. He had proclaimed to the world that he was a man, and somehow, the world knew...and so did he.

He lay spread-eagled on the granite slab, cupping his eyes to shelter them from the sun as his body soaked in its rays. For the first time since discovering his father's body, he began to feel some peace. He felt that his father, David Coulbron, even though he wasn't his biological dad, was gazing down at him at this moment, and he approved of what he saw. Then he slept as the sun crept its way to the vertical.

Jimmy awoke suddenly as he sensed a long-legged spider striding across his thigh. The youth laughed aloud and cupped his hand around the creature allowing it to crawl onto his palm.

"Hi there, Spidey. Now you're king of the mountain. Watch out, though. I'm so hungry I could eat you, legs and all."

The spider crawled to the tip of Jimmy's little finger and started to spin a line to the boulder. Halfway down, it seemed to run out of web-making material and it dangled helplessly. Jimmy lowered his hand and watched his new friend scamper away.

The feeling of depression had completely passed, and he felt elated. He knew how he was going to prove himself. Grabbing his clothes, he threw them far out over the cliff. He laughed as they were tossed about by swirls of wind and landed on trees or rocks. Then he heaved his leather boots over the side and watched where they landed.

Earlier on the way up the slope, he had noticed a diagonal fissure on the ledge and knew that it would offer enough of a hand and foothold. He eased his body over the edge and began to descend the ledge. He watched closely for safe places to grip and, where he could not see, he felt with his toes. In some places the drop was sheer, but he never failed to find a crevice to hold on to.

He glanced down between his legs and laughed again. He talked aloud to his body parts, "You guys better watch out or you'll get rock burn." Then he stared at the jumble of rocks at the bottom. Defiantly, he yelled out to the mountain, "This isn't so bad, you old heap of granite crap!"

It was hard, though, and the boy's fingers were bleeding before he reached the bottom. His shins were skinned and his chest was scraped. He crawled over the fallen boulders and stared upward at the cliff before shouting, "Next time, you son of a bitch, I'm climbing you blindfolded."

While retrieving his clothing, a slight bulge in his shirt pocket caught his attention. Remembering what he had put in there, he took out a recent family snapshot. He examined the faces closely. With extreme care he tried to repair the damage he had done to it that morning when he had deliberately plunged a pencil through the image of his face. Gently now he used a fingernail to unfold and smoothen the torn surface. Again he compared his face with that of his brother and father. Really, there was no discernible resemblance. Phil, like his dad, had brown, curly hair. His own was nearly black and so straight that it resisted being plastered down by any of the tonics and lotions that he had tried. Phil's face was narrow while his own was broad.

Earlier that morning he had the urge to cut his mother's image from the photo, to snip it into narrow slivers with a pair of scissors, and burn them in her own ashtray along with her cigarette stubs, but he had not. Now he was glad that he hadn't. He didn't hate her. He never had. It's just that he wished things had been different, more normal. He could see some similarity between his face and his mother's, especially in the eyes and mouth. His general features, though, were more angular and masculine.

Jimmy recalled the day the photograph had been taken on the previous Fourth of July, scarcely six weeks ago.

Wearing their red, matching bathing trunks, the brothers rushed up the beach to join the other family members after having swum in the lake. The water had been cool and refreshing, but the yellow beach sand nearly burned their feet.

"For heaven's sake!" scolded their mother. "How can we take a picture with you two looking like that?" She handed them a towel and searched in her purse for a comb.

Jimmy wondered why Phil scowled at his mother's remark and why he gave his face only a cursory wipe and combed his short hair with three strokes. This was enough, though, because Phil's damp curls snapped into position with little urging. Phil handed Jimmy the comb, and the younger boy whipped the tines through his hair repeatedly in a vain attempt to plaster down the errant strands. With his free hand he patted his hair trying to determine what it was doing. Noting that, as usual, it refused to cooperate. He smiled and said, "Sorry, folks, that's the best I can do without glue."

David Coulbron reached over, gently parted the boy's hair high on the left side, and pulled the remaining strands to the right. These bounced up forming a springy, irregular pompadour. Jimmy's father kept a happy smile as he did this, but the woman's face was dour.

The four of them stood on the beach with the lake as a background. His mother's sister Sharon wanted to try out her first roll of colored film. They lined up as a family group with the father, David, on the left. He had removed his shirt and undershirt earlier to soak up the sun. Jimmy noted the tan line on his father's forearms and was surprised at the paleness of his chest.

His mother, Lillian, stood next to her husband wearing a wispy mauve-colored summer dress and a wide-brimmed, matching hat. Her facial expression did not change. Nor did that of Phil, whose gray eyes seemed to be boring through the lens of the camera while his lips were rigidly pinched. He seemed to be enduring something painful.

Jimmy, alone, was truly at ease. The shutter caught him as he gazed up to the left at a circling seagull. Even his eyes, nearly black, sparkled in the sunlight and seemed to be smiling. His dark, full eyebrows arched as he looked up to the sky. His forehead was furrowed from the upward gaze, and several strands from his thick crop of hair began to rebel.

As Jimmy scrutinized the photograph he wondered why Phil had not grown a moustache as he had allowed himself to do. Then he remembered how downy his brother's facial hair really was and accepted the difference as normal. Before this day of self-reflection, he had never noticed how piercingly dark his own eyes were, nor how bronze-colored his skin was compared to that of his brother. Previously he had called it a suntan, but now he realized that, unlike his brother's tan his never went away, even in the winter.

In the photograph he was not quite sixteen. Phil was at least five inches taller than he at the time. Still, Jimmy's arms and legs were already stockier than his brother's limbs and his torso was fuller.

He tried to conjure up a mental image of his biological father, the one that he had never seen. He wondered how many times he had been with his mother, and what he had meant to her. He wondered if he were still alive. Finally, he supposed that it really didn't matter, but he would be willing to bet that the man was a handsome stud. Still, he knew that when he became a man, he would never make a baby and abandon it the way his father had. Nor would he ever sleep with another man's wife.

Fully dressed now, Jimmy chuckled to himself as he descended a dense stand of spruce. He knew this area well because just beyond him lay a new grove of olive-green aspen that he and Phil had logged over for pulpwood two years earlier. Sprouting up from the old root systems, the new growth stood like a miniature forest of buggy whips. He pictured himself growing taller to catch up with the trees.

Inside the new growth the boy heard a familiar musical chirp followed by a rustling of leaves as a covey of young ruffed grouse scurried for cover, dodging helter-skelter behind deadfalls, and diving into the safety of brush piles. The female parent, however, stood her ground, first trying a bluff by spreading her wings menacingly. Boldly she made short charges at the boy's legs. When this failed to deter him, she resorted to the old dodge of fluttering helplessly on the ground as though mortally wounded. The lad was familiar with this behavior, but still marveled at nature's way of protecting the young. As Jimmy approached her, she continued to distract her intruder by attempting to draw him away while dragging a faked broken wing.

Admiring her maternal instincts, Jimmy said out loud, "Good for you, Mama! You make a terrific actress, but I know that trick. Besides, I'm not some hairy monster who's going to devour your babies. Anyhow, they're such ugly runts – all legs and pin feathers – sort of like me. Watch out, though, because maybe I'll come back in October when they're bigger and put all of you in a pot pie. Nah, just a couple of you. I'll leave some for seed."

The brothers had done a small amount of hunting together with a twenty-two, but actually Jimmy preferred to observe grouse and snowshoe hares alive rather than in a steaming meal. Moreover, their mother didn't like wild game and refused to cook it. Sometimes while afield, they pretended to be woodsmen. Then they would erect a lean-to in the woods, sleep under the trees, and roast a rabbit or grouse on an open fire. Jimmy recalled these times with pleasure.

Then he wiped a tear from his eyes as he thought of Phil being so far away for so long and of his dad resting forever on the knoll overlooking St. Matthew's Church. He envisioned the mound of raw earth on the grave and knew that his mother would never visit it nor even have a stone erected in her husband's memory. Jimmy vowed silently to visit the grave often and that he and Phil would see to the monument.

The rest of the return route was so familiar he no longer needed to watch for landmarks. The trees were sparse in this part of the pasture which drained toward the lake. The boy began to sprint effortlessly taking giant strides. Reaching the first of the fieldstone fences he leapt gracefully across. Here and there he noted the remnants of split-rail fences an ancestor had erected.

Once dairying had been more important in the area, with a dozen or more family farms in the valley surrounding the lake. Lately, however, many farmers had sold their cows and taken jobs in the mines or in the state prison at Dannemora. The fields were becoming overgrown with brush and thistles. Along one side of his grandfather's back meadow, blackberry canes grew in abundance. Jimmy stopped to check them out, then realized they wouldn't be ripe until the end of August, just before the time school would start.

He took a short detour toward the leek spring, so called for the wild leeks that grew in the black, mucky soil where the water bubbled from the bottom of the shallow pool. Jimmy spread his body horizontally on a bed of ferns bordered with blue flag gone to seed. He shooed away a flotilla of water striders and sucked in great draughts of water directly from the pool. He splashed some water on his face and sank the fingers of one hand into the muck. He closed his thumb and finger around a leek, plucked it free, and rinsed it in the pool. He chewed it and swallowed.

He followed this water source downward as others joined in the race to the lake. Soon the streamlet became a brook that dissected a swampy meadow where patches of buttercups and daisies grew to the delight of bumble bees. He knew that tiny brook trout, too small to bother fishing for, inhabited this stream. He paused by a pool upstream from a log and stared into the depths of the water enjoying the illusion caused by the flow over the colored pebbles. He could see a six-inch fish holding itself motionless against the current, its orange and white fins rippling in unison.

Jimmy spread the wild hay apart in search of insects. He spied a pale green grasshopper nibbling a blade of grass and deftly scooped it up. Carefully he tossed it into the pool where it struggled to escape. Immediately, a trout arched through the surface of the pool and grabbed the insect. In that split second, the boy could see the red spots of the fish surrounded by circles of blue, reminding him of British aircraft insignias.

Continuing downstream the boy approached the remnants of Guillaume's sawmill. The stone foundation of the flat rocks was still visible, but nearly all of the wooden structure had been removed for use elsewhere. Jimmy picked up one end of a rotting timber which was studded with hand-forged spikes, the old square-cut ones. He allowed it to fall to earth and watched hundreds of black ants rushing to rescue their larvae by picking them up and transporting them into the burrows.

The millpond had silted in with black muck, and the water was barely two inches deep. Once it had been known as a good place to fish. In addition to the silting, the wooden spillway had decayed to the point that it could no longer retain enough water for any practical purpose. The boy wished now that he had lived in those days of expansion in the area rather than during its decline.

Only one small grove of second-growth trees separated him from the highway. As he headed for this, he was surprised to see swamp maple already turning crimson. His first thought was that it had been nipped by frost on that cool night when the moon was full. He realized, however, that it is not the frost that causes the color of trees to turn, although enough cool weather and diminishing hours of daylight will, for then the leaf factories cease producing chlorophyll. He had enjoyed his biology class last year and wondered what his junior year held for him.

It had been a hot, dry summer, but here in the mountain valley, temperatures were occasionally dipping into the upper thirties at night, and even greater changes were destined to come.

Chapter 9

The plan forming in Jimmy's mind as he headed toward the house was simple. That morning he had arisen early and gone directly to the barn to complete his farm chores prior to the mountain hike. He had milked the black and white Holstein, Daisy, and turned her out to pasture. He had fed the hogs and chickens before stashing his clothing and books in the back seat of Phil's Pontiac so that he could leave inconspicuously should his mother be at home. He had intended to leave a note for her but wanted to avoid any complications to his departure.

He approached the farm yard from the barn side and bent down to retrieve the splitting axe from the spot where it had fallen following Phil's attack on the preacher's car. Suddenly, turning the corner, he caught sight of Dodgson's car, and it unnerved him. Its headlights and windshield shattered, it lay there like dung defiling the gravel driveway in front of the house. Jimmy hadn't expected that because never before was it there in broad daylight.

Jimmy knew that David's Studebaker would not be there, his mother having wrecked it while driving drunk on the same day as his father's funeral.

"James," called his mother as she peered out the screen door, "come here, my darling."

The honeyed request seemed too fake to be genuine so Jimmy hesitated a moment, trying to gauge her intent.

"Oh, come on in, sweetheart, the Reverend wants to visit with you."

"Damn!" the boy muttered under his breath, considering the cultist less reverend than a viper.

Having skipped breakfast entirely, the boy was famished and had hoped to gulp down some milk and grab a peanut butter sandwich before leaving for good. He belched the taste of the wild leek he had consumed as it bubbled and foamed inside his stomach.

A wave of nausea struck Jimmy as Dodgson met him at the door. The man smiled so broadly his horse teeth bared, and the boy winced upon seeing up close the pock marks on the man's cheeks and the stubble on his chin. Dodgson wrapped his arms around the lad's shoulders and led him to the table.

Jimmy's nostrils stung from the combination of the man's whiskey breath and his stale sweat. He slumped on a kitchen chair and tried to conceal recurring dry heaves. Droplets of perspiration formed on his forehead and heat burned in his face.

"I'm fixing you something to eat, dear. You must be starved."

"Thanks, Mom, but could I just have a glass of milk? I don't feel so good. I think I'm going to heave. I'm gonna go lie down."

Dodgson was standing over him, "Looks like you scratched your face, Kiddo. Here, I'll wash the blood off for you."

Jimmy looked up into the man's bleary eyes and stared at the white matter accumulated in the corners of them. "No, uh, thanks. I can manage by myself, Mister."

Cecil Dodgson was not to be deterred, however, and he proceeded to wash Jimmy's face with a sour-smelling dish rag he found under the sink. Drool oozed down one corner of the man's lower lip.

At the first touch, the boy recoiled and tried to turn his head away. The man persisted clumsily, unaware of his own repulsiveness and the boy's distaste for him. "Relax, now, son. I'll have you spiffy in a jiffy." Then he laughed and belched all in one.

The boy squirmed to stand up, but the man pushed him down. Jimmy stared at the empty fifth of Three Feathers whiskey. It was flanked by two grimy tumblers which, together with the bottle, formed a centerpiece for the kitchen table.

Dodgson ran his fingers slowly through the boy's hair, trying to smoothen it down and brush out the weed seeds and stick tights. The boy cringed and, grabbing the glass of milk his mother offered, jumped up and ran upstairs to his room. He pulled the shades for his windows shut and stretched out on top of the covers. He drank the milk, then threw the glass against the wall, shattering it. He curled his body tightly in a ball and clenched his fists. Tears would not come, only the swelling in his throat caused by hatred and shame.

Downstairs in the kitchen, the adults conferred. "Even after we sell this farm," said Dodgson, "it'll be at least a year before I can get church members to come up with enough money to finance our kingdom in Montana."

"We can stay here until then if you're willing to take care of the goddam animals."

"Let's keep the kid here. He looks strong and can do a lot of work. For damn sure I'm not milking any cows or shoveling pig crap."

"I think he was planning to go live with my sister in Malone, but it doesn't make no difference to me. You're right about one thing, though. He is as strong as a bull, and he's never given me one bit of trouble. You and him will get along like bees and clover."

"The kid looks part Mohawk, Lil. He sure as hell doesn't look like your husband. Who's kid is he, anyway?"

"He's yours, you dumb ass."

Dodgson stared at her, his mouth open, "Huh? Well I'll be damned!"

"Why don't you pour me a goddam drink, Dodgy? Don't you know how to take care of your women?"

"The bottle's empty. Your husband have anything stashed away?"

"David? You gotta be kidding. Let's go to Tony's in Dannemora."

"Can't. Your other frigging kid smashed my headlights, and you screwed up your car royally."

"Well, let's take the kid's car."

Dodgson shrugged his shoulders and walked up the staircase. He eased open the door to Jimmy's room and saw the boy asleep, curled up on his side. He reached over and patted Jimmy's pants pocket, feeling for his car keys. The boy awakened abruptly and pushed the man's hand away.

"What are you doing?" he asked.

"Gimme your car keys. Your mother and I are going to town."

"No! That's Phil's car. You can't take it."

"He's the one who smashed my headlights and windshield so I'm entitled to use his car."

"Like hell you are, you whoring bastard," shouted the boy. He rolled over and stood face to face with Dodgson, ready to smash him with his fists the way his brother had done.

"Take it easy, kid. We're all bastards. You might as well get used to the idea. Now gimme the fuckin' keys."

"You try to take 'em, and I'll toss you down the stairs head first, you drunken slob!"

Jimmy was just as tall as Dodgson but not as heavy. No matter what happened, he was not going to relinquish Phil's keys to that man. The fact is he had them hidden in the shed.

Dodgson glared at him for what seemed longer than it really was. No more words were spoken. The man's face twitched several times.

Jimmy steeled himself to deliver a telling blow into the man's belly, but before he could do so, Dodgson turned slowly and walked downstairs. Meeting Lillian at the foot of the stairs, he said, "C'mon, woman. If we hurry, I can get the headlights fixed in town before the garage gets too busy."

"What about the broken windshield?"

"Pretend the top's down on the fuckin' convertible. You want to come or not?"

Jimmy watched from an upstairs window as his mother and Dodgson drove away. He walked downstairs and looked in the phone book for his aunt's number. He didn't know her all that well, but he knew she cared for him when he was little. He thought she would be willing to let him live with her until he could make other plans. He gave the operator her number and listened to it ring. There was no answer. This was not surprising since he knew she worked rotating shifts at the state hospital.

When Jimmy and Phil were young and their mother was feeling well, sometimes there were family get-togethers and Jimmy got to see his Aunt Sharon. She was older than Lillian by several years. Jimmy thought that she seemed pleasant enough. Often during family events she would go out of her way to spend some time conversing with him. Jimmy knew that his Aunt Sharon had no children of the own and that her husband was disabled.

Jimmy went downstairs and made himself a sandwich. He seethed inside, thinking about his mother and that bastardly preacher. A sudden image pierced his mind as he remembered the five-gallon can of kerosene that his father, David, kept in the cellar for refilling the barn lantern. He wondered if that would be enough to incinerate the house. Then, realizing that he would be the first one suspected, felt ashamed for even considering arson.

He went back up to his bedroom and returned with the twenty-two caliber rifle and a box of shells that he shared with Phil. He opened one end of the box of cartridges and poured a dozen of them in the palm of his hand. He fingered them, admiring the brass cases and lead tips. He wondered how anything so small could actually kill a person. Then, he shuddered involuntarily as he remembered the time last year when his mother had ordered Phil to shoot their sick kitten, and he had obeyed her. Carefully, he placed the cartridges back into their container and slipped the box into his pants pocket. He brought the weapon and ammunition to the barn and climbed the ladder to the hay loft where he hid them under hay. He wasn't at all sure why he was doing this. It seemed like the right thing to do, and he felt driven. He knew, at least, he was keeping the weapon away from that usurper and, if he ever had to use a gun, he knew where to find it.

Jimmy realized that his mother and her companion were unlikely to return until very late. He decided this would be a good time to drive to his aunt's house some thirty miles away, hoping to find her there. Phil's car was still loaded with Jimmy's belongings, and he knew he had no reason to stay.

He retrieved the key from its hiding place in the shed and turned the ignition key. He pulled on the choke part way and stepped on the starter button. The solenoid clicked and the starting motor began to grind, but the engine refused to fire.

The boy got out of the car and raised the hood, wondering if there might be a loose wire somewhere. Immediately, he could see that the vehicle had been tampered with. The distributor cap was ajar and the rotor was missing. The hatred rose again. It buzzed in his ears and pricked his face as he realized that that man, that bastard of a man, must have removed the part.

He sat for a long time in the front seat of the car as the afternoon wore on. He listened as trucks rolled down the highway, and he considered hitch hiking to Malone on one of them. He thought again of the rifle and bullets. Then, Daisy started bellowing, and he remembered that she hadn't been milked or fed that evening, nor had any of the other animals been cared for.

"They go off to swill booze into their guts and leave me with all the work," he muttered. "Well, they can go rot in hell, both of them." The cow bellowed again, and the boy relented. Just this time, he thought. Then I'm getting out of here for good.

He walked back up the hill to the basement door of the house and changed into his chore clothes. He stared at the can of kerosene. He lifted it, shook it, and noticed that it was nearly full. He set it down and picked up the milking pail.

The cow greeted him when he entered the yard by swishing her tail and watching him eagerly with her big eyes. He held open the barn door and patted the animal's neck as she passed by on her way to the milking stall. He poured a measure of grain into her feed box and straddled the milking stool. He didn't start milking immediately but first massaged the cow's udder for a few seconds to start the milk flow.

He had always enjoyed milking, having started when he was nine, learning how to strip the teats after his older brother had completed most of the task. By the time he was twelve, his hands were large enough and strong enough to do the milking alone. He and Phil alternated the task after that.

One reason he liked the job was because he knew that it strengthened his hands, and he wanted them to be like Phil's and his father's. The other reasons were intangible. Perhaps it was because during cold weather the animal's udder was warm, and it felt good to touch it or, perhaps, since the repetitive motion required no mental effort, he was free to think about important boy things. He sensed, too, that the animal enjoyed giving up her milk and that he was doing her a favor.

After he finished the milking, he set the pail aside and climbed up the ladder to the hay loft. He forked down enough hay for both feed and bedding. Then he realized that he had removed the hay close to the spot where he had hidden the rifle and box of cartridges, so he searched them out and hid them in the far end of the loft. He descended the ladder, scraped the dung out of the gutter, and gave the cow fresh hay to lie on. Outside in their pen, the pigs were starting to squeal so he slopped wet mash in their trough.

Inside the barn again, he was unsure whether or not he should turn the cow out for the night or leave her in her stall. Finally, thinking about Dodgson and his mother and the fact that they might not care for the animal properly, he unlatched the metal stanchion and herded the cow outside so she could drink from the brook and forage wild grasses.

He returned to the house basement with the milk, changed his clothes and washed his hands. He assembled the parts of the cream separator and poured half of the pail of milk into the stainless steel bowl of the machine. He placed a small container to catch cream from one of the spouts and a larger container to catch the skim milk from the other.

He grasped a handle with his right hand and exerted pressure to begin the rotation. It was difficult at first to start the heavy flywheel but, once it was up to speed, the handle moved more easily, and Jimmy switched to his left hand. He watched the thin, bluish-white skim milk start flowing first. This would be mixed later with ground grain and household scraps to make slop for the hogs. Soon cream appeared from the other spout and ran like a ribbon of yellow yarn into the container.

When he was finished separating, he refrigerated the milk and cream upstairs. Then he returned to the basement to wash the cream separator and set the perforated discs to dry on the rack. He wasn't doing this work for them. He did it because this was the way his father had taught him. He understood that if you have animals and equipment, you have a responsibility to take care of them properly.

Upstairs in the kitchen he picked up the empty whiskey bottle and tossed it in the trash can on the porch. He searched through the refrigerator and found some left-overs to eat. He moved to the living room and clicked on the radio. He started to listen to "I Love a Mystery" but soon felt tired and went to bed.

Sleep eluded him at first. His mind wandered through previous episodes of the radio mystery series in which he identified with the character, Reggie. Their exploration had taken him and his companions to a remote region in Venezuela where they climbed a rugged cliff. On top of this they discovered a plateau inhabited by prehistoric plants and animals.

The day dream fleshed itself out and merged with a real dream. Jimmy, a man now, struggled against clinging vines that tripped him and held him as Tyrannosaurus Rex attacked.

Chapter 10

Lillian complained constantly as the wind streamed through the broken windshield of Dodgson's automobile. He remained silent as he drove directly to the auto dealership where he had purchased the used Cadillac a few months previously. It was a busy day for the mechanic, and he could not have the repair completed until the following afternoon. The preacher was a slick operator when he was reasonably sober and so managed to wrangle a loaner vehicle from the manager.

He and Lillian drove off toward Tony's Tavern in a nearly new Chevy. Tony's was a nice enough place, having been refurbished right after the end of World War Two. They bypassed the dining area and moved directly into the bar. It was still early afternoon, and the bar stools were vacant except for those where two retired prison guards nursed their drinks. Dodgson and Jimmy's mother were the only occupants of the tables.

Soon, however, there was a shift change behind the walls of the prison and men, some still in their blue uniforms, hung their billed caps on wall pegs and brought the room to life. Two of the younger men took turns trying to outdo one another's score on the pinball machine. Two others played the shuffle alley game. The bartender pushed his cigarette farther into one corner of his mouth and placed a black leatherette dice shaker on the bar.

Three middle-aged guards walked in. They unbuttoned their jackets and loosened their ties. Each in turn shook the dice, and the tall one yelled, "Hey, hey!" upon tossing a seven which entitled him to a free drink. The bartender drew three glasses of Genessee beer. Several more bluecoats strolled in and soon all of the stools and several of the tables were in use.

Dannemora was far enough away from the reservation so federal regulations for Indians were not enforced there. Nevertheless, some of the guards looked at Dodgson sitting with a white woman, and they began grumbling to one another. One of the guards stood with his back against the bar and repeatedly smacked a leather sapper filled with lead shot into the palm of his hand. Noticing this, Gus McCurdy, the bartender whispered, "He's okay. He comes in here a lot."

"Who's the broad?" asked the tall guard.

"She lives up at Echo Lake. Her old man just died a few days ago."

"She sure wasn't in mourning for very long," sneered another.

"I hear she's good for a hot lay most anytime if you can get her slopped up enough."

"The way she soaks it up, I'm not gonna spend that much money for a lousy screw."

The guards turned their backs to the couple and started comparing the Yankees to the Brooklyn Dodgers.

"Hey, Gus," called one of the guards, "When you getting' television in here? I saw a set down in Albany last week."

"It's not gonna be long now. You can bet your sweet ass on that," said the bartender. "There was a man in town with a television truck here yesterday. He had a tower with an aerial or something on it, and he could crank that thing up about thirty feet in the air."

"You think he could pick up any stations?"

"LaPlante said he talked to him. Montreal comes in real good, but half the time it's in French. He got Syracuse, too, but it wasn't so good – full of white spots and wavy lines."

"Jesus!" said the tall man, "maybe we'll get to see the World Series. The Boston Braves are gonna take the National League this year."

"Ah, you're crazy, McGuire."

"Oh, yeah? Just remember they got Warren Spahn. Nobody can hit that lefty."

Lillian got up to use the restroom. On her return, she sat down at a table with three men. Dodgson watched her as she gushed shamelessly at them. One of the men placed his hand under the table and stroked her thigh. She smiled at him. Dodgson stood up and walked over to their table.

"This is my wife," he said to the men. "She's drunk."

He took hold of her arm forcefully and led her out of the room. "Where you taking me, sweetheart?"

"We're gonna do the river run and hit every joint along the Saranac."

Jimmy awakened when they arrived home and slammed the car doors. He listened as they argued about something, then headed up the stairs. He heard his mother fall on the steps and curse. He got out of bed and watched through a crack at the edge of his door. He saw Dodgson carrying his mother to the bathroom. He heard her retch and moan before she staggered to the bedroom.

The boy lay awake, breathing deeply and wondering about these crazy adults. Everything was quiet except the ticking of his alarm clock. Then the noise started, a rhythmical bumping of their bedstead against the wall. Immediately, he knew what it was, and he wished he wasn't there to hear it. He remembered and felt ashamed about what his mother had done to him and Phil.

The noises got louder. "Get off me. That's enough. Leave me alone."

Jimmy clenched his teeth and seethed in anger. He wanted to shout out. He wanted to smash Dodgson's face and crush his privates with his logging boots, but he knew he would have to hurt his mother at the same time. Once again, his mind conjured up the scene of a blazing inferno, and he thought of the kerosene. He was glad now that he had removed the rifle from his bedroom and placed it in the barn.

In the other bedroom, the noises diminished somewhat. Jimmy attached earphones to his radio and tried to tune in a station. All of the local stations had stopped broadcasting for the evening. Some country music started to come in clearly, "This is the radio station WWVA coming to you from Wheeling, West Virginia."

He had heard this station before late at night. Once Phil had explained that certain stations are allowed to increase their power at night and, also, that under certain conditions the radio waves travel farther. During the daytime, he could never capture that station. He listened to the old-time music that wailed out cheating hearts and death on the highway. The station drifted off and the boy slept.

Some early sun peeked through the edge of his window shade and struck the boy's eyes. He awoke with a start. There were no noises in the house. He shut off the radio and dressed. He fingered the five-dollar bill he had been saving to buy his mother a birthday present. He crammed it inside his wallet and poured the handful of change from his dresser into his pocket.

Downstairs he filled his belly with toast covered with peanut butter and with cold cereal smothered in the milk he had brought in the evening before. It was chilly out, and he wore his lined jacket. He walked into David's workshop and came out with some tools.

As he moved around to the front driveway, he was surprised to see a different car there. Then he looked closely at the license plate and could tell it was a temporary dealer's plate. So much the better, he thought. He raised the hood on the vehicle and removed not only the rotor but also the coil, and three of the ignition leads.

He closed the hood, sneered, and said out loud, "Let's see the Reverend Cecil Dodgson try to drive that bastardly car now."

Jimmy had planned to wedge a thin wire nail alongside the edge of the horn button so that it would be jammed on and blow steadily, but he noticed this wasn't necessary. The newer model had a wide, chromed horn ring. He took a piece of baling wire from the shop and wired the horn ring down so that it blared continuously. Then he stepped into the grove of maples to watch the fun.

Through the screen of leaves, he watched as Dodgson stood stark naked in front of an upstairs window. Jimmy could see him turn his head and yell something at his mother. The boy grinned and watched as Dodgson came down the front steps wearing David's bathrobe. He was bare-footed and winced as he stepped on the crushed stones of the driveway.

The man opened the car door and ripped off the wire. The blaring noise stopped, and he stepped out to glance around the yard. Ten yards away, Jimmy stood out in the clearing, tossing the car's coil up in the air and catching it.

"Why don't you try to start your car, Reverend? I'll bet it runs just as good as Phil's."

Dodgson took one step toward the youth and stopped when his feet hurt. "Gimme that, you little bastard."

"Fuck you, you old bastard."

Jimmy folded his arms for a moment as they glared at one another. Then he held the coil out tantalizingly with one hand and the spark plug wires with the other.

"Maybe you'd like to work out a little trade, preacher."

"Wait a minute. I'll get you your goddam part."

The man returned a few minutes later dressed in shoes this time. In the meantime, the youth had placed two pieces of board on the driveway ten feet apart. Jimmy pointed at one of the boards, and the man approached it.

"Put my rotor on the board and step back while I check it."

Dodgson complied, then said, "Listen kid, it wasn't my idea. It was your mother's."

"I don't believe a word you say."

The boy placed the coil and the wires on the board and stepped back. Each of them retrieved their car parts. They stood facing one another again.

Jimmy held his rotor in one hand and Dodgson's rotor in the other. He stretched them out saying, "Hey, look at this, I've got two of these little doo-dads. Guess I'll throw one away."

He made a gesture of tossing the man's auto part in the woods but actually held it in his hand. Dodgson advanced toward him, grumbling under his breath at being duped. Jimmy reached behind him and displayed a long thin knife in front of him. The man stopped short.

"You know what this is? This is the knife my father used to stick dirty pigs with – dirty pigs just like you, and I'm ready to do the same to you."

Dodgson stepped backwards several feet. "Okay, kid, take it easy. We can learn to get along."

"You hurt my mother, and I'll use this on you."

"Your mother needs help. She may have to go back to the hospital again."

"What are you talking about?"

"Didn't David ever explain things to you about her?"

"Explain what?"

"Well, you must know she's gone away a lot, don't you?"

"Yeah, so what?"

"If you want to you can check this out with her sister. She works in Ogdensburg."

"What are you trying to say?"

"Christ, kid, you don't know a goddam thing, do you? David's had to have her locked up a dozen times. She's even tried to kill herself three or four times. Look at the fuckin' scars on her arm. That's not from slicing baloney. If I don't look after her, who will?"

"I'll take care of her."

"Goddam it, kid, you can't. She wants to be with a man all the time. Any man. If she whores around too much, she'll get herself all syphed up."

"What's that mean?"

"It's a disease, a rotten, messy disease."

"How do I know you're telling the truth?"

"Ask your Aunt Sharon. She's a nurse. She can explain it a whole lot better than I can."

"Okay, I'll call her. Here's your rotor, and remember what I said. I'm getting the hell out of here, and you can learn to take care of the animals."

"Geez, kid. I like you. Try to relax a little bit. There's a lot about life you don't know. I can help you."

"Mister, I don't need your kind of help."

They each left the spot. Jimmy replaced the rotor in the Pontiac, snapped shut the distributor cap, and tried the engine. It coughed, then began to run, but roughly. The youth gunned the engine and roared out of the yard spewing two strips of gravel the whole way.

Chapter 11

Jimmy was angry with himself for abusing Phil's car by his rapid departure. He had never spun the wheels like that before. He knew it was his way of showing disdain for that man who was trying to take over his father's place, both on the farm and in his mother's bed. A few miles down the road, he slowed down realizing that if he got caught speeding and driving without a license, the state police might impound the car and give him a stiff fine.

The emotion of the moment diminished, and he began to pay attention to the sound and rhythm of the engine. It was obvious that the engine was missing, and the power seemed inadequate. He wondered if it might quit before he reached his aunt's house, and, if the car did manage to transport him to Malone, he wasn't certain he would find her at home. Moreover, the gas gauge barely registered a quarter. With less than six dollars in his pockets, he didn't want to waste any money on gasoline.

The engine sputtered several times but continued running. Jimmy noticed Mrs. Papineau's farm ahead and decided to pull into her yard to make repairs. He had a few tools along, and he knew her son Lawrence would have others.

As he turned into her yard, Jimmy saw his former baby sitter hanging up one of her house dresses on the clothesline. A brown and black farm dog barked and chased after the front tire of the car. The youth stopped the vehicle but left the motor running. He approached the woman and noted immediately that she looked older than he remembered her.

"Hello, Mrs. Papineau," he called.

She squinted at him and cupped her hand against one ear.

The boy walked closer and spoke more loudly. "Hello, Mrs. Papineau. I'm Jimmy Coulbron. Do you remember me?"

"Jim-mee! She squeeled. "Look at you. *Tu es un vrai homme, maintenant* – a real man!"

She rushed to hug him, although now, while standing together, her head barely reached his chest. She bent her head upright to look closely into his face. "I can't believe it. Come in and 'ave a cookie wit' me."

"Uh, no, thank you. I'm kinda in a hurry. I'd just like to work on my car for a while. Maybe I can borrow some tools from you."

"*Oui, oui oui*, but first you come inside. I want to know everyt'ing zat's 'appen' to you.

Jimmy gave in. They shared a panful of cookies fresh from the oven as they spoke. She regretted not having attended David's funeral, but she hadn't been feeling well. Jimmy filled her in on his mother and Dodgson as well as his sorry relationship with them.

"You poor *garçon*," she said, holding onto his hand. "Do you want a job?"

"What do you mean, Mrs. Papineau?"

"I need a man – a strong *homme* like you – to work 'round my farm."

"What's wrong with Lawrence? Isn't he still here?"

"Non, he is to get married, him, in a couple day, and zey to take over ze farm of 'er fazer. He will marry, him, zat Rabideaux girl in Altony, and, me, I'm to be left all alone. He could not wait, him. He move in wit' her, already. *Sacré*!"

Jimmy watched her bless herself.

"Gosh, I don't know. Maybe I could help out for a few days, but I'm thinking of moving to Malone."

"Me, I can not pay you much – just room and board and a few *piastres* a day.

"Well, uh, okay. I guess I can stay to help out for a while."

Jimmy asked the woman not to disclose his whereabouts to his mother or to Dodgson and, so, he assumed the position of chore boy and handyman at the Papineau farm.

That evening he went to bed upstairs with a certain amount of trepidation concerning the possibility of uninvited bed partners. He pulled back the top sheet but saw nothing moving. Next, he checked the mattress underneath the bottom sheet. The yellow stains on the mattress were evidence that Lawrence had slept in this bed. Each of the four casters was set in a bowl filled with what smelled like turpentine. Jimmy was glad he left most of his clothing in the car.

The air was unusually sultry that evening for so late in August. Heat lightening flashed on the horizon several miles away. The youth opened the bedroom window and adjusted the removable screen to fit the opening. This was inadequate to dispel the heat and humidity that forewarned of a possible storm.

Jimmy lay on the bedspread wearing only his shorts. Even with just the top sheet covering his body, the air in the room was oppressive. As soon as he stripped off the sheet, mosquitoes began sneaking in through gaps in the screen. They buzzed his ears like an attack by enemy night fighters. He took the insects as a personal challenge and honed his tactile sense so that he would recognize their touch on the fine hairs of his body. He would wait until an attacker began to insert its proboscis. Then he would smack it forcefully with his hand.

An owl hooted somewhere near the barn, reminding the boy of the ones he used to hear from his own bedroom window in the summertime. He wondered if his mother and Dodgson were out somewhere boozing it up or in bed again.

Jimmy's mind wandered back several years to a Sunday afternoon shortly after New Year's Day when he was ten. His father was at the mine working. The boys and their mother had finished a pleasant Sunday dinner complete with fresh-baked apple pie. Classical music was playing on the radio, and his mother's canary was singing its heart out perched on a wooden dowel braced across the inside of the cage. As it sang, it lifted its head, and its breast seemed to swell out. It trilled its melody as if it wanted to perform with the orchestra. Jimmy's mother was humming to the music as she knitted a wool sock for winter use.

Jimmy watched in fascination as his mother's fingers manipulated the strands of yarn and the needles simultaneously. She wasn't even watching what she was doing.

"Mom," he asked. "How can you do that so fast?"

"It's easy, Jimmy. Do you want to learn?"

"Sure, Mom."

He pulled a chair close to hers. She handed him a skein of blue wool yarn and instructed him on how to hold the yarn spread out with his wrists as she rolled the yarn into a ball. When she was finished, she handed him a pair of knitting needles and showed him how to cast on a line of loops before actually starting the knitting.

"Making socks the first time is fairly complicated. How would you like to start with a scarf?"

"Good idea, Mom."

Using the needles she offered the boy, his mother demonstrated knitting. "You hold the yarn like this with your two needles and place the needle in your right hand under this loop. Then you make another loop with the yarn over the needle, like this. After that, you use the needle to pull the loop you just made underneath, and you tighten the yarn up a little. Here, do you think you can do it?"

They worked together for a half an hour or so. When Jimmy had completed an inch of knitting, Phil came in and invited him to go skating with him on the lake. Together, they asked their mother for permission. She told them to be careful and to be home before dark.

A few inches of soft, fluffy snow covered the ice. Using a shovel and a scoop, they pushed this aside to create a skating rink. Because of recent thawing and sudden refreezing, the ice surface was smooth, and skating was enjoyable. Soon, two other boys joined them carrying a hockey puck and two sticks. Jimmy and Phil broke off sticks from brush on the shore's edge, and they played a game. At three-thirty the two other boys had to leave. Jimmy and Phil headed for home feeling refreshed and invigorated as they and their companions headed up the trail toward the Coulbron farm.

When the four boys approached the house, they were met by Lillian Coulbron. She brandished a willow switch and berated her offspring.

"I told you snots a thousand times not to go out on the ice unless your father was with you."

Then, she commenced whipping their legs and backs with the switch. She was so carried away with the punishment that her placement of the branch was careless and struck the boys' faces as well as their bodies. Even through their winter trousers and long underwear, the strokes stung sharply. Moreover, they felt embarrassed to have their friends witness their mother's behavior.

Inside the house, she verbally abused them, telling them how disappointed she was at having such inconsiderate brats for children. They both protested, reminding her that she had never forbidden them to skate alone and also that she had distinctly given them permission to go out this time.

She sent them to bed with no supper. In their bedroom, they stripped down and compared the red and blue welts which formed lines from the calves of their legs to their necks. They each had several marks on their cheeks from the tip of the switch which snapped around from their shoulders and stung their faces.

Their father had been working overtime at the time of the incident and later he was sleeping. The boys were too embarrassed to mention it to him, but later he noticed their subdued behavior and the way they avoided their mother. He examined the marks on their faces without questioning them. When he patted Phil on the arm as a fatherly gesture, he observed the boy wince and checked his bared back. Then he ordered Jimmy to remove his shirt.

"Did your mother do this to you two?"

They said nothing but, with their eyes downcast, nodded affirmatively.

Other irrational outbursts by their mother had preceded this one and more followed. She also would suddenly accuse her husband of seeing other women and being mean to her. Having overheard these attacks against their father and knowing that they couldn't possibly be true strengthened their love for him.

A cold front had moved in during the night, and it was chilly inside Jimmy's bedroom in the Papineau house as dawn broke. It was silent inside the house when he rose quietly and walked out to the barn to care for the animals.

When he finished his chores, he lit a cooking fire in the wood burning range using dried aspen splits.

'Pannycake wood' his father used to call it because it burned quickly and then went out without heating up the whole room. He pumped water into a blue enamel pot and brewed some coffee.

Soon he could hear Mrs. Papineau moving around upstairs. When she entered the kitchen, she seemed so lame the boy knew she was in pain. As soon as she saw him, however, she seemed to perk up and became jolly.

As he was standing next to the range, she hobbled over and hugged his shoulders. "You sweetheart," she exclaimed, "I could smell ze *café* way up ze stair. What you like me to cook for you?"

"Just cereal would be fine. I can do it, Mrs. Papineau. You don't have to wait on me."

"Don't be ze silly goose. What good is ze old woman if she cannot pamper young men like you? We are to have fried *patates* and egg and bacon and ever'ting else you want."

It pained the youth to see Mrs. Papineau limp as she hustled around the room to serve him breakfast. He helped by pumping water for her and stoking the range. He pared and sliced the potatoes so she could fry the *patates* and then set the table.

Meanwhile, she chatted constantly, "My fazer, him, he could not eat 'thout no grease. If we did not have no drippin' in the house, he say to me, 'Yvette, you go to ze store and buy me ze grease.' He like ze lard best. Of course, Crisco was okay, too. Sometime, he make himself ze grease sandwich."

"How did he do that, Mrs. Papineau?"

"Oh, my fazer, he just smear some bacon fat or lard on ze bread. Then he salt it and pepper it 'til it was black like *charbon* and eat it. Though, other time, him, he slice up ze grand *oignon* and cover zat wit' lot of *moutarde*. Course, it 'ave ze grease on it, too. *Mon Dieu! Mon Père, lui*, he could not eat 'thout no grease."

"You a pretty boy, Jimmee, but you too skinny. You stay 'ere wit' Yvette, and she fatten you up real good. I got ze nice hamhock, me, and I boil up ze pea soup for you and bake ze big panful of Johnny cake. You like zat, don't you, eh?"

"Uh..., yes, ma'am."

"Good for you, Jimmee. After ze breakfast you go into ze granary. You look next to ze trap door. You take zat sieve and use it to sift out ze oat you find in zere zat are mix' wit' ze yellow pea. You bring me a panful of ze pea and save ze oat for ze pig and chicken. I make you some good *habitant soupe aux pois* for supper. You like zat, eh?"

"Yes, ma'am. What does habitant mean?"

"*Habitant? He is ze petit fermier, a Quebeçois*. He has a petite ferme, him, and a *grande famille*. You talk French, don't you, Jimmee? Your fazer, him, he was a Coulbron. Zay was all French."

"I learned some from my father, but Mom didn't know any."

"Zen, me, Yvette Papineau, will learn you ze French."

"Thank you. I'd like that. Uh, *merci, madame*."

"You got to learn to not be so bashful, Jimmee. *Tu es timide. On parle Francais. Bien vite, et on parle beaucoup*. You don't talk enough. *Parle! Parle! Mon garçon*. You just say what you want to say. Never mind what ze people might t'ink. My fazer, him, he talk all ze time. He tell so many joke, him, I almost split ze gut. My mother, her, she learn no English. She talk ze blue streak, though. *Toute en français, elle*."

Yvette's oral capability in French was on par with her ability in English, with both vocabulary and sentence structure being non-standard. She was fluent in both languages, perhaps too much so. When she spoke in French, her words were both sprinkled with anglicism's and obsolete expressions. In both tongues she displayed a marked nasality and a harshness of both consonant and vowel sounds.

When conversing with her in French, Jimmy had some difficulty at first. Her speech was very unlike the Parisian pronunciation the high school teacher attempted to enforce. By relying, nevertheless, on his two years of school French and on what he had learned from David Coulbron, the two of them could converse moderately well in either language. He found his relationship with the woman emotionally satisfying, and he never tired of her jolly chatter.

Within a few days, his work at the farm assumed an easy routine, and he was able to spend time easing her workload in the house. Still, he recognized that she thoroughly enjoyed pampering him to the point of embarrassment. They continued to chat in both French and English with Yvette retelling jokes she had learned from her father. Jimmy appreciated the fact that she never brought up the incident where Jimmy bit her breast. Somehow he knew that she held it back in deference to his shyness.

The repair of Phil's car required two days of his spare time. First Jimmy removed the spark plugs, and examined them as he had observed both David and Phil do with their cars. Whenever he opened the hood of the Pontiac, he would marvel at the length of the vehicle's eight-cylinder engine and the spotless condition in which his brother had maintained it.

"Eighty-four horsepower," Phil had said. "That's twenty-four more than most Chevrolets had that year."

The youth cleaned and gapped the plugs and reinserted them. He opened up the distributor cap and held open the points. He saw immediately that they were pitted badly enough to affect the operation of the engine.

Jimmy's brother Phil was a stickler on proper maintenance, and although his vehicle was old, he kept it in as near perfect condition as his knowledge and level of expertise allowed. The younger brother had often observed his older sibling quietly with a degree of awe as he deigned to remove a part and disassemble it. The interior of a carburetor seemed very complicated to the boy. He wondered what each part accomplished. With a mixture of respect and common sense, he kept silent and observed. Often Phil would explain a process to him.

The youth was apprehensive about removing the points so that he could file them accurately. He worried that he might break something or lose it. Fortunately, Phil kept a point file in his tool box. Jimmy placed the set of points gently in a vice and meticulously filed them so that each of the pairs would mate as perfectly as possible. He blew away all of the metal filings so that they might not interfere.

He had no timing light and was unsure of how to use one. He wasn't certain what the correct gap between the points should be. He thought he remembered that it was supposed to be twenty-thousands, and using a gauge, set them at that amount. Earlier, when gapping the plugs, he had guessed at thirty-thousands, knowing that they weren't quite as critical as the points.

He was both exhilarated but anxious when he first tried to start the engine after his attempt at maintenance. He smiled when it fired immediately and continued to run. He drove out on the highway and noticed a definite improvement in the vehicle's performance. He drove it for a few miles and returned to the Papineau farm.

Chapter 12

On Sunday morning Jimmy drove Mrs. Papineau to ten o'clock Mass at St. Matthew's Church in Rock Mountain. He held her arm as she climbed the long row of steps and entered the sanctuary. She walked purposely up to a row of red vigil lights, removed a dime from her purse, and dropped the coin into a slot. She lit the candle and struggled to get to her knees without falling. Her lips moving rapidly, she uttered a prayer in French. Then she joined Jimmy in a pew. He kept wishing she would forego all of the kneeling and standing and just sit there to rest her joints.

After Mass, Jimmy wrote a letter to his brother but waited to mail it until he had Phil's latest address. He set the table while the woman heated some pea soup and made sandwiches for lunch. Afterward, she stretched out on a daybed in the parlor while the lad and the dog took a hike in the woods.

The dog was frisky and enjoyed having the boy there to throw sticks for him and pull on a rope. Together they romped through the pasture and into the foothills until late afternoon. On the way down a hill, overlooking the farm, Jimmy could see Mrs. Papineau's cattle milling around under a grove of basswood trees.

"*Va chercher les vaches, Gaston!*" he commanded, practicing his French.

Expertly, the dog circled behind the cows and drove them toward the fenced area next to the barn. Jimmy ran ahead and opened the door. There were only four milch cows. Their teats and udders swinging from side to side, they walked up the ramp leading into the barn and went in directly, each to her own stanchion.

The boy snapped the stanchions shut around the cows' necks and walked over to the attached milkhouse. He washed his hands and returned to the barn with a clean pail and milk can. He washed each cow's udder with a dampened cloth, knowing that the milk would be tested for bacterial contamination and, if care wasn't taken, Mrs. Papineau might lose her Class A milk permit.

He milked the cows one after another, pouring the milk into the large metal can. A calico-colored cat mewed softly and rubbed her body against the youth's legs. Noticing her dish on the floor, some twenty feet away, he tilted one teat and directed a stream of warm milk toward it. The cat ran over and lapped it up.

When the milking was finished, he loaded the filled milk can onto a wagon and hauled it to the milk house. He checked the temperature in the water bath of the milk refrigerator, and lifted the milk can into it. In the morning, he would place that can and the one from the next morning's milking close to the mailbox on the highway where it would be picked up and loaded on a truck for delivery downstate as far away as New York City.

After his evening meal on the eighth day at Mrs. Papineau's farm, Jimmy helped with the dishes, and the two of them sat in the living room to talk and listen to the radio. Outdoors, the dog began barking as a car drove into the driveway and stopped. Jimmy watched from the kitchen window. The driver extinguished the car lights and walked toward the house.

"You have company coming, Mrs. Papineau. I'll answer the door."

"Merci, Jimmee. Maybe it is my son, Lawrence, who comes to pick up his clothes."

It wasn't Lawrence, however, it was Dodgson. The youth snatched open the door and stood barring entrance to the house. The man stood on the porch. They looked at one another before either spoke.

"What do you want?" asked Jimmy defiantly.

"Take it easy, kid. I saw your car here yesterday so I knew where you were staying. Here's a letter from your brother. I thought you would like to have it right away."

"Well, okay, uh,...thanks. Now, you better leave."

"Jimmy, we have to talk."

"I've got nothing to say to you."

At that moment, Mrs. Papineau hobbled into the room. "Bring ze man inside so I can see him, Jimmee."

The youth stepped back and Dodgson entered. He removed his hat, smiled, and said, "Excuse me, ma'am. It's important that I talk to Jimmy."

"You come both to ze living room now so you can talk. Jimmee, you want me to go up ze stair?"

"No, Mrs. Papineau, sit down in your own chair. You can hear this, too. This is the man I was telling you about – Dodgson. He's living with my mom."

"*Arseyez!* Sit, everybody sit down," said the woman.

"Thank you ma'am. The boy has to know this."

"Well, say it. My favorite show is on soon," said the woman.

"It's about your mother, Jimmy. She's been gone all night and all day."

"Where did she go?" demanded the boy.

"Last night we were at Tony's. I left for a few minutes, and when I got back she was gone."

"She's been gone since then?"

"Yes. I asked the bartender about it. He said she left with two prison guards when I stepped out."

"Why didn't you follow them?"

"Follow them where? I never saw them go."

Mrs. Papineau observed the two of them intently. She noticed an imploring look on the man's face as though he was begging for help. She saw anger in the boy as he gritted his teeth and cast his eyes to the floor.

The woman had intended to remain silent during their discussion but, noticing the boy's emotional state, she took over.

"You, Mister Dodgson, does she do zis before?"

"Yes, a number of times, but whoever she goes with drops her off at the house before morning."

"You try to stop her?"

"Yes, of course, but I can't watch her every minute. The kid won't listen to me, but you must know that when she gets too bad, she has to go back to the hospital."

"Yes, I know zis because Mr. Coulbron, him, he told me. He did not want me to tell ze boy so I kept my mouth shut."

"Is it true, Mrs. Papineau? Is my mother crazy?"

"All zose time I stay in your 'ouse to take care of you and your brazer, it was because your mazer, her, was in ze mental ward. I t'ink your fazer, him, he should 'ave told you."

Jimmy raised his eyes and looked at Dodgson. "What do you think we should do?"

"I think it would be best if you call the police station instead of me."

"You could call from here, Jimmee, but I don't 'ave ze telephone. Maybe we should drive to your house together and call from there."

"No way! I'm taking Phil's car."

"I won't wait for you, Jimmee. Maybe you stay all night zere."

"We'll see, Mrs. Papineau. If I'm gone for long, I'll try to find someone else to do your chores until I come back."

When they arrived inside the house, Jimmy asked, "Why didn't you go looking for her?"

"I did, for Cripe's sake. Except for pulling cow tits and shoveling pig crap, I've been driving all over like crazy and asking everybody if they've seen her. I had to get someone else to hold my church service for me in Malone."

Jimmy walked to the phone and lifted the receiver.

Dodgson spoke, "Here, Jim, I already looked up the phone for the state police and wrote it down on this piece of paper."

"Yeah, I see it. Okay…thanks."

The youth phoned in the missing person report. The person who answered told him to wait there at home, and someone would come to talk to them soon.

After hanging up the receiver, Jimmy asked, "Why do you take her to places like that?"

"She wants to be on the move all the time, Jimmy. If I refuse to take her, she gets on the phone, and someone else comes here and picks her up. Guys, she always wants to be with guys. Then she stays out all night, and they dump her off here when they're through with her."

"She wasn't always like that."

"No, she wasn't. The problem comes and goes. David had a way to keep her calmed down most of the time, but, then she'd get nervous or something and go on a toot."

"Yeah, I know she's always had some problems."

"I met her in Malone the first time quite a few years ago even before you were born. She was there visiting her sister. She sat next to me on a barstool, and one thing led to the next."

"You must have known she was married, didn't you?"

"Not at first, I didn't. She didn't have a wedding ring on. She was very pretty and friendly. We got acquainted, and she started to come to my church services. After I found out that she was chasing after other guys when I wasn't around, it didn't seem to matter if she was married or not. I'm sorry, son, it pains me to tell you all of this, but I really do like her a lot. I always have, and I've never once hurt her."

"If only my father was still alive. He'd know what to do."

"He's not your father, Jim."

"I know that. Phil told me she doesn't even know who my father is. What's it to you, anyway, if I'm a dirty bastard?"

"Jim, you're not dirty. Don't say that. I'm a bastard, too, if that's any consolation. It's not the end of the world. Besides, she told me who your father is."

"Ha! I'm supposed to believe that? I may be a dumb bastard, but I'm not that dumb."

"Come here a minute, son. I want to show you something you'll find interesting."

Dodgson stood up and pointed toward the living room. Jimmy screwed his face into a sneer but followed the man into the other room. The man faced a three by five foot mirror and asked the boy to stand next to him. The man said nothing for several minutes as they stared at one another's reflection. Finally he asked, "Well, did your mother tell me the truth?"

Jimmy was stunned. A mixture of emotions confused his thinking. This unexpected revelation of his parentage was something he wanted to reject because of his hatred toward the man. Yet, he needed desperately to belong to someone. He studied the two faces carefully. Dodgson winked one eye. Jimmy did the same. The man wrinkled his nose, and the boy did likewise. They each frowned, then smiled. They bared their teeth. Their eyes turned away from the mirror's image, and they looked at each other.

Suddenly, the youth bolted out of the room and ran upstairs to his bedroom.

Not long afterward, a car pulled into the driveway, and three men walked to the porch. Dodgson let them in and called Jimmy to come downstairs. A tall state policeman in uniform and two detectives introduced themselves. They noticed that the boy had been crying.

The police interviewed Dodgson and Jimmy, asking questions. Then one of them requested a recent photograph of Lillian Coulbron. Jimmy removed a framed photograph from the wall, and the men left with it.

Chapter 13

The man and the youth sat at opposite ends of the living room, neither one speaking. From time to time Jimmy would sneak a furtive glance up at Dodgson before lowering his eyes again. Dodgson stared out the window, occasionally taking a deep open-mouthed breath. His eyes blinked often and seemed puffy from lack of sleep.

Dodgson reached beside his chair and picked up his guitar. He was about to start tuning it when he noticed Jimmy walk over to the telephone. He listened as the lad talked to someone named Perchy, said, 'Thanks' and hung up the receiver. Noticing the man's concerned look, the boy said, "In case you're checking up on me, I had to find someone to do farm chores for Mrs. Papineau until I can help out again."

"I'm not checking up on you, Jimmy. I'm just on edge. Who's this Perchy?"

"Perchy Garew. He's an older guy David knew from the mines. They used to talk French together sometimes. After he retired last year, all he does is go fishing and dig graves at St. Matthew's."

"Did he say he will do the work?"

"He said he'll be glad to have someone like Mrs. Papineau to speak French with and wouldn't charge her anything to do her chores."

"That's lucky for her. She seems like a good woman."

"She really is. I was worried about her because she's gotten so lame."

"How did you get to know her so well?"

"She used to take care of me and Phil when we were little."

"That's when your mother was gone?" the man asked.

Jimmy took a breath, and let it out slowly. "Yeah...when she was gone."

The man spoke slowly, "One of the detectives said they'd call as soon as they knew anything for sure."

"Yeah, I heard him."

Unknown to the man and boy and to the police at this point, Lillian Coulbron had been picked up wandering along a back road that morning. Her clothing was disheveled, her face was bruised, and she was incoherent. The older couple who found her delivered her to the hospital in Plattsburg. Hospital personnel cared for her but found no identification.

Later that day, Lillian was only vaguely aware of what had happened. When asked her name she only remembered her maiden name of Gonyea.

The two prison guards who had picked her up at Tony's Tavern the evening before brought a bottle of cheap whiskey along with them and drove to a secluded place in the overgrown meadow of an abandoned farm. After she was drunk enough, they took her out of the car and laid her on a blanket. They each took their pleasure from her as the other watched. When their desires were satisfied, they delivered her, drunk, to the house of a bachelor friend who invited in several more men and charged them ten dollars each. Hours later, two of the men dumped the woman ten miles out of town on the back road where she was found.

During the course of their investigation, the police checked the area hospitals, and it was the following morning before they were able to identify Lillian from her photograph.

The youth had gotten up early the day Dodgson reported his mother's disappearance to him, and now, as he waited downstairs for word about her, Jimmy's head nodded and he dozed off.

The man allowed him to sleep for a while, then shook his shoulder gently.

"What do you want?" complained the boy, only half awake.

"Please go to bed, Jimmy. No sense two of us staying up."

"I don't want to."

"It's okay if you go to bed now. It's late. Tomorrow might be a busy day. It's best if you get plenty of sleep."

Jimmy went to bed upstairs, but sleep didn't come immediately because he started worrying about his mother again. Then his thoughts shifted to school, and he recalled giving an oral report while standing in front of the class.

The students in English class had been studying Greek myths and legends and, by chance, Jimmy had been assigned the myth of "Oedipus". He felt a need to refresh his memory of the story. Gradually, the boy recalled it more and more clearly as he lay in bed – how King Laius of ancient Thebes was warned that he would be killed by his own son. To prevent this, he took the infant son of his wife, Jocasta, pinned the boy's legs and left him to die on the mountaintop.

David wouldn't have done that, no matter what, the boy thought. I wonder if Mister Dodgson would be that cruel to save himself.

The recollection continued. A shepherd found the boy alive and presented him to the royal family of Corinth where he was adopted and raised, bearing the name Oedipus which means 'swell-foot'. Jimmy pictured this affliction as a chronic, painful infection cause by the father.

As a youth Oedipus was taunted by a drunk concerning his parentage. Probably someone like Dodgson, Jimmy thought.

Oedipus went to consult an oracle who told him that he would kill his father to marry his mother.

I wonder where I'd be now if I had killed Dodgson when I first wanted to. In jail, I suppose. I've already slept with my mother. I might as well have married her.

Thinking King Polybus of Corinth was his father, Oedipus vowed never to return there. Maybe that's why my brother Phil ran away. He knew he would have to kill Dodgson if he stayed.

Jimmy had been intrigued by these stories when he first read them because as a child he once thought that destiny ruled his life.

He thought of how Oedipus continued traveling until he met a quarrelsome man, Laius, and killed him, not knowing it was his father. Then he was challenged by the man-killing Sphinx. After he solved her riddle, she killed herself. As a reward, he was made king of Thebes and given Laius' widow, his own mother, as his wife. After she bore four children by Oedipus, the truth came out. Jocasta killed herself and Oedipus blinded himself.

The youth wondered if his life was a re-enactment of the myth. Already he had thought about killing this man who claimed to be his father and had even pointed a knife at him. His own mother had seduced him when he was an infant, and she had already tried to commit suicide. Now she was missing. Dodgson seemed to be like the drunk who taunted Oedipus. There were so many coincidences. Still, at least, Jimmy thought, my own eyes and legs are fine.

Finally, the youth decided that the stories were more like fairy tales than reality, and he drifted off to sleep.

Jimmy and Dodgson still hadn't heard anything concerning Lillian at breakfast time. Either the man had risen very early or had not gone to bed at all. When the boy came downstairs and entered the kitchen, he smelled bacon cooking.

"No news yet, Jim," said Dodgson. "Have some pancakes and bacon."

"I don't want any of your damn food."

"Suit yourself, but maybe you should keep your strength up in case you're needed today."

"Needed for what?"

"God only knows, Jim. God only knows."

The boy's mouth watered and he forked several flapjacks on his plate.

"This is the best syrup I ever tasted," said Dodgson.

"It's crap. We made it last spring – me and Phil…and David. This is the darker batch. People say that the lighter stuff which comes first is better."

"Well, I think it's terrific, and they're too fussy. What do you think?"

"Nobody cares what I think."

"I do, Jimmy. And I'd like you to teach me how to make maple syrup. I remember my grandmother used to boil some down in a kettle out in the back yard when I was still living on the reservation."

"You used to live on the reservation?"

"Sure. I was born there. I left when I was younger than you are now."

"How come you left?"

"I don't know. I guess I was looking for my father."

Where was he?"

"Who knows? I never met him. Jim, I don't think you should hear this story."

"I think I'm entitled to know, don't you?"

"Maybe you're right, but it's not very sweet."

"Tell me anyway."

"Well, I don't remember my mother either. According to my grandmother, my mother was only fourteen when she had me. She wasn't married, and the guy she was hanging around with had already left her."

"Who was he?"

"I never found out. When I was your age, it bothered me, but I don't think about it anymore. Sometimes my grandmother would say he was a white peddler. Other times, she would say he was an Indian who went to work in New York City building skyscrapers. That's all I know."

"Is your grandmother still alive?"

"No, she died just before I moved away. Her sister still lives in Hogansburg. I visited her sometimes. I've got some cousins there, too, and also some relatives on the Canadian side."

"Are you all Indian? I don't think you look it."

"Your guess is as good as mine, Jim. Maybe it depends on which of my grandmother's stories you believe. Actually, I don't believe either one of them. I'd guess I'm full or nearly so. I don't know what that makes you. I do know it's enough that you could be registered as an Indian and live on the reservation. Does that bother you?"

"Nah, I don't care about that. What bothers me is that you didn't tell me sooner."

"Geez, Jim, I only found out about it a week or so ago, and I was too embarrassed to tell you. Do you believe me?"

"Well, I don't know – maybe."

"I didn't even know at the time of David's funeral. By the way, is David buried in the Rock Mountain cemetery?"

"Yeah, Phil and I are going to put up a monument for him as soon as we get enough money."

"Stone ones are pretty expensive. Maybe you could put up a wooden one for now."

"I'll think about it, Mr. Dodgson."

"Don't call me that, Jim. It's not my real name. I made that up when I opened the church in Malone. Reverend Cecil Dodgson sounded a whole lot better than Buck LeTarte."

"Is that your real name?"

"LeTarte was my grandmother's last name. She called me Buck. As long as we're here together for now, why don't you call me Buck?"

"I might as well." Jimmy wanted to learn more about his father's background, but his next question was interrupted by the telephone. The boy leapt to answer it. He talked with someone for a few minutes and hung up.

"Who was it?" asked Buck.

"Oh, that was just Clarence, a boy who lives across the lake. He wanted me to go fishing with him today."

"What's your pleasure, Jim? You want to do the dishes or the farm chores?"

"Well, if you're here to listen for the phone, I may as well do the chores. Maybe the pigs are lonesome for me. They're about my level of importance."

"Don't say things like that, Jim. Hold your head up. You're as good as anyone else – better than most. You've got a good head on your shoulders. You've got a strong body. You can make something of your life. You can have anything you want."

The boy simply shook his head and said, "Ha! What a laugh, but thanks for the lecture anyway." Then he went out to care for the animals.

Buck LeTarte watched from the window above the kitchen sink as Jimmy latched the fence gate next to the barn. He couldn't explain why he felt good whenever the boy was near, even when he was acting surly. Perhaps the lad reminded him of himself at that age and that subconsciously he wished to have another chance to relive a life that was on an increasingly rapid skid. He simply knew that being around the kid made him feel younger and more completely alive.

When Jimmy was heading toward the house carrying a pail filled with milk, he could hear Buck playing his guitar. Remembering his own instrument in the trunk of the car, he decided to retrieve it as soon as he refrigerated the milk. Buck noticed the boy carrying the guitar into the house and called him over.

"Show me your guitar, Jim. It looks like a good one."

Jimmy handed the instrument over. Buck nodded his head affirmatively and asked, "Mind if I try a few notes, Jim?"

"No, go ahead. It'll need tuning, though."

Buck strummed a few chords and said, "It's not bad the way it is. I never want mine tuned too perfectly because then, nobody would recognize me playing it."

The boy smiled a little, and the man began singing and playing the melody of a gospel song. Jimmy and Phil knew how to strum most of the more common chords but had never learned to play lead melody. He watched and listened intently and was impressed by the man's skill.

"This is an easy one to chord," said Buck. "It's just D7 and G with a C thrown in for good measure. Take my gitbox, and let's find out what we sound like together."

Jimmy stared at Buck's guitar for a few seconds. It was a handsome instrument, decorated with silver inlays. The boy did want to try it.

"Okay," he said. "I've got nothing to lose."

They were well into their third song when the telephone rang again. The boy laid Buck's guitar on the sofa and rushed to answer the call.

"They found Mom!" he shouted. "She's in the Plattsburg hospital. I'm going there right now."

"Wait a minute, Jim. We can go together in my car."

"I can go alone."

"Sure, but how are you fixed for gas?"

"uh...not too good."

"The reason I say this is because I didn't get much sleep last night, and I'd like you to drive. I might fall asleep at the wheel."

Secretly, Jimmy had admired Buck's forty-two Cadillac convertible. Although it wasn't new, it looked sporty, and it was in spotless condition now that the repairs had been completed.

"Well, then, okay," said the boy.

Buck tossed Jimmy the keys, they each grabbed jackets, and left. A few miles down the road, Jimmy announced, "You know, Buck, I don't have a driver's license yet. Suppose we get stopped by the police?"

"Don't worry. I'll take the rap. How old are you?"

"I'll be sixteen in two weeks – just before school starts."

"That's about what I figured. Pick up your learner's permit right away, and you can be driving legally before long."

The youth felt a certain pride driving the powerful vehicle and enjoyed its responsiveness to his commands.

The meeting at the hospital was painful. They found Lillian in an oxygen tent covered with tubes. Her face was discolored and, although she was awake with her eyes open, she did not recognize either of them nor respond to their questions.

Jimmy stayed with her and held her hand while Buck talked with hospital personnel. They told him that most likely she would be there for a week before she could be discharged. Buck felt obliged to inform the staff about her history of mental problems, realizing that she might have to be returned to Ogdensburg.

Before leaving the hospital, Jimmy telephoned his aunt in Malone to inform her of her sister's condition. She thanked him for the call and told the boy she would meet him at the farm before going to visit Lillian.

On the way home, Buck slept, snorting in his sleep occasionally. Jimmy pushed down on the accelerator and watched as the speedometer reached ninety and was still climbing. He held it there for a few minutes then allowed it to sink back to fifty.

He sneaked a glance at Buck to make sure that he was still asleep. Suddenly, it occurred to the boy that Buck seemed to be quite a different person from the one he had met a few days ago.

Chapter 14

After Buck and Jimmy returned home, the man went up to bed to get some sleep while the youth remained on the open porch trying to recapture, with his guitar, some of the sounds he had heard his father create. He could get the chording reasonably well, but the melody eluded him. The boy was impatient because it seemed to take a considerable amount of time for him to learn how to play a song by trial and error. Yet, Buck seemed to do it effortlessly.

He was about to put the instrument away for a while and find something to eat when he noticed his Aunt Sharon's car turn off the highway and head down their driveway. As she closed her car door, Jimmy noticed her staring at Buck's vehicle and, then, at Phil's older one.

"I see you have company," said his aunt, wrinkling her nose as she walked up the steps of the porch.

The boy stood up to greet her, expecting a hug. It was strange, he thought, that she merely shook one of his outstretched hands limply. She sat opposite him, her back to the barn. Jimmy offered her refreshments which she refused.

"Thanks for stopping in, Aunt Sharon. I know you're anxious to go see my mom."

"How bad is she, James?"

"I'm afraid she got beat up pretty bad, but the doctor thought there might not be any permanent damage."

"How's she up here," asked the woman while twirling a finger to denote insanity.

Jimmy winced upon seeing the gesture. "It's hard to say, Aunt

Sharon. She didn't speak to us. She didn't even seem to see us, and her body was really rigid, like she was in a trance."

"I'm sure she'll have to be committed again – maybe this time for good."

"Gee, I hope not, Aunt Sharon."

"She's beyond hope. Forget about her. Even as a girl she was always getting in trouble of one kind or another. I suppose you didn't know that she gave birth to twin girls just before she turned fifteen and gave them up for adoption. She was made pregnant by a boy who was just about your age now."

Jimmy's eyes opened in surprise. "No, I didn't know about that. That means I've got two sisters somewhere."

"That's right. Don't feel sorry for them, though. They're the lucky ones because someone else raised them. Alfie and I never could have any children, but my sister could breed like a sewer rat."

She continued as the lad listened dumbfounded, his mouth drooped open. "I offered to take the twins and raise them as my own, but she refused me and gave them to strangers instead. Mom tried to talk her into giving them to me, but she threw one of her tantrums, and Mom gave in. Did you know that your mother was locked up in Ogdensburg at the same time you were born?"

The boy simply shook his head in bewilderment.

"Well, she was. You were born in an asylum, you poor child and, right afterward, the doctors had her sterilized so she couldn't have any-more. They told David that you should be put out for adoption because they thought all of her boozing and running around might affect you. He wouldn't allow it. He was a living saint. That's what he was. What can I say?"

Jimmy squirmed uncomfortably on his chair as his aunt continued her tirade.

"Believe me, there's a whole lot more I could tell you about her, but you're too young to hear it just yet."

"Mom was good to us some of the time."

"How about all the other times? When you were younger, how did you feel knowing you had a crazy mother?"

"Well, I didn't really know it. I kinda thought all mothers were like that. Dad didn't even tell us that she was placed in the mental ward in Ogdensburg. He'd just say she was on a trip."

"That was his only mistake, and I can excuse him because he did it for you and Philip. He was a saint, for sure. What more can I say?"

"Yes, Aunt Sharon, he was a good man."

"I was the oldest, you know, but I was plain-looking. My mother and father favored her because she was so pretty. They gave her everything she asked for."

"I don't really remember your parents, Aunt Sharon. I was only two when they died. What was my mom like when she was young?"

"She was a spoiled brat. That's what she was."

"I'd like to talk to her psychiatrist sometime if that's possible."

"I can arrange that. That's Dr. Spencer. I've worked with him. He's the best psychoanalyst in the hospital."

"Would it cost me very much to talk with him?"

"I don't think it would cost you anything. She becomes a ward of the state when she's in there. The doctors want to talk to members of the family because that helps them understand the patients."

"That's good. Can you arrange it and give me a call?"

"That's the least I can do for you. I'm really concerned about this person she was seeing. Is that his car in front?"

"Yeah, that's Buck's car. He's sleeping now. He was up all night waiting for a call from the police."

"I don't want you staying here with him, James. I've heard a lot of bad things about him in Malone. If he won't leave, you can call the sheriff." Her voice was rising, and her comments went beyond a request and became a demand.

"Oh, Aunt Sharon, you know how people exaggerate. He's not so bad. He'll leave if I ask him to, but I think Mom needs him."

He wanted to tell his aunt that Buck was his biological father, but he decided to save that information until she could see them together.

"I don't understand how you can stand to have him in the same house. You know that he was having an affair with your mother behind David's back. Don't you have any respect for your dead father?"

Jimmy was upset by her forceful attitude, and he found it hard to control his temper. He spoke fast and harshly to her as tears flooded his eyes.

"It's not fair for you to say that, Aunt Sharon. I just lost the father I loved, and now I've got one I'm supposed to hate. But, for some reason, I can't force myself to hate him. Maybe it was Mom's fault more than his."

"What are you talking about, for goodness sakes?"

"Buck is my father now, and I don't want to lose him, too. With Phil gone, he's all I've got."

"Oh, Good Lord! I can't believe this nonsense. You send him away and come live with Alfie and me. You remember your Uncle Alfie, don't you?"

"I remember I stayed with you and him for a while when I was little. I was scared of him."

"What frightened you?"

"I remember he never went to bed at night. He'd just sit in his chair and smoke cigarettes. Then he would throw the butts in a coffee can half filled with water. It stunk terrible and looked goopy."

"Did he ever go into your bedroom at night?"

"Yes, that's what scared me the most. He kept moaning and groaning nonsense sounds, and I thought he was a ghost."

"But that was nothing to be afraid of. When he does that he thinks he's speaking in tongues. He's really a very religious person."

"Does he still go out in his boat in the river to re-baptize himself?"

"No, Jimmy. I sold the boat because I was afraid he would get drowned accidentally. He's much calmer now. He hardly ever roams around the house at night anymore. You don't have to worry about him. You could close up this house and go to a nice big high school in Malone where they have much more to offer than at Rock Mountain."

The lad thanked her for her offer but insisted on trying to work things out with Buck. She was peeved by Jimmy's refusal and was about to begin scolding him when she heard Buck cough as he started to walk down the stairway. The man walked out onto the porch barefooted and bare-chested. He rubbed his eyes to chase away the feeling of sleep.

Jimmy leapt up to introduce him and said, "Aunt Sharon, this is Buck LeTarte."

Deliberately, the boy stood side by side next to his father, grinning unintentionally. She glanced disdainfully from one to the other. Her nostrils flared as she spoke. "Well, James, if this is the way you want it, who am I to interfere?"

She turned and left without greeting Buck. Her unfair attitude reinforced the boy's feeling toward the man.

"Hmmm! Grouchy old broad, isn't she?" Must not be getting enough," mused Buck.

"What do you mean she's not getting enough? Enough what?"

You'll know soon enough, Jim, maybe too soon."

"Never mind her. Let's fix something to eat, Buck."

"You're a man after my own heart, Jim – or belly, I suppose. Oh, after we eat I'm going into town to look around and ask some questions."

"You mean Tony's in Dannemora? I'm going with you."

"That's not a good idea. It gets pretty rough in there sometimes."

"I've got a right to go with you."

"Yes, I suppose you do, but watch yourself and stay out of the bar…and keep out of the girls' pants too."

The youth's face reddened. "Oh, Buck, quit teasing me."

Chapter 15

Except for reiterating his request for Jimmy to keep out of the bar, Buck remained silent as he drove toward Dannemora. The boy took his cue from the man and said nothing. From the corner of his eye, however, he examined the expression on Buck's face. He could see that he was deep in thought, and he moved his lips as though he were forming questions to ask.

Jimmy stared more intently and saw for the first time that Buck possessed a unique, rugged type of handsomeness. Since the man was devoid of whiskers now, sober, and neatly dressed, the lad could see past the pock marks on his face and realized that, together with his way with words, he exuded a certain degree of charismatic charm. Jimmy recognized, also, that he was no longer ashamed to be seen with Buck and wanted to know him better.

They parked across the street from Tony's Tavern and headed inside. They sat side by side on stools facing the soda fountain. Buck placed a five-dollar bill on the counter and ordered two cola drinks. He swallowed half of his glassful in one gulp as though trying to get rid of it. He bared his upper teeth in an involuntary grimace that indicated his disdain for the sweet liquid and his desire for his usual beverage.

"You keep the change Jim, and wish me luck."

"Luck? What for?"

"Who knows? Maybe I'll need it. And now for the magical transformation. Watch closely, my boy," he said in imitation of W. C. Fields, "to this fabulous feat of prestidigitation because in a moment, you might not recognize your old man."

Buck deliberately messed his hair and tugged his shirt collar awry. He gave Jimmy a wink as he unfastened half his shirt buttons and rolled up one pant leg. Then he pulled his handkerchief out of his pocket, stretched it out and reinserted it halfway into his back pocket so that it dangled like a donkey's tail. He winked once more at the boy.

Jimmy watched, dumbfounded, as Buck staggered into the bar doing a convincing drunk act. His eyes squinted as though he were trying desperately to focus. He walked half sideways toward a round table next to which two men sat. The lad stood next to the doorway leading to the bar and watched but was unable to overhear their conversation.

Two girls walked into the café. One of them giggled and pointed at Jimmy. The other walked over and tapped his arm.

"C'mon, Jimmy. You're too young to go in there. Come sit with us."

He recognized the girls as two Dannemora cheerleaders he had met a few times before. Jimmy led them to a booth where he could face the bar and sat down. The girls sat on the opposite bench facing him. A young waitress sauntered over, snapped her gum, and leaned firmly against Jimmy's thigh while jiggling her leg as she took their order. The girls both wanted cherry Cokes which he paid for.

Jimmy watched as the girls sipped their drinks through straws and whispered to one another. He wished they would leave so he could see what was happening inside the bar. One of the girls was pretty, however, and petite. He caught himself viewing her carefully. Her hair was dark and cut short with waves and curls that seemed to defy control. She wore a face that struggled to keep from smiling. Jimmy wished that he had more time to get to know her better.

Her eyes sparkled, and he enjoyed the way the room lights reflected on her pupils. She had dimples on her cheeks the same place as his own. He stared at her fingers and marveled at how tiny they were in comparison to his when they each stretched them out on the table for a comparison and an excuse to touch. Her fingernails were painted dark red to match her lipstick. The rosy look of her cheeks, though, looked real. He wondered if she plucked her eyebrows. He hoped not.

"Well, Jimmy, will we be seeing you in your shorts this winter? asked the taller girl.

"How's that, again? Why would I be parading around in my underwear?"

The girls giggled again, and the blonde one spoke. "She's asking if you will be going out for basketball this year."

"Oh, I don't think so. I'm not very tall."

"That doesn't matter. You're taller than some of the guys on our team last year."

"I suppose I am. Well, maybe. We'll see, girls."

"Why do you keep looking toward the bar, Jimmy? Are we boring you?"

"No, no. Not at all. It's just that I'm waiting for someone who's inside."

"Say, Jimmy, we're having a little party at my house this Saturday, "the taller girl said. "We'd like you to come."

"Oh, yeah? What kind of party?"

"Just a party. You know, a couple of girls and a couple of guys. We'll make some fudge and Kool-Aid and popcorn and whatever you want. I've got lots of records and we can dance."

"I'm not much of a dancer, but I'm a first-class fudge and popcorn gobbler."

"Then you'll come?"

"I'm not sure. Things are kind of upset at my house right now. You probably heard that my father died. I'll have to give you a call. All right?"

The sound of a crash erupted from the bar, and Jimmy jumped to his feet. He rushed to the doorway, not knowing what to expect.

At first, his eyes saw everything as a blur. The lights were subdued, and it was hard to determine what was going on. A few people were running as if to separate themselves from what was about to happen. Others held their place at the bar or next to tables and took another drink.

Then he saw Buck splayed out face down on the floor. Two men stood over him, kicking him in the ribs. Buck seemed unconscious. Jimmy shuddered when one of the men sank his heel into the area of Buck's kidney. No one moved to help the fallen man but acted as though they enjoyed the novelty of this added attraction.

Jimmy entered the room in a crouch, selected one of the men as a target and struck him with a full body slam. Taken by surprise, the man rolled on the floor, writhed in pain, then doubled his knees to his chest. The other one stepped backward several steps and assumed a wide stance.

The momentum of this attack caused Jim to veer toward an occupied table. He spun around once, stumbled, and rolled underneath it, facing up. One of the men seated there kicked the lad's face deliberately. Immediately, Jimmy forced himself upward, upsetting the table and sending the two men sprawling.

Jimmy lost his footing and went down on one knee. He peered forward into a large pair of shiny black dress shoes. He recognized them as the type all of the prison guards wore. Quickly stretching his eyes upward he saw the blue pants legs, the round torso and finally the red, angry face of Buck's assailant.

Jimmy stood trying to face him, but the guard towered a full head above him. The man sneered and retrieved a folding fisherman's knife from his pocket. The boy watched as the six-inch blade was unfolded. Even in the weak light of the tavern, the polished steel gleamed.

"I'm gonna cut your nuts off, kid!" he bellowed.

Through the corner of one eye, Jimmy noted the bartender yelling in the telephone.

Another man approached within ten feet and said, "Here, kid, protect yourself." Then he tossed Jimmy an empty beer bottle which the lad caught. Judging from this man's expression, Jimmy knew the gesture was not meant as a favor but, rather, an attempt to liven up the brawl. He noticed Buck up on all fours, struggling to rise.

Jimmy grasped the bottle by the neck and smashed its base against the overturned table. Blood drained noticeable from the face of the guard when Jimmy thrust the fractured bottle towards the man's crotch missing it by a fraction of an inch. At that moment, his opponent lost stature in Jimmy's eyes. He knew him to be a coward.

The man stepped backward and, pretending magnanimity, announced to the onlookers, "I ain't fighting no crazy kid. Go home to your slut of a mother."

A flush of anger rose in the boy's face, and he wanted to retaliate with force.

"Keep your cool, Jimmy. Use your head." It was David's voice he heard breaking through the roaring in his ears. "Don't get suckered into anything."

Standing, now, Buck yelled, "Jim, come here!"

Still holding the broken bottle at arm's length and pointed toward the guard, Jimmy circled him and reached out his other hand to help steady Buck. He grasped one arm around Buck's shoulders and lead him out of the bar and into the café. The cheerleaders screamed upon seeing the blood flowing from Buck's face and oozing from the boy's cheek. He handed the broken bottle to the short-haired girl and winked. "Be seeing you around," he said.

Jimmy pushed Buck out of the tavern and loaded him in the back seat of the car.

Chapter 16

The two guards who assaulted Buck were joined by a third. This group exited the tavern from the delivery door, circled around, and watched as Jimmy and Buck sped away. They nodded to one another and climbed into a new green Chevrolet.

The youth floored the accelerator of Buck's car and headed west on the state highway. Then, remembering his brother's advice about babying a cold engine, slowed the vehicle. His heart, however, continued to race.

"How are you doing, Buck? You going to be okay?"

The man moaned, then spoke slowly and in obvious pain. "I will be – if you – can get me – to a doctor. I've got – some busted ribs."

"Oh, gosh! I should have thought of that. I'm headed in the wrong direction. The closest hospital is behind us in Plattsburg."

"Never mind – the hospital. Any doctor – can check me over – and tape my ribs."

"I'll head for Rock Mountain," Jimmy said. "Doc Manvel should be there."

While still in the village limits, Jimmy roared past the side street that led to the old iron mine. He knew that at one time prisoners referred to the prison, with its own iron mine as, 'Little Siberia', an apt moniker considering its remote location and the forced work imposed upon those incarcerated there. But that was many years ago. He didn't have time to entertain this thought because, in his rear view mirror, he could see the headlights of a car following them. Leaving the town site, the road rose steeply over Dannemora Mountain, then turned right before entering the steepest section, locally referred to as the

'Rock Cut'. Jimmy lost sight of the headlights as he turned, but, then, he noticed them creeping up on him in the Cut.

"Buck, I think we're being followed. What'll I do?"

"Floor this baby – we'll leave them – like they're standing still."

The drivers of many vehicles were obliged to downshift in order to drive up the steepest part of the mountain. Newer ones could manage it in high gear, but nearly all would lose speed. Buck's Cadillac, despite its age, surged forward when Jimmy's toe forced the pedal down. He felt the welcome pull of gravity against his back as he sank into the seat cushion and knew, without checking the speedometer, that he was accelerating. The headlights behind him gradually diminished in size until finally he lost sight of them.

Descending the reverse slope, Jimmy reconsidered his actions and wondered if the car behind them might be a state policeman instead of Buck's enemies. He slowed down on the curve where three high school students had been killed in a rollover last year and said his usual silent prayer for them.

The down slope continued until they approached a small lake. Straight ahead, Jimmy could see the two concrete shapes that formed the raised edges of a bridge. He knew that just beyond the bridge was a sharp left turn. He was allowing the car to slow so he could make the turn safely when headlights, once again, pierced his back window.

The vehicle was coming up very fast. Too late, Jimmy floored the accelerator. The speeding car overcame Buck's convertible and thumped the left front fender with a careening blow. Losing control, the youth struggled to keep the vehicle from crashing into the raised portions on each side of the bridge. Buck's car left the pavement and careened down a slope leading toward Stony River.

The stream was relatively shallow at this point, no more than a foot deep. Water spraying from the fan drenched the ignition components causing the car's engine to quit. The vehicle's front wheels coasted to the far bank, and the bumper nosed into the brush-covered slope.

Only moments before the crash, Buck had managed to climb over the front seat and, now, because of the force of the impact, his head lay on the dashboard amidst shards of broken glass.

Scant moonlight illuminated the scene. Recovering quickly from the shock of the accident, Jimmy was at once surprised to notice that the steering wheel which he still gripped had been bent forward several inches by the impact. He glanced toward his father and saw him slumped forward.

"Dad! Dad! Are you all right?"

Jimmy shook his shoulder, but there was no response. He opened the door of the driver's side and plunged into the current. Many thoughts flooded the youth's mind, but the one to drag his father up the far bank of the river was uppermost.

He felt certain that they would come back to finish them off, and he knew he must hide Buck in the bushes. He opened Buck's door and grasped him by the shoulders before dragging him out of the water. Keeping the man's head and shoulders high, he struggled backward, dragging his father with his feet dangling in the water while he clawed his own way up.

Jimmy soon found that he was unable to pull the man up the undercut edge of the slope. He jumped back into the river and hoisted his father's legs onto his own as he faced the inert body. Algal slime covered the rocks causing the youth's feet to slip as he pushed. Buck groaned and started to regain consciousness. Jimmy climbed up the bank again and dragged his father into the brush.

"What's going on?" muttered the man.

"Dad!Dad! You're alive." The boy hugged him.

"Where are they, Jim? Go watch – for them – but stay hidden. They plan – to kill us."

"Let me help you get farther into this thick brush, Buck. You can hide behind those rocks."

"Easy, Jim. I'm hurting."

Jimmy left his father hidden and rushed over to the ditch next to the highway. Once in position, he kept his head down low and did not move.

Waiting seemed to be the hardest part because of the uncertainty of what might happen next. The youth's body flooded with adrenalin. Blood surged through his arteries as he prepared himself for either battle or flight. He could sense the thumping in his chest and the swelling in his neck at each pulse through his carotids. His mind remained keen and tuned to every sensory input.

A cricket chirped in the stubble behind him. Down near the muddy shoreline of the lake, a shore bird called in its unique way. When he was a younger boy, he and his brother always called these birds 'sludgepumps' because of their eerie sound. Now, he knew they were some sort of rail or gallinule.

Then he heard it – the roar of an accelerating automobile. Its sound was picked up by the hollows in the mountains, amplified and distorted, then allowed to reverberate across the valley. Jimmy hugged the earth.

The car's tires screeched to a halt, leaving black streaks on the pavement. The driver rolled down his window and scanned the area. He noticed skid marks and overturned gravel on the opposite shoulder. He illuminated his spot light and swept its rays left and right before settling them on the reflection from Buck's rear window. The marsh hen made its sludgepump sound again.

One of the guards shouted, "Jesus! What was that?"

"Nothing you idiot. Nothing but a bird."

"Sh-h-h," hissed the driver, "I think I see something."

The man swung the ray of the spotlight slowly through the brush where Jimmy's father lay. Buck had seen the light as it penetrated his refuge. Now, it stopped moving and focused on the jumble of rocks that separated him from the man's view. Buck held his breath and waited. His chest hurt.

"Gimme the rifle," whispered the driver. "I see something in those bushes."

Grasping the weapon, the driver opened his door slowly and crouched as he made his way to the shoulder of the road overlooking the river. He knelt on one knee to steady his aim.

"This is just like shining deer at night, ain't it?" said one of the men inside.

"Shut up, Murphy!" said the other.

Jimmy was close enough that he heard the name distinctly. He studied the car closely and began memorizing its license number, 'PL29…'.

Then the boy noticed the driver take aim. He was about to shout a warning to his father when a shot rang out. Fire belched from the muzzle. Jimmy's hands searched desperately in the gravel for a rock to throw.

The copper-jacketed hunting bullet smacked a rock above Buck's head sending chips of stone flying in his face. The distorted piece of lead whined as it ricocheted before burrowing into the trunk of a willow tree.

The driver ejected the spent brass shell and reloaded.

Jimmy's fist rose back as he prepared to throw.

"God dam it, Larry. Pick up that friggin' brass. The state police will find it," yelled one of the men.

"Well, come here and help. I can't see in the dark. Bring the flashlight."

Jimmy relaxed his arm and waited. He didn't want to throw the rock unless he had to, knowing he would have to rise up and expose himself to the men in order to aim accurately.

The two men inside the car tumbled out and ran across the road. Searching with the flashlight, they combed the shoulder of the highway.

"I can't find the goddam thing in all this grass."

"Didja hit anything?" asked one of them.

"Nah, just a rock."

"Maybe they're still in the car."

"Can't be. Both doors are open. I can see inside, and I know they ain't no midgets."

Jimmy's ears picked up a sound of a heavy vehicle approaching from the east. He caught a glimpse of its headlight as it headed down the last grade. The driver downshifted, and, finally, one of the three men heard the truck.

"Somebody's comin'! Let's get the fuck out of here, quick."

They ran toward the car and roared off. Just as the green Chevrolet started to move, Jimmy rose up and fired the rock. It struck the trunk of the car smartly.

"What's that?" asked Murphy.

"Just a rock from the wheels, I think."

Chapter 17

The three men in the green Chevy headed back toward Tony's Tavern in search of liquid refortification. They drove silently until they reached the crest of the mountain where the sight of a yearling bear scooting across the pavement startled the driver. He braked the vehicle more violently than necessary causing all three occupants to lurch forward.

"Take it easy, McGuire. Yer gettin' too nervous."

"Yeah, you missed him by a mile. Turn around and try again. Ha, ha," joked the man on the right.

"Shut up!" shouted McGuire, beginning to realize the implications of his behavior toward the Indian. "I'll drive any way I want. I don't want to get no bear guts all over my new car."

"Take her out of gear. Let's see how fast she'll roll down the mountain in neutral."

"Yeah," said Murphy, "there ain't no traffic."

The driver, seeking to please his companions and keep them on his side in case of an investigation, depressed the clutch pedal and placed the shifting lever in the neutral position and allowed the engine to idle. He let out the clutch pedal and watched as the numbers on the speedometer climbed.

"You save lots of gas this way," said the one named O'Donnell. "I do this all the time. Just watch out for more bears." He laughed in his asinine manner.

Murphy drained the bottle of beer he held in his hand, opened the side window, and flung the container toward some rocks. "Let's see how far we can coast before you have to hit the brakes," he said.

New York State Trooper, Marvin Woods, having been informed

of the fight at Tony's by the bartender and alerted to the possibility of more trouble, left the tavern after talking to Gus and headed up the mountain. He was angry at having been called away from his late evening meal.

Climbing through the steepest portion of the grade, he floored his Ford patrol car, then slowed as he observed headlights approaching. He judged the distance to be closing much too fast. He swerved right instinctively and hugged the guard railing. His trained eyes bore into the faces of the three men and then concentrated on their vehicle through his rear view mirror as it careened, nearly out of control, down the center line.

"Damned fools!" cursed the trooper through clenched teeth. "They must be drunker than skunks."

He slowed his car even more and, noticing a pull-off where local residents often stopped to refill water jugs with spring water, made a U-turn. He accelerated smartly and went in pursuit of the speeder.

Trooper Woods overtook them on the street next to the tavern. He turned off his siren but left his red lights flashing.

"Get out of the car!" ordered the trooper. "Place your hands on the roof."

"Aw, Jeez, Woods," whined McGuire. "You know us. Hey, turn off them lights. Everybody's coming out of the tavern, and they're gonna see us."

Trooper Woods unsnapped the leather strap of his revolver holster and raised the weapon a few inches. He repeated his command. His eyes glanced right, and he noticed a rifle and box of shells lying on the back seat of McGuire's car.

Earlier Jimmy had stood on the bridge and watched the green car speed away, the occupants seemingly unaware of the thump caused by the rock he had just pelted it with. Headlights from the approaching truck loomed large as he stood on the center line of the highway. He heard a series of loud blasts from the vehicle's twin horns. The youth ran forward and jumped up and down, waving his arms frantically. The horns blared again as Jimmy prepared to leap toward the shoulder of the road.

At the last moment before impact, the driver swerved sharply. Having dived onto the gravel, Jimmy began to pick himself up. He rested on one knee and watched as the driver struggled to regain control. The youth noted that the truck was a tractor-trailer combination, and he feared that it might jackknife on the bridge. He stared, open mouthed, as the rear lights of the truck flashed on and off rapidly, and his nose stung from the acrid odor of burning rubber. He regretted having to endanger the driver's life but hadn't realized until now how large the vehicle was. He raced after the truck, fully expecting it to crash.

The vehicle negotiated the narrow passage between the sides of the bridge before entering the curve. Jimmy's lungs began to ache as he thudded down the concrete. He could see gravel spewing from the shoulder as several wheels on the right side of the truck left the pavement. It came to rest upright but with the cab sharply angled from the trailer so that both lanes of the highway were blocked.

Jimmy rushed to the driver's side of the cab and jumped onto the running board. Beads of perspiration had formed on the driver's forehead. He sat motionless, still gripping the steering wheel and staring straight ahead. The youth rapped on the window with his knuckles and mouthed some words.

The driver, recovering quickly from the shock of the close call, forced open his door. Jimmy sprawled backward and slipped part way down the incline of the ditch.

"You crazy fool!" screamed the driver as he walked toward the youth. "You damn near got us both killed!"

Jimmy stood up. "I'm sorry, sir. I'm sorry. Help me. We've has an accident!"

"Damn it! I'm running late already."

"Please, my father's hurt. We've got to get him to a doctor."

"All right, all right. I'll have to straighten my rig out first or somebody'll smash into us on this curve. Here, you know how to light these flares?"

"Yes, sir. I've done it before."

"Good. Put one on each side, a hundred feet out."

Jimmy lit the flares and placed them as told. He waited impatiently as the driver zigzagged his truck into a safer position and stood next to it with his flashlight.

"Okay. Now, where's your old man?"

"Follow me, Mister. Gee, I'm glad you've got such a good light."

Jimmy led the man to the far side of the river. When the driver noticed Buck's car in the water, he asked, "How in the hell did you get yourself in this mess?"

"Uh – we sort of got forced off the road by a bad driver."

"Yeah, I'll bet. Chances are you were flying too low. It's a hell of a spot, though. How bad is the other guy?"

"I think my dad's got some broken ribs, and he's cut up pretty bad. You'll see in a minute."

The truck driver shone the light on Jimmy's face. "You're smeared up with blood yourself, kid."

"Am I? I didn't know that."

"Have you been drinking?" asked the man.

"No sir!" said Jimmy emphatically as he rushed to his father's side. He found Buck unconscious, shook him, and placed his ear to his chest.

"He's alive!" Jimmy shouted.

Buck moaned and fluttered his eyelids, then raised one hand to shelter them from the glare of the flashlight. He saw everything through a glaze of red. Jimmy removed his handkerchief and wiped blood from his father's face.

"Never mind that," said the truck driver. "Let's drag him over to the rig. I think we can hoist him onto the back of the trailer together."

The marsh hen called again just as they reached the back door of the trailer. "That's a funny sounding bird," said Jimmy, releasing his grip on Buck's arm.

Buck moaned as they loaded him into the trailer. "I'd like to ride with him in the back, Mister. Do you know where Doctor Manvel lives in Rock Mountain?"

"Nope, you'll have to show me. I think your old man will be okay alone. Hop inside the cab with me."

"No, sir, I can't. I've got to stay with my dad. Just stop when you come to the gas station, and I'll show you where the doctor lives. Can I, uh, borrow your flashlight?"

"Okay, kid. You like your old man, don't you?"

"I, uh, yeah, sure, I do."

Doctor Manvel was relaxing in the living room, wearing his Chinese smoking jacket, when Jimmy pressed the button for the office doorbell. He sighed, placing his freshly-lit cigar in an ashtray, and set his brandy snifter on a coaster.

"Oh, dear", said his wife Edith, "I wonder who that could be at this hour. I do hope it's not another mine accident."

"Only one way to find out, Edie. Oof! I think I need a new chair. It's getting harder to get out of this one every time there's an evening call."

He removed his jacket and replaced it with a white smock. A stethoscope dangled from a top pocket. He left the room and entered a hallway that led to his medical office. Unlocking the door, he brushed back the curtain and noticed, first of all, the youth's bloody face nearly glued to the pane.

"Come in, son. Sit down."

"No, no, not me. My dad needs help. He's in the truck. We were in a car wreck."

"Edith," the doctor called, "bring the stretcher."

The driver and Jimmy boosted the doctor into the back of the van so he could examine Buck before moving him. The truck driver steadied the flashlight while Jimmy slid the stretcher alongside his father. Buck rolled his eyes away from the doctor's penlight and spoke unintelligibly.

Doctor Manvel and his wife held the handles on the front of the stretcher while the driver and Jimmy held the rear ones. Together, they carried Buck to the office.

"I don't know how to thank you enough, Mister – uh – what's your name?"

"It's okay, kid. People should help one another if they can. Everybody calls me Corky, Corky Allison."

"Mr. Allison, after my dad's feeling better, maybe you would like to stop by and see us. You drove right by our house. It's the third one you see at Echo Lake before you head for town."

"You got any fish in that lake?"

"Sure thing. I'll show you the best places. You could camp out on our beach if you'd like to stay for a while."

"I may take you up on that. We'll see. I go by here a couple of times a month on my way to Watertown. I've been thinking about taking a few days off."

"Gee, Mr. Allison, that would be swell."

Chapter 18

The four of them lifted Buck, still on a canvas stretcher, directly onto an examining table. Corky turned to leave. He shook Jimmy's hand, secretly hoping that someday he might have a son just like him.

"How about if I stop by on my next trip to see how you and your old man are doing?"

"I'd like that a lot, Corky, uh, Mr. Allison, and thanks a million for all you did tonight."

Tipping his cap and nodding to Mrs. Manvel, the young truck driver said, "Ma'am", and disappeared down the sidewalk. Jimmy watched from the window as the lights of the rig pulled away.

Edith Manvel took hold of the youth's arm firmly and led him to a chair.

"He's a real good man. I almost got him killed when I made him stop the truck to help us. I felt so stupid."

"Don't worry about that now, young man. Let us get your face scrubbed so the doctor can check you over as soon as he's finished with the other patient."

"Do you think my dad will be okay? It was a pretty bad car wreck, you know."

"The doctor is doing everything he can." She sponged the youth's face with soapy water into which she had poured a dark brown antiseptic. "Don't I know you, young man?"

"I've seen you before at school helping Doctor Manvel give shots and school physicals," said Jimmy.

"Yes, of course, that is why I remember you, but you don't live here in Rock Mountain, do you?"

"No, ma'am. I live on Echo Lake with my dad. I'm James Coulbron."

"But your father died recently, didn't he? And your mother…?"

"Well – uh – it's kind of complicated."

"All life is complicated, young man."

"I hope everybody's life isn't as complicated as mine has been lately."

Jimmy noticed the quizzical frown on the woman's face and sensed her desire to know more. He needed relief from the recent excitement and talking about it helped dispel the stress.

"Understand, young man, that I am not prying into your personal life. There are, nevertheless, some forms I am obliged to fill out."

"It's okay, Mrs. Manvel. I don't mind." He winced when she began scrubbing a laceration on his cheek with a small brush.

"I'm sorry, James, but there is some kind of grit or sand ground in here. What part of Echo Lake did you say you lived at?"

"There are no houses between Rock Mountain and Echo Lake. Ours is the third house in Echo Lake, and yes, the man I always thought was my father died not long ago."

He pointed toward the examination room. "Buck, here, is my real father – Buck LeTarte."

"Hmmm, I see, and is he from around here?"

"He used to live in Malone."

"And where is your mother?"

"Uh – she – uh – she had an accident. She's in the hospital in Plattsburg. You may as well know they'll be bringing her back to Ogdensburg soon. Maybe for good, this time."

"I see. Your father, I mean Mr. Coulbron, worked for the mining company, didn't he?"

"Yeah, for nearly twenty years. Uh, Mrs. Manvel, are you almost done with me? I've got to make an important phone call – in private."

"Of course, James. You just walk down that hallway and you will see our home phone. Then hurry back. The doctor will want to look you over and bandage your face."

"Thank you, ma'am."

Jimmy left the room and sought out the telephone. He removed his wallet from his back pocket and withdrew a card bearing the name and phone number of one of the state policemen who had interviewed him and Buck concerning Lillian's disappearance. He knew the information he was now able to supply would be of value to them.

The first thing the youth noticed after returning to the doctor's office was a live human body, its head and upper abdomen swathed in white, seated on a chair. Except for his eyes and mouth, Buck's face was bandaged. The top of Buck's head was sprinkled with white gauze like a bird's wings in flight. Buck's shirt had been cut away, and, now, his torso was covered around and around with adhesive tape from his armpits to just above his navel. His right arm was bent across his chest and supported by a sling.

Jimmy bent low and stared into his father's eyes. "You okay, Buck? You're going to be all right, aren't you?"

The man read the concern in his boy's face and in his words. "Can't keep – a good man – down, Jim. Not for – long, anyway."

"Try not to talk", said Doctor Manvel. "Don't cough and don't sneeze. Get lots of rest. Eat only soft foods because some of your teeth are really loose. You may lose one or two of them yet. You should be in a hospital for several days, but if you've got someone to take care of you, you'll be able to recover at home without any permanent damage. I'll come to see you tomorrow."

The doctor looked at the boy's face. "Not too bad, son. No glass fragments anywhere. That cut may leave a scar, but it doesn't need stitches. Looks like your face will be black and blue in the morning. Edith, please bandage the boy's cheek and give him some rolls of gauze and tape to bring home with him."

"Do you have a way to get home, son?" asked the doctor.

"I'll call David's friend, Perchy Garew. He'll give us a ride."

"Nonsense!" exclaimed Mrs. Manvel. "I will drive them home, myself."

"No, Edith, your night vision has deteriorated too badly," reminded the doctor.

"Humph! Indeed it has, but you mustn't allow these good people to think I am becoming a senile old woman, incapable of doing anything."

"Of course not, Edith. There is nothing wrong with your eyes except cataracts, and we will have those taken care of very soon, my dear, won't we?"

"I have no intention of wearing those horrid, thick spectacles some older people are obliged to wear. What will my friends think, for goodness sake?"

"Uh, excuse me, Mrs. Manvel, may I use your phone to call Perchy?"

"Yes, go ahead, James, but if he is unavailable I am driving."

The doctor shook his head and smiled. "Make your call, son."

It was a snug fit for the three of them in the cab of Perchy's aging pickup. Jimmy was glad that Mr. Garew did not ask him for details of the accident. Buck sat between the driver and his son, moaning slightly each time the vehicle bounced over a railroad crossing, but said nothing.

"It eez a good t'ng you call me when you did, Jimmee. I was jus' now leaving to go back to ze 'ouse of Madame Papineau, and pretty soon, me, I would not be 'ere."

"I'm glad you're helping her out for a while. Will you be able to help her out for a few weeks longer?"

"*Ça se peut* – maybe, but I still 'ave to dig ze big 'ole in ze *cimetière* for Fazer Orgebin when somebody he die."

"As soon as things get straightened out at home, I can help her again, Mr. Garew."

"You are a good boy, Jimmee, just like your fazer, David. I was very sorry when he die, him. He was one of my bes' friend, him, when I work in ze mine."

Man and youth, working as a team, walked Buck to the living room of the house. "We better let him sleep here on the sofa, Mr. Garew. After a few days he may be able to get up and go up the stairs to his bedroom. I can handle everything now."

"Okay, Jimmee. You want I should tell Madame Papineau about what 'appen to you?"

"Yes, but in such a way that she won't worry about us or fuss about anything. We'll be all right here."

"Okay, Jimmee, but what about ze wrecked *char* of Monsieur Buck? I 'ave ze friend who 'ave ze *grand camion* – a big truck. 'e would 'elp me to drag it 'ere to your yard."

"Uh, well, that would be nice of you two, but I was thinking of calling a tow truck from Dannemora in the morning."

"Zat would cost you ze big *piastre*. Let me see what we can do, me and my friend Alphonse Gagnier."

"Buck and I would appreciate it, but if it looks too hard, I'll get a wrecker."

After Perchy left, Jimmy removed his father's shoes and trousers, fluffed up some pillows for him, and covered him with a blanket.

"Are you hungry, Pop? Can I fix you anything to eat?"

"No, Jim. Mouth is – too damn sore. Just bring me – a can – to pee in."

"Gosh, yeah, why didn't I think of that?"

The youth took easily to his role as nurse. He spoon fed his father oatmeal in the morning and thin soups during the day. He emptied his urinal and read him the newspaper.

Each day Perchy and Mrs. Papineau would come early in the morning and again in the afternoon. The man would help with the farm chores while the woman cooked habitant pea soup and baked Johnny cake and, of course, molasses cookies. For Jimmy, it seemed like he was living with a family of four with three of them striving to heal the fourth member.

On the second day, a police detective arrived to take statements from Jimmy and Buck. They told the story plainly, exactly as it happened, from the ruckus in the bar to the shooting incident near the river. Jimmy described the green Chevy in detail, mentioning the possibility of a dent in the trunk lid as well as his partial recollection of the license plate number and the one passenger's name he overheard, 'Murphy'.

One evening, several days later, Buck was napping while Jimmy was out on the porch trying to perfect his fingering of a haunting melody. With the man's permission, he was trying out Buck's instrument, hoping that by means of the guitar's own spirit, he could coax forth the same sounds from it that his father was able to produce with seeming ease.

He watched as an automobile drove by slowly, having come from the direction of Dannemora. He heard the vehicle stop briefly before turning around and heading back in the opposite direction.

The August days had shortened, and now darkness was descending. A bat fluttered by in pursuit of a moth. The youth stopped playing the guitar because it was too dark to see the strings clearly. It was peaceful, and he hesitated to turn on the lights, not wishing to destroy the magic of twilight.

Once again, the vehicle slowed as it passed in front of the house. Jimmy thought he could see the face of a passenger staring at Buck's damaged Cadillac as it sat in the driveway in front of the dwelling. True to his promise, Perchy had arranged to have it towed there the day before.

Intrigued by the parading car's behavior, Jimmy left the lights off and squatted down on the porch. A third time, the same vehicle crept by. The youth wasn't certain but thought it might be a new model Chevrolet. This time, it stopped briefly as though someone were examining the premises. Slowly, the car drove off and continued out of sight. The youth continued to watch for fifteen minutes. During this time, no more vehicles passed by.

Jimmy went inside to check on his father. He turned on the lights and found that Buck was awake. He brought the man a glass of milk and tuned in a radio station.

"Uh, Buck, I'm going to take a long walk. It'll be a while before I come back. Are you okay for now? I'll check on you after a while."

"Sure thing, Florence Nightingale. I'm set until morning. If you're out walking with your girlfriend, give her a squeeze for me."

"Oh, come on, Buck. You know I don't have a girlfriend."

"Well, when you do, I hope you find one who can cook something besides pea soup and corn bread."

Jimmy laughed. "I'll try. How about succotash and fry bread?"

"Geez, I grew up on that. How about hamburgers and French fries?"

"I'll do my best, Buck. Gimme a break from the girlfriend razzing. You'll be the first to know."

Chapter 19

The youth had been lying in the haymow facing the house and the highway for some time. He knew that his father must be sleeping since all the lights were off. He tightened the blanket around his shoulders and thought about the night he had spent there with Phil. He wondered where his brother was tonight and what he was doing. He wondered if he was with a girl. He wondered if he would ever be with one himself but couldn't think of which one it might be, except, perhaps, the short cheerleader who lived in Dannemora. He wondered what she was doing right now. Maybe she was with another guy. Maybe she already had a steady. Maybe...she would turn out just like his mother.

Inside his pants pocket, he fingered the loose handful of twenty-two shells he had placed there. He released his grip on the bullets and peeled back the quilt. He reached for his rifle and rested the forearm of the weapon against the edge of the open haymow door. He brought the sights to bear on the chimney of the house. Silhouetted against the sky, it made an easy target.

Jimmy's eyes had grown accustomed to the light given off by the new moon. He wished he had a full moon, however, for then, he could be certain of his target. He tried to get a bead on the mailbox, but its outline was obscured by the way the trees and the fence line merged with it. He noticed a row of concrete guardrails and pretended to blast them away one by one.

The constant hum of an automobile engine caught his attention. Through the fringe of trees to the northeast he could see headlights approaching. Then, suddenly, the lights went out. From the sound of the engine it seemed as though the car was slowing.

Jimmy filled the clip of his rifle, chambered one round, and pushed on the safety button. He could see the shape of the car but not clearly enough to identify it by make. It stopped, and two men exited the vehicle. One of them raised the trunk lid of the car and withdrew a five-gallon fuel can. From the way the man used both hands, the youth knew it must be full.

He knew that he had to be certain. He could not allow himself to make a fatal error. There might be some other explanation for the men's behavior. He thought that, perhaps, they had simply run out of gas. He didn't want to hurt an innocent person, nevertheless his father was asleep inside that house. Somebody had tried to kill him before, and now it looked like they planned to cremate both of them.

He wondered how much the trajectory of a twenty-two bullet would drop in two hundred feet. He remembered that he and Phil had sighted in the rifle for one hundred feet. He realized that he would have to aim a little high but was uncertain how much. He considered aiming really high and firing over the men's heads to scare them away.

The youth's eyes bore into the dim light, trying to see more clearly. He mouthed some words, nearly speaking aloud. These men are crouching more as they get closer to the house. They've both got big hats on. I can't see their faces. The one in back is carrying the can. I wonder if it is kerosene or gas. The other one has a...a stick? No! It's a gun...a rifle or a shotgun.

Jimmy wished the guardrails were not there. They partly obscured his line of sight. As they passed behind each upright post, the men's images partly disappeared. In between the posts hung steel cables, linking them together. Fifty feet from the edge of the driveway, leading toward the house, the row of guardrails ended.

Jimmy aimed at the last upright and waited. He planned that once the first man stepped clear of the end guardrail, he would fire one round a few feet in front of him, then fire a round into the automobile so that he might be able to identify it later.

The first man stepped into the clear, and the youth began to take sight. Then, the quivering in his arms started. He could no longer hold a steady hand.

He mouthed the words 'buck fever' and relaxed his grip to take a deep breath. The men were closer to the house now. Jimmy aimed again, remembering to account for elevation. He had a perfect sight picture when he squeezed the trigger. Nothing happened.

"Oh, shit!" he hissed, "I forgot the safety."

"Oh, my gosh!" he thought. "Ten more feet, and I won't be able to see them at all."

He aimed again, released the safety, and fired. The shot was low. Gravel stung the faces of the two men. One dropped the metal can and ran toward the far ditch, closely followed by his partner. Jimmy sighted directly toward the top of the can, hoping that would account for bullet drop. He thought he heard bullets strike the can at least twice.

Jimmy reloaded and waited. He heard nothing. He saw someone coming out the back door of the basement, heading toward him, toward the barn. The person moved slowly. The youth's breath came in short gasps.

They must have gotten inside from the front of the house where I can't see them, he thought. They've already killed Buck. Well, they're not getting me. He raised the rifle again.

"Jim?" someone called softly. "Jim, where are you?"

"Oh, my God...Buck!" the youth whispered.

He gave a short whistle and waved from the barn loft window. He called softly, "Buck, come inside the barn."

Jimmy looked toward the house. A shadowy figure approached the can. Just before the man reached it, the lad fired again. This time, the bullet struck something that caused a spark. This ignited the gasoline can, and it exploded with a noisy whoosh.

The youth stood in horror as he watched the flaming body of a man running down the highway, waving his arms and shedding glowing bits of fabric before collapsing on the pavement.

Buck had not had time to heed his son's advice. Instead, he stood rooted to the ground watching.

"There goes another one, Jim. He's jumping in that car."

"I see him. I'm letting him go. I think he got the message."

"Well, I got the message, too. We're getting the hell out of here until things settle down."

"Where'll we go?"

"You got anything against living on the reservation?"

"Hell, no! Let's head out of here before somebody else comes. Should I call the lieutenant and tell him our plans?"

"Better not tell anybody. We don't know who all is involved in this. Some of these people work together."

Chapter 20

"Jim, go check how much gas you've got in your Pontiac."

"Why's that, Buck?"

"Because it's a fair haul from here to Hogansburg. It'll be harder for anybody to trace us if we're not seen. I'd feel safer if we have enough to make it all the way without stopping."

"Well, I already know the tank's pretty low, and the Rock Mountain station has been closed for hours. I don't think we could make it much farther than that."

"In that case, it's time to use the Oklahoma gas station."

"Huh? What's that?"

"That's what Preacher Pearson used to call it when he'd tell me to go siphon gas out of somebody's tank."

"A preacher had you steal gas for him?"

"It wasn't just for him. It was for all of us when we were on a tour. I'll tell you all about it when we get to the reservation."

"I'm holding you to that promise, Pop. I'll get David's siphon from the shop and drain what I can from the tractor."

"Fill as many containers as you can, even if you have to empty something else out. Then pour all the gas in the Pontiac. Put the cans and the siphon in the trunk because we might need to go on another midnight requisition."

"I know where there is a full can of kerosene."

"That's good. You won't even have to drain it completely or rinse it out. It'll all mix in. Sometimes we'd blend gas and kerosene together in one old tour bus if we couldn't get enough straight gas. As soon as that burned body is found, this place is going to be swarming with cops, and we better not be around to answer questions."

"What are you going to be doing?"

"I'm grabbing some clothes and food. Now, hurry."

"What'll we do with the twenty-two and shells, Buck?"

"Put them in the trunk of the car. Make it snappy."

Jimmy's mind buzzed with confusion. On the one hand he wanted to telephone the police lieutenant and inform him of everything. On the other hand, maybe Buck was right. He knew many of the police and jail guards did work together and even cover for one another whenever there was a scandal. Right now, the only person he could trust was Buck.

He backed Phil's Pontiac up to the back door of the basement where it was out of sight while they loaded it. He grabbed an empty gasoline can from the shed and drained the kerosene from the other can into a pile of gravel. He ran with them to Buck's car, then unscrewed the gas cap and inserted the rubber hose. He paused.

A little earlier, when the youth first saw the flaming man running down the road, he had wanted to try to save him even if the man had been intent on incinerating him and Buck. However, when the accomplice with the gun abandoned the burning man, Jimmy knew he must be already dead. Still, he could not stop himself from looking in that direction. He discerned the motionless body lying with half of its torso sprawled on the pavement. Small tongues of orange flame and greasy smoke licked on the man's hair and the remaining fabric of his clothing.

The boy shuddered. God help him, he thought. What a horrible way to die!

The raw odor of gasoline always nauseated Jimmy ever since the first time, as a young child, he had tried to siphon the volatile liquid. On that occasion, Phil, who was about ten, and his father were siphoning gasoline from the family's Model A Ford car to help out a stranded motorist. Phil had left the rubber tube inserted in the filler while he and his father carried the gas can away.

Little Jimmy had been watching from the kitchen window. Fascinated by this big men's work, he decided to go outside to help. He ran outside, climbed onto the front fender of the car and noticed the siphon dangling from the fuel tank. The tank was situated high on the firewall of the engine directly in front of the windshield to facilitate an easy flow of fuel to the carburetor.

The boy sucked on the hose and, at first, only inhaled fumes. He sucked again. Gasoline rushed into his mouth. He gagged and ran into the kitchen crying. He rushed up the stairs to his mother's bedroom and shook her. She seemed dazed and unresponsive.

"Momma! I drank gas. It burns."

"Leave me alone, Gad damn it! Go tell your father."

The boy ran back into the yard, screaming hysterically. He saw Phil walking back alone. The older brother noticed Jimmy's distress and ran to his side.

"What happened, Jimmy? What happened?"

He pointed toward the car. "Drank gas. Sick."

"Where's Mom?"

"Momma sick, too."

Phil noticed his little brother's body convulsing itself as it tried to retch. He thrust a finger deeply into the boy's throat and bent him forward until Jimmy vomited. He heard an automobile approaching and began to form a plan. He carried the boy inside the kitchen and forced him to drink a raw egg mixed with milk. Jimmy retched again. His eyes rolled in terror.

The ten-year-old scribbled a note to his father to explain what happened and rushed the boy outside. The first car had already driven by. Phil stood on the roadside next to the mailbox holding his brother in his arms. Another vehicle approached. Phil recognized the International pickup as that of a local fruit and vegetable peddler and waved him down.

The peddler, a middle-aged man, immediately recognized this as an emergency. He asked a few questions, then drove as fast as he dared toward Doctor Manvel's home in Rock Mountain, carrying the two boys. Phil rushed his brother inside without ringing the doorbell. Mrs. Manvel went over to them.

"The doctor is with a patient. What's wrong?" she asked.

"He drank gas. I made him throw up. I gave him raw eggs and milk, but he couldn't keep them down. It's all my fault. I left the siphon where he could find it."

Phil still cradled his brother in his lap. Tears welled up in his eyes. Jimmy no longer writhed in agony. He clung tightly to his brother's neck.

"I'll get the doctor. Don't worry."

Doctor Manvel laid the boy on a table and examined him. Then he sat him up and gave him something soothing to swallow.

He looked toward Phil and spoke. "You are lucky, son. I don't think he swallowed more than a few drops. You did all of the right things. I'm very proud of you. Now, we'll just have to let nature take its course. Where are your folks?"

"Mom's not feeling good, and Dad went with somebody to fix their car. He should be home soon."

"Good. In the meantime, you are in charge of your brother, and I know you will do what is right. I need to observe him for a little while. When you get him home, put him right to bed."

"Yes, thank you, sir."

Jimmy squirmed down from the table and grabbed on to Phil's leg.

"No, Jimmy, you have to rest on the table for a little while, and I'll hold your hand." He hoisted him back up.

"Edith, find out where these children live and drive them home in a half hour or so. And see if you can locate their parents. I've got to get back to my other patient."

"Of course, Doctor."

Phil was like that, thought Jimmy. He rescued me lots of times, and now I have to help Buck. Only Phil hates Buck. How's that for family complications, he asked himself.

Afterward while the youth drove steadily through the August night seeking safety in the reservation, his father removed the remaining bandages from his face with his one good hand.

"How about you, Jim, do you want your red badge of courage anymore?"

"Nah, I might as well rip it off now."

"How long did the doc say it would be before I can get rid of this damn sling?"

"I don't remember exactly, Pop. It's quite a while, though."

"I doubt if I really need it. It's just a crack. It wasn't snapped clean off, for Cripe's sake."

"Is there a doctor or medicine man where we're going?"

"I suppose so. Don't worry about it, Jim."

"Oh, oh! Here comes the first car. What if they don't see the body in time and run over it?"

"All the better for us. It makes the cops get confused. Of course, somebody coming from the other direction could already have found it."

"I wonder what happened to the gas can that blew up."

"Couldn't you see it on the road anywhere when you were siphoning, Jim?"

"No, I looked for it. It must have been blown sky high."

"The cops will probably find it – or pieces of it. I hope it blew to bits so no bullet holes show. Where did you put the empty shells, Jim?"

"I shot so fast I didn't think to save them. They must have slipped down into the hay. I don't think anybody will look there, will they, Pop?"

"Not likely. How come your friend, Perchy, and Mrs. Papineau didn't come to see us today?"

"Perchy said they were going shopping in Plattsburg and then to a movie. They sure must have stayed out late. His truck wasn't in their yard when we drove by. It's usually there most of the time."

"They're probably parked along some back road, smooching up a storm."

"Perchy and Mrs. Papineau?"

"Sure! Why not?"

"I don't know. I thought they were too old for that kind of stuff."

"You're never too old, Jim. And, maybe, you're never too young either. How about you, Jimmy boy? I'll bet you're making out like a stud horse."

"Aw, come on, Pop. You're making me blush."

"Well, that at least proves you'd like to do it."

"Oh, yeah? How old were you the first time?"

"Fourteen."

"Fourteen? Aw, Pop. At that age, you wouldn't even know what to do."

"That's true enough, but I didn't have to know because she sure did."

"Was she older than you?"

"Yeah, she was about twenty. That's when I was living with the preacher and his family."

"What was she like?"

"Well, she was pretty enough but kind of fat and not too bright."

"Was it just once?"

"Jim, maybe I shouldn't be telling you all this."

"Why not? You're the one who started it by asking me about my love life...or lack of it."

"Well, all right, I promise to tell you the whole story when we get settled at the reservation."

"I can wait. Besides, I can't believe how we're acting. I just killed somebody, and now we're telling sex stories. Oops! Here comes another car. No, there's two of them."

"Keep driving, nice and steady, Jim. Don't speed up. We don't want to draw attention to ourselves. You emptied both cans of gas into this car didn't you?"

"Yeah, we've got more than a half a tank now. That'll take us quite a ways."

"Just the same, we're going to top off in Malone. I know a guy there who owes me a favor, and he knows how to keep his mouth shut."

"Gosh, Pop, what are Perchy and Mrs. Papineau going to think when they find us gone?"

"I've been thinking about that. I'll go into town in the morning and call Perchy. I'll tell him I got called away on important business, and you had to come to help. I won't tell him where we are. I'll just say that we're heading for several places and that we'll call him again later. He'll understand. I'll ask him to take care of the animals."

They drove through the night silently now, and Jimmy allowed himself to feel some pride over the smooth running of Phil's Pontiac.

Chapter 21

"Okay, Jimmy boy," said Buck, "start slowing down. We're getting close to my cousin Bert's place."

"All I can see are junk cars and a couple of shacks."

"I said 'place' – not 'palace'. What did you expect – a mansion like the prison warden has? This will be a perfect hideout for us."

"Sorry. You're the boss, Boss."

"I've got to stop calling you 'Jimmy boy'. After what you did tonight you're 'Jim the man' as far as I'm concerned."

"But, Dad, I killed somebody. I feel rotten about that."

"Don't feel bad about eliminating evil from this world. Consider yourself an instrument of the Lord's vengeance because that is exactly what you are. Besides, if you hadn't been so alert, we'd both be nothing but charcoal, and those guys would be laughing their stupid heads off about it. They must be the same ones who ran us off the road and took a potshot at me."

"I suppose you're right, but I still don't like it. Should I park the car alongside that little house?"

"No, Jim, my man. Park right in the middle of those old cars. I'll go inside to wake up Bert – very, very gently. Sometimes he gets kind of trigger happy if he's startled."

"Oh, swell! More shooting."

"Nah, not this time – I hope. Take an old set of license plates off one of those junkers and put them on your car. That will confuse any cops that might come snooping around. Then, open your hood so that it looks abandoned."

"Sounds like a good idea. I'll toss some branches and a couple handfuls of weeds on top, too. What will I do with my real plates?"

"Bring them inside when you come with our clothes. The other stuff can wait until morning."

"Okay, Boss man."

The moon was beginning to sink into the fringe of trees to the west as Jimmy was completing his task. He dodged around an abandoned stove and a sink on his way to select a set of old license plates.

Maybe this Ford, he thought. Good grief! These plates are from thirty-eight. That's ten years ago. I hope the bolts aren't too rusted to get off.

The job done, the youth appeared at the back door of the house carrying a suitcase. He stopped suddenly when he saw a man, clad only in undershorts, standing in the doorway holding a shotgun in one hand and a kerosene lamp in the other.

"Who's the kid?" he demanded of Buck.

"This is my boy. Come on in, Jim. Meet your Uncle Bert."

"Uh, hello, Uncle."

Bert placed the gun behind the door and gave Jimmy a firm shoulder squeeze. "Welcome to the reservation. If I knew you were coming, I'd have had a feather ready for you."

The man chuckled and ushered the youth inside. Jimmy was uncertain of what to say so he remained silent.

"He looks just like you, Buck. I didn't know you had any kids."

"He's been living with his mother. She's sick now."

"What the hell are you doing here, Buck? I thought you were living in Malone."

"I was. It's a long story. Jim and I are hanging low until things blow over. Don't tell anyone we're here."

"That's too bad. I was going to introduce Jim to some kids his age. School's starting soon if he wants to go."

"I'm afraid not, Bert. That will have to wait."

"Fine with me. You guys hungry? I can get Cora out of bed to fix you something."

"No, thanks, we're okay for now. We've got a box of food in the back seat of the car. Jim will bring it inside in the morning.

Bert tapped the cast on Buck's arm with his finger tips. He squinted first at Buck's face, then at Jimmy's. "Oh, oh! What's this all about? Looks like both of you have been fighting with wildcats."

Instinctively, the boy fingered the partly-healed scar on his cheek and looked at Buck's more serious ones.

"We got cut by flying glass from the car windshield last week. Seems like we went on a side trip and ended up in the river."

"You mean you smashed your neat convertible?

"It's repairable. At least I think so, Bert. How about your cars? Why don't you get one of them patched up and the others hauled away? You could sell the worst ones for scrap to pay for the repair."

"Yeah, I suppose you're right. I'll get at it one of these days if it doesn't interfere with my hunting."

"I'm pretty good with cars, Uncle Bert. Is it okay if I take a look at them tomorrow?"

"You're welcome to try, so be my guest."

"Thanks, Uncle Bert.

"Well, let's all get some sleep. You guys are going to have to double up. There's only one extra bed," said Bert, pointing to another room.

"That will be fine, and thanks."

The bedroom was tiny, as was the rest of the house. A four-poster double bed nearly filled all of the floor space.

"This was my girls' room," announced Bert while striking a wooden match to light the lamp on the dresser. He seemed a bit embarrassed at offering the ornate bed with its flowered quilt to the men. "They're both married and moved away now."

Jimmy stared at the pink roses that papered the room and looked for a place to set down the suitcase where they wouldn't stumble over it. Buck undressed and hung his clothing on pegs on the wall. Taking his cue, the boy did likewise. Buck cupped one hand around the chimney of the lamp and puffed out the flame.

Although it was scarcely two hours since Jimmy and Buck had left Echo Lake, it seemed much longer to the youth. He lay on his side, facing the pink roses, and shuddered as he remembered the sight of the man in flames. He listened as his father started to snore softly, then dozed off himself wishing he was a full-blooded Mohawk like Bert.

It was nearly noon when the youth awakened, groggy, his sleep having been interrupted by dreams. He had not heard his father leave hours earlier. He was about to pull back the covers and get dressed when his Aunt Cora opened the door and stepped into the room. She smiled and sat down on the bed next to him.

Feeling self-conscious, Jimmy hugged his arms around his knees and looked at his new aunt. She was about the same age as his mother but shorter and with darker hair. His nose wrinkled as the pungent odor of ammonia wafted in through the open door.

Noticing his frown, the woman smiled again. "Oh, that's just from my new permanent. My sister just gave me one of those new cold waves this morning. Do you like it, Jimmy?"

"Oh – oh, yes, it's – uh – very nice. It looks good on you."

"Thank you. I'm your Aunt Cora, in case you didn't know. The men have gone into town for something. I'll bet you're starving."

"Well – uh – yeah, I guess I am a little hungry."

"Boys your age are always hungry. I didn't have any sons but I did have brothers so I know that for sure. My daughter Madge may stop in this afternoon. You'll get to meet her."

"Uh – Aunt Cora, maybe that's not such a good idea. My dad and I are kind of in trouble and are hiding out from everybody."

"Don't worry, Jimmy. It's for sure that nobody in this family will say anything. Now, hop out of that bed and let's get something in your belly. I can hear it growling. Come on, now, don't be bashful."

"Uh, Aunt Cora, I've got a little problem – and I don't have any clothes on."

"Oh, you men are all alike – as bashful as can be. I'll give you some privacy. You can use the thunder mug, if you want, or go to the outhouse."

"Uh – thank you."

As soon as she turned to leave, the youth pulled on his trousers and headed to the outside toilet, bare-footed and bare-chested.

Leaving the outside biffy, Jimmy noticed that the Pontiac was still where he had parked it. He wondered if his Uncle Bert had managed to crank up one of his junkers or if he and Buck had hitch-hiked to town.

He noticed the wash basin and towel on the porch and began to wash his face and hands. When Cora stepped out of the kitchen and stood next to him, Jimmy smelled the hair-curling chemicals again.

"Do you like venison and fry bread, Jimmy?"

"I like just about everything, Aunt Cora. I've never had much deer meat, though."

"If you stay around here for a while, you'll have to get used to it – or go hungry."

"Did Uncle Bert shoot the deer?"

"Oh, sure. He was sitting right here on that rocking chair last week when the dog chased it out of the woods. We'll have to eat it up pretty fast or give it away because we don't have a refrigerator."

"I'd like to go deer hunting with Uncle Bert sometime if we happen to stay here long enough. I've only got a twenty-two, though, and that's too small for deer."

"Well, that all depends. Sometimes Bert uses a twenty-two when he goes shining, but, never mind about that. He's got all kinds of guns. He can loan you whatever you like."

"Do you think he'd take me with him sometime?"

"I'm sure he would. He's always been sorry he didn't have a son of his own to drag into the woods or go fishing with."

"Gee, that would be swell. I'll ask him tonight."

Jimmy looked over toward an elm tree and noticed a beagle lying next to the base of it, panting in the shade. "Is that your dog?"

"I guess so. There's a couple of those mutts that come and go whenever they want."

"I thought deer season didn't start until November."

"Maybe so, but your Uncle Bert makes his own rules when it comes to hunting and fishing."

Seated at the kitchen table, Jimmy watched as his aunt placed two skillets on a kerosene-burning range. She struck a match to ignite the burners and adjusted the fire until a circular blue flame licked the heating grid. The youth continued to observe as his aunt wiped a chunk of sowbelly around the inside of one pan and allowed it to begin melting for a few seconds before removing it and placing it aside. Then she scooped several large spoonfuls of lard in the other skillet. When the first one began to sizzle, she placed an inch-thick slab of round steak in it and seasoned it with salt and pepper. Then she sliced up a huge onion and spread it alongside the meat.

By the time the other skillet had begun smoking, Jimmy's mouth started to water. She lowered the heat and walked over to the sideboard counter where she began cutting pieces of rising dough into triangular shapes with a butcher knife.

"Can I help you, Aunt Cora? You look awfully busy."

"You can if you want to, but I'm not used to men doing the cooking." She handed the youth a large fork. "Here, you watch the steak and turn it when it gets done enough for you and stir the onions."

He tended to the meat and watched as his aunt placed the wedges of dough into an inch of sizzling hot fat. Bubbles foamed around the edges of the fry bread, and she turned each piece once, then removed them individually and placed them on several thicknesses of newspaper.

"You know how to make pan gravy, Jimmy?"

“I’m not sure. I think my mother used to make it sometimes.”

“Well, in that case, I’ll teach you now. There’s nothing to it. Place the steak and onions on that platter and bring me a can of flour.”

The youth did as he was told, and the woman continued. “Now, take a couple of big spoonfuls of flour and sprinkle them in the pan of meat juice.”

She watched carefully. “Okay, good, that’s enough. Turn the heat up a little bit. Okay, now stir the flour with the spoon. Good, now, get about a cupful of water from the pail next to the pump, and pour it in. That’s right. Now, stir in some more and taste it.”

“I think it’s pretty good just the way it is.”

“Okay, then, shut off the knob on the burner, and let’s eat.”

Jimmy broke open a piece of pan bread and watched the steam escape. He sopped his bread in the venison gravy. “This is really good, Aunt Cora. Can we have it again, sometime?”

“Of course, now make sure you eat enough to last you until supper time. I miss not having my girls around everyday so I’m going to fatten you up instead.”

“If I keep this up, you’ll have to roll me out of bed in the morning like I was a big ball.”

He looked at his aunt. In a way she reminded him of Mrs. Papineau when she was younger. His aunt was darker skinned, of course, and nowhere near as heavy. He decided it was their genuine friendliness and the attention they gave him that created an impression of similarity.

He thought about his mother and knew that, by now, she was a patient in Ogdensburg again. He wondered how she was getting along and if she would ever be released from the asylum. He was certain that he and Buck would try to visit her as soon as it was safe for them to leave the reservation.

Chapter 22

Jimmy reloaded his plate with venison and gravy. He watched as his aunt rose from the table and filled a large enameled pan with water from the pump. She placed this on top of the kerosene burner and lit it with a wooden match.

"As soon as I finish eating, I can help do the dishes, Aunt Cora."

"No need for that, Jimmy. This is woman's work. I know you can't wait to go out and play around in those old cars so go to it."

"Thanks, I will, but I was wondering why you don't use the wood stove outside to cook and heat water with."

"When it gets colder, I will. Sometime in October, Bert will get one of his brothers to help him carry the stove inside and hook up the stovepipes. I like to use the oil better in the summer. It doesn't make the kitchen get so hot."

"That makes sense. Uh, Uncle Bert has six old cars out in the yard. Do you know which one of them was working last?"

"Well, let's see now," she said, walking over to the window.

The youth arose and stood beside her.

"You see that pointed-nosed one on the far side?"

"Hey. Yeah! That's a Lincoln Zephyr. Last night in the dark I thought it was another Ford."

"I think there's a Ford out there somewhere."

"I see it. It's right next to the Zephyr."

Cora was amused by the excitement in the boy's face and in his speech. "You better go check them out, Jimmy, before they rust away."

"Do you know what was wrong with the Zephyr, Aunt Cora?"

"Well, now, I can't be completely sure, but I think that's the one that got real hot and boiled over. Bert put some water in it, but after that it wouldn't start anymore. It's too bad because it was a real nice car."

"The body's in great shape and the tires are like new. Maybe I can get it running. How about the Ford? What was wrong with that?"

"Hmmm, that's the one that growled so much. Bert said the rear end was shot. He took it apart and started to fix it but gave up because the parts cost too much. That's when he decided to get the fancy one. He traded somebody a whole pile of mink pelts for it. He was saving them to make me a fur coat, but I told him to go ahead and get himself a car if that's what he wanted. It didn't last very long, though."

"Does Uncle Bert have any tools around? I've got some in my car, but not enough."

"Knowing Bert he probably left them where he used them last. Go look inside the station wagon."

"Thanks, Aunt Cora, I'm gonna check out all the cars."

She smiled and watched him sprint across the yard. Three mongrels followed behind him in single file. Cora returned to her dish washing and hummed an old French reel.

Jimmy stopped to pet the dogs. One of them licked a drop of gravy from the lad's knee. Another sniffed deeply into his crotch.

"Go on, you mutts, get out of the way. I've got work to do."

His mind was racing now. He remembered that his brother Phil had once told him about a man who had taken the small engine from a Ford and installed it in a Lincoln Zephyr during the war to save on gasoline because of rationing. He thought, perhaps, he could do the same. It made sense to him. After all, the Lincoln's engine was shot, and the Ford's motor was okay when the rear end went out.

He walked over to the Lincoln and noticed one of the back doors was open. While he was standing alongside it, one of the bitches hopped inside and curled up on the cushion as though she belonged there.

"Get out, you lazy mutt! Go chase a rabbit or something."

Jimmy closed the door soundly and raised the hood. He examined the vee-twelve engine. To him, it looked just like a Ford vee-eight that had been stretched. Once he had overheard a mechanic in the garage in Rock Mountain complain that this was not a reliable engine and a person should avoid buying one unless he was looking for trouble.

He returned to the Ford station wagon and studied the engine carefully. He wriggled underneath the car to check out the motor mounts. The beagle-looking dog joined him underneath and licked his face.

He reached over and petted her gently. "Okay, lady dog, if you want to cool off in the shade, it's fine with me. Only don't get in my way – and stay out of the back seat."

The youth was disappointed when he saw the Ford's battery. The terminals were coated with crusty white residue, and the side casing appeared to have frozen during the winter and cracked. He used a steel file placed across the battery terminals to check for sparks on each of the abandoned vehicles. Two of the batteries were missing while the others were lifeless.

Jimmy removed the battery from Phil's car and attached it to the cables of the Ford. He checked the engine for oil and the radiator for fluid. Both were adequate for now.

True to form, his Uncle Bert had left the key in the ignition. Jimmy held his breath as he turned the key. He watched the needle of the ammeter rise. The gas gauge registered nearly a quarter. He depressed the clutch and placed the shifting lever in neutral. He pulled on the choke, pumped the accelerator, and tried the starter. He allowed it to grind for several seconds and, then shut off the key, not wanting to run down the battery.

The youth walked over to a pile of tin cans beside the house and selected one which appeared to be cleaner than the others. He removed the siphon from the trunk of the Pontiac and withdrew a cupful of gasoline. Returning to the station wagon, he removed the air filter and poured a few tablespoons of gasoline into the throat of the carburetor. This time, when he switched on the ignition and tried the starter, the engine fired immediately. It raced for a few seconds, then stopped.

Jimmy felt encouraged by this and hurried to re-prime the carburetor. It fired again, backfired defiantly, but then continued to run roughly. The boy jiggled the choke rapidly and pumped on the accelerator. The sound of the motor smoothened out, then threatened to stop. He pushed in the choke halfway, and it continued to run. He allowed it to run for a few minutes before turning off the key. When he tried again, moments later, it started and ran reasonably well.

His mind continued to race. He realized that he still had some work to do on the engine but, at least, he knew that the Ford would run. He was certain that he could clean the spark plugs and set the points himself and that, perhaps, his Uncle Bert or Buck would buy some fresh oil and antifreeze.

The dogs followed him as he walked over to a pile of firewood and removed the axe from a stump. Noticing one of the clotheslines dangling on the ground, he cut it free with the axe, coiled it and hung it over his belt. The dogs frolicked around him expecting to be taken on a hunt.

At the far edge of the meadow Jimmy selected three straight maple trees with five-inch diameters. He chopped them down and limbed them. The beagle, which had been ranging farther than the other dogs, scented a snowshoe hare and ran off bugling. The two larger dogs were not interested in this chasing game but lay near-by watching the boy.

Jimmy called them over, petted them, and began fastening a crude harness for each of them with the clothesline. He connected each of them to one of the poles and hoisted the third one on his shoulder. The animals struggled at first to move the poles but soon were able to keep abreast of the boy.

When they were approaching the house, Jimmy noticed his aunt outside hanging up some laundry. She stopped long enough to notice him drop his maple pole and unhook the dogs from theirs.

"Are you building a log cabin, Jimmy?" she asked.

"No, no, Aunt Cora. The poles are for a tripod – to work on the car with. I, uh – sort of borrowed one of your clotheslines. I'll put it back up for you right away."

"Don't worry about it. I've got plenty of space for my laundry. Come inside for some cocoa and cookies. I don't know when the men will be back."

Seated at the kitchen table, Jimmy explained his plan to his aunt. She smiled at his youthful enthusiasm.

"I can do it, Aunt Cora. I know I can. All I need is for Buck or Uncle Bert to help me hoist the engines out and plop the Ford one into the Lincoln Zephyr. It should fit easily enough."

"Well, it certainly would be nice to go to a movie again without asking someone to take me."

"I'll need a chain or a real strong rope. Those motors are heavy."

"You can look in the barn. Bert used to have one of those things with ropes and pulleys."

"Oh, boy! Rope blocks. That'll be slick. Excuse me, I've got to get back to work."

"Watch your time, Jimmy. We're going to be eating supper in one hour, and I want you all washed up by then."

Bert's brother stopped his pick-up and let the two men out. Walking across the yard, they noticed the tripod that straddled the front end of the larger car. They could see the youth bent over working on it. Rope blocks were attached to the top end of the tripod.

"Jeez, Buck, your guy doesn't waste any time, does he?"

"Hell, no! Kids need something like that to stay out of trouble. Besides, who knows – maybe he can get something running. I was never any Christly good at it."

Chapter 23

The two men walked into the house without interrupting the youth's work on the cars. They sat at the kitchen table poring over the latest copy of the Malone Evening Telegram.

"About time you two fine country gentlemen came home. My stew has been ready for an hour," said Cora, half in jest.

"Thanks, Honeybunch," said her husband. "Take a look at this picture."

"Oh, that poor man!"

"Poor man, hell. He was trying to burn a house down last night with Buck and Jimmy in it. He got what he deserved," said Bert.

"Oh, my God! Did Jimmy see it happen?"

"See it? He's the one who torched the guy – only it was an accident."

"You've got to go tell the police all about it, Bert."

"Impossible! According to the newspaper, the dead man was a prison guard named McGuire. Buck thinks he's the one who picked a fight with him in Dannemora and is responsible for the assault on Jimmy's mother. Sometimes the police and the guards cover up for one another. Right now, Buck can't trust anybody but us."

Cora raised her hands to her ears as though she didn't want to hear anymore. "But what about Jimmy? He didn't say a thing about it to me except that he and Buck were hiding."

Buck stood up and patted her shoulder. "You don't have to worry about him, Cora. He's tougher than you think. He's no kid anymore."

"The best thing for him is to stay away from that place and live with us for a while. Let him do something different and meet different people", Bert said.

"He told me he wished you would take him hunting."

"I sure will, and we'll go fishing out on the St. Lawrence. Maybe we can snag a big Muskie like the one I caught last year."

"Shhh! I see him coming to the porch to wash up for supper. Don't spoil his day," Cora said.

The two men left the kitchen, taking the newspaper with them. Jimmy poked his head around the corner of the screen door. "Excuse me, Aunt Cora. Do you have a scrubbing brush I can use? I can't seem to get my greasy hands clean with only this soap."

"Of course, Jimmy. How's your job going?"

"Really great! I'm ready to hoist out the Zephyr motor."

"That's fine, dear, but that's enough repair work for one day. Maybe tomorrow the men will help you."

"That would be swell! Oh, oh! Here comes somebody in a car."

"Don't worry. That's only Madge and the baby. Maybe they will stay for supper."

The men walked into the kitchen and sat down.

"Hi, Dad," said Jimmy. "Hi, Uncle Bert. Wait until you see what I'm doing. I hope you approve of it, Uncle Bert."

"I see you've got a tripod all set up. Are you ready to do some hoisting?"

"Yes, Sir! I'm gonna pull the motor out of the Zephyr tomorrow morning."

"Buck and I will give you a hand, but you're the boss. I can't tell a piston from a pisspot."

Jimmy stood up when his Aunt Cora opened the door and greeted her daughter and grand-daughter. Madge handed the infant to her mother and smiled at everyone.

"Hi, Uncle Buck," she said. "I haven't seen you in quite a while."

Then her eyes focused on the youth. "And who is this handsome heart throb?"

"Madge, this is my son, Jimmy."

The young woman came over and hugged Jimmy. "Hey, now I've

got another kissing cousin. You better watch out, though, Jim. The girls around here will be snatching your pants off."

Cora scolded her, "Come on, now, Madge. You're making the boy blush. He's not interested in girls yet – are you, Jimmy? He'd rather work on old cars."

"I sure hope he likes to hunt and fish because I need a partner," said Bert. "I'm getting too old to do this all alone."

Embarrassed by this sudden attention, all Jimmy could do was cough nervously.

"Eat up, everybody, it's ven'son stew. The potatoes and carrots are from the garden. Madge, you make sure to take home some of that ven'son in the shed. There's hardly enough ice left to cool a hamburger."

"I plan to build a new ice house this fall – a bigger one with lots of sawdust," said Bert.

"That would be nice, dear," said Cora, knowing that the job was unlikely to ever get finished.

"I'll help, Uncle Bert," said the youth. "I'm pretty good with a hammer and saw."

A siren wailed as a state police parole car sped down the highway. Everyone sat motionless and waited until it passed.

"Probably an accident somewhere," said Buck. "Pass the stew, it smells terrific."

"We already had venison once today. I could eat it every meal," said Jimmy.

"You won't be disappointed as long as you stay here," said Madge. "I've eaten so much I'm afraid I may start to grow horns."

"Antlers," corrected her father, "bulls have horns and bucks have antlers."

"Not this Buck," said Jimmy's father.

Later that evening after Madge had left and the others had gone to bed, Buck handed his son the Malone newspaper so he could read it himself. Jimmy read the front-page article avidly, devouring each word. He raised his eyes and discovered his father staring at him.

"So it was McGuire who got fried," said Jimmy. "He's the one who shot at you. Then, the one with him last night could have been the one they called Murphy. I wonder if the police have questioned him."

"If they have, he's sure to have given them a pack of lies," Buck replied.

Jimmy pointed to the news article. "It says here that the inhabitants of the house closest to the fire are missing, and the police are investigating."

"Dad, do you think we could get Uncle Bert and his family in trouble for sheltering fugitives?"

"I don't know. Nobody is calling us fugitives yet."

"Yeah, maybe they're dragging the lake for our bodies or something."

"They will be asking a lot of questions and will be looking for this car. That much is certain. It's likely they will try to contact your brother in the army."

"Oh, gosh! I hope they don't. I don't want Phil to be worried. Maybe I should write him another letter."

"You can't. They would trace it back here."

"But suppose we got somebody to mail it to Phil from Montreal or even farther away than that?"

"That might work, Jim. Let's think about it in the morning. Also, we should hide that Pontiac some place better."

"We might be able to get it inside Uncle Bert's barn if we widen the doors. The walls are kind of falling down anyway. Hey, how about our animals? I haven't been able to call Perchy yet."

"Don't worry about it, Jim. I took care of it today. We called somebody I know in Syracuse, and they are relaying the message. We could be here for quite a while, Jim. If the cops start nosing around Hogansburg and asking questions, we'll head into Quebec. I've got cousins there, too."

"That's fine with me, Dad. I'll get to practice my French some more."

"Maybe you'll have to learn Mohawk."

"Are there still people here who speak it?"

"Quite a few, especially on the Quebec side."

"Can you speak it?"

"I could some – when I was little, but I've forgotten a lot of it."

What Buck and Jimmy could not know was that their situation as far as the state police were concerned, was not as precarious as they imagined. Working together, Trooper Wood and Lieutenant Carruthers, the man who had interviewed them about Lillian's disappearance, had shared information which tended to exonerate the two of them from any crime.

In fact, it was Trooper Wood who was first on the scene following the explosion. He had placed McGuire, Murphy, and O'Donnell under surveillance since stopping them for speeding down the mountain. McGuire was out on bail pending a hearing for drunken driving and carrying a loaded weapon inside a vehicle.

An undercover operator, following McGuire and Murphy, had watched as they filled a can with gasoline and placed it in the trunk of McGuire's Chevrolet, the same one Jimmy had identified as belonging to the men who had forced him and his father off the road.

Trooper Wood had followed them over the mountain at a discreet distance. When he saw the sudden flare of light in the sky, he wished he had been following more closely. By the time he saw the still-smoldering body of McGuire, Jimmy and Buck had already left.

In the morning, Wood discovered the burst gas can with bullet holes in it and pieced the scene together in his mind. He knocked on the front door of the Coulbron farmhouse. When no one answered, he tried the door and found it unlocked. Noticing cupboard doors in the kitchen and closets upstairs left open, he knew the inhabitants had left in a hurry. He realized, also, that this was their second close call and didn't blame them for fleeing.

He knew that he couldn't watch O'Donnell and Murphy constantly, and, since he didn't yet have enough evidence to arrest them, decided not to search aggressively for Buck and Jimmy. He realized that in time they would show up and, if he asked too many questions now, they would only hide somewhere else. Yet, eventually, they would be needed to testify against Murphy and O'Donnell. Then, too, the assault against Lillian Coulbron seemed to point strongly in the guards' direction.

Chapter 24

At false dawn the youth climbed out of bed without waking his father and carried his clothes into the kitchen to dress. The house remained silent while he donned a jacket and pumped himself a glassful of water to drink. He closed the door gently and stepped out into the first breeze of the morning. A young aspen tree fibrillated its heart-shaped leaves in applause to announce the arrival of dawn while the sun oozed orange and peeped over the horizon.

Hearing a whimpering sound near the old vehicles, Jimmy hurried over to check it out. The three dogs he had seen yesterday were nowhere in sight. Instead, an obviously pregnant part-collie bitch pawed at the back door of the Lincoln Zephyr. Even through her long coat, he could see the swollen breasts.

She wants to have her littler in the back seat of the car, he thought, and from the looks of things, it's going to be soon.

The animal responded appreciatively when the youth knelt to pet her face. "I'm sorry, girl, but this car is going to be up and running soon. It's not a maternity ward. Come on with me. I'll make you a bed in the barn. There's straw and feed sacks in there."

When the animal refused to follow, he started to lift her up and carry her inside but she barked in pain and convulsed her body.

"Oh, oh!" he said out loud. "You're going to do it right now, aren't you?"

He laid her down gently and petted her. "It's okay, girl. I'll bring some bedding for you."

When the lad returned with gunny sacks and an old quilt, he noted that pink-gray amniotic tissue was already protruding past the animal's vulva. Silently he thanked David Coulbron for having allowed him to observe kittens and calves being born.

The membrane was nearly transparent where it stretched, and the youth smiled as the brown and white muzzle of a puppy appeared. One by one the mother dropped her litter. She licked each one dry and spread out her belly so they could nurse.

Jimmy stared awestruck at the cuteness of the five pups. He wanted to cuddle each one of them but knew that the mother's duties came first. He grinned at the sight of the round bellies and the pink tongues. He was unable to tear his eyes away as they nursed and the mother continued to lick them.

Cora appeared on the porch, a spatula in her hand. "Come to breakfast, Jimmy. We're having pancakes."

He didn't want to leave the pups, but he knew their mother could care for them better than he could. Besides, his mouth had begun watering at the sound of the word 'pancakes'.

"Aunt Cora," he called, "come over here for a minute. I'd like to show you something."

She walked over to see what the boy was pointing to and noticed the smile that curved his lips.

"Well, now, isn't that something special?"

"I watched them being born, Aunt Cora. Aren't they cute?"

"Cute as a bug's ear, Jimmy. Since you were the midwife, you get the pick of the litter."

"You mean I can have one? My mom would never let us have a dog. She said they were too much trouble."

"Of course, you can have one. In fact, you can have them all if you want."

"Gosh, I don't know about that. But I for sure would like to have this one," he said, pointing to the first one born.

His left forearm still encased in the plaster that Doc Manvel had applied the night of the wreck, Buck was washing his face in a white enameled basin and examining the scars on his forehead and cheeks with the aid of a small, framed mirror. Bert stood behind him, trying to share the glass. As soon as Jimmy and Cora entered the room, Bert finished combing his hair and slapped the lad on the shoulder.

"Well, old buddy, I suppose you've got the car running already."

"I'm afraid not, Uncle Bert. I kind of had a delay. I had to be a midwife for one of the dogs."

"Oh, yeah, that must be the one I call 'Missy'. She's a good watch-dog. You want a pup?"

"You bet I do! Can I have one, Dad?"

"Why not? It looks as though your Uncle Bert just might be able to spare one."

Bert gave his cousin a wry grin. "One? How would you like a half dozen?"

Buck shook his head, "No, no, no! One is perfect."

When the three of them reached Missy and her litter, she wagged her tail as if to welcome them into the presence of her family. Jimmy placed the puppies in a cardboard box and carried them to the barn while the mother and the two men followed.

The lad laid them gently on a bed he had prepared. Cora arrived with a pan full of food scraps and milk for the mother.

"I'll go get her some water," Jimmy said, as he rushed out of the barn.

Buck waited until his son was out of earshot, then spoke, "You're right, Bert. It's good for the boy to be here right now where there's so many new things happening. He's been through hell and back in a very short time. It has been one shock right after another."

"He's lucky to have you, Buck. I never figured you as a family man, though," said Cora.

"Neither did I, but here I am, and you know what?—I like it. "

"How about his mother? Is she going to pull out of it this time?"

Buck just screwed up his face in a grimace and shook his head. "Jim and I don't even dare to go check up on her – what with this burning and everything."

"What are you doing about your church in Malone?" asked Cora.

"I've got somebody covering for me. He's a young guy who just graduated from Bible school. He asked me if he could help. I'm thinking about turning the whole business over to him. I was getting worn down trying to change people who didn't want to change. I'm the only one who was changing and it definitely wasn't for the better. I was a mess until I met the kid. He rubs off on me. I don't even hit the sauce anymore."

"Well, good for you, Buck," said Cora, hugging him. "You take good care of that boy, or I'll take him away from you."

"Don't worry about that. I need him more than he needs me, and that's no lie."

"Here he comes," said Bert.

Cora returned to the kitchen to wash the dishes while Jimmy led the way to the tripod and began to explain his plan. After hearing about the proposed engine switch, the men looked at each other and shrugged their shoulders.

"Sounds good to me," Bert said.

"Will that Ford motor have enough power?" asked Buck.

"Well, yes and no. It all depends on what a person expects. You see the Ford only produces sixty horsepower and the Lincoln is rated at over a hundred. Plus – I figure the Lincoln weighs at least a thousand pounds more. It's going to be sluggish on the hills, but that's what they have lower gears for. It will never make it over Dannemora Mountain in high gear, but it will make it – if you have enough patience."

"At least," Bert added, "the gas mileage should be better."

"You bet it will! I think you'll be able to go a hundred miles for the cost of seventy-five."

"Well, then, Mr. Engineer, let's get to it," said Buck. "What comes first?"

"The way I've got it figured, we'll raise the engine of the Lincoln

Zephyr first and lay it down on some boards next to that old Hudson. Then we'll move the tripod over to the Ford and pull its engine but leave it suspended. We'll push the Ford out of the way and push the Lincoln right where the Ford was. There are other ways to do it, but I'd rather not have to put both motors on the ground and then have to skid one of them. What do you suggest?"

"I think your way will save time," said his father.

"So do I, Jimmy, except for one thing," said Bert. "Although these ropes might be able to hold up the Ford motor, the Lincoln motor looks twice as heavy. You see that splice right there? That's where it broke the last time I used it. I don't trust it."

"Even if I strip off the heads and all the little parts?"

"There's an easier way, Jimmy. I know somebody who has a set of chain falls. He works on motors all the time. After dark we can go down in your car and pick them up," said Bert. "Then we'll hide your Pontiac inside and not use it until it's safe."

"That's great! The chain falls will have a greater mechanical advantage than these rope blocks. I'll let the Lincoln rest for a while and concentrate on disconnecting the Ford. That way we can do the switch first thing tomorrow morning."

"We're going into town again this afternoon with Bert's brother. Is there anything you need?"

"Uh, just oil for the Ford engine, and oh, yeah, if you go to the garage, see if either of these batteries will take a quick charge."

"We'll take care of it. You want to come with us?" asked Bert.

"No thanks. I've got lots to do right here. Besides, I want to check in on the pups."

The process of engine switching proved to be a much more onerous task than the youth anticipated. One problem popped up as soon as the previous one was solved. Hoses cracked or did not fit. Wires broke and had to be spliced. Parts had to be filed to fit properly. The two men offered encouragement and helped with heavy lifting but refrained from interfering and offering too much advice. They were confident that, in time, the lad would succeed. More importantly, they knew he had to do it on his own.

The youth worked until dark each evening and, then, brought parts inside to work on by lamplight. Three days of rain added to the delay of the project's completion so that more than a week passed before Jimmy was ready to test his work.

One evening during supper Buck asked, "Say, Jim, you've got a birthday coming up pretty soon, don't you?"

The question surprised and flustered the youth. "Well, uh, I guess I sort of forgot about it."

"Forgot about it," said Cora. "Nobody forgets their own birthday. When was it? Come on, now."

"It was yesterday. I didn't want anybody to fuss."

"Fuss! Jimmy, I love to fuss. I'm baking a cake for you tomorrow, and there's even enough ice left to make homemade ice cream."

"I'll turn the handle," said Buck.

"There's something else that is going to happen tomorrow, Uncle Bert."

"What's that, Jimmy?"

"I'm going to test out your Lincoln-Ford. I could have done it today, but it got too dark on me."

"You've got all kinds of secrets, don't you?" kidded Cora.

"Come on, Jimmy," said Bert. "Let's all go check it out right now! Cora, where's the flashlight? Come on, everybody."

Jimmy and Bert sat in the front seat while Buck and Cora sat in the back.

Buck thought to himself, even if it only goes fifty feet, I'm satisfied.

"We really should have daylight, you know," said Jimmy. "There's dozens of things that can go wrong. Wires could be crossed. Something might not be tight enough. I don't think we should go out on the highway yet. I'll just drive around the meadow sort of slow."

He started the engine and allowed it to warm up for a minute before switching on the headlights and driving past the gate leading to a grassy field. They joked as the vehicle made one complete tour of the plot of ground. Then quite suddenly, a thin stream of water began to spray out from the front grill, curve back because of the wind, and splatter against the windshield. Jimmy stopped the car abruptly.

"That's just what it did the last time I drove it," moaned Bert.

"Not exactly," said Jimmy. "It's not overheating this time. Look at the temperature gauge. It's on normal. I think it's just a leak in the radiator."

Everyone piled out to investigate.

"See, here," said the young driver. "It's no big deal. I can solder it with a blow torch in the morning, but we will still have to take short trips for a while until all the little problems show themselves and get corrected."

"Good job, Jim," said his Aunt Cora, patting him on the back. "I'll pay for your ticket if you take me to the movies in Cornwall on Saturday."

"It's a date, Aunt Cora.

Chapter 25

That night after the kerosene lamp had been extinguished in their tiny bedroom, Jimmy and Buck lay side by side in the four-poster. Jimmy felt better than he had in many weeks. The car ran. It really ran. He had said he could do it, and he did. He did it for Bert and Cora, he thought at first, but then he realized that he was also doing it to prove something to himself – to prove that he was a worthy person – to prove he was a man, and a man is like David – somebody who does things for other people without hoping for a reward.

As he lay there that evening, he felt that no one could be as lucky as he was. He had had David for almost sixteen years, and now there was Buck. He did wish that somehow Phil could learn what Buck was really like.

"Dad," he whispered, "are you awake?

"Sure, Jim. Something troubling you?"

"No. No troubles. Do you remember your promise?"

"What was that?"

"You promised to tell me all about living with the Pierce's."

"That's a big order, Jim. I don't know if you can stay awake that long."

"Try me."

"Okay, just remember that you asked for it. If you start to get bored, start snoring."

"I won't get bored. I promise."

"Where do you want me to start?"

"The beginning is a good place. Tell me what it was like when you lived with your grandmother."

"Hmmm! That's a tall order, Jim. I remember I was alone a lot playing with pots and pans or clothespins – whatever I could find."

"What was your grandmother like?"

"I wasn't very close to her. It was like she took care of me because she had to."

"Was she mean to you?"

"No, no! Not mean, just unconcerned. I tried to make her like me by dragging lots of firewood in from outside. I picked up feathers I found and brought them to her."

"Feathers?"

"Yes, I thought they were pretty – you know, from blue jays and gold finches. She made things from them. You can't believe how naïve I was. I didn't know anything about the outside world."

"What do you mean, Dad?"

"Well, for example, modesty. That doesn't come naturally. You have to learn it. Once a week Grandma would have me heat water on the cook stove and pour it in the wash tub. She would use the water first, and then I would. One time, not long before she died I was still in the tub when several of her lady friends came to play cards. I remember I was big enough that it was hard for me to fit in the tub. When I finished taking my bath, I just walked over to the ladies to see what they were doing."

"I'll bet they were embarrassed."

"No, not at all. One of them got up and dried me with a towel. She whispered something to me about what a big boy I was becoming, but I didn't know what she was getting at."

"How old were you?"

"I'm not sure. Let's say that I was changing. "

"Okay. Enough said. I get it. What did you live on – money, I mean?"

"I guess I don't know. There never was any that I can remember. Relatives dropped off food for us, wild game mostly or fish. Sometimes all we had was cornmeal or flour so she made meals from that."

"You said before that she made maple syrup."

"Yes, every spring. Even when I was very little, I helped carry buckets of sap. The trees were all around us, real big ones. Somebody, I think it was Bert's father, used to tap the trees for her. She boiled the sap down out in the back yard in an iron kettle suspended by a tripod just like you used to lift the car motors. I hauled the wood and helped keep the fire going."

"How are you related to Uncle Bert?"

"He's my cousin, the son of my mother's older brother."

Maybe he knows who your father is."

"No. We talked about it when we were kids, but he barely remembers his sister. Don't worry about it, Jim. It doesn't matter anyway."

"Okay, well, anyway, we've got something in common. I always liked maple syrup time."

"I don't remember if I liked helping make it or not. I certainly liked eating it. Grandma LeTarte used to make something she called Indian pudding. It was a lot like Mrs. Papineau's Johnny cake. I used to soak it in maple syrup. That was the only sweet stuff I can remember except for maple candy and 'cheer'."

"'Cheer'? What's that?"

"I think it's French. It means 'pull' or 'taffy' or something like that."

"'Pull'? That would be 'tire' in high school French. Come to think of it – that's the way Mrs. Papineau pronounces it, too. Dad, did you have lots of friends in those days?"

"No, very few. Sometimes, one of my cousins would stop over for a visit, or I would visit them – especially Bert."

"Did you go to school?"

"Ha! Not much. I was supposed to, but I didn't have any decent clothes, and Grandma didn't make me go. After a few years I was so far behind the other kids that the teacher thought I was retarded. Anyway, I quit going entirely when I was about twelve."

"By that time you must have been on your own a lot. What did you like to do?"

"Best of all, I liked to go fishing in the big river."

Enough moonlight shone through the window that the youth could see the smile on his father's face.

"What would you catch there, Dad?"

"A lot of pike. They were easy to catch. I think they were as hungry all the time as I was."

"What was the biggest one you caught?"

"Oh, boy! Was that a monster, but it wasn't a pike. It was a muskie – darn near as long as I was – probably bigger around because I was a skinny little runt."

Jimmy was excited now because fishing was his passion as well. "How did you catch it?"

"There was a certain spot I used to fish all the time. It was a point that went out into the current. On the downstream side there was a bay filled with weeds. That's where the pike seemed to be, but it was a bad place to get all tangled up in. One day I was stillfishing with worms and I caught a sucker, and I wondered if I could use it for bait to catch a big pike. I wasn't using a pole of any kind, just a long hand line, a sinker, and a big hook. The sinker was really a steel nut I had found. Anyway, I would coil the line up very carefully and swing the nut and bait around over my head. Then, I'd let it go out over the water into the current but close to the weeds."

Jimmy had never heard his father speak with such enthusiasm before, and this made him feel good to know the man was enjoying the telling of the story.

"Is that how you caught the big muskie?"

"Not quite. This time I decided to make the bait go farther out if I could. There was a strong wind behind me so I corked a big bottle and attached it to the line as a float. I hooked the sucker through the lips and tossed it all into the water as far as I could. The current and the wind carried the bait out about two hundred feet."

"How long was it before the muskie hit?"

"Nothing happened for a long time so I tied my end of the line to a branch and went home for supper. I was planning to go back right away, but Grandma had some work for me so I had to leave it overnight."

"Did you expect to find your line broken or snapped on something in the morning?"

"Yes, and I also feared that someone else would have found my line and stolen it. It was the only piece I had. Anyhow, I sneaked out of the house real early and rushed out onto the point. Right away I could see the bottle - I think it was a brown Clorox bottle. It was being pulled completely underwater for a short time, and then it would pop up and zing along in a straight line for a while before stopping. I knew I had hooked onto something big."

"How long did you have to fight him, Dad?"

"About a half an hour, I guess, but first I tied my end of the line onto a dry log. I had heard that if you threw the log into the water when you had a big fish on, it would help tire it out without breaking your line."

"Is that what you did?"

"No, I didn't have to. When I started pulling on the line, the fish kept coming my way until I had half of my line coiled up beside me. From them on we tugged back and forth. Sometimes he had almost all of the line straight out but, then I'd get some back. After a while, Bert and his father showed up to go fishing there, and they helped me pull it up the shore. When they first saw me, I was up to my waist in the water wrestling with the monster."

"Gosh! How big was it?"

"Bert's father had a car so we drove down to the grocery store and weighed it – fifty pounds exactly, counting the sucker that it swallowed. There were other people in the store, and everybody was congratulating me. After that, everybody started to call me 'Big Fish.'"

"So, you became a hero for a while."

"That's for sure. Bert's dad drove me home. When Grandma saw that fish she screamed really loud and hugged me. I think that was the first and last time."

"How old were you when you caught the big fish?"

"I must have been about thirteen because Grandma died the next year. I found her dead and cold in bed. After the funeral Bert's father, my Uncle Vince, asked me to live with him. I realize now that I should have, but I was all mixed up and wanted to go look for my father."

"Where did you think you would find him?"

"I remembered one of Grandma's stories that my father was a reservation man who went to New York City to build skyscrapers. She said he was tall and handsome except for one crossed eye. I thought I'd just go there and look for him. I had no idea how big New York was."

"Did you ever make it to New York?"

"No, not until many years later. By then I didn't care anymore. I don't hold it against him. I suppose he was just like me. He never knew I existed."

Jimmy reached over and squeezed his father's hand. "I'm glad you found me, Dad."

"Jim, I bless that day every night before I fall asleep."

"Me too, Pop."

"I'm the one who is getting sleepy, son. Do you mind postponing this until later?"

"No, I guess I've had enough for one night. Good night, Dad."

Chapter 26

During the twenty-five years since the death of Buck's grandmother and his sudden departure from the reservation, many changes had occurred both in the physical appearance of the place and in the man's understanding and acceptance of the vagaries of life. As a child he had fled the closed environment of the reservation in search of a father. Now, as an adult, he has returned to the reservation and is having thoughts about giving up his ministry and livelihood because he has found his son. He felt as though he may now be atoning for both his father's sin and his own by learning to treasure the boy.

While Bert was driving down the dusty road in his Lincoln-Ford, Jimmy squirmed left and right in the front passenger's seat, trying to be the first to spot the log house where his father was raised. His father and his aunt conversed in the back.

Bert said, "I haven't been down this way in quite a few years. I'm sure the roof of the house has collapsed by now. If the brush hasn't grown up too much, we should be able to find the foundation."

He slowed the vehicle, turned right and nosed the car into a narrow lane. He tried to continue but alder brush was scraping both sides of the vehicle, and the front bumper was bulldozing saplings.

"Sorry, folks, but this is as far as we go. We're gonna have to hoof it from now on."

"How far is it, Uncle Bert?"

"Not far, Jimmy, only about a hundred yards or so."

At his uncle's suggestion, the lad had selected one of the adult dogs to accompany them on the trip. Now, he lifted the animal off his lap and opened the door. Immediately, it began ranging left and right along the path, its nose and eyes alert. The people hiked along, sometimes stepping over the trunks of fallen trees and pushing aside branches that tried to bar the way. A covey of young grouse exploded in front of the dog and zigzagged upward through openings in the trees.

"Uncle Bert," the boy asked, "did anyone live in Grandma LeTarte's house after she died?"

"Well, there was a young couple who lived in it for a year or so. After they left, I started using it for a hunting and trapping shack. It was pretty close to the river so I camped out in it a lot when I was your age. I kept patching the roof and fixing it up for a while, but, then my dad took a job in Massena and I went there with my parents."

"Why did you come back?"

Bert laughed and stopped walking long enough to hug Cora. "This is what brought me back, Jimmy. I was trapped by a designing woman. You better watch out, or the same thing will happen to you."

"Come on, Bert," said Cora. "Tell the truth. We met at a dance, and you swept me off my feet."

"Any regrets, Sugar Plum?"

"No regrets. I have everything I want."

They approached a small clearing surrounded by brush and small trees.

"Well, this is it, everybody. What's left of the house must be over there."

"What happened to the big maple trees?" asked the youth.

"Oh, they were all logged off twenty years ago," said Bert.

Jimmy surged ahead through the brush followed by the dog. "Hey, here's an iron pump. This must be where the well was, and here's some logs and part of a window."

He was disappointed that the building was no longer standing as he clambered over the tumble of logs that once supported the side walls of the structure.

You're standing in the kitchen now, Jim," said his father.

"Yeah, I can tell. Here's the cook stove."

"My room was right here in this corner."

Cora had remained outside the site of the fallen building, not wanting to step on a nail or be surprised by a snake. "Look here, Jimmy!" she cried. "You might be interested in this."

The youth joined her and saw her pointing to an overturned iron kettle. His father joined them. "That's the one Grandma used to make maple syrup in."

"Can I have it, Dad? Can I have it?"

"Let's pull it out and take a look. Be careful of the handle, Jim. That might be weak."

"Yeah, it's rusted right off, but the rest of it is okay. I bet I can make a new handle."

Bert said, "You can have it, Jim, but how are you going to haul it to the car? It must weigh a hundred pounds."

"We can do it. We can lay out two poles like a stretcher, and lay it upside down on them. If each of us holds on to one corner, that's only twenty-five pounds each."

That afternoon at the home of his aunt and uncle, Jimmy spent several hours cleaning and removing rust on the kettle.

Once again in bed, the youth gently poked his father in the ribs. "Well, Pop, are you ready to start chapter two of 'The Adventures of Buck LeTarte', or is this one of those stories that I'm too young and innocent to hear?"

"Well, son, it is a little raw in parts, but you're man enough to handle it. Where was I?"

"Your Grandma died and Bert's father asked you to come live with them."

"Yeah, that's the way it was. After the funeral I went back inside the house and made a bundle out of some of my clothes. I tied a stick on it, just like bums do. I went in Grandma's room and found her secret cache of Hershey bars. I remember there were six of them. Then, I simply took off hitch-hiking for New York City."

"Wow! That must have been scary."

"Let's face it. I was really stupid. I was lucky, though; I made it to Plattsburg the first night and only ate two of the candy bars. Whenever somebody dropped me off, I'd keep walking until I got picked up again. Every time I passed a brook that looked clean enough, I'd fill my belly up with water."

"You're lucky you didn't get sick."

"Ha! Who said I didn't? I had stomach cramps and diarrhea so bad I had to ask one driver to let me out at Cadyville."

"How old were you, Dad?

"Younger than you are now – fourteen and a half. I was pretty little and skinnier than a two by four."

"What happened in Cadyville?"

"I saw a big tavern. I didn't know what it was, but I thought I might be able to find something to eat so I sneaked around the back and hit pay dirt."

"What did you find?"

"Wooden cases filled with returnable beer bottles and pop bottles. Lots of them still had some dregs in them. By draining everything from one case into one bottle, I could usually get nearly a bottle's worth. I must have drunk three bottles of beer and a couple of pop. I tried to avoid the ones with cigarette butts in them. Then I found some stale popcorn in the garbage can and a pickled egg."

"You were the one who must have been getting pickled. That's not exactly a balanced diet for a kid."

"It gave me a little courage, though. I walked right in the back door of the tavern and asked the bartender for a job. He looked me up and down. He told me I was kinda scrawny, but he handed me a pail and told me to empty all of the slops from the cuspidors into it."

"Yech! Spare me the details."

"Okay, anyhow after I dumped the third one, I got really sick and threw up all over the place. Everybody at the bar was watching me, and they laughed their fool heads off."

"Oh, gosh! I'm getting sick just listening to you."

"Good thing it was summertime though. I staggered down the hill to the cemetery. It was deserted, and I was woozy drunk so I slept it off hidden behind some tomato plants. After I woke up, I hitched a ride directly to Plattsburg."

"What's the first thing you did there, Dad – look for another tavern?"

"No, that was later. I saw a tall monument – sort of like the one in Washington, only this one had an eagle on top. I saw some tourists going inside, and I watched them for a while. They would climb the steps together and then look out over the town and the bay through a wide slot underneath the eagle."

"Yeah, I know where that is, only I don't think people can go up any more. I don't know why."

"I'll bet I do. There's too much pigeon poop up there."

"How do you know that?"

"Because I went up, and that's where I spent the night. After it got dark, nobody else came up so I curled up under my bundle of clothes. It wasn't too bad except for the noisy, messy pigeons. And it smelled like every tourist had taken a leak up there. I don't doubt that some of them had."

"I'm glad it's not supper time because you sure know how to spoil a guy's appetite."

"Hey! You asked for this story. Are you backing out already? You're more than a year older than I was when this happened."

"I'm sorry, Dad. I was just kidding. Come on. Go ahead."

"Early in the morning the pigeons woke me up with all their wing flapping and cooing. I added my donation to the ammonia smell and ate another Hershey bar. Then I went across the street and walked a ways until I found another bar. Did you ever try to drink stale beer filled with flies at six in the morning? No? Well, you learn real quick how to strain them through your teeth."

"Dad, you've got to be making this up."

"No, Jim, it's the truth. There weren't very many bottles outside so I sneaked in the back door and stole a six-pack of full ones and a bottle opener. I drank two bottles and wrapped the rest in my clothes bag."

"Did you keep heading south after that?"

"No. I almost ended up going to Montreal. I walked down to the railroad yards. There were two trains on the siding without engines on them. I hid inside a boxcar on one of them and waited. Pretty soon a steam locomotive came along and hooked onto the other one and headed north to Canada. Mine brought me to Troy, New York. By then I was out of candy and beer so got out and wandered into a residential section of town."

"What exactly were you looking for?"

"Food. Something solid to eat. I still had the runs and one son-of-a-gun of a headache."

"I can imagine you were in bad shape by then," said the youth grimacing.

"Anyhow, I walked completely around the block looking for an easy touch. Earlier, on the way south I had met another guy about twenty on the train. He told me that when you're bumming to avoid any house that has a big wood pile or a vegetable garden because they'll put you to work before they feed you."

"Did you have to watch out for anything else?"

"Dogs. Big dogs and yappy little dogs and people with lots of kids because they're too busy to help strays who wander in. After a while I learned to look for grandmother types."

"Is that what you found in Troy?"

"Yes, and I did pretty well – at least I didn't starve or have to drain beer bottles anymore. After about a week of this, I found something even better. This was a preacher's wife – a remarkable woman. I pretended to stagger up to her door while she was watering her roses. I took off my cap and held it to my chest and asked for something to eat."

"'Please, Ma'am,' I said, with a quaver in my voice, 'Would you have a crust of bread I could have?'"

"Right away I added, 'I can eat outside, Ma'am, so I don't dirty up your floors.'"

"'Oh, you poor child,' she said."

"I was such a little runt, I looked like I was eleven or twelve. I only weighed about eighty-five pounds."

"I wasn't very big a year ago either, Dad."

"Well, you are now and still growing. You'll pass me up pretty soon."

"That's because you're learning to be such a good chef."

"You are lucky you survived my feeble attempts at cooking."

"What happened at the lady's house?"

"Oh, boy! Maybe I shouldn't tell you everything."

"C'ome, Dad, you promised."

While telling the story, the man felt a particular closeness to the lad as though he saw himself whenever he looked at him. Other times, it was like watching a movie with himself as the star.

"There I stood like a lost waif right out of a Dicken's novel. The pretend name, Mrs. Dogwood, flashed through my mind, and I knew I was in luck. She thought my fake staggers were due to extreme hunger."

"'You come right inside this instant, you poor thing. Go wash your face and hands in the bathroom sink,' she commanded, and naturally I obeyed. My hands were so filthy I had to soap them three times. When I looked in the mirror, I almost didn't recognize myself. I scrubbed my face and tried to slick down my hair. I didn't want to soil her fancy towels so I dried myself with toilet paper."

"You must have been quite a sight."

"I was. She handed me an apple to help stave off starvation while she proceeded to cook me a meal. While I wolfed down the food, she watched me and drank a cup of tea."

"Was the lady's husband around?"

"No, he didn't come home until after supper time."

"So you were there for a while?"

"I'll say! I stayed with them for five years."

"Five years? How did that happen? Did they adopt you?"

"Just about. That day after I finished my third helping, I told her I couldn't pay for my food."

"'Oh, yes you can,' she said. 'You can repay me by taking a bath while I wash your clothes and mend them.'"

"'But Ma'am,' I protested, 'I don't want to make any more work for you. I better be moving on.'"

"'Oh, no, you are not! You are going to get cleaned up. Land's sakes! What would your mother say?'"

"'I never had a mother, Ma'am – or a father.' I could see her heart melting. I didn't know one person could feel that badly for someone else. She wiped her eyes and smothered me with a hug. I really didn't mean to do it as a trick, but I clung to her and pressed my head against her breast. This comforted me a great deal, but I was embarrassed because I started to cry."

"'Don't you have anybody?' she asked."

"'No, Ma'am. My grandma used to take care of me, but she was buried last week.'"

"'So she kept you with her?' the woman queried."

"'Yes, I answered her.' Then she drew me a big tubful of hot water, handed me a bar of soap, and told me not to come out for at least an hour. Do you know that was the first time I used a real bathtub?"

"Yeah, you said you used to use a washtub once a week."

"That's right, and remember I didn't know what the word 'modesty' meant."

"What did you think of the lady's big tub?"

"I thought she must be rich to have such luxury. I could stretch my body straight out like I was swimming in the river."

"After a while the water cooled off. I dried myself off and walked into the kitchen completely naked. I didn't know any better. It never bothered grandma or her lady friends."

"I'll bet it bothered the preacher's wife. What did you say their name was?"

"Pierce. Actually, she didn't see me in the buff because she was down in the basement. However, her daughter sure did. She looked me up and down like she was planning to buy a stud horse."

"How old was she?"

"Well, let's see now. I'd say somewhere between eighteen and twenty."

"And you still weren't embarrassed?"

"Not one bit – just surprised because I didn't know she lived there. I said, 'Hi', like I belonged. She told me her name was Prudy and that she thought I was cute. Then, we heard her mother coming up the stairs so she wrapped a towel around me and whispered that her mother was very old-fashioned and didn't like to see people without all their clothes on. She said that it didn't bother her one bit. That was my introduction to modesty. Prudy was promising to teach me some fun games when her mother came in."

"What did Mrs. Pierce do?"

"She almost dropped her teeth. She told her daughter – Prudence was her full name for Cripe's sake – to go pick up their order at the grocery store. Prudy winked at me as she left. Her mother handed me some of the preacher's underwear and socks. They were about ten sizes too big. Then she had me put on his bathrobe."

"How did you feel about all of this sudden attention?"

"I went with the flow. I just let things happen without thinking about it. While I was taking the bath, she had been washing my clothes in the basement. She hung them to dry and mended all of the worn spots. After I was all dressed, she handed me some books and asked me to read to her."

"How well could you read?"

"Very poorly – about like a second-grader. She didn't criticize me though. In fact, she praised me every time I got two words right in a row."

"When the preacher came home, what did he think about your being there?"

"He was not very pleased. That's for sure. I overheard them arguing in their bedroom that night. She insisted that God had sent me to her because she had been praying for another child for years and now that she was too old to have her own, a miracle happened."

"Did you think of yourself as a miracle, Dad?"

"Hardly! More like a curse. Do you mind if we postpone this adventure until tomorrow night, Jim?"

"It is your call, Dad," said the youth. "And thanks for telling me so much. It's lots of fun to listen to."

Chapter 27

The next day Jimmy and his father returned to the site of Grandma LeTarte's house. They poked through the ruins as the man spoke about his life there. Jimmy discovered little of interest among the shattered dishes and broken furniture.

At the boy's request, they began following the path leading to the river. The woods gave way to willow brush and, finally, grassy meadows. A mixed herd of dairy cows, some black and white Holsteins, others red and white Ayrshires, cropped grass next to the water's edge, each with its tail to the wind. One of them took a long draft of water before rejoining the group.

"Dad, why do they almost always seem to be facing in the same direction?"

"I think it's part of the herd instinct, Jim. They stay with the group for protection from predators. Like fish in a school or birds in a flock, they are constantly observing signals from one another so that they seem to behave as one."

"Do people have a herd instinct?"

"What do you think, son?"

"Well, I hadn't actually thought about it before but, yeah, I think that sometimes people do act as though they were part of a herd."

"How about your Uncle Bert and Aunt Cora?"

"Nah! They're individuals. Maybe that's why I like them so much."

"How about you, Jim. How would you classify yourself?"

"I'm not sure yet. I guess that's something I'm still working on – you know, things like who I am now and who I want to become when I'm a man."

"Tell me, Jim. Are there any advantages to being one of the herd?"

"Gosh, you ask hard questions."

"Do you want me to stop asking questions?"

"No, don't stop. Sometimes I ask myself the same type of serious questions, but now, with you here listening, I have to think more carefully and not try to fake an answer."

"In that case, what do we call our human herd?"

"Uh, society?"

"Yes, society – all people in general – as well as smaller groups we associate with more frequently. You haven't answered the question yet. Do we need society?"

"Sometimes it makes rules we don't like, and sometimes we know that those are bad rules. Still, if we don't obey them, we could get in trouble. It puts people in a bind. Society isn't always right."

"Is that the only way you see it?" Buck pushed on.

"No, not really. I know that without an organized society we wouldn't have schools and hospitals. To have things like that, people have to know how to work together for the same purpose."

"What else bothers you about society?"

"Oh, mostly little things – like how some people think they have to follow the latest clothing fashions or all read the same books – dumb things like that."

"Is that what you really think?"

"I'm not sure. This is hard. I need more time to think it through better. You know, Dad, you're always surprising me. Today you sound just like a college professor."

"I had a professor once who used to ask me these same kinds of questions."

"What? I didn't know you went to college."

"I didn't graduate, but I did attend for a few years. Never mind that. Come on! We're almost to the spot where I caught the big muskie. I'll race you to the end of the point."

Within a few yards, the youth surged ahead, but then held back in order not to embarrass his father.

"Whew! I'm winded," Buck puffed. "This is the spot. I was standing right here when I set the hook, and we pulled the fish in on this side. I was lucky it had swallowed the bait so far it couldn't spit it out."

Jimmy stared out across the water, trying to imagine his father as a child. He looked down at the shoreline. "Look here, Dad. Somebody had a fire, and look at all of the fish scales and bones. They still catch fish here. Uncle Bert said he was going to take me fishing tomorrow. Maybe I can talk him into trying our luck here."

"I imagine people were catching fish here thousands of years ago."

"Dad, did you ever find any old Indian things here along the lake shore – you know, like arrowheads?"

"Of course. The shoreline is a good place to look. I used to have a boxful of stuff, but it's all gone now."

"Gosh, that's too bad. I would like to have seen it. Maybe tomorrow I can come back and see what I can find."

"Sure. Just remember what your cousin Madge said about the girls around here snatching your pants off."

"Oh, she was just kidding. How long are we going to stay on the reservation?"

"We have to stay here until it's safe to return home, and I don't know when that might be. I keep watching what's going on in the newspapers. So far there hasn't been any mention of an organized search for us. The newspaper reported the burning as an accidental death. Are you anxious to leave here?"

"Not really. It's just that school has started, and everybody at Rock Mountain High must be wondering about me. If I go to school around here, somebody will want to see my old school records, and then the police might find us."

"If I were you, I wouldn't worry about missing school. You can always make it up. I managed to catch up without any trouble, and I missed a lot of school."

"I've been wondering about that. How did you do it?"

"Mrs. Pierce taught me to read better, and after that I read everything I could lay my hands on. The librarian knew me by sight and called me by my first name. She helped me find all kinds of interesting books. I lied about my age, and I enrolled in the tenth grade when I was with the Pierces. At first I had to fake it, but I paid careful attention in class. I got good grades."

On the way back to the car Jimmy continued to press his father about his early years, and somewhat reluctantly the man continued.

"You know, Jim, I try my best to be completely honest with you but, still, some things are embarrassing and maybe I should skip over certain spots."

"A promise is a promise, Pop. I'm not a little kid anymore."

"You're right, but I don't want to be setting a bad example for you. You know – do as I say, not as I do."

"Let's make a deal. I won't keep secrets if you don't."

"Fair enough. Where was I?"

"The Pierce's daughter was going to show you some fun new games."

"Oh, oh! That's what I thought you wanted. Oh, well, I might as well tell you. Have you ever been laid, Jim?"

"Laid? What's that?"

"Have you ever slept with a girl?"

"Oh, that kind of laid. I – uh – guess not."

"Why do you hesitate, Jim? Remember, no secrets."

"Uh, well, it's just that Mom used to do things to Phil and me. Things she shouldn't have done."

"I thought as much. Don't worry about it. It has to happen sometime. When it happens doesn't make too much difference, and, maybe who it happens with the first time doesn't matter either. Most young guys think of virginity as a burden – like a pimple on the end of their nose. They want to get rid of it any way they can."

"You said it happened to you when you were pretty young."

"It was the second night I stayed with the Pierces. The parents had some kind of a religious crusade to go to that night. Prudy and I were supposed to go, but I had a cold and she pretended to be sick to her stomach so we were home alone."

"And you got laid, but how did you know what to do?"

"I didn't know. In fact, I was so naïve that I hadn't even started playing with myself yet – you know, the way boys do."

"So what happened?"

"We each went to bed in our own rooms, but pretty soon she came into my room with a panful of fudge and sat down next to me. I had never tasted fudge before and thought it was really terrific. Afterwards she said she was lonesome and wanted to sleep with me. She knew exactly what to do, and I was too dumb to know what was happening. I thought it was great, and after that we did it whenever we had a chance."

"What was she like?"

"She was quite pretty but not too bright. She was kind of on the hefty side. Compared to her, I was a shrimp."

"Weren't you afraid to get her pregnant?"

"Not a bit. I didn't know anything about that."

"You didn't know where babies came from?"

"No. I was completely unknowledgeable about sex."

"So she tricked you into doing it."

"Well, let's just say I was willing to be seduced. I didn't stay dumb forever. After a while I knew the score. I also found out that her mother had had her fitted with a diaphragm because she knew her daughter was no angel. They kept this secret from the preacher. He would have thrown both of them out of the house."

"Did her parents ever find out about the two of you?"

"Several years later but, by then, I had already started college. Mr. Pierce not only threw me out, he wanted to have me arrested. There was nothing he could do because we were both adults, and Prudy wasn't about to press charges."

"Before that, what happened? You said the family travelled around a lot."

"That's right. The Reverend didn't have a specific church, but he was an ordained minister of some kind. He would send out a lot of letters to churches all over, telling about himself and what he called, 'The Singing Gospel'."

"Is that how you learned to sing and play the guitar?"

"That's right. Mr. Pierce bought me a second-hand guitar at a pawn shop and taught me how to play gospel songs. I went with them all the way to Texas."

"How did you travel? Did he have a car?"

"He did have a car, but when we were on tour we used an old converted school bus that we could eat and sleep in."

"Is that when you learned how to snitch gas?"

"I'm sorry to say so but, yes, he showed me how. It soon became my responsibility to keep the fuel tank filled. Every time we stopped some place, I got out the hose and gas can."

"Didn't you ever get caught?"

"No, but I got chased a couple of times and even had to abandon a full can of gas. Mr. Pierce kept an extra one for emergencies."

"If he was a preacher, how did he justify stealing gas?"

"He didn't use the word 'stealing'. He called it 'requisitioning for the Lord'.

"Is that how he made a living, travelling around and preaching?"

"Sure. Whenever he preached at a church, we would all sing and play gospel songs. Then there would be a collection. If no churches in a town wanted us, he would talk to a farmer outside of town, and we would put up a big tent. That's what he liked best because then he could do some faith healing by laying on of his hands. Once in West Virginia he even handled rattlesnakes."

"I suppose you learned a lot from him."

"Yes, I did. After I dropped out of college, I picked up with a girl, and we went around preaching and singing on our own. We were doing pretty well, but she left me for another guy in Missouri. After a while, I didn't like myself or what I was doing, but I wanted to help people who were down and out. The depression was still on when I hit Malone, and I started a church there."

"How well did it go?"

"Not very well. I hardly made expenses. I operated it like a mission and, at first, the other congregations welcomed me and made donations to my cause. Later some people dropped out of their church and joined mine. From then on I was blacklisted, but there were still individual volunteers who donated food and helped serve meals. We had some cots in back for people to sleep. I thought I was helping people and maybe I was at first. I could feel myself changing, though. I was being changed more by my parishioners than I was changing them. I was drinking so much I knew that in a few years I'd be looking for handouts myself."

"Is that where you met Mom?"

"Yes, that was after I started the church. I swear to you, Jim, I didn't know she was married at first. I met her in a bar. She was very pretty and seemed lonesome. I know I was lonesome and needed someone to love."

Both man and boy were becoming uncomfortable with these personal revelations. Still, the man wanted desperately to redeem himself in the eyes of his son and held nothing back. The youth was having mixed emotions. Somewhere in the back of his mind, he was still blaming Buck for his mother's problems and was trying to punish him. On the other hand, he realized that his father had struggled through tough times and wasn't completely responsible for the way his life had turned out.

An uncharacteristic burst of anger clouded Jimmy's thinking, and he lashed out, "Well, I know one thing for sure, Mr. Buck LeTarte. I'm never going to make babies and abandon them – no matter what!"

Immediately, he wished he had not spoken those harsh words, and he bit his lips so he would say no more. He expected his father to be angered by his remarks, but the man didn't respond for several moments.

"Jim, do you hate me because I'm an Indian or because your mother and I cheated on David?"

"Buck, I don't hate you! It hurts me when you say that. At first, I thought that I was supposed to hate you. What else could I think? If you were me, what would you think? I was afraid of you and even more afraid of what was happening to my whole life."

"I'm sorry I hurt you. It's all right for you to be disappointed in me, Jim. I deserve your criticism. I accept it. I don't deny that what I did was wrong. A man – a real man – is responsible for what he does and should never hurt another person. On the other hand, this is not a perfect world filled with perfect people. I do know that some good things happen by chance. Take you, for instance."

The youth lowered his eyes and stared at his knees. "I'm sorry, Dad. I didn't mean to say that to hurt you. It just blasted out of me."

"It's best to let it out, Jim. I don't pretend to be a saint. I've made plenty of mistakes, and I'll probably make more. I'm convinced, though, that it is possible to turn a mistake around so that good comes out of it. There is no doubt in my mind that you and me being together is good for both of us, no matter how you came to be. I suppose there was a time way back then when you were no more to me than a few moments of pleasure. Whoever said that the Lord works in mysterious ways didn't know how right he was."

"I apologize, Dad. I wasn't thinking straight."

"You don't have to apologize, Jim. I'm the one who should apologize to you. Since I've grown to know you as a young man, I've received a tremendous amount of enjoyment every day just watching you grow up. I pray that some day you will really accept me as your father. I didn't know what I was missing, and I owe David a tremendous debt for the fine way he raised you. If Lil had told me sooner that you were my son, I would have found a way to watch you grow up from a distance without interfering with your life because I know that I wouldn't have been as good a father as David."

Buck took a deep breath and continued walking silently toward the car. Jimmy glanced over and noticed the tears glistening on the man's cheeks. The youth asked no more explicit questions, nor did the man offer more explanations to justify his past behavior.

Chapter 28

Buck led the way back to the car, and Jimmy followed at a distance of some yards. Neither spoke nor made any attempt to acknowledge the other's existence. Buck drove, his eyes seemingly glued to the pavement. Both he and his son, however, would each furtively stretch his eyes toward the face of the other person and stare briefly at him while trying to read his mind, and, at the same time, trying to erase from that mind all things he may have said or done that had clouded the relationship.

Each knew he had caused the other one distress, and he needed relief from the feeling of guilt that it engendered. Saying, 'I'm sorry' was not enough. Retribution would require time and patience as well as trust and introspection. The father-and-son friendship had grown remarkably fast due to a period of unusual stress and mutual need. Ironically, in a calm and settled environment, the unresolved issues re-emerged.

Jimmy's mind raced as he renewed his memory of his short relationship with his father. Faintly, at first, he recalled having first seen the man while he was preaching in the mission church in Malone when his mother had taken him and his brother there with her. Jimmy was quite young then, only seven or eight. He did not see Buck again until the evening of David's funeral. That memory flashed like a movie scene to the time he and Phil had seen Buck lying naked in bed atop his mother. He shuddered upon recalling how enraged Phil was as he pummeled this stranger who had moved into his dead father's bed. He could see and almost smell the blood on Phil's face from the blow his mother had delivered with a lamp. Bit by bit Jimmy remembered each encounter up to this moment. Now he talked silently to himself, trying to comprehend the implications of all that had happened.

He has tried hard to be good to me, thought Jimmy. He has been fair and understanding. He tried to help Mom. What more does he have to do to prove himself to me? How could I have said what I did to him? How could I have been so ungrateful? Without him, I wouldn't even have been born, but, still, he is one of those who was cheating on David. God, how I wish my dad were still alive! I miss him so much, and I miss Phil. Right now, my life is tied up with Buck LeTarte whether I like it or not – but I do like it – only I don't know how to say it to him, and I don't know how to explain it to David. I try to talk to David at night just before I fall asleep. I can't just forget the man who raised me, and I can't forget my brother. What if Buck decides he's got better things to do and doesn't want to bother with a mouthy kid like me? What if he kicks me out? What if he moves away for good? I won't have anybody. I don't want him to leave.

The intensity of the man's introspection equaled or exceeded that of the youth. My own kid saved my life, he thought. He dragged me out of the river – and what's even more important, out of the gutter. Without him I have no self-respect – no reason to live. Without him I'm nothing but a bum. If I lose him, I lose everything. He used to chatter all the time when we were together. Now, he won't even talk to me. God! How I need a drink!

As Buck drove the Lincoln-Ford, he steadied the steering wheel with the fingers of his immobilized left hand while he steered with his unencumbered right arm. He knew the plaster would have to stay on his broken arm a while longer until it was healed more completely. He had wanted to allow his son to drive them to the site of his grandmother's house that day but had not because of the possibility of an accident that might lead to an embarrassing investigation.

He allowed the car to coast to a stop in front of Bert's house. Neither driver nor passenger exited the vehicle immediately but instead, they sat motionless with their eyes boring into the windshield. Each wanted to speak, but the words for reconciliation eluded them.

Each ached for the other one to break the deadlock. Finally, their eyes met in a prolonged gaze that feebly managed to say a few hopeful words for them.

Jimmy swallowed nervously, coughed, and went into the barn to play with the puppies. Cora met Buck at the door and asked him how their day went.

"Mixed," said Buck.

"Mixed? What does that mean? Did the car break down?"

"The car is fine. Jim did a good job on it."

"What is it, then? Did you have an argument?"

"No, not an argument really – just some words. He doesn't accept me as his father."

"That will take time, Buck. He's still grieving for his other father."

"I'm afraid, Cora. I'm afraid I'll lose him, and I'm afraid of what will happen to me after that."

"It will work out, Buck. I know it will. He loves you. I can tell."

"I hope you're right. Lord! I hope you're right!"

"Of course I am, after Bert comes home, we'll all have supper and a birthday party for Jimmy. Wait until you see the cake I baked!"

"He wanted to apply for his driving license on his birthday. Now he can't because of me and the mess I got us into. I didn't even think to buy him a present. What kind of a father am I?"

"You've never had any practice being a parent. Besides, kids don't measure their parents by the number of presents they get. Just be his friend, and be there when he needs you. I wish I could have given Bert a son. He wanted one so much. He was a good father to our girls, though."

During the meal Buck and Jimmy each tried to put on a pretense of happiness, but it was clear to Cora and Bert that the former sense of camaraderie between their two guests was strained. Bert felt worried. He knew his cousin well enough to see signs of an impending explosion. The man was emotionally stretched and, without support, he would be too weak to resist returning to the bottle.

At the end of the main course Cora uncovered the birthday cake which she had hidden under a cardboard box on a shelf. She carried it triumphantly to the table and placed it in the middle for all to admire.

"I'm sorry, Jimmy," she said, "but I could only find seven candles. I'll bet you're good at math, though, so let this bigger one stand for ten, and the others are ones."

"I like that idea, Aunt Cora, and the cake is beautiful! Thank you."

She motioned to Buck, and he rose to get the ice cream maker from the shed where he had helped make the dessert.

"Ta dah!" he exclaimed while presenting the metal cylinder containing the frozen treat. "I get to lick the paddle."

Jimmy beamed. Buck was acting just like David used to. His mother had seldom remembered the children's birthdays nor made preparations for them. David, however, always did. Jimmy tried to catch Buck's eye and somehow indicate his thanks, but the opportunity did not present itself.

Bert started singing the birthday song and the others joined in. When they finished, Buck began slowly singing 'For He's a Jolly Good Fellow' while the others mouthed the words. Cora handed the youth a knife and instructed him to cut four slices with a double one for himself.

Bert observed his cousin as he massaged his temples with his fingertips, first the right side, then the left.

"I'll help you with the dishes, Aunt Cora," said the youth.

"Not now you won't, because I'm going to stack then on the counter until we return from the movies."

"Where do you want to go this time?" asked Bert.

"I checked in the newspaper this afternoon. We've got three choices. There's a good one in Cornwall called 'The Treasure of Sierra Madre'. In Malone there's one with Ronald Colman called 'A Double Life'."

"How about in Massena?" asked Bert.

"Well, that's an older one. It's 'The Lost weekend'. We saw it already."

"Yeah, me too," said Buck. "The fact is I could have acted the part better than Ray Millard. After all, I've had more practice with the subject matter. You three go ahead. I think I'll stay here and listen to the radio or read a book."

"It's your birthday, Jimmy," Cora said, "so you get to choose."

"Okay. I've never been to Cornwall before. How do we get there, Uncle Bert?"

"We take the Cornwall Bridge. Cornwall's right on the other side of the Saint Lawrence. Will the old Zeph take us that far?"

"It will, if we all cross our fingers," Jimmy said, smiling.

Jimmy looked at his father. "I wish you would come, Dad."

"Thanks, son, but I've got a bad headache. Go and have a good time."

Bert felt torn. He wanted to stay with Buck, afraid to leave him alone when he was showing signs of his problem. Yet, it was the boy's birthday, and going to the movies was one of the few things his wife asked of him.

Buck watched through the window as the automobile his son had repaired headed out toward the highway. Bert was driving while Cora and Jimmy sat next to him, all of them snugly compressed in the front seat. He placed the palm of his free hand against his temples again, one at a time, and pressed hard. His face wrinkled in a grimace while his eyes closed tightly. Then he massaged his temples with his fingertips in hopes of exorcising the devils that tormented him.

In the past, headaches often preceded the man's drinking binges, and, once again, he needed relief. He knew that Bert never kept liquor in the house so he ransacked the cupboards until he found a bottle of Cora's aspirin. He pumped himself a glassful of water and swallowed six of the white tablets. Cora had not had time to put away her cooking ingredients, and Buck's eyes focused on the bottle of vanilla extract. He twisted open the metal cap and smelled the liquid. His head pounded violently and his hands shook as he sucked the bottle dry and searched the shelves for any other substance that might contain alcohol. He belched after consuming the lemon extract. He searched for some cough syrup with codeine, but there was none anywhere in the house.

He walked into the living room and turned on the radio. The exaggerated and prolonged sound of a crash came from the speaker. "T'aint funny, McGee," said Molly.

Buck flicked off the radio and took a flashlight to check on the puppies. When he entered the barn he noticed the bitch wag her tail. He squatted low and petted her head. The pups were entwined with one another sleeping. He swept the beam of flashlight toward Phil's Pontiac. His head pounded.

Out on the highway Buck checked the gas gauge as he headed for Massena. He planned to have just a few belts to chase away his headache and be home long before the others.

After the three moviegoers returned home, Jimmy ran to the barn to visit the puppies. He noticed the barn door ajar and stared open-mouthed at the spot where the Pontiac had sat. A sense of dread invaded the boy's thoughts. He feared that Buck had gone for good, and that it was his fault. Tears forming in his eyes, he petted the mother dog and picked up the puppy he had selected as his own. He brought the puppy to its mother and walked slowly into the house.

"Buck is gone," he said and rushed into his bedroom.

Bert took a deep breath and exhaled. "I could see it coming. I should have stayed here with him."

"Where do you think he went?" asked Cora.

"To the nearest bar where he won't be recognized. Once he starts drinking, he doesn't know when to stop."

"They're not supposed to sell to Indians around here. Where do you think he went?"

"I don't think he'd go toward Malone. He probably went in the other direction."

"Go look for him. Please, Bert, do it for Jimmy. Buck might get in an accident or something."

"Okay. Make me a cup of strong coffee. This may take a while. I'll go talk to the boy."

Bert tapped gently on the youth's door. "Are you awake, Jim? Can I come in?"

"It's your house, isn't it? I can't stop you."

Bert ignored the taunt and eased open the door. He noticed the youth stretched out on top of the covers face down and fully dressed. He could tell the lad had been crying.

"Jim, I'm going to look for your father. Everything will be all right. Don't worry."

"No, it won't! He's gone. He'll never come back, and it's all my fault. I drove him away."

"I don't agree with you, son. Above all, don't blame yourself. Getting along with other people and understanding them is the hardest thing you'll ever run up against in your whole life. You know that your father is not a bad person, don't you?"

"I don't know what to think anymore."

"Sometimes I don't either. I do know that people need one another, and that sometimes, in spite of that, they do things that make everybody sad. We have to do the best we can."

Bert held out one of his hands and patted the boy's back.

"Thanks, Uncle Bert. If you do find him, tell him..."

"Tell him what?"

"Tell him... Tell him I love him."

"Why don't you come with me? Then you can tell him yourself. It will mean more."

"You're right, Uncle Bert. Yes, I'd like to come."

"Good! Now hop out of that sack and slug some coffee with me. You and me are on a rescue mission, buddy."

Chapter 29

Upon first stepping out of the house with his uncle Bert, Jimmy was surprised at the brilliance of the stars. The moon had hidden itself hours earlier, but a lone planet continued its path along the heliacal arch, and the boy wondered if it might be Mars, the god of war. He shivered when a gust of wind flapped open the front of his light-weight jacket.

Bert started the engine of the Lincoln-Ford. In the glow of the instrument panel lights he could make out the glistening in Jimmy's eyes.

"We'll try Massena first, Jim. That okay with you?"

"Sure, Uncle Bert, and thanks."

"Don't worry, Jim, we'll find him. There are only so many places he could be."

"But suppose he crossed over and went into Canada. Then what?"

"There's nothing stopping us from going there, too. Besides, I've got friends across the border who will help."

From then on there was silence inside the vehicle except for the hum of the automobile engine. Bert turned on the heater, glanced once again at the boy, and drove steadily west.

When they saw lights indicating that they were approaching their destination, Jimmy broke the silence.

"How many bars are there in town?"

"Oh, I don't know, Jim. Not too many. They'll be easy to spot. Not much else is lit up this time of night. There's one right ahead. You see that pink neon sign on the left?"

"Yeah, I see it. It says R & J Taproom. There are a couple a cars parked in front. There's a...Stop! That's it. That's Phil's Pontiac parked right in the middle."

Bert eased his car to a halt. Neither he nor Jimmy had had time to look at the three cars parked across from the bar.

"Oh, my gosh, Uncle Bert! He didn't even change the old license plates. Those are so old it's pathetic. He's lucky the police haven't noticed them yet."

Bert pulled ahead, made a U-turn, and parked behind the Pontiac.

"Well, come on, Jimmy. Let's go face the music."

"No, Uncle Bert. I don't want to see him again this way. You go. I'll climb in the back seat and wait."

"Sorry, Jimmy, but there are some things in life that you can't hide from. And this is one of them."

Bert excited his vehicle and peered into the windows of the Pontiac to see if, perhaps, Buck might be passed out inside. As Jimmy was looking into the window from the other side, a sudden glare from the spotlight of a white Ford blinded him. This was followed by one short wail from the siren of the patrol car.

Jimmy and Bert froze as two New York State Troopers approached them, each brandishing a long flashlight.

Jimmy's heart thudded with fear. He longed to run but his feet were paralyzed.

"Stay there!" Bert whispered. "Don't move, Jimmy!"

The spotlight still shone on them when the troopers approached. It was nearly impossible for Jimmy to see what was going on because of the glare of lights. Suddenly he was surprised by Bert's calm manner.

"Good evening, officers. How can we help you?"

One state trooper stood a few feet from Bert and shone the flashlight directly into his eyes. The other crowded against Jimmy so closely that he was forced to step into the gutter and lean against Phil's car. Again he thought of running.

One officer flashed his light toward Bert's Lincoln-Ford and asked, "Is that your vehicle?"

When Bert nodded affirmatively, he demanded, "Let's see the registration."

While Bert was reaching for his wallet, Jimmy was expecting to be slammed against the car and frisked by the other officer. Instead, the man spoke almost gently.

"Is this your car, son?"

"Uh...no, it's my brother's. He's in the army."

Jimmy noticed the other trooper examining Bert's license and registration and, then, handing it back to him. He motioned to Bert to move over toward Jimmy.

"Let's all go inside. There's someone else in there I want to talk to."

Jimmy's mind was racing. He recalled the sudden flare of exploding gasoline and the sight of McGuire burning to death on the highway. Bert led the way into the tavern with Jimmy and the two state troopers following closely behind.

The inside of the room was gloomy and smoke-filled. A half dozen patrons lined the bar. Others sat on chairs around tables or in booths. Jimmy's nose flared from the unpleasant odor of stale beer and regurgitated stomach contents. Almost immediately he spotted his father sitting alone in a booth. He just sat there with a bottle of Coke in front of him.

At almost that instant Buck looked up and noticed the four who had just entered the room. He stood up, took a swig from the bottle of soft drink, laid it down on the table, and walked toward his son. He stretched out his right arm as though to shake hands. Jimmy rushed up and grasped his father in a big bear hug.

"I don't know what's going on here tonight," one of the troopers said, "but let's go talk in the patrol car."

Only then did Jimmy recognize the officer as the one he had spoken with at home when his mother was missing. Outside again, the officer pointed down the street.

"On second thought, it's crowded in the car. The lights are still on in a diner. Let's go have some coffee."

Inside the café the two state troopers smiled at the waitress and ordered coffee for everybody. Jimmy caught Bert's attention to try to ascertain what was happening. Bert simply shrugged his shoulders and raised his eyebrows to indicate a lack of knowledge. Even so, the boy began to relax.

"You are James Coulbron, aren't you?" Lieutenant Carruthers said.

"Yes, sir."

"I have some sad news for you, son. Your mother died in the hospital this morning, and I'm sure you will want to make arrangements. We were pretty certain you and your father were hiding out around here somewhere, but we didn't have any reason to look until today. We are going to need you to testify against some people next week so we would appreciate it if you would move back to your house at Echo Lake where you are closer to the court house."

Jimmy's mouth opened in surprise. "You mean we didn't have to run away?"

"Yes and no. We never had any specific charges against either one of you, but until our investigation in Dannemora was finished you were wise to disappear. I'm sorry about your mother."

"Thank you, sir."

Jimmy was seated in the booth between his father and his uncle. They each held his arm as he laid his head on the table top and slowly began sobbing.

Jimmy's mind seemed to keep generating loud buzzing noises in an attempt to obliterate all comprehension of what was transpiring. The officers continued to question Buck for several minutes and then departed. Only two thoughts registered in the boy's mind. His mother was dead, and his father was stone sober. At that moment the latter thought seemed more important.

"Come on. Let's go home and get some sleep," Bert said. "You fellows start off, and I'll follow."

Buck rose to leave, but Jimmy didn't budge. He hadn't heard over the roaring in his ears. Bert shook the lad's shoulder to release him from his shocked state. Jimmy looked alternately from Bert to Buck.

"Uh, well, guys, maybe we oughta go home now, huh?"

Chapter 30

A golden slit of sunlight pierced a gap in the curtains of the bedroom where Jimmy lay sleeping. The boy's uncle Bert and his father were seated at the table eating breakfast while his Aunt Cora was preparing a food basket for her guests' return trip to Echo Lake. The ray of light was only able to find Jimmy's left eye, the other being sheltered by a fold of the blanket. The lid of his eye began to flicker and consciousness fought against dream for mastery of the youth. Abruptly, he sat upright, not immediately recognizing his surroundings, then scolded himself mentally for having slept late on a day which he knew would demand much from him.

Cora watched from the corner of her eyes as Jimmy entered the room still buckling his belt. His hair was flattened down and moist on one side from having been compressed during sleep. He tip-toed up to the men, approaching them from the rear, then silently touched each of them on the shoulder as a friendly greeting. He smiled at his aunt before stepping outside. Moments later he returned and pumped water which he rubbed vigorously into his hair.

"Aunt Cora," he said, "One thing's for sure. You're pretty enough to be in the movies."

"I'll agree to that," Bert said. "My honeybunch should be dressed in pearls and mink."

"No, thank you. That's not for me. Here, Jimmy, take this plate of pancakes to the table, and help yourself to the maple syrup."

"Thanks, Aunt Cora. Buck – uh, Dad, how long do you think the, uh, business in Ogdensburg will take? I mean Mom and all."

"That's hard to say, Jim. I think we may get home pretty late, maybe after dark. How about if we find a phone and you call Perchy and

Yvette and tell them we're coming…maybe you should tell your aunt Sharon, too. She's pretty worried."

"Good idea. Um, uh, Dad? Mom should be buried next to David, shouldn't she?"

"Whatever you want, son. You're in charge."

As he ate breakfast, Jimmy's mind raced ahead, envisioning his mother's funeral, his return to school in Rock Mountain, and his future life with Buck at Echo Lake. His thoughts were interrupted by his Uncle Bert.

"Well, Jimmy, your pup should be ready to leave its mother in about a month. Are you coming back to get it then?"

"Yes sir, Uncle Bert. Remember it's the one with one brown ear and one white one."

"And bring your twenty-two along. It'll be a good time for us to hunt some rabbits and partridge."

"Oh, yeah, for sure."

Bert winked at the boy. "And just maybe we'll run across something a little bigger to shoot."

After eating breakfast, Jimmy excused himself to tend to the dogs and to hug the puppy that would soon be his own. He replaced the license plates on Phil's Pontiac while his father gathered up their belongings. Moments later he noticed Cora carrying a picnic basket and placing it inside. Then she hugged him and placed a roll of dollar bills in his pants pocket.

A tear rolled down each cheek as she whispered, "Here, take this, Jimmy. You're going to need it. I wish it was more. And you make sure to come visit us as often as you can."

He returned the hug with genuine affection and shook hands with Bert, then climbed into the passenger's seat of the Pontiac. As soon as Buck sat behind the wheel, he winked at his son and asked, "Friends?"

"Yes, Dad, we're friends."

In Malone they stopped to pick up Sharon at her house. Upon seeing the youth she clasped his shoulders and clung to him.

"Oh, Jimmy, I'm so sorry for you. And where have you been? I was scared to death when I saw your picture in the newspaper and read the story. When you didn't answer the phone, I drove to your house and saw Mr. LeTarte's wrecked car. I was worried sick."

"I'm sorry I worried you, Aunt Sharon, but there was nothing I could do. I'll tell you all about it later. It's a real long story."

Together they started driving to the hospital. She and Jimmy shared the back seat while Buck drove. His aunt held his hands as a gesture of sympathy.

"I was with your mother when she died, Jimmy. It was painless. The doctor said it was a massive stroke."

"I don't understand why I had to lose both of them. They were too young to die."

"Those things just happen sometimes. Maybe it was God's will."

Jimmy heard her but didn't respond. He was unable to accept that as a valid explanation. He felt that there had to be more to life than to live or die at the whim of an unpredictable Creator. He felt that life should make more sense.

Sharon knew that her sister's body would still be in storage in the hospital morgue and wished to spare the boy the anguish of seeing his mother's dead body before it had been prepared for burial.

"Jimmy, I've been thinking things over, and maybe it would be best if you wait to see your mother until after she is at the funeral parlor."

"Won't they let me see her now?"

"They will if you insist, but why don't we go to the funeral home now and make arrangements? I have one of her pretty dresses that she left in my house. She can be buried in that if it is all right with you."

"Well, uh, yeah, I guess that would be the best way. When will they pick her up?"

"They will be at the hospital an hour after we talk to them, and you can see her tomorrow afternoon."

"Should we have the wake in our house like we did for David?"

"You can, but I would recommend that you use the chapel at the funeral home. Many people are doing it that way now. They will explain everything to you there, and I'll be available to help."

The arrangements were concluded quickly, Jimmy having selected a handsome mahogany casket identical to David's. United as father and son, Buck and Jimmy headed for home.

On the way they stopped at Rock Mountain so Jimmy could explain to the grave digger, Perchy Garew, where he wanted to have his mother buried.

"I sink I can do it ze way you want, Jimmee, but first you talk to Fazer Orgebin because he must approve everyt'ing I do."

"Okay, Mr. Garew. Where can I find the priest?"

"You should find him in ze oblate now, in 'is 'ouse."

Jimmy thanked the old French-Canadian and sprinted up to the priest's house while Buck remained in the car. He was perspiring freely as he approached the front door. He noted that the main door was open and that the screen door was crawling with fat, pesky flies. He was raising his hand to press the doorbell when he saw Father Orgebin standing only a few feet inside the vestibule. Seeing the priest through the screen reminded the youth of the first time he saw him in the confessional. This time, however, the man's head was raised high as he drained the last drops from a whiskey glass.

The boy tried to stifle a nervous cough, but Father Orgebin turned and saw him. Quickly the priest hid the glass behind him and said smoothly, "Come in, my son."

Ten minutes later Jimmy rejoined Buck after first slamming the car door and muttering to himself.

"What's the matter, Jim? What's wrong?"

"Oh, it's that stupid priest. He says he won't hold a funeral service for my mother because she had lost her faith. Not only that, he won't let her be buried next to David because that's on consecrated ground, and it's reserved for good Catholics. It sounds spiteful to me. It doesn't make any sense at all. Mom wasn't responsible for some of the things she did. He said she has to be buried somewhere else."

"Don't worry, Jim. We'll work something out. She doesn't have to be buried there. How would you like to have her buried in Malone where her sister Sharon lives? The minister who took over my church will be happy to conduct the services right at the funeral chapel there."

"Dad..."

"Yes, son."

"I'm glad you're helping me with this."

Part Two

Chapter 31

A few weeks had passed since Lillian's funeral, and Buck and Jimmy fell into their routine of cooking, cleaning, and doing farm chores. Although the boy completed his chores without complaint, Buck could tell that Jimmy was having a hard time adjusting after his mother's death, and thought, perhaps, that the promised puppy might be able to help him.

Right after Jimmy finished his chores the next day, Buck said, "Say, Jim, I think that puppy at Uncle Bert's is probably old enough to leave his mother. How about you and I make a trip to the rez and pick him up?"

"Oh, Dad, that would be great! Can we go today?"

"That's what I was thinking. Are you sure you know which puppy is yours?"

"Sure do. He was the first one born, and had very distinctive markings. C'mon, Dad, let's get going!"

The trip to the rez was filled with chatter, and Buck was glad to see his son had something to look forward to again. As soon as they arrived at Bert's, Jimmy dashed away to find his puppy, and came back shortly with the squirming pup. "Look, Dad, look how much he's grown already! Isn't he great?"

Aunt Cora made lunch for them, then packed some snacks and supplies for the dog. It was almost time to leave, but Jimmy had mixed feelings about leaving his Aunt Cora and Uncle Bert. Although he was eager to return to the farm with his pup and to join in school activities again, he had really enjoyed living on the reservation and being treated like a man. Finally, it was time to go. Jimmy gave Uncle Bert a firm handshake and promised once again to return for fall hunting. Cora's eyes were moist with tears, and she hugged the boy. She whispered in his ear, "Stay good, Jimmy. We love you."

"You drive," Buck said, "It's your car."

The Pontiac started to purr immediately, and everyone waved. The return journey was underway. They drove silently except for nervous coughs. After a time Buck began to hum a melody and then to sing. Smiling, Jimmy joined in the song, an old gospel tune they had practiced many times. As they approached Malone, Buck asked, "Jim, do you want to stop by and visit Lillian's grave?"

"Yes, I'd like that. Thanks, Dad, this is a very sad time for me."

At the gravesite the first thing they noticed was that Sharon had had a small stone installed. A bouquet of plastic flowers sat in a vase next to the stone.

"When we come by again, I'll plant a real flowering plant for her." Buck wrapped his arm around Jimmy's shoulder and said, "I loved her, too."

Later passing the Rock Mountain School Jimmy slowed, then stopped. He gazed at the windows. They seemed spectral. A shiver ran through Jimmy's body. Although it was a school day, no students could be seen. He recognized several of the teachers' automobiles.

Arriving at the farm, Jimmy and Buck noticed Perchy Garew about to climb into his pick-up. They both saw Buck's Cadillac parked in the driveway. It looked immaculate, repaired and polished. Perchy got out to greet them.

"You been gone long time, eh? The animals, them, they all fed and okay. I go now to do ze chores for Cherie."

"Cherie, who's Cherie?" asked Jimmy.

"Oh, dat just de fun name I give Miz Papineau. I live dere now wit 'er. I was lonesome, me. Now, I feel good."

Inside the house they enjoyed the picnic lunch Cora had provided. Then Jimmy went down to the barn, not so much as to check but rather to say 'hello' to the animals. When he had greeted them all and left the barn, he could hear Buck tuning his guitar.

Rather than go into the house, however, Jimmy decided this would be a good time to go fishing, even though August was a lousy time to dig fishworms. The soil was too warm and dry. All of the big night-crawlers seemed to be evading Jimmy as he tried the usual places. In May and June he could usually find enough for a few hours of fishing simply by turning over flat rocks in the pasture or by spading inside the chicken yard. He noticed dampness next to the ditch that drained the cesspool. The odor wasn't pleasant but the enriched earth relented and yielded a bumper crop of fat, healthy-looking fish bait. Within a few minutes the boy had filled nearly half of his coffee can.

Inside the house Buck was picking his guitar while singing 'Jerusalem'. It comforted him to sing the old songs and kept his mind off other things. Jimmy admired the man's mature voice and his wide range of tones from tenor to bass. Jimmy's singing, in comparison, was that of a young untrained tenor only recently released from the threat of adolescent voice breaking. His voice was clear, though, and had a charming bell-like appeal. Buck had been teaching him to play melody on the guitar and to harmonize with him while singing. This had helped bring the two of them closer.

When Jimmy returned to the house with the can of worms, he interrupted Buck's playing. "You wanna go fishing?" asked the boy.

"I haven't gone fishing in thirty years. I used to get some nice pike in the Saint Lawrence when I was a kid."

"Well, we don't have any pike or muskies in this lake, but I can try to get some brook trout out of Owl Pond. Phil and I used to fish there."

"Is this a good time to fish trout, Jim?"

"Not really. It gets better in a few weeks as the weather cools off, but then pretty soon the season closes."

"Tell you what. I'll come by and watch, but you have to do the catching. How do we get there?"

"There's two ways. We can follow Big Bay Brook up or we can walk along the D and H tracks until we see the pond."

"You decide. Let's eat first, though."

"I was thinking we could bring some sandwiches instead. That way we'd get there sooner."

It had been overcast all day and, now, as they parked the car next to the railroad tracks, a fine mist began to fall. The tracks approached the pond close to the inlet forcing them to skirt the long edge of the pond to reach the beaver dam where Jimmy wanted to fish. "This is the deepest spot in the whole pond," said the boy. "We almost got our limit here last time."

The animal-made dam was the largest either of them had ever seen. Old maps showed that it had existed for over a hundred years. The beavers could not have chosen a better location. A broad, flat plain extended some distance toward the west, disappearing into a tangle of black spruce and tamarack. This was bordered left and right by scraggly willows first and then maturing aspen. There was no shortage of food supply for the flat-tailed rodents. Their lodge rose out of the water twenty feet in front of Jimmy and Buck. Freshly chewed aspen sticks decorated the top of the lodge while others floated on the still water.

Water did not overflow the top of the dam, rather it oozed and seeped through chinks in the mud and vegetation the beavers had plastered against sticks and logs. The fishermen could have walked on top of the dam, but that was precarious. Instead, they hopped across small boulders that interrupted the brook as it gurgled at the base of the dam.

"Are there any trout in the stream here?" asked the man.

"No, Buck. The water's too warm for the first quarter of a mile or so. Then, too, there might not be enough oxygen. I'm not sure why. Anyhow, once you get past the falls, there's lots of them, but they're kinda small."

The boy led the way to the side of a low hill where he could cast over the dam. He was disappointed not to see any trout rising on the surface. "Maybe they're hiding from the rain," he chuckled.

Jimmy hadn't bothered to carry much fishing equipment, simply a container of hooks and a hank of fish line. At the shore's edge he selected an alder stick, three-quarters of an inch thick at the base, and cut it off with his jack knife. He sliced off the branches and tested to see if the pole was supple but still strong enough to land a fish. He attached the line half way down the pole first, and wrapped it along in a spiraling fashion all the way to the tip where he tied it again. He measured this line so that it was twice the length of the pole and then attached a snelled trout hook. Buck smiled to himself as he watched, recalling that he had done it the same way as a boy.

The young fisherman skewered a purple and pink nightcrawler onto the hook and stretched his line straight up the bank. Then, using the pole, he heaved it out and it plunked on the surface, forming concentric circles which rippled their way toward shore. He waited impatiently, but there was no interest shown by hungry trout.

For more than an hour the boy cast and recast his line, frequently refreshing his bait. Meanwhile, an early darkness began to settle upon them as the light rain continued. Suddenly, the boy's line tightened and seemed to head straight toward the beaver lodge. "Holy smokes!" he shouted. "I think I've snagged a beaver."

"You catch it and I'll cook it," kidded Buck.

"No, it's a fish all right, and it's big, but it doesn't fight like a trout."

"Maybe it's a sucker."

"Here it comes. Hey, it's a bullhead, and look at the size of it. Must be over two pounds!"

"Did you ever catch any bullhead here before, Jim?"

"No, but, then, this is the first time I've fished here in the dark."

"Well, now, as long as they're biting, I'm going to fish too. You have any more line?"

"Sure, Dad, and lots of hooks, too. Oh, boy! This is fun. Take whatever you need."

The fishing got faster now, and both were hauling the whiskered pouts onto the bank. "Youch!" called out the man. "That son-of-a-gun stabbed me!"

"Yeah, that's happened to me lots of times. It takes about a week to heal. Here, Dad, I'll show you which fins to watch out for. You see these two next to his whiskers and this one on top? They're the only ones with spines. Hold 'em like this."

"I wish you had told me that before I almost got stabbed to death."

"Hey, I thought you knew. You're supposed to be the Indian around here." They laughed, enjoying the camaraderie.

By then, it was nearly pitch black. "We ought to build a fire, Jim, I can't see a darn thing, and it's cooling off."

"You're right. Let's just leave our lines out and build it together. Here's some birch bark, and there'll be dry stuff underneath that balsam."

"You're a better Indian than I'll ever be, Jim."

They sat now, father and son, with their backs close to the fire, enjoying in silence, neither wanting to break the spell.

Finally, Jimmy admitted, "They've quit biting. I suppose we have to go."

"Yes, and we're going to have one hell of a time trying to find our way to the railroad track."

"We could wade the brook all the way back to the lake, but then we'd still be more than a mile from your car."

"I've got a better idea. We've got a good fire. Let's build some kind of a shelter under that old spruce and spend the night."

"Hey, great! And we can fish in the morning."

Jimmy's acceptance of his biological father had not come quickly. It grew bit by bit out of a mutual need. A routine had developed in which the boy took care of the outside chores while the man cooked meals and cleaned. Once a week Buck attended AA meetings, often speaking to others about his past and his hopes for the future. Jimmy was getting geared up for his junior year at Rock Mountain High School, and was worried because few of his clothes fit him any longer.

Chapter 32

Jimmy was in the woodshop attached to the garage when Buck entered. "What are you doing there, young buddy?"

"It's a maple cross, Buck. David always liked maple trees. He'd say, 'This is the best kind of tree there is. They give us food, they give us firewood, they make homes for birds and animals, and they live a long time. You can't beat that.' In order to tease him, Phil or I would remind him that oak trees produced edible nuts, made excellent lumber, and lived even longer than maples, but he would always stick up for maples. Of course, the only oaks anywhere nearby were a half dozen that my Great-uncle Frank planted from acorns during World War One.

"The cross is for David's grave, isn't it, Jim?"

"Yeah, it's only temporary, though. Phil and I are going to have a stone engraved as soon as we can save enough money."

"Didn't David have any insurance?"

"Not much. Barely enough for the funeral. I asked the undertaker where we could buy monuments around here. He gave me a couple of addresses, and I've been calling around. One guy said we wouldn't have to pay for it all at once. We could make payments every month instead, but right now, we can't even afford that."

Buck thought that, despite the precarious state of his bank account, he could offer to pay for a monument. Still, he realized that this was something very sacred that the boys needed to do on their own so he did not interfere with their plans.

"I wasn't at the funeral," said Buck. "Is David buried in Rock Mountain?"

"Yes, his father enlarged the family plot there. It's supposed to be near the grave of his great-grandfather, Guillaume, but that grave for him and his wife only had a wooden marker and they rotted away. So, now, nobody knows exactly where they are. I suppose that someday a grave digger will rise up out of the pit he's digging with two skulls and say, 'Well, looky here, what a nice looking couple.' Then Guillaume will rattle his bones and say, 'Hey, sonny, don't get smart with me. I'm the one who made your grandmother's first pair of shoes exactly a hundred years ago today.'"

Then the boy smiled sheepishly and added, "I don't want David's grave to just disappear like that."

As he sanded on the wood, Jimmy announced, "I'm going to make the cross round so it resembles a tree more. Then I'm going to varnish it and carve his name. It should last a couple of years, don't you think?"

"I'm sure it will, Jim." It was the man's turn to become misty eyed. "I've got to go practice. See you when you're finished."

Later, from the open window, the boy could hear him playing and singing, 'Amazing Grace'.

Although Buck didn't seem to push their music practice sessions, it seemed to Jimmy that they were becoming both more frequent and more serious. It did surprise him, though, when the man asked, "How would you like to take piano lessons after school starts?"

"I don't know. I never thought about it. A couple of girls in class last year and one of the boys were taking lessons in the afternoon class. It would be kinda hard, though, because I've got my chores to do then and also I 'd miss the school bus."

"Jim, if you're willing to give it a try, I can pull tits for you and shovel a little crap. Besides, by then you'll have your learner's permit and will be driving legally for a change. Your Pontiac still purring?"

"Pretty good. Actually, I'm not driving it much, but I do keep the battery charged up just in case."

What surprised the lad more, though, was Buck's announcement a week later. "Hold onto your privates, kid. We got our first gig on

Saturday. We're providing the entertainment for a Methodist fellowship group in Massena. It's only a free-will offering, but it's a start."

"Buck, I'm not ready for that. I'd pee my pants singing in front of a group of people."

"You won't have to do much singing or peeing. I'll take care of the songs, and you take care of your waterworks. You just come in on the choruses and echo me once in a while like you did last night when we were singing 'In the Sweet Bye and Bye'. It's like your first piece of tail. After the first time it's easy."

The boy gave a wry smile and said, "You certainly have a way with words, Buck. You better not say something like that during a performance in a church. They'd string you up."

It surprised Jimmy that as soon as they started playing, he found his worries were groundless. "Smile!" Buck had told him. "You smile constantly like a blooming idiot and I'll look sad and serious. That'll be part of the act."

Earlier, the boy had worried about what he would wear. Buck had told him to just wear his best clothes even if the pants were three inches too short. After all, the girls wouldn't be staring at his socks because they would be too interested in that bulge in his crotch. Buck's statements like that always caused Jimmy's face to redden. Then the man would laugh and punch the boy's arm gently, but Jimmy actually liked it and only pretended to complain.

At the church that night, Buck introduced them as a father and son duet trying to do God's work on Earth. The audience was a mixture of Sunday School teachers and students of all ages. Buck started out singing 'Just a Closer Walk with Thee' while Jimmy strummed the chords and tried to maintain his smile. Considering Buck's coarse remarks that the girls would be only interested in his crotch, he took comfort in knowing that his front was safely hidden by his guitar.

The boy knew that their routine was supposed to end with Buck's rendition of 'Amazing Grace', but after they finished that, the audience applauded thunderously and demanded an encore. Buck's ad-libbing and patter between acts had kept the audience's attention, but still they were not satisfied. Then Buck pointed at Jimmy and said, "And now what all of you wonderful young folks have been waiting for so patiently, here is the handsome and talented Jimmy LeTarte singing 'It Is No Secret'." The teenagers and preteens clapped very hard, and the shy lad was forced into his first solo.

As the refreshments were being served afterwards, the kids Jimmy's age crowded around him asking endless questions. He was inundated with offers to attend parties and requests for autographs. Others requested copies of his phonograph records of which there were none. Buck winked at him knowingly as he went over to talk to the minister.

The offering only produced nineteen dollars, barely enough to cover expenses, but Buck was satisfied, knowing that word of their performance would spread quickly and, also, the minister promised to give him recommendations.

Buck wanted the two of them to go on tour, covering a circuit surrounding the Adirondacks, including Watertown and Glens Falls, but avoiding Malone for obvious reasons. After Labor Day, however, school was in session, and except for nearby towns like Elkburg and Dannemora, their act was only available on weekends.

Evening shows sometimes found them too far from home to drive all the way back. Then to cut expenses, they would hunt up a house in town with a sign saying, 'Tourists'. Often they were recognized and given a free meal. If not, they would start playing and singing in their room, in which case they would be invited downstairs to play for the owners. This never failed to provide a hearty breakfast the next morning. "You see, Jim, I told you that the Lord would provide."

"I don't know, Buck. You can con them into feeding us, and sometimes they won't even let us pay for the room."

"Look at it this way. Do you feel good doing it, and are they getting their money's worth?"

"I suppose you're right, but it's not like a real job."

"We're entertainers, Jim. That's our job for now. Later, if you want to, you can rot your lungs out with silicosis and bust your balls in the mines. That's not for me."

"I don't know what I really want in life. I never expected this, but it is kinda fun most of the time. Maybe in a couple of years I'll join the army like Phil. That'll give me time to grow up. Were you ever in the military service, Buck?"

"No. When World War Two started I tried to join up. I really wanted to enlist, to do my part, but I couldn't pass the physical. I've got a ticker that sounds like a thrashing machine falling apart."

"Take care of yourself, Buck. Maybe you should get checked out by a doctor. I don't want to lose you, too."

Chapter 33

Now Jimmy wished that he hadn't sent Phil that photo of himself and Buck in their new costumes. A girl from one of the church groups they performed for had a crush on Jimmy and snapped a photo of him and Buck standing next to the man's forty-two Caddie convertible. Buck wore an old-fashioned black suit which made him look like an eighteen-eighties preacher while, for contrast, Jimmy sported a flashy cowboy outfit complete with boots and spurs. The boy had explained to his brother all of the fun they were having traveling around and singing.

Phil, however, was upset by this and rushed back an angry reply. He ordered his brother to 'send that drunken Indian back to the reservation,' claiming that he was trying to steal the farm from them. He said that he would notify both Father Orgebin and the county welfare department if Jimmy didn't get rid of Buck. Then Jimmy would end up in an orphanage or a foster home. He insisted that Buck couldn't possibly be his real father and that he must be lying.

Jimmy was shocked by his brother's attitude, thinking that if he only knew Buck he wouldn't feel that way. He wrote back to Phil in Fort Dix just as Phil was finishing his basic training. He explained that Buck was a good man and that he trusted him.

Phil's next response was a succinct threat. "If he is not out of there when I come home on leave at Thanksgiving, both of you are in big trouble."

At first, the boy was reluctant to show the letters to Buck but saw no other manner of treating the problem. He watched Buck's eyes as he read, trying to guess his thoughts. "Well," the man said finally, "looks like I better move on. I don't want to be the reason that you have a falling out with your brother."

"No, there's got to be another answer."

"In a way, your brother is right. You're still a minor. Maybe they can take you away from me and farm you out with strangers."

"Let 'em try. I'd run away for good."

"Then, the county might confiscate your farm, and you would both lose it. I think we have to go see a lawyer. It's possible there is a way you can get a judge to give you your right of majority."

"What does that mean?"

"It means that, under certain circumstances, an underage person can petition the court to give him adult status."

"How do you know stuff like that?"

"There are a lot of things about me you don't know. I already told you I had started college once. Even before that I had discovered libraries. I can thank Reverend Pierce's wife for that. I read everything I could get my hands on in those days."

Buck located an attorney in Plattsburg who would consider the case. He laid his cards on the table as the boy watched. The lawyer was optimistic, suggesting that if he had some credible character witnesses, Buck could be appointed Jimmy's temporary legal guardian. Buck had obtained affidavits from three of the ministers whose churches they had performed in and the problem seemed to be solved for the time being.

Less than a month later, Buck watched as a mouse-gray Plymouth business coupe rolled into the driveway. Noticing the sign painted on the car door attesting to the county welfare's ownership, Buck emitted a quick, "Oh, oh." Just as she was about to knock on the door, Buck began playing and singing 'Nearer My God to Thee.' For several minutes he pretended to not hear her thumps on the doorframe. When he did open the door to the woman, Buck was the epitome of gentility and charm.

She was a tall woman about thirty-five. Her black hair was pulled back so severely that Buck wondered how she could close her eyes should the need arise. Her hair terminated in a neatly-swirled bun that was held in place with three hat pins. Buck ascertained that she was possessed with more than her share of insecurity and had, most probably, never lain with a man. She wore a gray skirt that was too long even for the extreme styles of the day. Both the collar and the cuffs of her white blouse were fringed with dainty lace. A scented yellow handkerchief dangled from her left wrist. Over the blouse she wore a tailored gray jacket.

She sniffed several times conspicuously as though expecting to be struck by some disgusting odor. Finding none, she accepted the man's polite offer to sit. "Please, Miss, may I offer you a brisk cup of tea?"

"Oh, my! Uh, no thank you, no thank you. I've only got a minute. The welfare department has been receiving complaints that an underage person is living here in an unsavory atmosphere. I'm authorized to investigate."

"Of course, my good woman, I understand completely. How may I be of service to you?"

"According to our records, James Coulbron's father died recently and his mother is a resident in a mental institution."

"Not exactly. I'm afraid both his mother and father have died."

"Doesn't he have an older brother?"

"Yes, but his brother Philip is a soldier."

"Under the circumstances, perhaps the army can release the brother from service since he is the closest of kin."

"I believe his brother intends to become a career soldier. An army barracks is hardly a fitting place for a boy to grow up. The language of those soldiers is absolutely shocking."

"In that case, I'll wait here until the boy returns, and I'll transport him to the county home until other arrangements can be made."

"I'm afraid James would not agree to that, nor would I."

"If you try to interfere with the law, I will call the sheriff."

"Let me pour you that cup of tea now, Miss. You are going to need it for your long trip back – alone."

"May I use your telephone?"

"Of course, Miss, but why bother?"

"What do you mean?" she snapped.

"Simply that I am James's legal guardian now."

"What? What do you mean? No one told me that. I'll need some proof."

"Of course," said Buck smoothly as he handed her the document.

As she turned to leave, Buck brushed his palm across her fanny. She stood transfixed, ramrod straight, then slowly turned her head and gave him a wry smile. "And oh, yes, I may have to check back on James again, soon."

He said nothing, simply raised his eyelids wide and circled his eyes around once.

Buck realized that Father Orgebin might be harder to convince, trained as he most probably was on how to appeal to a young person's sense of idealism, not to mention every clergyperson's store of pat rejoinders. This would be one encounter the boy would have to survive on his own, although the man did not doubt that he could handle it.

Having graduated 'summa cum laude' after his long enrollment in the college of hard knocks, the ex-preacher possessed an uncanny ability to judge human nature. In Miss Alice Wehrmann, he saw a beautiful woman who only lacked his expertise to unlock her potential and free her from years of repression. It would be a challenge, he realized, but felt himself equal to such an interesting task.

Alice grew up as an only child born to the Reverend Gerhard Wehrmann and his wife, Bertha. As a newly-ordained minister of the Reformed Church, Gerhard and his wife had emigrated to Saint Louis, Missouri, to begin his service as pastor of his flock.

Soon afterward, Bertha gave birth to a healthy, active infant girl whom she tolerated rather than adored. When the girl was four years old, incidents occurred that embittered the father and caused him to take out some of his frustrations on his wife and daughter. The

World War had started in Europe shortly after they had departed the old country, and now resentment and prejudice was building up in America which, by itself, was preparing for war involvement in order to "make the world safe for democracy."

During his sermons, Gerhard's English pronunciation was more Gothic than biased members of his congregation were willing to accept. Several times, just as he began to speak on the pulpit, long-time parishioners got up and left. On two occasions, neighborhood youths smashed stain-glass windows in the sanctuary and painted hate slogans and symbols on the front door of the church. Bertha became frightened when anonymous persons called during the night and threatened to "kill all dirty Krauts."

Gerhard resigned from his Saint Louis church and accepted a call from a small parish in Texas. From there the family moved to Minnesota, and finally New York State. Financially, these moves were disastrous. They dragged debts with them from one small town to another.

Alice grew up in this strict, unhappy household. She learned to sew and crochet, to knit and cook. She attended all of the funerals and weddings her father performed, and was, at all times, expected to behave like a proper young lady whose father was a minister of the Gospel. She was duly confirmed as a Christian, sang in the church choir, and taught Sunday School.

Sex, in any of its guises, was never a topic of conversation in the Wehrmann home. The closest attempt at sex education occurred when six-year-old Alice was taking a bath and her mother soundly admonished her by saying, "Young ladies never touch that part of their body!" At the age of ten, she was told that ladies should never be completely unclothed. In order to bathe, she was obliged to cover her top half with a towel or shift while she soaked the bottom half before attempting to bare the top. This, of course, was bathed with a dampened cloth.

Her first menstrual flow, although light, frightened her so much that she burned her bloomers in the furnace. She felt that she had caused the bleeding because of those few times she had explored her anatomy with the hand-held mirror and had dared to touch herself while washing. A month later, she did confess the flow, an announcement that her mother took matter of factly.

"Of course, you silly *ganz*! All young women must suffer through this curse." Then the mother handed her some sanitary pads and instructed her on their use.

"Do men have to do this, too?"

"*Ach du liber!* I told you that this was a woman's curse. Men are made different. Must I draw you a picture?"

After high school, in which she excelled academically, she could look forward to very few career choices her parents might allow her to consider. One of these was to marry a minister; the other was to become a teacher. Neither of these appealed to her, but she agreed to try one year at a state normal school primarily because it would be a chance to get away from the oppression of her home.

During her first month in college, she developed a romantic obsession with a young man in her education class. Their first date was a stroll at dusk along the banks of the campus pond. As they sat side by side, hidden under the willow branches, she realized that she had never before felt so happy. When the handsome young man kissed her fully on the lips, she knew ecstasy. When he placed his groping hands inside her panties, she was horrified and screamed in terror while her would-be lover ran away, perhaps more frightened than she.

Other collegiate strollers discovered her there, sobbing uncontrollably, and helped her to her room. The next day in class, the young man wished to apologize and make amends, but she refused to talk to him. She still thought he was handsome but that, surely, he must be a demon in disguise and, so, she avoided not only him but all men. Instead, she sought consolation by engrossing herself in romantic novels.

After the first semester, with her parents' permission, she switched to a course that would lead to a career in social work. After graduation, she was employed in several locations until taking the job in Clayton County. Often obliged to work with disadvantaged and dysfunctional families, she became aware of many of the unsavory aspects of life. In addition, she could not help but notice that there were some happily married couples with beautiful children, and she began to yearn for this.

When Alice's father died, her mother came to live with her. She quickly made herself unwelcome by opening her daughter's mail and grilling her endlessly about her relationships, all the while complaining about how unfair life is for women and how cruel-hearted men are. In fact, she wished that she had never left Germany just because a man wanted her to.

When the mother's senility became untenable, Alice moved her into the county nursing home, and her life returned to normal. She involved herself in her work and in church activities. She kept close tabs on her clients and shared occasionally in their good times, but knew in her heart that something was missing.

She was first attracted to Mr. Buck LeTarte when she overheard him singing a Gospel song as she waited outside on his porch. She was further impressed by his impeccable manners and swarthy good looks. Although she tried desperately to maintain a professional demeanor, she was thrilled when he showed her some attention. Now that her parents finally had no direct control over her behavior, she was ready and willing to experience real life. Moreover, she longed for a loving man to possess her. The first time she saw Buck and Jimmy together, she fantasized that this was the boy she could have given birth to years ago, and that this was the man she wanted to spend the rest of her life with.

Chapter 34

"How's school going," Buck asked one morning as Jimmy waited for the bus.

"It's okay. I kinda like my French class best, but Mrs. Eggleston must be sick or something. We have a lot of subs. There's a rumor going around that we're getting a new teacher."

"It'll probably be some dried up prune, although you might get lucky. You never know."

"When did you say that Father Orgebin was coming?"

"Around eight o'clock tonight. I suppose I better bake some cookies or something so the good padre can keep his strength up."

Jimmy could see the school bus approaching so he grabbed his sack lunch, waved to Buck, and ran up the driveway toward the highway. For a fleeting moment, he thought of their former bus which was an old Chrysler stretched limousine with two sets of fold-down jump seats. At that time the driver was a gruff-sounding local farmer. "You kids always have to cross in front of the bus where I can keep an eye on you," he had informed Phil and Jimmy on the first day of school. Then he would point a gnarled finger across the highway toward their house.

It bothered the six-year old boy that, after school, his older brother always beat him to the cookie crock and would tease him for being so pokey. Accordingly, during class, he formulated a plan wherein he would be first today. He would sit in the front seat of the bus and, then, when Phil walked in front of the bus as directed, he would dash around the back and scoot across the highway.

His plan worked up to a point. As he ran past the rear bumper of the Chrysler, he glanced left. Good, he thought, there were no cars coming. He glanced right, directly into the radiator of a moving gravel truck. The truck's massive bumper was such that it picked the boy up and tossed him into the sod-covered ditch. Jimmy was unconscious at first, then awakened to see Phil running toward the house and his mother coming out only to faint in the driveway. The truck driver rushed to help the boy. He squatted down close to the boy's face to see if he were alive. Seeing this enormous face staring at him, Jimmy clenched his fist and punched the man's cheek.

David was at the mine working when his wife called. He rushed home to drive Jimmy to the hospital. The boy was alert the whole time but filled with aches and nausea. A doctor took his blood pressure and checked for broken bones. Jimmy squirmed as a nurse skinned off his underwear and tied a hospital gown on him. Later he suffered the indignity and embarrassment of being given a pan bath by a strange woman. He was feeling somewhat better now and becoming feisty. "Stop looking at my bug when you're washing me," he told her.

"Don't worry," she said. "I've seen lots of little boys' bugs. I won't hurt it. Here's the cloth. You can wash it yourself. I promise not to peak." He was released from the hospital the next afternoon but told to rest for a couple of days.

This was the beginning of a concept of divine protection that was formulating in the boy - first getting hit by the truck and, then, all of the other incidents. He thought often of the close calls, like nearly drowning and surviving the car wreck. He recalled the time Phil was felling a large birch, and it crashed to earth so close it scraped Jimmy's thigh. During those years in elementary and junior high he thought a lot about destiny ruling his life. When he was about ten, he once stood on the edge of a highway as automobiles and trucks whizzed by him only a few feet away. I don't have to worry, he thought. If I wanted to I could step out right in front of a car and God would save me.

Two very different, recurring dreams began to plague the boy when he was fifteen. One was that he could will his body to rise up off the ground for several feet. Then, effortlessly, he could flow in whichever direction he wished as others watched in awe. The phantom image was a pleasant one, and he always welcomed its arrival. The other dream was more of a nightmare, a succubus perhaps, from which he awakened with his arms and legs twisted about in odd positions and with his body soaked in sweat. He would find himself in a crowded room filled with strangers. Suddenly he would notice that he was completely naked. No one else seemed to take notice of this but, still, he would rush toward the door only to find it locked. In desperation, he would grasp the doorknob leading to a closet in which he hoped to hide. The whole door would pull loose from its hinges, and everyone would watch him holding it by the doorknob. Then he would look to escape through the window but would see hordes of faces peering through from the outside. There was no escape.

Recently, however, he had decided to face the demon. Now, when he would awaken after the ordeal, he would consciously continue the fantasy, forcing it to go wherever he wished. Sometimes he would clothe himself in exotic finery like a king or prince. Other times he would cause everyone else to become nude along with him. Once he attempted to mentally disrobe only those women he considered the most beautiful, but this embarrassed him and he never repeated it.

Jimmy greeted Mrs. Dupre as he boarded the bus and smiled at the other passengers. The bus was actually a large suburban with real wood sides and doors. It carried only eight to ten students depending on their size. The driver was a pleasant woman and the kids all liked her. She had two daughters, both older than Jimmy, whom he considered very pretty. He had even had wet dreams about the younger of the two and felt embarrassed every time he saw her. He was glad she was older than he and didn't have any classes with him. The older daughter had graduated the year before so he seldom saw her any more.

Jimmy was now the oldest boy to ride this bus so he usually sat with the next oldest fellow, Clarence Clement, a ninth grader. With Phil gone, Jimmy appreciated having Clarence to talk to although he thought they had little in common. "Can I come to your house after school this afternoon? I'd like to talk with you about something," asked Clarence.

"Sure, Clare, but only for a while. I'll be busy later."

French class was a waste of time that day. The substitute teacher knew very little of the language, and she kept mispronouncing 'bonjour.' She did announce, however, that their new teacher was coming soon and that the principal was making plans for the class to take a trip to Montreal.

As the boys had arranged, Clarence got out of the bus with Jimmy, and they walked toward the house. "Hey, Jimmy, I heard that you sang at the youth fellowship in Dannemora last week. My friend Tommy was there and said that you guys played really neat."

"Thanks, Clare. We have lots of fun doing it."

"Do you guys play and sing any other stuff, you know, western ballads and country tunes?"

"Sure, but just for ourselves."

"Did you know that I've been taking accordion lessons for four years? I'd like to come and practice with you guys, sometime."

"I think that would be okay with Buck. He's a nice fellow."

"I'm sorry your dad and mom both died. What is Buck to you anyway?"

"He's my real dad. He's been away a lot. David was my foster father."

"But you still have his name, don't you?"

"Yeah, but I'm thinking of getting it changed to LeTarte."

"That'll seem strange – to change your name."

"I don't know. Lots of strange things have happened lately."

"When's your brother coming home?"

"He was supposed to come home for Thanksgiving, but there's been a problem.

"What's that?"

"The darn nut. He's in the guardhouse. He smarted off at a drill sergeant, and they had a fight. Phil knocked him on his ass, but now his own ass is in a sling, so I guess I won't be seeing him for a while."

"They don't fool around in the army."

"If Buck was here we could talk to him now, but he's gone to buy some groceries. You want me to give you a ride home?"

"Hey, great! I was expecting to hitchhike."

Jimmy gave his friend a tour of the farm, then he led him over to the shed to check out the Pontiac.

"Boy, I can hardly wait until I get my own car," said Clarence. "My dad lets me drive the tractor, though."

Jimmy reached for the keys hidden next to the rafter, and they started out. "You know, Clare, this was Phil's car, and he gave it to me. Now he wants it back, and he doesn't want me to drive it anymore."

"How come, Jimmy?"

"He's mad at me for something I don't want to talk about."

Chapter 35

Father Orgebin arrived on schedule wearing his usual black habit, complete with a Roman collar. Upon seeing him walk up the steps to the porch, Jimmy thought he should learn to relax once in a while. He's always in that black uniform. Old Father O'Connell used to come here to go fishing on Saturdays and he would wear just old clothes like everyone else.

As usual, the house was spotless, and the aroma of freshly baked cookies permeated the kitchen. The priest knocked on the screen door a little too forcefully. Dutifully, Jimmy greeted him and hung up his black Homburg.

The cleric smiled wanly and shook hands with both Jimmy and Buck. Buck excused himself saying he had business to attend to in town. Jimmy felt a shiver of apprehension creep over his body.

"Well, now, my son, let's get right down to business."

Immediately Jimmy was repelled by the smell of whiskey on the man's breath. He looked into his watery eyes and couldn't help but stare at the starburst veins on his ample nose.

"Yes, Father. That's a good idea." The priest hovered close to him, so close the boy felt uncomfortable.

"You know I haven't seen you at Mass since your father's funeral. Are you having problems at home?"

"No, Father, there are no problems here."

"I see. How do you explain this disturbing letter I received from your dear brother, Philip, who is doing his duty helping to protect our great nation?"

'He surely lays it on thick,' thought the boy. 'Is he trying to make me feel guilty about not going to Mass or not running away to join the army like Phil?'

The priest handed the letter to Jimmy, and told him to read it. First, however, the boy lay out a tray of cookies and poured each of them a cup of coffee. "Cream or sugar?" he asked.

"Bless you, my son; a little of both, if you please. My, what delicious cookies. Did you make them?"

"No, Father, Buck is the cook around here."

"I'm glad you brought up his name. I'm afraid he may not be a good influence on a growing lad like yourself. Did you know that he passed himself off as a minister of the Lord in Malone, but he's really just another Indian off the reservation?"

"Of course I know that, Father, but Buck is not in the religion racket anymore. And he's not just another drunken Indian." The boy's voice was rising now, and the priest could sense his emotion.

"Holy Mother the Church will welcome you back with open arms. The saints and holy angels will pray for you, my son."

"I don't believe in angels anymore, Father, or leprechauns, or the boogey man either."

"This is all because of the bad influence you are receiving. Didn't the good sisters tell you that you would lose your guardian angel if you went to a Protestant church?"

"Have some more coffee, Father, you have to drive home in the dark."

"Yes, thank you, my son."

"I don't mean to be disrespectful, but the truth is that the religious instruction we received at Saint Matthew's was little more than a joke."

"My son, I'm sure everyone put forth their best effort. Why, the holy bishop himself took time from his busy schedule to confirm you."

"Yes, that was two years ago, and I remember it perfectly. He arrived in the back seat of a big black Cadillac limousine. He had a young priest as a chauffeur. The bishop was all dolled up in a fancy outfit full of gold thread, and he had a silly fish-head hat on. Just the Sunday before that you asked everybody to donate as much money as they could to build the bishop's new home. Didn't you know that there was a strike on and everybody was broke?"

The priest went on the defensive. "You should know that the people bought that car for the bishop."

"Then, if he was really the good man you say he was, he would have sold that Cadillac and driven around in an old Ford. He's begging for a fancy new house while the people here can't even pay their rent."

"Oh, my son, my son," Father Orgebin said in exasperation.

"You didn't know that the bishop was so interested in getting on to more important things that he forgot to slap my face like he did everyone else. That was supposed to give us the strength to resist temptation and be a soldier for the Lord. The sisters, good and otherwise, tried to teach us some songs that were better suited for kindergartners. Then, they would drill us on things no one would remember like the 'Seven Beatitudes.' I remember when Tadpole Johnson asked Sister Martha to explain what the sixth commandment meant. She got all red in the face and told him to ask his father. That's when we all knew it was about sex."

"So, sex is your problem, is it? Don't stay away from the church because you have normal feelings. God will give you the strength to remain pure."

"I don't have to worry about remaining pure because I'm not a virgin. My own mother took that away from me."

He made the 'Sign of the Cross', then, saying, "Heaven protect us."

"Let me tell you what our sex education consisted of. In school all we had was a filmstrip on frogs mating. All of us had seen dogs stuck together several times, and it used to be my job to bring our cow over to the neighbor's yard and hold Daisy's rope while the bull mated with her."

"Every Friday afternoon, we were let out early to walk over to Saint Matthew's for religious instruction. Sometimes we had the sisters. Other times we had the assistant priest or some new young priest right out of seminary. One of them thought that it was his responsibility to teach the boys some sex education. We wanted to learn all right. We paid attention to him, but it didn't amount to anything. It was like the blind leading the blind. Some of us knew more about it than he did. One day, for instance, he said that you have to be careful when you walk behind a woman because the feminine curves of a woman's behind can sexually excite a man and cause big problems. Why couldn't he say that you might get a hard on? Another time, he said that he had heard our confessions and knew that the very worst sin boys and girls our age could commit was something called 'jerking off.' He claimed it was a mortal sin and, if we died with that on our consciences, we would go straight to hell. Every guy I knew played with himself and didn't think it was wrong. Most guys would confess it once or twice. They would say their penance of five 'Our Fathers' and five 'Hail Marys' and the next day be pleasuring themselves again."

"Another priest asked us one time to write an essay that would explain what the sex organs were made for. This was for both the boys and the girls. Everybody wrote down what they knew about human reproduction and felt pretty pleased with themselves when they submitted their writing. A week later, though, after he had had time to read all of the essays, the priest was madder than heck because the kids had emphasized the reproductive side of these organs rather than the elimination side. He was sputtering so much he could barely speak, and his face was all red. He told us we shouldn't be thinking about such things at our age."

"Did you know, Father, that once I wanted to become a priest so I could help poor people all over the world? I wanted to be a missionary."

"That's marvelous, my son. Perhaps I can still help you."

"Father, would you like a drink? Buck said he had thrown out all the booze, but he missed one of my mother's bottles of rye." Jimmy noticed an involuntary flick of the cleric's tongue as it parted his lips.

"Oh, no, my son, but I thank you for asking."

"It's all right, Father, I know how to keep my mouth shut. "

"Do you now? In that case a wee bit would be welcome among friends. We are friends, are we not?"

"I don't mind being your friend." Jimmy deliberately had dropped the name 'Father' this time as he sensed his respect for the man diminish. He handed the priest the bottle and a tumbler. The man filled it half full, then added a touch more.

"God allows us to relax in moderation. Of course, we must be discreet about it, mustn't we?" The man took a healthy slug of whiskey and resumed. "Now, tell me, Jimmy, my lad. How is it that you lost your interest in a religious vocation? The Holy Church always welcomes sincere young men into the priesthood."

"First, let me tell you about another thing one of the assistant priests told us. He was talking about vocations. He said that the word 'vocation' meant a calling from God – how marriage was both a vocation and a sacrament because it was blessed by God."

"This is all true, my son."

"Then he went on to say that not being married was also a vocation, so it was all right to be a bachelor or a spinster."

"Yes, that's right. What are you getting at, James?"

"Just this, and this is where I disagreed with him. He claimed that Holy Orders was a greater vocation than marriage and that priests and sisters and brothers were especially blessed by their vocation. There is nobody I've ever met, priest or otherwise, who was more of a saint than David, the man who raised me."

"Oh, it's a pity you have such little faith. The Bible says that our faith should be like that of little children."

"I don't believe that either. God gave us eyes and ears because he knows we need them, and he expects us to use them. He gave us a brain, also, and he expects us to use that as best we can. He also gave us sex organs so he must expect us to use them as well."

"Is that why you decided against a religious vocation?"

"No, I could have lived with that. I finally decided against it when I learned that your Holy Mother the Church doesn't allow bastards to become priests, and that's exactly what I am, a dirty rotten bastard. Buck is my real father. My mother was a whoring tramp who was locked up in the asylum."

"I see," said the man of cloth sucking in his breath and pouring himself another drink. Then, as though to console the boy, he placed his hand on Jimmy's knee and patted it. Not being rebuffed by that familiarity, he moved his hand slowly along the inside of the boy's thigh and then snugly up to his privates where he began fondling. For a moment Jimmy sat gritting his teeth, then, abruptly stood up. "You better be going now – Father. Don't drive in the ditch on the way home. I wouldn't want that on my conscience." Feeling disgusted, the boy left the room.

Chapter 36

Jimmy lay trance-like on his bed in a state somewhere between slumber and awareness as blissful sensations coursed through his body seemingly powered by a force pump which caused surges of raw testosterone to be infused into every fiber of his being. Eminating from his loins, the sensations would divide into two distinct paths – one oozing its way through his viscera, heart and lungs, then lodging briefly in his throat before exploding into starbursts of pleasure. The alternative path seeped simultaneously through his thighs, continuing past his calves and feet to suddenly expend their energy into the air through his toes. He would have liked this altered state to continue but, gradually, full awareness came bringing with it a dull, nagging sense of fullness in his privates which begged for release. He regretted not being totally asleep because then the pressure might have been released by spontaneous emission.

Ever since that fateful night of the funeral when the boys discovered their mother in an uncompromising sexual situation and especially after the talk he had with his older brother, Jimmy had been vaguely aware that he was capable of fathering a child. It remained an unimportant bit of knowledge because he had no real need for it. Recently, however, his sexual urges had become nearly impossible to control.

Like all boys, he had experimented with self-pleasuring when he was younger. Now, however, after having admitted to Orgebin that he had once considered the priesthood as a career, he was uncertain if complete celibacy was something of which he was capable.

Accordingly, he had taught himself to fall asleep quickly by mentally reciting multiplication tables as he lay in bed. This sing-song repetition often would focus his thoughts long enough to blot out spurious thoughts and insistent sensations. Prayer helped him also, but the hypocrisy he had noted made memorized prayer meaningless. Only those silent orations he composed himself had any real effect.

More than a month had passed since he had adopted this regimen of denial. For whatever reason the nighttime emissions had also ceased. In daytime he was usually too busy to be affected. Yet, increasingly, spontaneous erections and insistent tickles plagued him mercilessly. Sometimes he would unknowingly grab at his privates as though trying to dissuade a biting insect. Once during English class, when called upon to read his essay aloud while standing in front of the class, he noticed the familiar bulge and tried vainly to conceal it with his writing tablet. All of the boys, at least, recognized the problem but had little sympathy for the afflicted one.

This plan for sensory obliteration in bed using math lessons began to fail. On those evenings when he did manage to fall asleep quickly, he would awake an hour or two later, with a throbbing organ and with a sense of great pressure in his groin. He would struggle with the bed clothing, rolling the quilts into a ball and squeezing them repeatedly with his arms. Then he would punch the pillows with his fists. On one occasion, he punched the wall hard enough to skin his knuckles as his fist punched a hole in the gypsum wallboard.

Buck had been awakened by the boy's struggles, and not aware of its cause, worried about him. Buck went to the bathroom to relieve himself and flushed the john. Hearing this, Jimmy felt embarrassed that his father had heard him. He sat silently in bed with the bed coverings spread helter-skelter around him.

Buck rapped gently at the door. "You okay, Jim? Sounds like you're having a nightmare."

"I wish I were. Come on in. I need to talk, Dad."

The man flicked on the lights, causing the boy's eyes to squint. 'What's up, son?"

"Pointing to the erection making a tent out of his sheets, Jimmy said, "This damn thing is what's up every night, and I can't get any sleep."

"Yeah, that's a whopper all right, but it shouldn't be a problem. The real problem comes when it doesn't act that way anymore. Actually, pronging out like that is what it's supposed to do. Too soon – all too soon, you may start to lose some of that power."

"I know I can jack off if I want to, and nobody will be the wiser. I used to do it, but I don't want to feel like a little kid anymore. I want to be in control of my body."

"I suppose I'm not the best person to try to give you advice for this kind of a problem because I seldom denied myself that kind of pleasure. I started young and kept at it. I can't even remember all of the women I've screwed."

"I trust you more than anyone else. Some of the guys talk about getting sex, but I think they're exaggerating a lot."

"Oh, I suppose some are, and some aren't, but I do know one thing."

"What's that?"

"They keep sane when they have to by using the five-finger solution. Guys like us just weren't cut out to be monks. But, hey, it's got to be your decision, and as long as I'm giving out free advice, how about when you're with girls? Sometimes things can happen mighty fast. When those hormones start hopping, they have a mind of their own and they want to take over. If you get intimate with a girl, use a rubber or you could have big trouble. Some of these farmers around here have big shotguns."

"Oh, come on, Dad. I'd never let things go that far."

"Just the same, I'm going to buy you some rubbers. You see that you use them when the time comes, and it'll come sooner than you think. Remember, too, that girls can be more aggressive sometimes than guys, so don't let yourself get trapped into a situation you don't want to happen."

"Not long ago, I couldn't wait to become a man. Now, I don't like everything that goes along with being one."

"How about if I pay a woman to come over to spend the night with you and show you the ropes. I'll stay in town that night so you can be alone with her. Of course, in a week you'll be pounding holes in the wall again."

"Uh, uh. No, I wouldn't want to do that, but thanks anyway."

"Have you tried a cold shower? I heard that works."

"Hah! That's nothing but a joke. I tried it once. My thing just got harder, and I got hornier than ever."

"Did you ever study about evolution in science class, Jim?"

"Yeah, some – not a lot."

"Okay then, try to imagine what life was like in caveman days. People didn't live very long then – what with saber-toothed tigers and cave bears gobbling them up. There were lots of accidents and diseases but no real doctors. Most people didn't live to be thirty unless they were extra lucky. So, what I'd like to figure out is how they could have children and take care of them long enough so the kids could survive on their own."

"I've never thought about that. I imagine that they would have to get married when they were very young – as soon as they could make babies."

"I think you're right. You've probably heard about something called 'survival of the fittest.' Those people who were the horniest and started having babies right away had the best chance of passing on their genes. In other words, nature made us ready to reproduce at fourteen or so. Unfortunately, our society now says, "Hold on there! Put a snap clothes pin on that thing. You've got to have an education so you can get a good job. Go to college and all that."

"Hey, maybe if evolution continues, in a million years things will change and future kids will stay kids longer."

"Could be, Jim, but I doubt it, and we won't be around to find out. You okay now, Jim?"

Yeah, I'll survive, I guess. At least my thing is resting for a change."

In the days that followed, Jimmy thought often about Buck's words concerning the gap between what nature had decided for him and what society demanded of him. In this way he was able to reach an accommodation between his sense of idealism and reality.

The boy appreciated the way Buck was never evasive when he asked him a question or needed advice and, so, it wasn't unusual for him to question the man about other areas. It was in this vein that a question concerning immortality arose. One evening after supper the two of them were carrying on a friendly conversation. "Dad, do you think that David is in heaven?"

"I guess it doesn't matter what I think about that. Each person has to decide whether or not he believes he's going to live after he dies. Nobody knows the answer to that question. The way I look at it David lives on in your memory because he set a good example and taught you to be a good person. I'll live on in you because you carry my seed. That way your children will be part of both you and me. That's enough immortality for any man. Why be greedy?"

"I'm confused about religion. Sometimes I feel like a hypocrite. I haven't gone to Mass since David's funeral. I'm singing in Protestant churches even though Father Orgebin said I would lose my guardian angel. The fact is, I don't think I ever had one."

"Jim, how many angels can dance on the head of a pin?"

The boy looked at him quizzically. "What do you mean?"

"I mean that I'll believe in angels when I see one. For thousands of years self-appointed people have been trying to have power over other people. They think that it's their mission in life to tell other folks what to think and how to behave. Maybe it's a greater sin to lust after immortality than it is to lust after immorality."

"What do you mean?"

"Think of it this way. Craving to have eternal life is kind of selfish, isn't it? What's wrong with living a life where you hurt no one, do some good for others and then, when you're worn out, make room for the next generation. A person lives on in someone else's memory. David is more alive to you than your mother because he meant more to you."

"That's true enough. I try to forget about her, but I think about David every day. Buck, what was it like when you were 'fleecing the suckers', as you used to say?"

"To me it was just another job. I had learned the trade and apprenticed under Reverend Pierce. I also picked up a lot on my own in the College of Hard Knocks. I appealed more to the poor folks, who felt out of the mainstream, sort of the dregs. Some of the 'high class' congregations didn't want them around smelling up the place. I gave them what they needed – some solace, some dignity, some fellowship. They weren't getting it anywhere else. I don't feel bad about anything I did then, and I sure as hell didn't get rich."

"In a church congregation how many of the people really belong for strictly religious reasons?"

"I'd guess about twenty percent. Of course, a person can be sincere one day and not the next."

"Why do people go to church, then?"

"It's primarily a social gathering. You meet people, work on a committee, get involved in do-goody things. It makes you feel good about yourself. Many people like to feel morally superior to others. Conspicuous church attendance and participation in church activities is one way to do that. It also helps to explain why the leadership of every denomination tries so desperately to instill in their congregation that theirs is the one true religion. They all say the same thing."

"A lot of people would get awfully mad at you for saying things like that."

"No one likes to see his own hypocrisy exposed. It's like stripping them naked. They would get so mad they would try to do some very unchristian-like things to me. As for our rigidly-righteous friends, they are in constant fear that someone will expose their shortcomings. Oftentimes, the real reason for their righteousness is to cover up for some of the dirty, rotten things they've done in the past or are still doing. After all, if you teach Sunday school, sing in the choir, and donate to the overseas missions, who's going to believe bad gossip about you? What I've just said to you about religious honesty is also what is in their own minds but left unspoken."

"That's no way to live. How about the good Father Orgebin? Do you think he's afraid I'll tell what he tried to do to me?"

"Of course he's afraid. I hear he's being transferred to a parish somewhere out of state. My guess is that he's been involved with other boys and the bishop knows it. They'll avoid a scandal by foisting him off on another parish."

"I feel that I should say something to the authorities. Of course, I'd get razzed in school and everywhere else."

"I'm afraid it wouldn't do any good. I know you want to protect other kids, but around here people would say that I put you up to it. Naturally, Orgebin would lie to protect himself, and the bishop doesn't want a scandal to break out in his backyard. You might feel better if you write the bishop an anonymous letter. He probably knows the score, and will take action if there have been enough other complaints."

"Buck, are you down on all church goers?"

"Hell, no. The truth is that in the long run they do more good than harm. There are thousands of fine folks attending church every Sunday."

"Maybe we should go to some church and get involved if we can."

"Fine with me. How about if we visit each one in rotation to get the lay of the land? We've already sung in several of them, but haven't attended services in many. Of course, you might have your eye on that gorgeous daughter of Pastor Fields. A pretty skirt will convert a guy faster than anything else I can think of."

The lad smiled and gave the little smirk that revealed his dimple. Again, Buck became aware of how much he loved the boy and how glad he was they were together. This bonding had come late in their lives, but by now it was complete.

"Do you believe in God, Buck?"

"Absolutely. I see proof of it every day, all around me. It's fall now, and the earth is going to rest for a while, but we know when the spring comes, everything comes alive again. There can be no doubt about a Great Spirit. One seed sprouting is enough proof for me.

Chapter 37

Jimmy walked along the junior high wing of the school corridor looking for Clarence's study hall. The door was open so he walked in and inquired of the teacher the boy's whereabouts. Informed that he had just left for the lavatory, Jimmy thanked her and continued his search. The washroom appeared to be empty at first, but then he noticed two sets of boys' feet inside one of the sit-down stalls with the door closed. That's odd, he thought, wondering if Clarence was one of the stall's inhabitants. He was about to call out when he noticed one of the sets of shoes disappear as though the owner was standing on the stool to hide.

Jimmy left silently and walked to the end of the corridor. After a few moments, he saw Clarence leave and return to his room. Then, a senior boy Jimmy knew slightly exited the same washroom and disappeared down a stairway. He thought little of this, considering it was a kid prank.

There was usually a fifteen minute wait between the time of school dismissal and the arrival of their bus. Walking outside the perimeter of the building, Jimmy noticed Clarence from a distance walking with the same senior boy he had seen earlier. They headed toward the bleachers and ducked underneath the risers, hidden from his view. Jimmy approached the bleachers from the opposite direction expecting to meet them as they came out. When they did not exit, he peered inside. Alex Rushton, the basketball captain, was sitting on a rickety wooden chair with no back. Clarence was kneeling between the older boy's thighs facing him, his head bobbing up and down rhythmically.

At first, Jimmy wondered what was going on. Then, as his eyes became accustomed to the gloom, he noted that Alex's pants had been pulled down.

A nasty word came to his mind – the same word his mother had used against Phil the night he interrupted her illicit coupling with Dodgson. He knew what the word meant but thought that such behavior did not really happen. He thought it was only a joke but, here and now, Clarence was doing it to another guy.

Suddenly, Jimmy felt ashamed for having witnessed such a private act and left silently, unseen. Later, in the bus, he was not able to sit with Clarence for fear his face might reveal his knowledge and sat, instead, alongside the bus driver and chatted with her. He decided to question Buck about it as soon as he could bring up enough courage.

That night as Jimmy lay in bed trying to fall asleep, his mind turned to Clarence and Orgebin. He remembered that he had often seen the two of them on the altar offering Mass. The priest wore his sacerdotal garb, while the boy had on a three-quarter length white robe, incongruous with the black tennis shoes and white star decorating each ankle. He wondered if it was vaguely possible that there was more than a priest-altar boy relationship going on. Then, he thought of what he had accidentally seen under the bleachers as well as the inebriated cleric's shameful pass at him. He shuddered, then dismissed the thoughts as gentle sleep overcame him.

Buck was bustling about in the kitchen, humming now and then, alternating this with risqué jokes. The percolator blub-blubbed monotonously, and a thin cloud of steam arose from the skillet filled with home fries while the man expertly folded over a ham omelet. Jimmy's mouth began to water in anticipation as he walked to the sink to wash his hands from milking.

"Well, Jim, how did tit pulling go? After I separate the cream today, I'd like to make some butter. If there's enough cream left, maybe you could dig a small chunk of ice out of the sawdust, and then we could make some ice cream tonight."

"That would be fun, but I don't think there'll be enough for all that. Daisy's starting to dry up already. We're gonna have to have her bred, but maybe she's getting too old. I remember when she used to give lots more milk this time of the year."

"How old is she?"

"I'm not sure. She's the only cow we ever had."

"Who's got a breeding bull?"

"Gilberts. Either Phil or I used to lead her over and wait until old Ferdinand took care of her."

"You mean you watched, you naughty boy?"

"Buck, they're just cows. They're not people. Besides, you have to stay there and drag Daisy out of the pen after a while or Ferdie would keep on pestering her. We never dared go in with them because he's such a mean old monster – must weigh a ton."

"How much does the breeding cost?"

"It was five bucks last time."

"I think the farmer should pay you for keeping his bull happy."

"It doesn't work that way. Nobody cares if the bull likes it or not – or the cow either."

"It sure must be tough being a cow. She only gets it once a year and can't even pick out her own sweetheart. On the other hand, I'm beginning to know how she feels except nobody's pulling on my tits twice a day."

"Buck, can I ask you something that's kinda embarrassing for me?"

"That's what I'm here for."

"Well, I don't quite know how to say this, but I saw something behind the school yesterday that I don't understand, and I wish I hadn't seen it."

"Come out with it, Jim."

"Two guys from school were doing something nasty. It was a sex thing. I never knew that people really did that. It seemed disgusting."

"Jim, you've got a lot to learn about life. Don't feel bad about what you saw. People do all kinds of different sex things together. That doesn't make them bad people. Some young guys, and girls, too, I suspect, aren't sure who they are, or what they are, or what they want to become, so they experiment with sex for a while. A few of them decide that they like it that way and continue to do it the rest of their lives."

"But, Buck, when I see these guys again, how am I supposed to act toward them?"

"There's no reason to avoid them. Pretend it didn't happen. Just be your old self."

"Okay, Buck. Oh, uh, Clarence Clement wants to practice with us some evening. He's pretty good with his accordion."

"Sure, Jim. Glad to have him. Oh, oh, here comes your bus."

It turned out that Clarence played extremely well for a person his age and had an extensive repertoire of country music. His father had given him a ride to Jimmy's house. Jimmy and Buck admired the boy's expensive piano accordion and asked him to give them a demonstration. Clarence played "The Tennessee Waltz" flawlessly and with feeling. Buck's mind was already gearing up for more possibilities on how to advance their musical careers. The boy followed this with "Your Sweetheart Waits for You, Jack", then ripped into "The Beer Barrel Polka."

The three of them played together for several hours, kidding and joking between gulps of home-made root beer. Then, Clarence announced that he had promised his parents he would be home by eleven.

"Here, kids, take my car," said Buck, tossing Jimmy his keys. Jimmy liked driving the big Caddie and loved the solid roar of its massive vee-eight engine.

Once they were out of sight of the house, Clarence said, "Open this baby up. Let's tear up some cement."

At that moment they were passing the spot where he and Phil had demolished David's car, and, remembering this, he did not respond to the other's urging. "Not this time, Clare, we're not in a hurry. By the way, you really played well tonight. Can you come practice again?"

"Sure, most any time. You know my dad runs the resort and dance hall on our side of the lake. Well, this year we raised too damn many turkeys. We can't sell 'em all so we're going to have a raffle and dance. Pop wants me to play for the dancing, but I don't know how to call for the square dancing. Hank Garceau said he would call."

"How does a dance and raffle work? I've never been to one of them."

"My old man said that nobody's done it around here in a long time, but it was common when he was a kid. Everybody who wants to square dance buys a bunch of raffle tickets, but first we bring the bird out that is going to be won so everybody can see it. Then we play three dances. The last one is a fast breakdown. Then someone pulls the winning number out of a hat, and the winner scoops up the live critter. We save one big gobbler for the end. Most of the rest are hens or small gobblers."

"That sounds like fun. What with Thanksgiving coming up soon, it would be a good time to win a turkey."

"Yeah, that's what Pop said. How about if you and Buck play with me? You already know most of the songs, and so does he."

"I'll talk to him about it."

Jimmy had been trying to formulate in his mind a careful way to question Clarence about Father Orgebin in order to find out if he was actually involved in improper behavior with boys.

"Say, Clare, what's it like being an altar boy with Orgebin?"

"It's a lot of fun. He takes us on trips, and we play in his basement. He's got a lot of games and a shower."

"What do you need a shower for?"

"You know, you get all hot and sweaty, running and chasing around."

"Do you think I'm too old to become an altar boy?"

"I don't know. You'd have to ask Father, although Alex didn't quit until basketball started this year. He said he was too busy."

"That's Alex Rushton, isn't it?"

"Yeah, you know him, don't you?"

"Oh, sure. You and he are pretty good friends, aren't you?"

"He's my big buddy. When he's around, nobody messes with me."

As a guess, Jimmy tried another tactic. "Did Father Orgebin ever show you guys any of his, uh, art pictures?"

"Oh, you mean his boob and dink show. How did you know about that? He said it was just for us altar boys who were getting special sex education from him."

"Oh, he's shown me some things too, and we've done some things together – lots of fun. He showers with you guys, doesn't he?"

"Sure, and he shows us the proper way to wash everything, and I mean everything."

"You know he could get in a lot of trouble if the bishop ever found out what he was doing with young men. Didn't he ever say this was a sin?"

"He said we were special, so it's not a sin as long as nobody finds out about it, and we all pledged not to tell."

"But you're telling me, aren't you?"

"You seemed to already know all about it."

"Yeah, I did."

Jimmy didn't like the idea of sending an anonymous letter to the bishop but could think of no alternative. Now, he was convinced more than ever that he had to do this for the boys' sake. Deep inside, he wished that he had never found out about it.

Chapter 38

After Jimmy finished sanding the maple cross which was to serve as David's temporary monument, he handcrafted a method to attach the horizontal bar to the vertical upright, recalling how he had observed David similarly make half laps to reinforce wooden fences. He joined the two members by temporarily holding them in place as he bored two holes using a bit and brace. He tensioned the nuts on the threaded side of the steel bolts against both a lock washer and a press washer, then gave them another twist with a Crescent wrench.

He tested his work for sturdiness, and finding no looseness, applied a coat of spar varnish to the wood and admired it as it gleamed while drying. Suddenly he noticed, in miniature, his own reflection and thought of Christ's image that Saint Veronica saw imprinted on her veil when she wiped His face on the way to Calvary. This unnerved him a bit, but he continued with his work. At the base of the structure, which would be covered by soil, Jimmy applied a liberal amount of creosote as a preservative. Buck watched from the back porch as the boy struggled up the hill with the finished product, his back bowed by his burden. The man felt a strong surge of pride as he watched, knowing full well that this was no time to interfere. When he reached the steps, Jimmy saw Buck and paused, smiling, though winded from the effort. He rested the butt end of the cross on the lawn, and it towered above him. He awaited Buck's comment.

"Mighty fine cross, son. Mighty fine."

"Thanks, Dad. I was thinking at first that I could tie the cross on the top of the Pontiac to transport it to the cemetery, but maybe that's not such a good idea. What do you suggest?"

"Well, we could lower the top of my convertible and lash it in there. You could steady it, while I drive. That would give the town's people something to gossip about for years."

"Thanks, but no. I don't want anybody laughing about this."

"Maybe you know somebody who'll loan us their pickup truck."

"Hey! Yeah. Clarence's pop has one. I'm going to give him a call."

That afternoon both Clarence and his father helped with the transport and installation of the cross next to the mound of earth where David's body rested. Jimmy was glad that neither the priest nor the cemetery worker, Perchy Garew, was there to give advice or interference.

A few nights later the wind picked up and whipped off the remainder of the birch leaves that had been clinging to their branches, sending them swirling until they plastered themselves against any object they happened to strike. Rain fell in waves, horizontally striking the side of the house that contained the boy's bedroom. Intermittent snow pellets, mixed with the rain, rattled the spectral panes and the whole structure creaked eerily.

In the morning there was a small accumulation of snow everywhere but not enough for school to be closed. During class the next day the boy worried that the elements may have softened the soil he had tamped around David's cross, causing it to tilt or fall. For this reason, he had driven himself to school in the Pontiac.

Jimmy seldom drove the car now that Phil had reneged on his gift, but Buck told him that it was better for the car to be driven occasionally than to be stored, just so long as he kept up the maintenance of the vehicle. He worried a lot about Phil now because he had stopped answering the boy's letters. Jimmy didn't even know if his brother had been released from the guardhouse and was still stationed at Fort Dix.

Avoiding the priest's residence, Jimmy parked in Perchy's yard next door. The boy recalled that Perchy's real first name was Medor and that the nickname reflected his love for catching perch in nearby Castle Lake. He liked the old fellow who served as grave digger and groundskeeper of the cemetery. He had visited with him on occasion, and out of respect always avoided using the nickname. The old man may have noted this and, being lonesome, had given Jimmy a standing invitation to go fishing with him anytime.

The man's way of speaking always attracted the boy's attention, sprinkled as it was with French syntax and Quebec *'patois'*. He liked the way the old man always pronounced the second syllable more strongly than the first, the same way Mrs. Papineau did.

On the day that they erected the cross, the last thing Jimmy did as they drove away was to glance up the cemetery knoll and see the top of the cross peeking through the tombstones. Now, as he walked the path, his fears were realized. The cross was no longer in sight. Hurrying toward the family plot, he saw Perchy bent over the cross. He had it placed on a sawhorse and had already sawed off the horizontal portion into sixteen-inch long rounds.

"What are you doing, Mr. Garew? That's my father's cross. Did the wind blow it down?"

"*Non, mon Garçon*, she stand good against ze win', but ze Fazere, him, he make me tear it down."

"But why? It was a lot of work to make that."

"*Oais, ben sur*. Zat a bootiful job, alright, but ze Fazere, him, he don't 'low no mon'ment more high zen zat of ze monseigneur."

"That old bastard Orgebin doesn't have the right to decide that. Which one is the monseigneur's monument?"

"Zat big fancee one, ober zere, wiz ze statue all ovair."

Jimmy could not remember Monseigneur Riley, but knew from hearsay that he had been a popular Irish priest throughout the region and was being considered for elevation to the position of bishop just before his untimely death several years ago.

"Orgebin must have known this was David's cross. It's got his name on it," shouted the distraught boy. "If it was the wrong size, he could have called me, and I would have shortened it. He's a son of a bitch."

"*Oais, oais, peut-être que c'est vrais,* but he don't want no more wood cross here – only stone. He say to me, 'You cut zat up and burn it in your wood stove today. I varee sorry, Garçon, but I must obey ze fazere. You want I should put ze wood in your voiture?"

"No, Mr. Garew. It's not your fault. Just save me that piece with David's name on it. Maybe I'll make a lamp or something with it. Here, let me cut it."

"Maybe you won't go to fish wiz me, now."

"It's okay. I'll fish with you. How about if we go fishing through the ice during Christmas vacation?"

Oais, ben sur. Zat good idée. *Dieu te benisse, mon garçon."*

"Mr. Garew, it may be a couple of years before I can afford a headstone for David. How will I be able to keep track of where he is?"

"Viens, icitte. You see ze steel rod, all of zem, *un, deux, trios, quatre*. Also, I have ze map in my house. Map of ever' bodee."

"How old is the map?" inquired the boy.

"Varee, varee, varee ancient. Viens, I show you in my house."

The boy was excited now as he entered the low-ceilinged structure. Medor Garew carefully unrolled the old map, its edges yellowed and frayed, and spread it on the kitchen table. Jimmy traced with his finger the path to the family plot and there discovered, not ten feet from where David lay, the exact location of the graves of his great-grandparents. He vowed silently to provide a stone for them as well, and, borrowing a paper and pencil, sketched his own map of the family plot.

Jimmy was hoping that his French classes would move along faster so that he could learn to converse entirely in French with the old man. He knew the old timer would enjoy it and that he would as well.

Chapter 39

One of the prevailing activities in most small towns is gossip, and, if sociologists were called upon to measure this as a product, they would find in Rock Mountain a bumper crop. Thus, the death of David Coulbron and the subsequent incarceration of his wife in the state mental hospital, and then death, provided local tongue waggers with hours of entertainment. Coupled to this were rumors of the woman's sexual exploits that went back for a number of years.

This line of conversation extended, quite naturally, into the ranks of the school faculty. Since mining towns have tended to attract immigrants over the years, the second generation population of the village was sprinkled with a variety of white European ethnic groups. With such a conglomeration of nationalities to meet with daily, an easy acceptance of differences existed. Intermarriage among these groups was frequent. One common denominator in the town was the preponderance of Catholics. This did not extend to the town's elite which consisted of mine managers, engineers, and other upper-staff personnel. Some of the elementary faculty members were local, but most of the high school staff came from some distance.

In this atmosphere, the only prejudice that existed seemed to be directed against Indians. The relative closeness of the Mohawk reservation tended to reinforce this bias. Newspapers rarely failed to headline each altercation which occurred on or near the reservation that happened to be brought to their attention. Local taverns prominently displayed signs warning that it was contrary to federal law to serve alcoholic beverages to Indians. There were, nevertheless, several persons of mixed French-Canadian parentage who enjoyed reasonable immunity from this prejudice.

It is understandable then that discussions in the faculty lounge not infrequently centered around James Coulbron, his recent loss, and his living arrangement with Buck LeTarte. Most teachers came to the lad's defense in consideration of his high grades and good deportment. A few, however, predicted trouble. Among these was a math teacher named Alvin Bascomb.

Alvin Bascomb could be seen at lunch time savoring his tuna fish and dill pickle sandwich as he extolled the virtues of early retirement. He exaggerated the success of the real estate business he was attempting to expand and bragged that in three years he would be able to kiss this dump goodbye, longing as he did for a respite from the daily grind of facing squirrelly adolescents.

The students at Rock Mountain considered Mr. Bascomb the least competent teacher possible. Because of the relative isolation of the village, its paucity of cultural enlightenment and low salaries, the overall quality of instruction tended toward mediocrity, but he had never been able to approach even that level of performance nor did he care to.

Jimmy first encountered Bascomb during the boy's sophomore year while attending his geometry class. The man's usual method of instruction consisted of facing the blackboard as he copied in chalk the identical theorem printed for that day in the students' textbooks. The main respite available to the students from this tedium came about as a result of the man's obnoxious habit of periodically tightening the muscles of his circum-anal sphincter. The effect of this was that his posterior visibly twitched every few minutes.

Boys outnumbered girls in the class three to one, many of the girls having opted for home economics or business courses. After the first day of Bascomb's performance, the boys began sniggering among themselves, referring to the pedagogue's twitch as 'an advanced case of touchhole chiggers.' In private conversations they referred to him as 'Chiggers, the twitcher.' Sometimes the more entertaining among the scholars would organize a lottery in which the person who most nearly guessed the number of Bascomb butt twitches during the first ten minutes of class would win the pot. This had the serendipitous result of keeping their minds occupied and the classroom relatively composed, or so the instructor imagined. In reality, much adolescent funfare managed to be accomplished behind the man's rounded and prominent backside.

Tadpole Laschinsky, for instance, appropriately seated in the back row, would unbutton his fly and expose himself in order to wiggle his insignificant peanut to the amusement of the other boys. Still others drew gross pictures of Bascomb, with or without trousers as the whim struck them.

Booger Janulavcich, the class's best artist, could always be seen with the latest issue of his favorite funny book, 'Plastic Man,' lying prominently on his desk as, in large size, he meticulously drew twenty-foot-long penises at the appropriate location on the body of the superhero. These artistic additions eventually occupied each frame of the comic book. Sometimes the appendage would be drawn in such a way that it wrapped serpent like around a woman's leg or, perhaps, the bad guy's neck as suited the story and the capriciousness of the reincarnated Michelangelo.

Jimmy was aware of this behavior and, although he didn't entirely approve, he never chided his companions and, at times, he may have chuckled. For the most part he focused on the task of learning. In June, when the time came for State of New York Regents Examinations, the frolic makers still seemed oblivious of any impending disaster. As a result, Jimmy was the only boy to pass the course along with two girls. The remaining twenty-six students failed and were obliged to repeat the course.

The following year, Jimmy signed up for intermediate algebra, hoping that a replacement math teacher had been hired. This proved, however, not to be the case and, once again, Mr. Bascomb orchestrated his brand of boredom. Not infrequently the students noticed errors in his calculations on the blackboard and called them to his attention. At first he would attempt to ignore them. If the students persisted he would attempt to bluff his way through by proclaiming that he deliberately created errors to keep them on their toes and force them to pay more careful attention. He fooled no one, including himself.

On rare occasions he would try to treat the students to one of his friendly discussions on topics unrelated to mathematics. So it was on a particular day that his chosen topic centered on the future of atomic energy. With great enthusiasm he expounded on the extent that our future would be enhanced by the development of this marvelous advance in technology. He predicted automobiles that would run for a million miles on a single pellet of uranium and steam plants that would create electricity so cheaply there would be almost no cost to homeowners.

Jimmy, however, and a few of his classmates were skeptical, primarily due to Bascomb's easy acceptance of atomic energy and his rosy predictions. Their thinking was that if he, of all people, was in favor of it, there's got to be a hitch. Jimmy suggested that since we are dealing with the unknown, there was a need for caution.

"Don't be ridiculous," the man thundered, as if sheer volume implied correctness and intelligence. "Our scientists are the best in the world. They created the atomic bomb, didn't they?"

At that point, Jimmy said, as an aside, "That's what I'm afraid of."

Immediately, Bascomb walked beside him and slapped him soundly across the face.

Although his face stung and his head snapped from the blow, he did not immediately react except to recall David's advice 'Keep your cool. Use your head.'

"The good book says we should turn the other cheek." Then the boy turned his other cheek toward the teacher who promptly smacked that one. Rising quickly, Jimmy floored him with one blow to the jaw. The students roared their approval and began throwing their books at the fallen teacher.

Struggling to rise, Bascomb seethed, "You half-breed son of a bitch, get out of my room."

Jimmy stood over him, breathed deeply to compose himself and said, "With the greatest of pleasure, you dung heap."

Mr. Wagner, the high school principal was aware both of Bascomb's shortcomings and of Jimmy's good record. Yet, when Jimmy sat down in Wagner's office to explain the incident before Bascomb could color it with his version, the principal felt himself in a bind. There were only two other occasions during his tenure when students struck a teacher, and in both of those cases the student was expelled from school. He knew that he would have to report this to the members of the school board at their next meeting.

Chapter 40

Jimmy returned to his next class, and the day continued without incident except for friendly back slaps from other boys who had heard of the Bascomb brouhaha. The final period of the day was reserved for physical education which, for the boys in the three upper grades, was taught by the principal who served likewise as basketball coach.

In view of sloppy weather out of doors that day, the instructor reverted to a rough and tumble game of basketball. On these rare occasions, Coach Wagner acted as referee. After taking attendance, he dribbled a basketball to the center circle, tested it for bounce, and swished a two-hander through the hoop. This always impressed the younger boys whose arms had not yet achieved the growth or strength to do that. During the years any of the boys could remember, he had never missed such a shot.

Normally the members of the basketball team were exempted from participating in physical education during season. Sometimes, however, one or more of them would show up at class time to help referee or to play. On this day senior student Alex Rushton suited up and joined in the game. After noticing Jimmy make several good shots, Alex called him over to talk.

Remembering the incident under the bleachers, Jimmy was reluctant to meet with him, yet under the circumstances could not refuse. "You've got a good eye, Coulbron. Why aren't you out for basketball? We could use you."

"I've thought about it, but I'd miss my bus and have to hitch hike and then, too, I've got work at home."

"I've seen you driving your own car. You don't have to take the goddam bus, for Christ sake."

"Gas costs money. Besides Buck and I are on the road a couple days a week."

"I saw you guys when you played at that frigging turkey raffle. How long has Clarence Clement been playing with you?"

"He just started. He plays a mean squeak box."

"What else do you play with him?" asked Alex maliciously.

"What the hell are you talking about, Rushton?"

"Just remember what I'm saying. You keep the fuck away from him, or you'll answer to me."

"Simmer down. He's just a kid, but he's got a mind of his own. You don't own him."

"Just because you gave Bascomb a sucker punch doesn't mean I can't put you in your place. All of you musicians are a bunch of fairies." Then Alex stormed off.

Jimmy wished that he had stayed. He wasn't afraid of the older boy. Although Alex was much taller than he was, Jimmy thought that Rushton's arms and legs looked like toothpicks. He was all length with little muscle development. Jimmy, on the other hand, had hardened his whole body through years of farm work and logging.

All of the basketball players were in the same study hall and, not infrequently, they would con the teacher into letting them go to the boiler room ostensibly to help the custodian with one task or another. Harry Granger also served as bus mechanic in the shop across the alley so the boys could normally plan on using the boiler room as they saw fit.

The study hall teacher suspected that the boys went there to smoke, but since she was a smoker herself, was not unduly concerned. Besides, if she got rid of them, and, if a few others went to the library, she would feel justified in sneaking a smoke for herself in the teachers' lounge.

The boys found the boiler room vacant, but none of them had any cigarettes. They rummaged around Harry's cluttered desk and came up with his package of Red Man chewing tobacco. Some brands of the chew were flavored with ordinary molasses while the better ones contained genuine maple molasses. Neither Harry nor the boys were connoisseurs enough to tell the difference; still, if there was one thing that boys did know how to do with both impunity and gusto, that was to spit. "Time or distance, this time?" asked one of the group.

"Distance," said Rushton, he being the undisputed champion in long-range spitting.

"No way," said the others. "It's got to be for speed."

They each anteed up their quarter and lay it on the desk.

Rushton glanced up at the second hand of the wall clock and announced his intention of being score keeper and time judge as well as participant.

"Gentlemen, on your mark, get set, go!" he yelled.

The contest had scarcely begun when Mr. Wagner, the principal and coach, walked in. Caught up in the competition of the moment, no one noticed his arrival. He sized up the situation quickly, and struck by the sophomoric nature of the contest, suppressed a smile, then commanded in a carefully measured voice, "Men, as soon as you have a winner, empty the ashes and clean out all the clinkers from the boiler. Then sweep the floor and report to my office."

Wagner had no real wish to punish the boys but knew it was necessary to give them a scare. They arrived at his office looking sheepish. The man pretended to be upset and disappointed in their behavior.

"Clean up your act!" he told them. "Report to the gym on Saturday at nine AM. Wear old clothes. You're going to scrub and polish the gym floor. Now get out of here!"

Jimmy was worried on the way home about how to tell Buck about his encounter with Bascomb and waited until after his chores were done.

"Dad, what would you say if I told you that I slugged a teacher today?"

"Hmm. That's a tough one. Did he deserve it?"

"Definitely!"

"Do you feel badly about doing it?"

"No, not at all. He had it coming, but I might get expelled from school over it. Maybe he could have me arrested."

"Jim, there are worse things in life than taking some hard knocks. I'd rather you be a man who can live with himself and not be a cringer. Whatever happens you'll face it like a man, and it sounds like that's what you did today. Besides, worrying doesn't solve a damn thing. Let's have a good supper, play a couple of songs, and have a good night's sleep. Tomorrow will have to take care of itself.

Chapter 41

Miss Alice Wehrmann considered it to be in her personal best interest to keep the name of James Coulbron included in her case list, according her an excuse and opportunity to continue interviewing the boy's charming guardian. Her arrival for those rendezvous always occurred at a time when the young client was most likely to be absent.

Had it not been for the sign on the door of the county welfare automobile, Buck would have been hard-pressed to recognize the woman at the time of her second visit. Certainly he would not have recognized her by her physical appearance. Gone was the bun-and-hatpin hairdo, it having been replaced by a shoulder-length cascade of rippling auburn waves. Instead of her previous bodily attire, which emitted mixed messages at best, Miss Wehrmann's current outfit emoted smartness and allure.

Buck, having endured several months of monk-like denial of feminine companionship, was quick to erase from his memory the first encounter he had endured with the social services lady. It may be sufficient to say that a certain dreaminess suddenly appeared in the behavior of each of them.

Jimmy first noticed the changes in Buck's language. It appeared as if his vocabulary had been sterilized in an autoclave. Even more apparent were his long periods of quietude and reflection, as if sweet memories were being relived and new fantasies being created. The fact that Jimmy's father had also taken a full-time custodial job in the county offices also struck the boy as having a hidden agenda. When the boy noticed the new Buick Roadmaster as he walked down the driveway, he assumed it belonged to a visitor until he saw the unmistakable grin on Buck's face.

The boy's first inclination was to scold. "Dad, you can't afford a car like that. Your old one was good enough. Daisy has completely dried up, and there are no vegetables left in the garden. We haven't even played anywhere in two weeks."

Buck smiled, stood up, and hugged Jimmy's shoulders. "The good Lord has gone and done it again, my son. Let's go for a ride – you drive."

At school the road was bumpier. Mr. Bascomb, the mathematics teacher, stormed past the secretary and barged into the principal's office. He demanded the immediate dismissal of 'that half-breed Coulbron.' Flecks of saliva splattered on Mr. Wagner's face and eyeglasses from Bascomb's mouth as he spoke.

"If you don't act, I will," he threatened. "I'll go directly to the school board."

"I plan to discuss this myself with the chairman of the school board prior to our regular meeting on Monday. In the meantime, I order you to have no contact with James Coulbron, nor he with you. You two will keep your distance."

Principal Wagner, having spent much of his service time during World War Two as a drill sergeant was not one to be intimidated by the likes of Bascomb.

The local gossip mill worked overtime grinding out bits of fact and fiction. Old stories about the Coulbrons and Reverend Dodgson, as well as ones about Bascomb, were related with enthusiasm as the participants in this drama savored each taste of the rehash. This lead to a large crowd of concerned citizens demanding entrance into the school board chambers, forcing the proceedings to be held in the school gymnasium.

Prior to the scheduled meeting, the school faculty conducted a meeting of their own in an attempt to form a united front. After discussing the issue at length, with Bascomb playing the role of victim and chief character assassin, the resulting vote of expulsion was divided evenly on two fronts. With the exception of Bascomb, all of the teachers who knew Jimmy as one of their students voted in his favor. The others, who feared more outbreaks of violence against teachers once the walls of discipline had been breached, voted against him.

The final decision, however, was not in the hands of the faculty alone. Students made it clearly understood that they wanted a representative at the meeting. Since Father Orgebin had been transferred to an administrative post on the bishop's staff in Ogdensburg, he was unable to attend. Two of the board members had more pressing matters to attend to, leaving three to carry out the task.

Both Bascomb and Wagner were there, of course, along with other faculty members including the substitute French teacher. Some of the overflow crowd had suffered through Bascomb's classes during the fifteen years he had been at Rock Mountain and wished to have their say. The remainder were present in hopes of more salacious insight. Not a few of these had amply fortified themselves for the upcoming ordeal with their favorite rotgut. Buck did not attend, believing that his presence might rekindle old prejudices. One other person appeared, strictly, so it seemed, on behalf of the welfare department. For this occasion, Miss Alice Wehrmann wore her most businesslike outfit and hair style.

The members of the school board sat on wooden folding chairs in front of a battered oak desk. The spectators daydreamed or dozed through the board's old business involving bids for bus engine repair, federal commodities for school lunches, and similar tasks necessary for the smooth functioning of a school.

In due time, new business came up on the agenda. To start the proceedings, the school board chairman called up the principal to give some background of the problem and to present the charges. Mr. Wagner presented this factually, then took it upon himself to call to the school board's attention James' nearly perfect attendance record prior to the incident and the fact that if his grades continued as they had in the past, he stood a good chance of being a candidate for class valedictorian next year.

As he sat down, Bascomb sneered, "Not if I can help it!"

This was followed by several shouts of, "Now, you're tellin' 'em, Bascomb," and "We don't want no half-breeds trying to take over from decent people."

The teacher representative told about the faculty caucus on the matter and that the results were inconclusive.

Mr. Bascomb was given the opportunity to express his views. He launched into a vitriolic attack against Jimmy, claiming that the ungrateful brat had attacked him without provocation. At this point, one student in the audience yelled out, "You're a liar, Bascomb!"

The moderator hammered on his gavel and demanded order.

Finally, Miss Wehrmann raised her hand to speak and was recognized. She spoke eloquently, mentioning her professional need to visit with Jimmy and his guardian. She mentioned the exemplary home life she had witnessed in his household and of a loving family relationship. She extolled the lad's good manners and tractable nature.

As usual in such cases, the board voted to table the discussion and make their decision later. Everyone understood this to mean they would mull the political pros and cons amongst themselves until they could justify their decision to the voters. Although disappointed in the dearth of new revelations during the meeting, the townspeople continued to discuss their expectations concerning the outcome of the board's decision with great fervor.

Chapter 42

Alex Rushton barged out of the second-story boys' lavatory, forcing the door so violently it collided with Jimmy's shoulder. The two confronted one another. Rushton glared. "You want that little freak? He's all yours!" Then the gangly youth stormed off.

Jimmy entered the room and found Clarence standing in front of a sink trying to stem the flow of blood from his nose. It was obvious the younger boy had been roughed up and was crying. His face was tear-streaked and flushed, his clothing ruffled. Jimmy said nothing at first but grabbed paper towels to wipe off some of the blood. Then he started to apply pressure on the area between the boy's lip and nose.

"Ow! Oh!" Clarence yelled.

It was then that Jimmy noticed the splits on both of Clarence's lips. "Come on, Clare, I'll help you to the nurse's office."

"No! Alex will wreck me for good if anybody finds out about this." He spoke this between sobs and frantic but gentle dabs with the paper towel at his mouth and nose.

"Okay. We won't go to the nurse's office, but you've got to let me apply pressure. I know it's going to hurt, but you're tough. You can take it."

The bells in the hallway were sounding as Principal Wagner oversaw the flow of students into the classrooms. He was a stickler for promptness and frowned as several of the latecomers rushed so as not to be caught. He turned to re-enter his office when he observed a blur of color as a student appeared to be sneaking out of the building. Since he hadn't signed any passes for anyone's early dismissal, he decided to intercept the violator.

The school secretary was surprised to see him dash toward the window, then rush out the door. “Rushton.” he muttered as Alex Rushton walked up to an old Pontiac at the far end reserved for students and visitors. The principal watched as the youth unfolded his pocket knife and made a deep gash on a front tire of the vehicle. Air did not immediately escape, but a reddish bubble formed from the tube and swelled ominously. The perpetrator glanced left and right then headed back into the schoolhouse.

Wagner intercepted him in the hallway, spun him around, and pinned him to the wall with a viselike grip against his Adam’s apple.

Inside the washroom Jimmy had managed to stop the bleeding and cleaned up most of the splatters. Clarence’s shirt, however, was a mess and his face still swollen. They waited there as the minutes ticked away, then Clarence suggested, “Maybe if you told Mr. Wagner that I wasn’t feeling good he’d let you drive me home.”

“Sure, but won’t he want you to see the nurse first?”

“I’m pretty sure she’s at the elementary school this afternoon.”

Wagner was alone in his office when Jimmy entered. Before he had a chance to speak, the principal thundered, “What’s that smear of blood on your face? Looks like you’re in trouble again, Coulbron. If you smacked another teacher, you’ll find yourself in reform school. I stuck my neck out for you once. I won’t do it again.”

“No, not today, sir. I was helping Clarence Clement. He was having a bad nose bleed. Sir, his clothes are all bloody. Can I drive him home right now? I’ve got my car, and he lives right across from me in Echo Lake.”

“Is yours the old Pontiac? If it is you’ve got a tire to change first.”

“Yeah, that’s mine.”

“What in hell is going on between you and Rushton?”

“I’d rather not say, Mr. Wagner. It’s personal, and I can handle it.”

“Well, I hope you can handle him because you and he are going to meet in the gym tomorrow morning at seven o’clock sharp with me as a referee. You better know how to box.”

"I'll be there. How about Clarence, sir?"

"Oh, all right. Now get out of here and, for Christ's sake, try to keep out of trouble."

The boys hurried to change the tire on the car before any other students could see them, then drove toward home. Clarence still uttered a sob occasionally and wiped a tear, "I thought he was my friend, Jimmy."

"He's not your friend. He was just using you. I know all about you and him. It's not your fault, Clarence. It's that bastard Orgebin. You guys wouldn't have even thought about this stuff if he hadn't shown you."

"I'm sorry, Jimmy. If my parents find out, they'll kill me."

"Nobody's finding out. Now, tell me exactly what happened in the can."

"He wanted me to let him do it to me the other way, and I wouldn't let him. He slapped me up, and I started crying. Then he pounded my face. I'm afraid he'll try again."

"We'll see about that! I've got my own score to settle against him."

Principal Wagner arrived at a quarter to seven to unlock the school. Jimmy was there waiting. They walked into the gym together, laid out several mats, and took out two sets of boxing gloves. "Well, now," said Wagner. "Let's wait for Mr. Rushton."

A half hour went by without any sign of Rushton. "You ready to talk about this yet, Coulbron?"

"No, sir. It's best that you don't know. If the people around here knew, there would be big trouble, and you would be caught right in the middle of it. A lot of people would get hurt."

"It's my business to know. I'm calling his house."

Alex Rushton's mother answered the phone and informed him that her son was sick in bed. Wagner was on his way over to see for himself when he was interrupted by a salesman he had previously promised to meet at that time.

Since he hadn't had an opportunity nor the necessary finances to purchase a new tire, Jimmy took the school bus in the morning. Clarence was not there and Jimmy worried about him. Likewise, Rushton was absent. At lunch time one of the basketball cheerleaders delivered a note to Jimmy:

Meet me after school alone in the alley behind the boiler room. You know who.

The girl was awaiting his reply in writing. Although he wanted to have it out with Rushton, he sensed a trap, thinking that bastard had his chance so I know he's yellow. He'll have his whole team there ready to beat the crap out of me. I can handle one or two of them but not the whole damn bunch.

Jimmy turned the paper over and scrawled:

Nuts to you!

Then he folded it and handed it to the messenger. "Make sure that the creep gets this."

"You better be careful, Jimmy," she said. "He means business."

"So do I. Now, go do your dirty job."

Principal Wagner felt so frustrated by Rushton's refusal to meet Jimmy with the gloves on, that the next morning he escorted his basketball center to school and marched him to the gym where Jimmy waited. Also in attendance as spectators were the other four game starters and Clarence Clement.

The bout didn't last long. After the second round, Rushton was bleeding freely and stumbling blindly while Jimmy danced around him jabbing and twisting his gloves with each thrust. He remembered the tussle he had in elementary school, and sank his right fist into Rushton's solar plexus. Rushton sank to the floor and crawled away on all fours. He covered his head with his gloves and cringed in a fetal position.

His team mates stared at him, sneering. As a group, they walked over to Wagner. “Coach,” said one of the forwards, “it’s time we elect a new captain.”

Clarence rushed onto the mats to untie the winner’s gloves.

Chapter 43

The members of the Rock Mountain District Free School Board met in secret session in the back room of the Sweet Taste Café to mull over school matters before meeting as an official group where voters might be present. This wasn't illegal at the time but was frowned on by some. Over sticky pastries and insipid coffee, they hashed over two matters – one was the teacher slugging incident; the other, the teacher contract extension.

After lengthy discussion and licking of sticky fingers, the honored group decided that since this situation smacked of political overtones which might affect their re-election, they decided to take the invalorous way out. They turned the decision over to the principal. After all, they argued, he is the chief disciplinarian, and they should not interfere in his decision-making. Now, on to more pressing problems.

Board secretary Wayne Paulachek revealed information his daughter had told him about her math teacher's incompetence, she being present at the time of the incident between Bascomb and James Coulbron. Mrs. Koivunen, the lone female representative, and also the youngest, related that she had had Mr. Bascomb as a teacher some years ago and felt that she, too, had been shortchanged in his classes. These comments, together with the principal's written reports, confirmed their decision to not renew Bascomb's contract at the end of the school year. If they could not find a suitable replacement, they could always do some reshuffling of faculty.

Jimmy awaited the results of the school board's decision, and realizing that he could be expelled, he began to reminisce about his days at Echo Lake and Rock Mountain High School. Sixth grade was the last year that Jimmy had attended the little one-room school at Echo

Lake, the district having decided during a town meeting to send the scholars from seventh to twelfth grade to the village high school at Rock Mountain.

This iron mining village spread out on the western slope of the mountain and extended across a flat before dipping steeply down the mountain toward the shore of Crystal Lake.

The style of house construction and the structures' locations gave an indication of their age. The very oldest homes were squat log buildings crafted from round logs. These were irregularly spaced among conical-shaped heaps of gray ore tailings which rose more than a hundred feet high in several locations.

Ore-bearing rock had been blasted loose from within the bowels of the mine and hauled, first by mules and later by electric-powered ore cars. Emanating from the powerhouse at ground level, thick woven-steel cables spun over two gigantic pulleys on top of the headframe and were attached to the mine elevators. One of the cars transported helmeted miners to and from diggings; the other hauled ore to the surface.

On the surface stood the concentrator where the shiny crystals of black magnetite, embedded in the granite, was removed by means of grinding and magnetic separation. Although some of the waste rock could be used for road construction and other purposes, most of it had simply been disposed of by dumping it outside the mine. Conveyor belts extended in a radial pattern from the mine so that, not infrequently, the gray dunes encroached peoples' yards right up to the foundations of the houses.

In this dismal setting it was not uncommon to see first generation grandmothers, their white hair covered with babushkas, tending beds of red roses and pink petunias while thinking, perhaps, of their husbands who had perished suddenly in accidents at the mine or succumbed more slowly to the silicon dust that invaded the life-sustaining sacs of their lungs.

One can assume with reasonable certainty, and by the stories told by old-timers, that over the years as the piles of ore tailings grew, miners and their families were obliged to surrender their homes to the approaching dunes. Legally, this posed no problem to the mine owners since this was, in every sense of the term, a 'company town', that is to say, controlled. The Crystal Mining Company could do no wrong.

On the other hand, a strong measure of paternalism compensated, in part, for the company's behavior. Rent was very cheap, practically subsidized. Neither the grocery store nor the gas station overcharged unduly. Coal, for heating, was reasonably priced and delivered to one's door. Health care, although rather basic, was provided essentially free by the company doctor, old Doc Manvel.

Except for the oldest of the houses, those inhabited by aged widows and pensioners, there was running water and a sewage system which operated with reasonable efficiency. Those without the modern conveniences relied on a strategically-placed town well and individual privies.

Perpendicular to the log homes, stretched Pullman Avenue, aptly named after the railroad passenger cars which had been bulldozed into place as temporary homes about the time of the Great War when a need for additional housing arose. The rail cars had been gutted of seats or sleeping lofts and replaced with partitions and made into snug homes.

On certain prominent and tree-lined streets, there rose a dozen or more cast concrete duplexes, rather stark on the exterior but said to be 'very nice inside.'

A hodge-podge of other styles peppered the hillside and extended down to the flats. The level area had been created by filling in a watery swamp fed by Greenwater Creek. The fill for the capital improvement of the townsite came, as one might expect, from huge piles of ore sand. The tailings had the added attraction of being uniform in texture, making it easy to bulldoze and spread. In time, the sand fill could even be coaxed into producing a passable lawn. Excluding frogs and water striders, no inhabitants of the area objected to the project.

The twenties was a time of relative prosperity and high employment. The company therefore, decided to construct a new high school out on the flats. This was a concrete block structure whose façade was covered with rose-colored stucco and metal curlicue decorations on the windows.

Behind the school lay the school grounds. The sand, intermixed with swamp muck, had become reasonably well compacted over the years by thousands of young feet. Overrun with pig weeds and Canada thistles, it provided a place for softball games and a general expenditure of excess energy.

The fact that there was no playground equipment in working condition except for three swings did not strike the inmates of this establishment of learning as unusual. This was their school and, since it was the most palatial building most of them had ever seen, they had respect and pride in it.

Despite this, noxious fumes tended to invade the corridors and classrooms on those days when the coal-fired furnace was not operating correctly, although the interior was spotlessly clean. The narrow-slatted maple floors gleamed with new varnish each September. No flaking paint could be seen except for a few high spots on the ceiling of the combined gymnasium and auditorium.

On the other hand, the cafeteria was quite dank and musty. No food was cooked or even served here any longer. The coal-burning ranges had not been fired up in years. The kitchen had been closed during the depression of the thirties when many men were out of work and students could eat at home more cheaply. Only the bus students ate there now, usually in three separate corners so as not to have to associate with 'them other bums.'

The building had been well furnished when it was first built. In the chemistry room students sat at lab tables that had individual sinks for experiments. The table tops were impervious to acids and other spills. By the time the forties arrived, however, two decades of reluctant scholiasts had vandalized the sinks and scratched their initials on every available inch of the desks' surfaces. One microscope, nevertheless, was still capable of focusing. This was now kept locked inside the teacher's desk.

In those halcyon days, the school even boasted of a football team and a band. The team equipment and the musical instruments had been donated by the mining company. During the depression so many boys quit school to look for work that the football program was dropped. The band continued, peopled mostly by girls and junior-high boys. The girls also took pride in their glee club, and not a few managed to pierce their fingers in the treadle-powered sewing machines.

There were four social groups in Rock Mountain High School. The children of the upper mining staff considered themselves as the chosen ones, and more than a few of the faculty members showed them favors that they denied other scholars. Grading practices may also have entered in since school board members nearly always came from the elite of the community, and insecure teachers sought to placate them.

The offspring of the miners needed someone to look down on so the lowest social status was foisted upon the bus kids. There were three separate bus routes and, rather than joining together to oppose the town snobs, one group of country kids would often behave fractiously against the others.

The divisiveness was most strongly apparent among the seventh and eighth graders so that by the time students were in their junior year, the student body had melded more or less into one.

As a seventh grader, Jimmy learned to enjoy the full hour given for lunch break. He would eat his sack lunch in the cafeteria or, on nice days, out on the steps of the auditorium. Then he would walk uptown to the general store. The downstairs was for groceries, but upstairs a great variety of goods were to be found and stared at. Several times Jimmy had bought inexpensive earrings or bracelets for his mother, which she never chose to wear.

Only once during his first few years at Rock Mountain was Jimmy ever harassed at school. Three town boys Jimmy's age had begun following him from school to the store while calling disparaging remarks along the way. He said nothing the first time. The next day when they repeated their action, he confronted them outside the store, lifted their leader up, and threw him to the ground. Then he knelt on his chest, and placed his fingers and thumb on the opposite sides of the boy's windpipe. This lasted only a few seconds before Jimmy stood up and asked, "Who's next? How about you, Stephanovich?" The three ran away.

Mining at Rock Mountain began around the time of the Civil War as the digging of ore to supply the needs of local forges and blacksmith shops sent workmen to pry or blast loose chunks of rich black ore. There were several outcroppings of iron ore in the area, and each of these became pockmarked over the years until serious attempts at underground mining started in earnest with the building of a narrow-gauge railroad right to the site of the diggings.

Coal and iron interests in Pennsylvania possessed the capital to exploit and develop the mine. Nearby at Crystal Lake they built a Catalan forge where the ore was reduced to iron with the aid of locally-produced charcoal. The lumps of iron were formed into blooms through a steam-powered stamping process to produce wrought iron, much in demand by an expanding nation. The wrought iron, in many ways similar to steel, found its way into many products from locomotives and bridges to small tools and decorative filigree.

Later a blast furnace, also fueled by charcoal, would replace the forge bringing with it greater efficiency but also increased denuding of the forests. Jimmy knew the location of several of the abandoned charcoal kilns and even talked to old timers who had worked as charcoalers, arranging the hardwood logs into carefully placed piles, covering them over with sawdust and sod so that a barely smoldering fire would carry out the process. By Jimmy's time, however, coke from Pennsylvania had replaced charcoal.

Thousands of acres of hardwood trees were cut down to feed the hungry forge first and following that the blast furnace. The softwood forest supplied timbers for the mines, railroad ties, and building material for homes. Not far away at Plattsburg, the demand was for pulpwood for paper products. All of these drew heavily from nature's storehouse. Then, because of forest slashings left in the woods and a series of dry years, forest fires erupted, further reducing the forests.

Jimmy and his brother Phil were born too late to see many of the great trees. They did, however, marvel at the huge blackened stumps that served as monuments to them. In their place a second growth of birch and aspen predominated, sprinkled heavily in places with dark spruce and hemlock while cedar and tamarack filled in the lower, swampy sites.

Benevolent nature acted to restore the forests so that trees of respectable size flourished once again. Here and there, on certain southern slopes, favored by early morning sun and rich soil, groves of gnarled maples and handsome smooth-barked beeches of considerable size still grew.

This, too, both village and forest, was Jimmy's world.

Chapter 44

The get-together after school started off innocently enough. Tadpole had passed the word around to Jimmy that a few of the guys were going over to Vera's house to talk into and listen to her new wire recorder. None of them had used one before. Even the school had not accepted this technological advance as being of sufficient educational value to justify the expense.

Three classmates, Vince, Charlie, and Tadpole, hopped into the car with Jimmy, and they drove over to Vera's house. Her parents having gone shopping in Malone, the kids were free to relax. The three other girls had already arrived when the boys swaggered onto the front porch. Margie invited them in, then joined Helen, Marlene, and Vera in the kitchen as they giggled and stirred up some lemonade.

The boys sprawled their gangly arms and legs on the overstuffed chairs and on the sofa. They kidded one another while tossing decorator pillows around which they were pretending were big breasts as they pressed them against their own chests. Tadpole extracted the straight pins from one of the crocheted doilies which served to protect the upholstery from hair oil and perspiration. With no girls watching at the moment, he rolled the doily into a cylinder and jammed it into his crotch creating a dainty white phallus. It was unstarched, and when he released his grip, the pretend appendage drooped limply.

The boys howled in laughter.

"Poor Tad," said Vince, "he doesn't have much to begin with, and now he can't even keep it up."

They heard the girls coming, and Tad tossed the doily behind the sofa.

"Ah, refreshments," gushed Charlie. "I hope you got passion fruit in that juice."

"Yeah!" said Tad, "he needs it to get going every morning."

"You guys!" complained Helen half-heartedly. "It's just plain, old-fashioned lemonade."

"I'll bet it's made with virgin lemons," quipped Vince. "I've always wanted to squeeze a virgin, uh, lemon, that is."

"You probably wouldn't know how," said Vera.

Tad countered with, "I'm willing to learn, willing to squeeze, and willing to please."

"Oh, you guys!" said Helen again.

Vera plugged in the wire recorder and placed it on the coffee table which she carried into the center of the room. Then she connected the microphone, unwrapped the mike cord, and inserted the power cord. "C'mon, everybody, let's sit around in a circle."

"I know a game we could play around in a circle."

"Shut up, Tad," whispered Charlie.

The kids took turns speaking into the microphone and listening to the playback, each exclaiming, "I don't sound like that, do I?"

In truth, the quality of the recording was poor. It sounded treble-pitched and was distorted rather comically; yet it was innovative and exciting for them.

It wasn't long after the introductions and preliminaries that the boys began telling raunchy jokes into the microphone and laughing riotously after each punch line. Jimmy remained aloof from most of this, smiling occasionally and not complaining. He enjoyed the give and take of other teenagers but, being a country kid, school was his only chance to socialize, other than talking with Clarence and riding the school bus.

Vera noticed the glasses were empty so she gathered them up and brought them into the kitchen for refilling. She laid the tray on the counter and glanced around to see that the swinging door had closed completely behind her. Then she reached up and opened a cabinet door, revealing one of her mother's vodka bottles. After unscrewing the bottle top, she poured a slug of the colorless liquid into each glass, giving the boys an extra measure. Then she added the lemonade and stirred the glasses with a spoon. She tasted a spoonful and gave a little smile. Shrugging her shoulders once, she walked into the dining room, and played the role of friendly hostess.

When she returned, Charlie was telling the story of the lumberjacks way out in the woods who solved their sexual needs by making love to a wooden barrel. The only problem being that they each had to take his turn one night a week sleeping inside the barrel.

"Oh, you guys! I'm not going to listen to this," Helen protested as she squatted closer to Tad and held his hand.

"Come on, Jimmy," coaxed Marlene. "You haven't told a single story yet."

"I guess I can't remember them very well."

"Don't be a spoil sport."

"Well, okay, but remember, you asked for it."

By this time the teenagers were beginning to feel the effects of the alcohol, although, except for Vera, they were unaware of the cause of their diminished inhibition.

"Well, this story takes place in an elementary school room where little Johnny, who's not too bright, sits in the back row."

Vince poked Tadpole, remembering Tad's lewd behavior in Bascomb's class.

"Anyhow, the teacher is very enthusiastically teaching about punctuation. 'Today's lesson is on exclamation points'. She explains that exclamation points are used to attract people's attention or cause excitement. Then she asks, 'Who can think of a word that would cause excitement?'

"Little Susie, the teacher's pet, raises her hand and waves it violently."

'That's nice, Susie. Come up and write your word on the board, and then make an exclamation point right after it.'

"Susie goes to the board and writes 'Halt!' 'Very, very good!' says the teacher.

"This continues with words like 'Fire!' and so forth until the little darlings can't think of any more exciting words. The teacher is ready to go onto other things when Johnny raises his hand.

"Yes, Johnny, what is it? Do you have to go to the bathroom, again?"

The teenagers all laugh at this, and Jimmy continues. "'No, no,' says Johnny. 'I want to write on the board, too.'

'All right, but hurry up.'

"Johnny walks to the board proudly and draws two dots followed by an exclamation point."

"The teacher is very surprised and asks, 'What's so exciting about two periods?'"

"'I don't know,' says Johnny, 'but my big sister came home from school yesterday and told Mother that she had missed two periods. That caused an awful lot of excitement in our house.'"

This time, it was the girls who doubled up in laughter, but Vince and Charlie didn't get it so Tad had to explain it to them.

Once again, Vera refilled the enriched lemonade and the stories continued until they grew bored with the activity and abandoned the recorder in favor of paring off for hand holding and mild petting.

Vera sidled up to Jimmy and snuggled next to him, sighing seductively. Feeling happy and relaxed, he went along with this although he had never considered the girl particularly attractive. Soon the couples drifted out of the room one at a time and went elsewhere in the house.

Vera took Jimmy by the hand and led him to the basement. He noticed a rec room filled with old furniture and a phonograph. She smiled and put on a record. The music of 'Kiss of Fire' began slowly, its beat obvious, and Vera took hold of Jimmy's hands to dance. She held him close and gyrated her body against his groin. She sang with the recording, 'I know I must surrender to that kiss of fire.'

Jimmy moved zombielike, his head fuzzy from the drinks. Vera led him to the sofa, unbuttoned his shirt and massaged his chest. She felt his pectoral muscles and biceps while humming in appreciation. They lay side by side and petted.

He thought of Buck's admonition, 'It'll happen sooner than you think. Use a rubber.' He could feel the pressure rising in his privates.

"Vera, wait."

"I can't wait. I'll kill myself if I can't have you right now."

"Okay, okay. Hold on a minute. In my wallet. I've got a rubber."

She reached over his body, pulled out his wallet, and handed it to him. Then she unbuttoned his fly and skinned off his trousers and shorts. She kissed his aroused member lightly, then gave him a juicy, smothering French kiss on the mouth.

Immediately, two odors assaulted him – the smell of liquor on her breath and the perfume – his mother's perfume. The memory of his mother molesting him made his face burn. Vera had her blouse and brassiere off and was rubbing her nipples in his face.

Roughly he pushed her away from him and stood up, facing away from her.

"I can't," he said. "I'm sorry, I just can't."

He dressed quickly while Vera made fun of him. She stood directly in front and shouted, "Next time, I'll find me a real man!"

She flung the condom in his face saying, "Here, little boy, go blow up your balloon."

He drove away, his face stinging with shame, and left his classmates behind. Soon he realized that he couldn't see well enough to drive safely. He was trying to focus on the center line. It seemed to keep jumping all over the road. A car approached from the other direction and swerved out of his way, its horn blaring.

Jimmy allowed his car to slow to a crawl. He noticed a section of the old road which had been abandoned when the state realigned it before spreading concrete. He eased the car off the pavement and down the old road where the engine stalled on a hill. He shut off the ignition and slept.

It was dark when he awoke. His head throbbed, and he shivered from the cold. He stepped outside to relieve himself, and the dry heaves started. His face felt flushed and his mouth watered. Then the vomiting erupted. He smelled the alcohol on himself and retched even more violently.

He thought about Buck, knowing he would have had supper ready hours ago and would be worried about him. He wondered what time it might be and how he got himself in this mess. He didn't know how he could explain it to anyone. He wondered if Vera would tell the other girls about his inability to be a man, or even worse, tell the guys.

When Jimmy turned off the highway and was heading down the drive to the farmhouse, he flicked off the headlights, not wanting Buck to know he was coming. It surprised him to see that dawn was breaking already.

He walked into the kitchen because Buck had left the lights on. He read the note saying that his supper was covered and on low in the oven. He removed the pie tin filled with pork chops and mashed potatoes, and he smelled them. His stomach revolted at the smell of food, and he struggled to keep from retching. He placed the food in the refrigerator, shut off the stove, and tip-toed up the stairs.

At first he thought that Buck was asleep, but as he moved past the man's open bedroom door, he saw his eyes blink. There was no sound except that of his stocking feet on the hall floor. He undressed quickly, tossing his shirt and slacks on the floor, and burrowed himself into the safety of his bed.

Chapter 45

"Dad, the cow's almost dried up. I guess we're going to have to buy milk pretty soon," said the boy at breakfast.

"Okay, Jim. I'll pick up a couple of quarts on the way home from work. Can you think of anything else for me to pick up?"

"There's a list on the refrigerator. We are all out of meat."

"I'll get some steak or something."

"Yeah, that would be fine, but we do have a couple of pigs left."

"Now, Jim, old buddy, I don't think a pig will hold still for long enough if I plop her onto a sizzling skillet."

"Haven't you ever butchered a pig? It's no big deal."

"No, I haven't. I told you that you're the farmer around here. Can you do it?"

"I've never done it alone. I've helped David and Phil lots of times."

"I suppose I could help if you're sure you know what to do. What do you do, shoot her?"

"No. David was really good at sticking them. He showed me exactly how to do it so that the animal doesn't suffer. They just seem to fall asleep. I've still got the knife he always used."

"Let's talk about it tonight. I've got to hurry or I'll be late for work."

"Sure, Dad."

Jimmy washed the breakfast dishes and got ready for school. He rarely took the school bus anymore, now that Buck was giving him a monthly allowance. Their income from the band had diminished because they only played an occasional weekend engagement. In addition to the gospel shows, however, they played at a few bars and filled in at square dances. Buck also was called upon to sing at weddings and funerals by people who had heard him play at churches.

Now, whenever they did play and sing together, Alice, the social worker, always came with them. Jimmy would drive the big Roadmaster while Buck and Alice sat in the back seat. After the first of these trips the boy decided to turn the rear view mirror up high enough so that he wouldn't be distracted by the amorous activity which was occurring behind him. There was nothing improper, but it was obvious to the boy that his father and girlfriend were very much enamored of one another.

Jimmy had wondered how Buck could afford such an expensive car. One evening he came right out and asked, "Dad, did you win a jackpot or something? I don't see you making payments on your Buick, and I know you didn't have that kind of cash."

"Well, son, when you've got it, you've got it. I guess I've still got it."

"Got what?"

"Sex appeal! The ladies still have their eyes on me, and from what I hear, they're after you, too."

"Are you saying that Miss Wehrmann gave you cash for that car?"

"No. She did loan me the money, though. I'm paying her back from my monthly checks. Enough of that story. Are you ready to tell me what happened that night you got in so late? I suppose you finally got yourself laid real proper."

"I didn't mean to pry about the car, Dad. As for my coming home so late, I've been trying to think of a way to explain it."

"You don't have to if you don't want to."

"I do want to. It's just that it's so darn embarrassing. I nearly got myself in bad trouble. This will sound like I'm making excuses, and maybe I am. It's all mixed up in my mind."

"Don't hold it in if it bothers you. Let it out. That way you can get rid of it."

"Okay, I got so drunk I was weaving all over the road and almost smashed into another car. That's why I pulled over on the side of the road and slept it off."

"How do you feel about the drinking now?"

"I was as sick as a dog then, and now I'm ashamed that it happened."

"You're under age. Where did you get the booze?"

"That's just the point. We were at a party, and one of the girls must have spiked our lemonade. We were having a lot of fun for a while. Then things got out of hand."

"Do you want to tell me about it?"

"A girl undressed me and wanted me to make love to her. She was all over me."

"Did you want to do it?"

"My body wanted to, but my mind didn't. I remembered my mother, and I felt too ashamed to do it."

"You probably wouldn't have enjoyed it anyhow. Sex is no good when you're drunk. You did the right thing. Your time is coming. You don't have to rush it."

"You should have heard her when I refused her. She kept yelling at me and shaming me, telling me I wasn't a man. She'll probably tell everybody in school about it."

"I seriously doubt that. She may be more ashamed than you are. Besides, in another year or so you won't even be associating with any of these people. You'll each be going your own way. And your way is going to be the best college we can afford."

"College? Me?"

"Why not? You've got the brains for it. You could be a doctor or a lawyer, anything you want."

"Gosh Dad, I don't know."

"Think about it. Ask your principal about scholarships."

"Okay, I will."

David Coulbron had always waited until after Thanksgiving to butcher a hog. That way refrigeration was less of a problem. Sometimes he would bring the fresh hams and bellies to a man who would cure them by soaking them in brine and smoking them. Other times, he would simply hang the carcass upside down from a beam in the garage, and the family would consume it from the bottom to the top, starting with a neck roast and ending with pan-fried or broiled fresh ham. Jimmy and Buck decided to try the latter method since the weather was now staying below freezing much of the time.

That Saturday, Jimmy rose early and built an open wood fire close to an overhanging limb of a beech tree. Buck watched as the boy rolled a fifty-gallon steel barrel next to the fire. He braced a stout elm plank between the trunk of the beech and a small boulder so that the barrel rested at a forty-five degree angle with the open end of the barrel facing upward.

"What's that for?" asked the man.

"You really are a greenhorn about butchering, aren't you?" he said with a smile.

"It just seems so complicated. Why can't we just stab the animal, cut off a chunk, and fry it up?"

"I suppose you could if you were starving to death, but you should bleed the carcass thoroughly and cool the meat right away before it spoils. Besides, we have to shave her."

"Now, hold on right there. I admit to being a greenhorn, but you must be pulling my leg. Why do you have to shave the pig?"

"You wouldn't have to but, if you didn't, you'd have pig bristles on your ham and bacon. Of course, you could always use them as toothpicks."

"Okay, okay, you're in charge. I'll believe everything you say. What's next?"

"Water. We can take turns hauling from the creek on the other side of the barn. There's a nice little pool there where the cow drinks. Watch out for my little rainbow trout, though."

"Why, is it vicious like a piranha?"

"No, I just don't want him to get scooped up by mistake. He's sort of a pet. I think he hangs around the pool because sometimes there are pieces of cornmeal on the pail when I dip it in to get water, and the trout seems to expect that. It comes out and eats the cornmeal. Once I scooped him out by mistake but put him back right away. He's really pretty with a rosy stripe on his side."

"I promise to watch out for him. Where's the buckets? I'll bring the first load."

"Inside the shed. You can use the shoulder yoke to make it easier to carry the water. It used to belong to David's grandfather. He hand-carved it out of maple."

Jimmy split more firewood while Buck hauled water and poured it into the barrel. When the man sat down to rest, the boy finished hauling water.

"I think we should go have our breakfast now. The fire is really roaring and, as soon as the water starts steaming, we should take care of the pig."

"Does the poor critter get a last meal before the execution?"

"Not really. I will coax her out with some corn meal though."

"Why do you keep saying 'her?' Why not kill that horny old boar over there?"

"David said that you shouldn't butcher an older boar until after he's been stripped for a while."

"Stripped? What do you mean stripped?"

"You know – castrated."

"I suppose you know how to do that, too?"

"I could if I had to, but I was thinking that maybe we should sell him as a breeder. Some day we may have to get rid of all of the animals."

After breakfast, Jimmy stoked the fire again and seemed satisfied that the water was heating properly. Buck had hauled two more pails of cold water and this was standing to one side.

"Well, fellow executioner, do you want to select the victim or do I have to be the bad guy?" asked Jimmy.

"How about eeny meeny miny mo?"

"Okay with me. These sows were never named, and I can't tell them apart anyway."

Jimmy walked into the pen carrying a pail filled with a small amount of grain. He called "Pig, pig," and showed the pail to the animals as he backed out the gate. Both tried to follow, but as soon as one came out, Buck closed the gate against the other. The sow followed the pail to the slaughtering area next to the fire.

The boy allowed the animal to eat a few mouthfuls, then instructed Buck to hold her hind legs as he grasped one front leg and pulled it toward him. The sow slipped to her side and Jimmy petted the back of her neck. He readied David's thin, long knife and laid it next to him as he pressed against the side of the animal's windpipe. David had taught him the spot, and immediately he sensed the pulsing. With his finger tips he followed the carotid artery of the sow down to the point where the heartbeat seemed to diminish.

The pig did not struggle because Buck kept its hind feet from digging in. It grunted peacefully. Jimmy held the knife in his teeth while he made one last check for the pulse, then with slow slices he made an incision through the skin. He placed the blade tip at the site of the incision and angled it toward the animal's heart. Almost effortlessly, he pressed the blade into the artery so that it punctured the aorta.

He removed the blade and laid it on a stump. Immediately great spurts of blood gushed from the wound, at first arching a foot or more from the opening but then in decreasing amounts. He knelt to one side so as not to soak his work clothes and glanced up at Buck. He saw the man's face blanch and his eyes began to flicker.

"Okay, Dad, you can let go. Why don't you rest for a minute on the stump?"

Buck was close to fainting and followed his son's advice.

"They sure have a lot of blood, don't they?"

"Yeah! That's a fact. Mom used to make pudding from the blood when she was feeling better."

"Pudding? You mean blood pudding?"

"Sure, only we called it *'boudin'*. Some people would wash out the pig's intestines and force the pudding in to make sausages, but Mom just poured it into a bread pan to harden. Then we'd slice it and fry it."

"I suppose that now you're going to tell me that you could make that, too."

"No, I never watched her make it. I was too busy helping David with the gutting and scraping. I think she used to put small pieces of fat in the blood and cook it with nutmeg and cinnamon. I used to really like it. You can buy it in the store if you want to try some. It'll be in sausage links, though."

"Thanks, but no thanks."

"Then, you probably wouldn't care for the head cheese either."

"I don't want to even hear about that."

Jimmy used the knife to slice an opening between the bones of the sow's back legs and the tendons. Then he inserted a three-foot hardwood branch about an inch and a half thick between the bone and tendon. He tossed a rope over the beech limb above them and tied one end to the stick.

"Okay, partner, let's hoist away."

Pulling together on the rope they raised the carcass of the animal and submerged it in the steaming water. Then they slid it out onto the slanted plank. Jimmy took a wide-bladed butcher knife and scraped against the bristles. Some of these were shaved off but most resisted.

"Gotta give her another bath. The bristles haven't softened enough yet."

Once again the carcass was dipped into the hot water, this time a bit longer. When they tried scraping against the bristles the second time, they shaved off easily. Together they rolled the animal onto a wooden table consisting of planks laid across two sawhorses. They scraped steadily, tossing the cut bristles onto the thin layer of snow that covered the ground. Whenever the bristles seemed to become difficult to shave, the boy would scoop a pail of hot water from the barrel and splash it on this carcass.

When the scraping was finished, they stood back to admire their work. "What's next, partner?" asked Buck, wiping his brow with the back of his hand.

"We'll tip the barrel over so it's out of the way, then we'll lift her up again and gut her."

They left the leg spreader attached and now they hoisted the carcass, then snubbed the rope to secure it. The animal was raised high enough so that the disembowelment was easier. First, the boy cut carefully around the anus and vulva of the sow. This being freed, he took a cord from his pocket and secured it around the dangling flesh.

"That's so that she doesn't have an accident on us and mess up any meat."

"Yuck! Now I know why I'm not a farmer."

"Look at it this way, Dad. If a person is going to eat meat, he should do some butchering at least once to know what it's all about. Otherwise, he should become a vegetarian, but then he might start feeling sorry for the poor little string bean babies he was gobbling up."

"I guess you're right, Jim. This is surely an education for me."

Carefully, the boy opened the abdominal cavity using two fingers inserted inside to slightly lift the skin and press back the intestines at the same time.

"When David was doing this he would always say 'Thirty years a butcher, and I never split a gut.' I hope I don't split one now. That would be a mess."

When the intestines began to tumble down, he reached up inside the body cavity to finish cutting around the anus and reproductive organs. He pulled this into the cavity so it dropped out along with the rest of the offal.

Buck had expected the intestines to smell bad and was surprised to only sense the odor of fresh meat. He noticed the maroon kidneys lying next to the backbone, and was amazed at the size of the liver as well as the fact that it looked bluish.

"How about liver and sow belly for supper, Pop?"

"Well, I'm not so sure. Oh, what the heck. Liver and sow belly it is. I might even invite Alice."

"I'd like her to come to have dinner with us, but let's wait until we have some nice pork roast or some chops."

"Good idea, Jim."

Buck watched as his son completed the evisceration, saving the liver but discarding the rest. The boy used a handsaw to sever the head and then sloshed cold water inside the body cavity and over the outside to hurry the cooling.

A little earlier when Buck was scraping the belly he accidently sliced off a nipple. Holding it up, he asked, "What am I supposed to do with this?"

"Well, you could save it to chew on when you're lonesome. Maybe it'll remind you of an old girlfriend."

"Hey, kid, you got to watch yourself. You're getting worse than I am."

They smiled at one another, enjoying the repartee and work that continued to strengthen the bond. "What do we do with the head and guts?"

"I'll just haul them into the woods with the sled. The crows will take care of them in a couple of days."

They lay the carcass on a tarpaulin and skidded it into the garage where they hung it once again to finish cooling.

Chapter 46

Miss Faye Morgan was a college student with plans. She had no intention of wasting her time becoming so involved in frivolous co-ed activities that her real-life goals were compromised or delayed. It's not that she viewed her classmates' sorority involvement disdainfully nor their idle chatter about boyfriends with derision, it was simply that she knew that she wished to have the opportunity to teach high school students as soon as possible. Her vehicle for achieving this goal was the foreign language section of the education department at New York State Normal School at Albany.

She had a boyfriend who was a business major there. In a way, she was hoping that taking a job up north would help cool down a relationship that was growing more heated than she wished.

When she was in high school, two teachers had inspired her. One was Miss Fairbanks who taught her math, the other was Mr. Maubrey who had actually lived for a year in Paris and now was teaching high school French. Although she enjoyed all of her classes, her exposure to foreign language and foreign culture seemed to be special, and she wanted other young people to share this exotic experience. Mr. Maubrey had infused in her the noble love for teaching by his daily example.

For her, he was the epitome of gentility. He was suave, cultured, and so very sophisticated. He was moderately tall. His brown hair was immaculately trimmed as was his mustache. To Faye Morgan, his voice seemed so powerful, so mature, so in charge. Yet, this adolescent adoration on her part was strictly limited to academic considerations. She summarily dismissed any romantic fantasies concerning her teacher, which inadvertently crept from time to time into her psyche. He was her psychological mentor only, her model. Because of him, she too, would inspire young men and women as they were approaching adulthood.

The young man in her life, Ronald Swanson II, was a daddy's boy using college as an opportunity to have some fun and grow up while waiting his chance to follow in his father's footsteps in the family business. She had known him in high school, and for now he added a certain diversion from her academic life.

The availability of summer sessions at Albany State Normal School made it possible for Faye to shorten the time she spent in college. At first she had intended to graduate in three years, but certain advanced classes were not offered when she needed them, and, as a result, she did not graduate until the end of the first semester of her fourth year.

Normally, a new teacher would have all summer to select a teaching position. Graduating out of the normal sequence complicated this. She had resigned herself to the possibility that her first real teaching would be as a substitute. When she saw the announcement that there was a full-time opening for a French teacher just as she was about to receive her diploma in December, she phoned Rock Mountain immediately to arrange an interview with the principal.

The Delaware and Hudson train that headed north from Albany was powered by a steam locomotive. Directly behind the engine was the coal car, followed by a single passenger car, a mail car, and three enclosed box cars with the red, wooden caboose bringing up the rear. The first stop was Troy. Here the train juggled back and forth on a siding, abandoning two of the box cars and replacing them with another.

Miss Morgan was aboard that December morning along with a smattering of other travelers. At the Troy station, one passenger departed and was replaced by two others. She watched as her train huffed past a row of open cars filled with black chunks of a substance she did not recognize.

"Excuse me," she said to the two men who had just boarded, "Could either of you gentlemen tell me what is in those cars?"

"That's coke, ma'am. It's hauled here on barges on the canal. Some of it comes by train, though. Most likely we'll be hooking on to them and dropping them off at the iron mines near the blast furnaces up north."

"Oh, really! What mines do they go to?"

"Well, there are several. I suppose they'll drop some off at Mineville first, then go on to Rock Mountain. They'll use the same cars to haul the pig iron down here."

"You must live around here."

"Yes, ma'am. You see over there by those tall smoke stacks? I work in that steel plant. The rumor going around is that the blast furnace at Rock Mountain is going to close soon, and then the company will only ship its sintered ore here."

"I see. Won't that put people out of work there?"

"I suppose so. Maybe some of them could get jobs here because we'll have to expand."

"Yes, I do hope so."

She was glad that she had long, cotton stockings covering her legs and overshoes over her shoes because outside the temperature struggled to reach ten degrees. Inside the day coach, a pot-bellied stove attempted in vain to moderate the temperature. There was no conductor on board, and so Mr. Garrity, the fireman, was obliged to stoke the coal stove each time the train stopped at a station or refilled with water at a conveniently placed storage tank. It wasn't every day that a passenger the likes of Miss Morgan was aboard, and, on this occasion, the onerous task was lightened.

"I beg your pardon, Sir," she said, "will the train be on time at Rock Mountain?"

"Oh, yes, Miss. Four o'clock sharp. Are you visiting relatives there?"

"No, I'm interviewing for a teaching job at the high school. Do you know if there is a good place to stay at Rock Mountain?"

"Well, there is a hotel. Whether it's good or not, I can't say. It's right above the bar, and some of the miners who room at the hotel can get pretty rowdy. Most of the single teachers live at the teacherage. They have rooms in a duplex right across from the school. Maybe you can stay there. If not, telephone Mrs. Manvel, the doctor's wife; she knows everybody and will find you a nice clean place to spend the night."

"Why, thank you. What is Rock Mountain like?"

"It's a mining town. What more can I say? If it's your home, I suppose you learn to like it. Oh, say, I've got some hot coffee up in the cab. Would you like some?"

"Thank you, I really would. I did bring a lunch along in case I get hungry but the coffee would be marvelous."

From her window seat on the right side of the car she had watched the mists of water vapor steaming on the Hudson River, and now she observed them again as they crossed the Mohawk River which was part of the Barge Canal system. Briefly she recalled snatches of her courses in American history, how this area had been important during colonial days. There were stories still told of Indian massacres and of the French and Indian War battles as well as the defeat of British General Burgoyne at Saratoga. She had read all of Fenimore Cooper's 'Leather-Stocking Tales' and tried to imagine living then and meeting Indians. She was heading into 'Deerslayer' country, and she smiled as she thought about the Deerslayer and Uncas as well as Chingachgook and his lovely maiden, Hist.

The train was slowly backing now, and Miss Morgan's head jerked as the cars coupled with those carrying cars of coke. She brought along a road map so she could keep track of their travels. She could see that her train would lead them through Saratoga Springs where she had vacationed with her parents. She recalled the fun she had swimming in Saratoga Lake and luxuriating in the hot waters of the spa.

Here the D and H track split with the western branch heading into the middle of the Adirondack Mountains. She wasn't sure if other mines were in that region or if it was primarily for use by tourists. She knew her train would take the eastern branch skirting the Champlain Canal as far as Whitehall and, then, along the long tongue of Lake Champlain as far as Plattsburg. From there, the tracks turned east and began their climb into the mountains.

When the train stopped at Glens Falls to take on water, Miss Morgan alighted to stretch her legs. Although the wind whipped around her ankles and several inches of snow hindered her walk, the air was clear. Only a thin screen of cirrus clouds streaked the sky and warned of stormy weather in the offing. For a minute, she wished that she had taken the New York Central as far as Plattsburg and then switched to the D and H but, oh well, she thought, the die is cast so I'll live it out to see where it leads me.

The engineer shuffled cars around again at Mineville while Miss Morgan took a break inside the station. She searched toward the east, trying to get a glimpse of Mt. Marcy, the highest peak in the state, but couldn't be sure which one it was. She knew that not far to the northeast was Lake Placid, once the site of the Winter Olympics. She thought of the 'Movietone News' reel of the event she had seen as a child and of Sonja Heine movies. She wondered if the Olympics would ever be held here again.

The trip seemed interminably long so she was happy to reach Plattsburg, knowing that only one more leg of the trip remained. The elevation at Plattsburg was low, and now the labored ascent began. Leaving the narrow Champlain lowland, the train threaded its way up the river valleys and passed through the hills. She admired the broad expanse of snow and ice covering Echo Lake. Once there had been a station near the shore of Echo Lake with a hotel and a few houses. Now only the wooden water tower remained. She could see huge icicles drooping from the sides of the tank as the fireman pulled the water spout in position atop the locomotive for refilling. From this spot, the train labored steadily as it wound its way, serpentlike, past the highway three times, screaming at the approach of each unguarded crossing. After one more steep grade, the village of Rock Mountain burst into view.

Her appointment with Mr. Wagner had been set for nine o'clock in the morning in his office. At the station she asked for directions to the hotel, then walked down the street past a row of railway coaches converted into homes. She peered down into the tumbling waters of Dead Mule Brook. She could not miss noticing the hotel since it was the only three-story building in town. She noticed that this same structure housed the miners' taproom, the Sweet Tooth Café, and the barbershop. In time, she would learn that all businesses here were strictly company owned and operated. The hotel stretched out at an angle from Pullman Street creating a sort of plaza between it and the general store. Immediately behind the store lay the stables, rarely used now but giving evidence of bygone days.

Miss Morgan glanced up to admire huge flakes of snow drifting gently to earth. The sun had already hidden itself behind Abair's Peak and soon it would be dark. At that moment colored Christmas tree lights in a display inside the store were turned on and glowed warmly. This gave her a good feeling as though it presaged pleasant things to come.

She carried her small suitcase into the lobby of the hotel and set it down. No one was at the desk. She glanced around noticing several deer heads mounted on the wainscoated walls. Overhead on the tin-sculpted ceiling a four-bladed fan drooped, waiting for summer before being reactivated. A pink neon sign announced 'Men's Bar' from which the odor of cigarette smoke and stale beer emanated. She waited a moment and then placed her finger on the bell. A short, round man with black slicked-down hair, which had been parted in the middle, picked nervously at his pencil-thin moustache and rushed to the counter.

He leered at her, eyeing from top to bottom, on the way by. Now, he gave a gapped-toothed grin and announced, "Are we ever glad to see you. We didn't expect you until tomorrow, though. I've got your room all ready."

"What do you mean? Just whom are you expecting?"

"Why, you're Judy, aren't you? You'll be, uh, working right upstairs."

"For your information, my name is not Judy, and I have no intention of working here. Now, show me a room."

"Um, uh, didn't Mr. Panelli send you?"

"Of course not. Do you have a room or don't you?"

"Well, we're almost full up. I could let you stay for one night. That one is reserved for Judy."

"I see. One night will be just fine. I'll take it. Is your dining room open?"

"I'm afraid you're out of luck on that account, Miss. We haven't used the dining room for ten years. Uh, what did you say your name was?"

"My name is Miss Morgan, and I'm here to apply for a teaching position."

"A teacher? Oh, my, yes, I see. Er, the café next door is pretty good. You'll be staying for the night then?"

"Yes, I plan to."

Lino Alfredo, the combination bartender and hotel clerk, hummed as he handed her the guest registration form, still studying her intently. There was a spring to his step as he carried her bag to the room and showed her in.

"I'd open the drapes," he said, "but it'll soon be dark. You are in luck, though. There are only two rooms in the whole hotel with a private bathtub and a toilet. The other one is permanently reserved for company executives from downstate. You'll notice that the water looks rather rusty, but it's fine for bathing."

Miss Morgan glanced into the stained tub and into the unflushed toilet. "I see. It will suffice for one night. Now, if you'll excuse me, I need to freshen up before dinner."

Several men ogled her as she passed by the bar on her way to the café. She was hungry and tired from the trip, making the hearty meal that was served all the more enjoyable. After eating, she would have liked to explore the town, but darkness had set in and the wind had picked up so she hurried up to her room to soak in a hot tub of water.

She found the water to be so hard that she completely exhausted the sliver of soap that the management provided. A thick scum of reddish precipitate formed in lieu of bubbles and clung to her body like iron filings to a magnet. The water was hot, however, and it relaxed her.

Miss Morgan donned her nightgown and dried her hair by combing it as she sat next to the steam radiator. She stripped back the sheets suddenly, praying that she would not see anything scurrying for cover. 'Well, at least there are no bedbugs that I can see', she thought. She did not like the musty smell of perspiration on the pillow nor the lingering odor of cheap perfume so she covered it with her towel and extra blanket. The mattress seemed reasonably acceptable, and she dozed off wondering what the school and faculty would be like.

She awakened suddenly from a deep sleep when she perceived someone pounding on her door. Still groggy, she pulled on her robe and unlocked it. A man, obviously intoxicated, pushed it open, mumbled something, and started to barge in.

She didn't have time to become frightened, and simply said, "Out you go, Buster!" and pushed him into the hallway.

She relocked the door and placed a wooden chair at an angle against the doorknob. Then she looked out the window to see if there was a fire escape. There was none. Instead she discovered an inch-thick Manila rope with one end attached to the ceiling for use in emergencies. The rope was knotted at intervals to facilitate descending. A previous inhabitant of the room had apparently entertained himself or herself by creating the hangman's noose. Miss Morgan shuddered upon seeing this at first, but then placed it around her neck and stared into the dresser mirror. She smirked wryly and made faces in the reflection wondering what kind of career noose she might be getting into.

During the night, she heard several other raps on the door. Some of these were timid little pecks, other forceful as though expressing frustration. Getting no response, the callers would rattle the door-knob to test its level of security. After the third reawakening, the tired teacher pushed the heavy wooden armoire against the door and the dresser against that. Then, for added protection, she searched through her purse for a hat pin which she stuck conveniently into her pillow. In time the requests for personal service ceased and she slept.

Chapter 47

In the morning several of the miners from the afternoon shift complained to Lino and wondered what in hell was going on around there. The hotel manager explained that they would just have to be patient and the new girl would most likely be there that evening. This seemed to calm them for the moment. Then Lino explained that Miss Morgan, who was temporarily occupying the 'service room' was, in fact, a high-class lady, a teacher, completely out of their league. He, however, was going to take her for a drive in his car that very morning. He didn't know for sure if she would accept the offer for a ride to the school that he planned to give as soon as she came downstairs. Several of the men guffawed their disbelief and some dollars exchanged hands in the form of a wager.

They stood at the end of the bar closest to the lobby and swilled glassfuls of draft beer as they waited to ogle the lady when she descended the staircase. Adolph Pauchnik hawked up a gob of throat congestion heavy with silicon dust, puckered his lips, and expelled it into a brass cuspidor. Lino nervously fingered his moustache and was poised to spring as soon as she opened the door.

Faye Morgan met him halfway down the stairs and allowed him to carry her suitcase.

"Don't worry about your luggage, Miss Morgan, I'll guard it with my life. It's bitter cold outside today Miss, bitter cold, and it's a good five blocks to the school. It's best if I give you a ride for your appointment."

"Why thank you. That would be very nice of you, and it will give me time for breakfast."

As she walked out on her way to the café, Lino gave a big open-mouthed wink to the onlookers and told them to kiss their money good-bye.

"Sheee-it!" exclaimed Pauchnik, hawking and spitting again.

Lino Alfredo rushed out to start his Studebaker and turn the heater on full blast. When Miss Morgan exited the Sweet Tooth Café, he was waiting for her outside. Inside, the beer drinkers would have to serve themselves to the tap labeled Rheingold.

During the short drive to the high school, Mr. Alfredo chatted constantly. "Oh, you'll love the children here in Rock Mountain. They're well brought up. If they don't behave, we beat the cr…, uh, we know how to discipline them. Mr. Wagner's a good principal – runs a tight ship – no fooling around, no siree."

"Yes, I'm sure."

"Now, when your meeting is over, you just call me at the hotel, and I'll come down to give you a ride back."

"Fine. I'll appreciate that. I'm planning to spend most of the day looking around the school and visiting classes. Then, I'll catch the afternoon train back to Albany."

The principal was at his usual place watching for hall stragglers when the first bell of the day was about to ring. Miss Faye Morgan thanked Lino for the ride and walked up the front stairs leading into the school. She was impressed by the neatness of the building and the orderly passing of the students. Inside the office she greeted the school secretary, smiled, and took the seat offered.

Mr. Wagner entered the office a few minutes after the nine o'clock bell stopped ringing and invited the prospective new teacher into his inner office. She handed him her credentials, and he scanned them briefly before speaking.

They exchanged pleasantries for a few minutes, but the principal seemed upset upon learning that she had spent the night in the hotel. "I'm really sorry about that. It was an oversight on my part. My intention was to invite you to stay at the teacherage across the street."

She assured him that the hotel accommodations caused her no inconvenience, although in the future she would prefer an alternative arrangement.

"I see in your records that you just graduated and that this would be your first real teaching experience."

"That is correct; however, I practice taught in both French and mathematics in the public schools of Albany."

"How do you intend to handle your discipline problems, Miss Morgan, since you are only a few years older than some of your students? Let's see, why, you're not quite twenty-one yet according to this."

"My twenty-first birthday is in four months. I hardly believe that my age will prove to be a problem. I get along very well with adolescents and they with me."

The interview continued for a half hour with Mr. Wagner being impressed with her scholastic accomplishments.

"The job is yours if you want it. You could start tomorrow if you are ready, but why don't you think it over for a few days before you decide?"

"If I were to take the position, what would my duties be?"

"You would have three classes of French and two of sophomore English, plus a study hall."

"But I'm not certified in English."

"Yes, I know, but in an emergency such as this, we do the best we can. The other teachers will help you get started."

"Well, I suppose I could handle it all right."

"Oh, one more thing, since you are certified in math, I'd like you to tutor one boy in intermediate algebra three times a week. I want to make sure he passes the New York State Regents Exam in June."

"How much difficulty is he having with the subject?"

"Actually, none at all. It's a personality conflict with his teacher. His name is James Coulbron, although sometimes he goes by the name of LeTarte. If you are interested, Miss Fourcell will show you his records."

"Yes, thank you. I would like to see them before I decide. I'm taking the train back this evening. I'll phone you on Monday, one way or the other."

Mr. Wagner gave her a tour of the school and then left her on her own to visit classrooms. In the French Two classroom she winced as the substitute teacher consistently wrecked havoc with her mispronunciations. Miss Morgan thought to herself, 'good grief! I'll spend all of my time reteaching everything.'

Finding qualified substitutes was a serious problem. Fortunately, there were a few retired teachers in the area who agreed to help out. Often, when they were called upon to fill in during teacher illnesses, it was not in an area of their expertise. Such was the case for the French classes.

When the substitute teacher called upon students to read aloud in French from their textbooks, Miss Morgan was pleasantly surprised because the accuracy of the students' pronunciation exceeded that of the teacher's.

"Next, said the teacher, *"Mon-sewer James Callbroon."*

Miss Morgan was even more pleased when James read aloud several paragraphs of the lesson. She studied his serious manner and the full attention he gave to his recitation. At the moment she didn't connect his name with that of the prospective math student she might tutor.

That morning while eating at the café, Miss Morgan had also ordered a sandwich and an apple which she now removed from her purse as she sat with the rest of the faculty in the teachers' lounge. These teachers, for the most part, seemed pleasant enough, their ages ranging from twenty-five to sixty-five.

According to custom, the lady teachers occupied one table while the men occupied another. Directly behind her, Miss Morgan could not help but overhear a certain Mr. Bascomb criticizing a decision by the principal.

"Do you know what that idiot did this time?" he asked rhetorically. Not waiting for a response, he continued, "He didn't expel that half-breed Coulbron kid. All he did was expel him from my class. He hasn't heard the last of this."

"Is that James Coulbron he's talking about?" Miss Morgan inquired of one of the lady teachers.

"Yes, that's Jimmy all right. I have him for junior English. He's a doll."

"Well, what's the problem?"

"The women teachers love to have him in their classes, but some of the men are sort of afraid of him."

"Why is that?"

"Could be because he's stronger than they are. He bopped loud-mouth Bascomb in the schnozola a couple weeks ago. Knocked him flat on his fanny. From what I hear he had it coming."

"I see."

Another teacher asked, "Are you going to take the job?"

"I think so, but Mr. Wagner wants me to think it over for a few days."

"Well, if you have Jimmy in class, give him a hug for me. I had him last year for English."

Chapter 48

When Miss Morgan finished her tour and class visitations in the high school, she looked out the front windows and was pleased to see that it was still a beautiful sunny day. She could see a slight melting of the snow on the street, and there was no wind. She changed her mind about calling the hotel manager for a ride to the railroad station. With two hours remaining before the departure of the D & H train, she decided to check out the accommodations at the teacherage should she decide to take the job offered.

She walked across the street and sounded the doorbell. A middle-aged woman invited her in and assured her that, indeed, there was a room available. Miss Morgan informed her that since she wasn't certain whether or not she would be teaching in Rock Mountain, she was only looking for now. She found the room to be barely adequate. It was clean enough, but it was tiny and cluttered with cheap furniture. The linoleum covering the floor was worn and showed several cracks. What upset her the most was the wallpaper. Four walls filled with large pink roses would be too much to bear.

She asked to see the bathroom, and when she found out that she would have to share it with five other lady teachers, she knew that this was out of the question. Having grown up with three older sisters who spent a good share of their time primping in front of the mirror or reading romance magazines while sitting on the stool, made a private bath a priority for her. She thanked the woman and continued her walk up the street.

Passing through a pleasant stretch of two-story houses, she noticed the shingle that announced the entrance to Doctor Manvel's office.

She remembered the railway fireman's information that Mrs. Manvel might be able to find her a room in an emergency.

She wasn't sure if she should try the office door or the front door in order to speak with Mrs. Manvel. She rang the bell for the front door. A pleasant, gray-haired woman answered. After Miss Morgan introduced herself and presented her dilemma, the woman's eyes opened wide and she said, "My dear, let's have a cup of tea."

What followed was one of those instant cases of mutual friendship. Each woman felt at ease and seemed to find in the other person someone to share ideas with. When Miss Morgan related her adventurous evening in the hotel fending off hormone-stricken miners, the older woman roared with laughter.

"Oh, I suppose we should stop some of those shenanigans that go on there but, then again, maybe we shouldn't."

"Why is that, Mrs. Manvel?"

"Call me Edith, dear. About ten years ago, Father Orgebin got some of the good citizens all roiled up about the hotel 'service room', and they complained to the sheriff about it. He conducted a raid, arrested the girl, and threatened to put Mr. Alfredo behind bars. Some people thought the problem was solved, but a week later there were two unsolved rapes. Before that, there hadn't been any assaults for many years."

"What happened then?"

"Well, the 'personal service room' was reopened, and there have been no more problems. That's not to say that I approve, but it is the lesser of two evils."

"Have you thought of someone who might rent me a room, Edith?"

"I certainly have. Put down your tea cup and follow me."

Mrs. Manvel led her up the staircase to the upper story. "This was my son's room. He is a surgeon in New York now. My daughter, Rebecca, had this room over here. It's so nice and cheery, don't you think?"

"It's lovely. What does Rebecca do?"

"Oh, didn't I tell you that? She is an artist, a lovely girl."

"I would love to meet her."

"You will, perhaps. Now, you will notice that there is plenty of closet space. And here is the bathroom. There is both a tub and a shower. My son, Bobby, insisted on a shower like they had at school, but Rebecca always used the tub."

"It's a lovely upstairs."

"Yes, it is, isn't it? Did I show you the outside stairway entrance?"

"No, I don't believe so."

"It is right here, dear. Arvin had it installed after the children moved away. He thought we might rent out the upstairs as an apartment. Oh! I haven't shown you the kitchenette. Honestly, I don't know what is happening with my brain these days."

"Mrs. Manvel, I'm sorry – Edith – I'll have to hurry now. I must pick up my luggage and catch the train to Albany."

"How silly of me. Of course. I have been here for thirty-five years now. One would think that I should know when the train departs. Now, tell me, my dear, is it absolutely necessary that you return on the train this evening?"

"No one is expecting me tonight, and my ticket is good anytime."

"Then it is settled. We have so much visiting we can do after dinner. You will stay in Rebecca's room. I will telephone Mr. Alfredo to have him deliver your luggage here. Now, as for your apartment rent, whatever you would have paid at the teacherage will be sufficient. Of course, you will be expected to dine with us on occasion, as our guest, if that pleases you."

"Edith, I can't impose on you like this."

"My dear, at my age, I don't propose anything that I do not sincerely want. Now, tell me about yourself."

"Well, I really want to teach, especially French, but English will be fine also."

"Yes, dear, please go on."

"I know this is silly, but I'm addicted to classical music. I even bought myself a high-fidelity phonograph last year. I couldn't afford it, but I bought it anyway."

"Splendid! It would please me very much if you were to bring your phonograph here and play it as loud as you want. It won't bother Arvin. He is so hard of hearing, he won't even know it is on."

That would be marvelous, but..."

"No buts. Can you drive?"

"Yes, but I don't have a car."

"No matter, we have two of them. If you like, we can go to the symphony in Montreal next month. It is not that far. Also Burlington and Plattsburg have concerts fairly often."

"I would like that, Edith, but I haven't yet signed a contract."

"Now, I'm not trying to tell you what to do, but you would find your life here interesting. And one more thing. I am not an old – what do you call it – 'stick in the mud.' If you should be inclined to wish to entertain a young gentleman upstairs from time to time that is certainly fine with me. I don't expect you to sacrifice your social life for an old lady."

"You are a remarkable woman, Edith."

"Thank you. Did you know that I gave up my chair in the New York Philharmonic to marry Arvin?"

"No, I didn't know that. What instrument did you play?"

"Can you imagine, I played the oboe? When Arvin and I first moved here, I would go down to the high school and demonstrate the oboe during band rehearsals. The band director was all in favor of it, but I couldn't interest a single student into taking lessons. One of the clarinetists tried it once but the other students laughed at her, and she quit. I even offered to give her my instrument."

"That must have been a disappointment for you."

"Yes, like you, I love music, and I miss it. Still, I don't regret my decision to marry. I raised two lovely children. My son, Bobby, has given me a granddaughter, and she will be my musician."

"I certainly hope so."

That evening Miss Morgan and Edith Manvel joined forces to create a gourmet meal using the old China and the fine crystal. Dr. Manvel searched in the cellar and returned triumphantly with his best bottle of wine. Only twice during the evening was he interrupted by medical phone calls. In the unfolding of the afternoon and evening, Faye Morgan found a sponsor and Edith Manvel, a soul mate.

Chapter 49

About the time of Miss Morgan's visit to Rock Mountain High School, the principal, Mr. Wagner, called Jimmy into his office. "James," he said, "I'm going to level with you because I think you can be square with me. First of all, understand that all of us are walking on a tightrope all of the time. Sometimes, it's more like a spider web. Things are going on around here that you may not be aware of. I've given you a break because I believe that you have a great potential. Many members of the faculty thought that I should have expelled you from school permanently. On the other hand, several members of the faculty came to your defense. As for me, I only really know you from physical education class. I can see that you are a competitor when you want to be, but, also that you like to see other kids succeed. Is there anything you would like to say?"

"I really am sorry that I hit Mr. Bascomb. I've thought it over in my mind a thousand times. The truth is that I feel sorry for him. The first mistake was made when someone hired him to teach. He just can't do it. He doesn't know how."

"James, this is strictly off the record. I agree that Bascomb should not be allowed to be a teacher, here or anywhere else. I know that, you know that, and by now, everybody in town knows that. Now, this is a secret that I believe I can trust with you. He will not be teaching here next year, come hell or high water. He's got a contract and so we'll keep him on until the end of the year. There's nothing else we can do."

"I'll keep my mouth shut, Mr. Wagner, you can count on that."

"Understand, James, that I'm placed in an awkward position. It is imperative that I maintain the support of my faculty. Many of them are very upset about the fact that you hit a teacher."

"I'm sorry I'm such a problem, Mr. Wagner."

"I'm not blaming you, son. If I'd had your guts when I was a kid, I would have hit somebody like Bascomb myself. However, and this is important, if there is another incident involving a teacher, you're out of here. You got that?"

"I understand."

"One more thing. As a punishment, you are expelled from Mr. Bascomb's algebra class."

"I expected that, and it's okay with me. I don't blame you. It's my problem. You've always been fair with me."

"I don't want you to fall behind your class. If you want to work hard, you can still take the algebra Regents exam, on your own, of course. Maybe there is a teacher here who can give you some help, on their own time."

"I'd appreciate it, sir."

"I know you would. Now get out of here before I change my mind – no, wait a minute. Come on back."

"Yes, sir?"

"How is your mother doing?"

"Oh, didn't you know? She died in September."

"I'm sorry, son. This must be very hard for you. Who is this Buck LeTarte you have been staying with? Do you get along with him all right?"

"Buck's my real father, and we get along swell."

That's good to hear. It's very important for a boy your age to have a good relationship with an adult male."

"I couldn't ask for better."

"What is your brother doing?"

"Phil's in the army, Mr. Wagner, but he never writes any more. I don't even know if he's still at Fort Dix."

"Contact the Red Cross. They can locate him for you. All they need is his army serial number and his last known address."

"Hey, that's a good idea. Thanks a lot."

"One last thing, James."

"Yes, sir?"

"You aren't involved in any sports this year. I think that sports are good for kids. How come you aren't in basketball, for instance? I see you in physical education class, and you are a better shot than some of my starters."

"It's hard for country kids, sir. The bus leaves at four fifteen. Your practice goes until six. I've thought about it, but then I've got chores to do at home. We've got a farm. Town kids don't have to worry about things like that."

"Okay, I understand. Maybe next year we can work something out."

"Sir, I appreciate everything you've done for me. It's been a rough year for me, a real rough year – more than you know. I think that next year will be better. At least, it looks that way."

"What are your plans for this summer?"

"Everything's up in the air. It's kind of complicated."

"What are your thoughts about baseball? Do you ever think of playing on the town team?"

"I like to play softball in phy ed. My other dad, David, used to take my brother and me to the town games."

"Jim, you probably know that I'm the coach for the Rock Miners' team. Guys who are going into their senior year like you are eligible to play for the town. Of course, we've got older guys, too, but we're able to compete with the best of them all over northern New York. If you can work it out, there's a place for you. There are professional baseball scouts at these games. Several of our former players are signed up with farm teams, and one of them is a pitcher for the Dodgers."

"Gosh, Mr. Wagner, I'd like that, but it's so complicated right now. Things are all up in the air."

"Son, I trust your judgment. You do what you know is right, and if you need help with anything, come see me."

Shortly after Jimmy talked with the principal, Tadpole Laschinsky stopped him in the hall. "Jimmy, old buddy, how you doin'?"

"Above ground, Tad, you?"

"I'm soaring! I've got a hot one on tonight if I can get wheels."

"You and Helen are really hitting it off, aren't you?"

"You betcha, buddy boy. Tonight's the night. I'm gonna slip it in."

"Why are you telling me?"

"You got wheels. I need 'em. C'mon, loan me your car tonight."

"Gosh, Tad. It's not my car to loan. It's really Phil's car. I don't even have any insurance. If something were to happen, I'd be up a creek."

"Okay for you. I thought you were my buddy. Never mind. Keep your old wreck. I'll find my own wheels."

Jimmy tried to explain the situation, but Tad stormed off.

At that time, for a high school student to have an automobile was unusual. In fact, only a few of the students at Rock Mountain had their own vehicle. Upon rare occasions some of the others were able to borrow their parents' car for use at a school activity.

Alex Rushton was aware of this, and after his humiliating defeat in the boxing ring by the underclassman Jimmy Coulbron, he strove to upgrade his social status with the purchase of a 1937 Hudson Terraplane, certainly one of the more ugly looking vehicles of the period. Anxious for acceptance, Alex was only too amenable to a loan when Tad Laschinsky made his request.

Chapter 50

It was no longer necessary for Jimmy to get out of bed so early every morning ever since the cow dried up. He took advantage of this on Saturday mornings by sleeping quite late. When he did come down for breakfast that morning, Buck asked, "Do you know an Arnold Laschinsky and a St. Vincent girl? I didn't catch her first name."

"Yeah, sure. That's Tadpole and Helen. Why do you ask?"

"There was just an announcement on the radio. Seems like they're missing. They didn't come home last night so their parents notified the sheriff. There's a search going on. Do you know anything about it?"

"Just that Tad wanted to borrow my car. He said he had a hot date."

"You figure they may have eloped?"

"No, I don't think so. Tad said he was going to borrow somebody else's car just for one night. Maybe they got stuck somewhere."

"Could be. There were six inches of very slippery snow that fell last night."

"Wait a minute! I know one place they might be."

"Where's that?"

"There's a spot on the old road between here and Rock Mountain that some of the kids go to for smooching. There's one really steep hill on it. They could have slipped into the ditch."

"Finish your breakfast, and we'll go check it out. I've got new snow tires and chains if we need them."

"Maybe we should throw a couple of bags of sand in your trunk along with a tow chain and a shovel."

"Good idea, Jim."

The heavy Buick did have good traction but, even so, the automobile seemed to swim from side to side as they drove down the highway. Several times Buck had to make sudden corrections on the steering wheel to counter a skid.

Jimmy pointed out the entrance to the old road as soon as they approached it, and Buck nosed the car in for a few yards.

"Nobody's been through here since the storm started last night. We're gonna have to put the chains on."

"That won't take long with two of us working, Dad."

Even with the added gripping power, Buck had to drive cautiously. "Where is this lover's lane you were talking about?"

"Up ahead on the right there's a kind of meadow where the old charcoal kilns used to be."

Immediately after Buck stopped the Buick next to the clearing, Jimmy shouted, "There it is! That's Rushtons' car. Tad must have borrowed it from him."

Buck didn't want to risk getting the Buick stuck by driving off the roadbed onto uneven ground so they hiked toward the car.

"I'll bet they got stuck and walked home. I suppose they're both home laughing about it right now."

Buck said nothing but hurried toward the silent vehicle.

"Oh, my God! They're in there, Jim."

"No, they're not."

"Look here in the back seat."

What the boy saw chilled him. Helen lay on the seat facing up. Tad was facing down on the floor. Both were partially nude. Jimmy stood there unable to move or speak.

Buck snatched open the door and rushed to the girl to check for a pulse.

"She's cold," he said. "Dead for hours."

Then he felt the boy and looked up at Jimmy. He said nothing but simply shook his head.

"What happened, Dad? What happened?"

"Carbon monoxide poisoning. Notice how blue they look. Look at the ignition switch and the gas gauge."

"The switch is still on, and the gas tank registers empty."

"No windows open, either," said Buck.

"Oh, God! It's all my fault."

"Your fault? How could it be your fault?"

"Tad wanted to borrow my car, and I wouldn't let him so he borrowed Rushton's piece of junk."

For the first time since they had been together, Buck spoke harshly. "Stop taking on all of the world's problems onto yourself. Bad things happen, and we're helpless to prevent it. Besides, your own muffler is starting to act up. I heard it rumbling when you drove it yesterday. So forget that nonsense, and get your own car fixed up."

Jimmy was surprised at Buck's sharpness but knew he was right. "Oh, Dad, what are we going to do?"

"We'll go home and call the sheriff's office. What else can we do?"

"But everybody will know what happened – and why. You know this town. Nobody can keep a secret around here – not even the sheriff."

"How well do you know the families, Jim?"

"I know that Helen's family is super religious. Almost every time I went to Mass with Phil and David, I'd see her mother on her knees, reciting a Rosary in front of a statue of the Blessed Virgin. If she ever finds out what really happened, it would kill her."

"How about the Laschinsky boy?"

"He was one of my best friends. I've been in their house dozens of times."

"Okay. Here's what we're gonna do. If you don't want to help, I'll do it alone. We're going to dress them completely and put them in the front seat. Then nobody will know. Not the sheriff. Not the parents. Just you and me."

"Oh, Dad! Do you really think we can get away with it?"

"No reason why we can't."

"I don't think I could dress Helen."

"That's all right. You dress the boy. I'll take care of the girl."

Jimmy waited until Buck was finished, then he helped him move her body to the front seat. Tears welled up in his eyes as he clothed his classmate. Then he lifted him alone and placed him behind the steering wheel. He moved his hand to shut off the ignition.

"No. Leave it on," said Buck, "and don't open any windows. The sheriff will need the evidence."

Except for concocting a story about looking for a Christmas tree to cut, Jimmy remained silent all of the way home. Buck called the sheriff's department with the unfortunate news.

Home wakes were the custom at Rock Mountain, and since the Laschinsky and St. Vincent families both lived on Pullman Avenue, there was considerable activity in the area that night. Buck did not know either family so he stayed home. Jimmy went early to Helen's home. When he walked in a young priest was leading the group through the Holy Rosary.

Jimmy was surprised when Helen's mother got off her knees and, while still fingering her beads, grasped the boy in a hug as though begging for his strength. Her cheeks brushed against his lips, and he tasted the salt of her tears. He hugged her firmly for a few seconds, then spoke, "Helen was such a good girl, Mrs. St. Vincent. I know she is with God now."

The mother clung to him for a few moments longer before returning to the group of mourners facing the priest. Jimmy knelt in order to mouth the rapid prayers more as a sign of respect to the family than for religious devotion.

He knew Tad's family better and was welcomed as though he were a family member. After paying his respects to the parents, he stood in front of the open casket, staring intently at the boy he knew so well.

He disapproved of the way the boy's hair was immaculately combed and of the powdery makeup on his face. It surprised Jimmy to see Tad dressed in a suit and tie. He had never seen him that way before. The crystal Rosary draped so meticulously over his fingers seemed incongruous. He uttered a silent prayer. "I'm sorry, Tad. God bless you." Tears came now so he sat in a corner to hide them.

Distant relatives of the dead boy filled the room, chatting and renewing family bonds. One woman had cornered two young girls and was reciting the grim story of another girl who, long ago, was crushed when a load of logs fell on her. Jimmy gritted his teeth, wanting to shout, "Shut up! All of you, shut up"!

Out on the porch, for moments at a time, men smoked cigarettes and passed around a bottle of whiskey.

Tad's father came to sit next to Jimmy. "I want you to be a pallbearer, Jimmy – you and some of the other boys in Arnold's class. Can you give me some other names?"

Jimmy no longer tried to suppress the tears. They flowed down his cheeks as the father spoke. "Thank you so much for asking me, Mr. Laschinsky. I'd like to do that. I'll make you a list before I leave tonight."

The father shook the boy's hand and went off to greet the priest who had just arrived. Jimmy didn't feel like kneeling through another Rosary so he drifted out onto the enclosed porch. Several high school boys were standing around not knowing what to do. Jimmy listened as Alex complained about having his car impounded by the sheriff's department.

By that time the town gossipers had spread their versions of the tragedy far and wide. Unwisely, Tad had bragged in advance to school chums concerning his expected sexual adventure with Helen. As soon as the other teenagers noticed Jimmy they began pumping him for information.

"What did they look like when you found them?"

"Is it true what I heard?"

"What do you think happened?"

He replied to each of them the same way. "Their car got stuck, and they left the motor running too long. The windows were closed so they were asphyxiated by carbon monoxide."

"I heard that Tad was tearing off a chunk, that true?"

"No. Not true. They were side by side in the front seat."

"I heard that Rushton's muffler was all shot to hell."

"I don't know anything about that."

Several of Tad's closest friends arrived, and Jimmy led them in to talk with the father about serving as pallbearers. Then, he left.

The next morning Buck drove Jimmy to Plattsburg and helped him select a suit, the first he would ever own.

The two families had decided on a double funeral to be held at St. Matthew's Church, and every pew was filled. Latecomers were herded up into the choir loft or stood mutely along the side walls next to the Stations of the Cross. Jimmy and the other pallbearers followed the undertaker's instructions and carried Tad's casket into the sanctuary, then laid it on a stand next to that of Helen.

Five altar boys accompanied the priest, each carrying a different sacramental item. The priest lit the incense and caused it to sway back and forth around the caskets of Jimmy's young friends. Family members and students began to cry. Jimmy felt numb. He thought about the drinking party at Vera's house when he noticed her dabbing at her eyes with a handkerchief. He wondered what she was thinking about and whether or not she had told about their personal encounter. He looked for Clarence but couldn't see him. He noticed Buck near the back of the church. Then he thought about David Coulbron's funeral in the same place and said a silent prayer for him.

The earth was not yet completely frozen so the gravedigger had managed to open two holes on separate plots. Jimmy stood next to the Laschinsky family after Tad's casket was lowered. Earlier he had tucked a rose inside each of the caskets and now he tried to visualize the petals pressed against the bodies.

Mrs. Laschinsky grasped his hand for support on one side while her husband wrapped his arm around her shoulders. She wept uncontrollably.

Jimmy glanced over toward the knoll where the Coulbron family plot lay. He noticed a small wooden cross in front of David's grave and knew that Perchy must have placed it there after Father Orgebin transferred to Ogdensburg.

Chapter 51

Buck walked into the attached garage, turned on the overhead light, and stared at the two halves of the hog carcass that were hanging from a wooden stringer. On the day of the butchering, Jimmy had taken David's handsaw and divided the carcass into two equal parts by sawing down the center of the spinal column from the tail to the neck. He and Jimmy had decided to thoroughly consume one-half before starting on the other. Side one was now two-thirds of the way through the loin. Buck used the saw and the butcher knife to hack off four thick chops, trimmed them and carried them into the kitchen.

It had been cold inside the garage, and now he wished he had put on a jacket. He soaked his hands in warm water until the tingling stopped, and then washed them. The chops were semi-frozen but would cook up nicely. He smeared some of the hog fat around the inside of their largest cast-iron skillet and arranged the chops in it to begin heating.

A good-sized pan full of potatoes was steaming on the stove as was one containing canned corn. Just to be sure, he placed a half loaf of bread and a jar of peanut butter on the table. He had intended to serve cookies for supper, but when he opened the tin, he noticed that a quarter of the batch had been consumed already. Seeing the brown crumbs on the table, he smiled, and opened a can of peaches instead. Buck knew that he wasn't much of a cook, but during the time that he and Jimmy had lived together, he had learned how to satisfy the appetite of a teen-aged boy – nothing fancy, just lots of it. Boy, hell, he thought. He's more of a man than I am.

The ground behind the house sloped downward toward the barn so that the concrete south wall of the cellar was exposed. This wall contained two windows and a heavy wooden door. After finishing his farm chores, Jimmy always re-entered the house through the basement door, took off his chore clothes, and washed in the laundry tub. He dressed again, flattened his hair down with his hand and joined his father.

"Smells good in here, Pops. Are you sure there's enough food for both of us?"

"One chop is enough for me. If you need more than three of them, you'll have to go cut some more or fill up on peanut butter."

"Nah, I'm not too hungry tonight. Are you going out with Miss Wehrmann after supper?"

"Not tonight, Jim, she's got a meeting to attend."

"I'm not prying now, because I like Miss Wehrmann a lot."

"You're beating around the bush again. Go ahead and say what's on your mind."

"I was just wondering how you two are getting along."

"That's a fair question. Let's just say you're going to look good in your new suit soon."

"When's that and why?"

"Next month when you're my best man."

"Uh huh! I knew something was getting serious. Where's the wedding going to be?"

"We haven't decided anything yet. Alice doesn't have any relatives around here. She's thinking of having it in the Presbyterian Church in Plattsburg so the people she works with can attend. One more thing – she wants you to sing at the wedding."

"You sure she wants me to sing?"

"It was her idea, Jim, and I'd like it, too. It would mean a lot to both of us."

"Sure, I'll do it. Did you buy her a ring yet?"

"I sure did. We're doing this up really proper – wedding dance and everything."

"Do I get to kiss the bride?"

"If you don't she'll hunt you down and kiss you because you're the reason we found one another."

"I'll let her catch me, Pop."

"You know, Jim, you and Alice are the two best things that ever happened to me. After we met last August, I started to straighten up, and Alice has kept me on the straight and narrow ever since."

"I don't know what I would have done without you, Dad."

"Hey, I'm burning the pork chops. Let's eat."

During the meal Jimmy said, "Since you're going to be here tonight, is it okay if I call Clarence to see if he wants to practice? He's been asking if we would teach him to play some gospel songs."

"That's fine with me. Does he have a ride?"

"Usually his dad can bring him. If not, I'll go after him."

"Say, I just had an idea. If we could get one more player besides you and Clarence, you could play for our wedding dance. I'd just as soon pay you guys as someone else who isn't half as good."

"I think Clarence would like that. He's been trying to get more experience."

After Jimmy finished the dishes, he remembered the letter from the Red Cross that he had brought into the house earlier. He could hear Buck in the living room tuning his guitar. The boy slit open the envelope and read:

Dear Mr. Coulbron:

We are sorry to inform you that we have been unable to locate your brother, Philip.

According to the U.S. Army records, he was discharged from military service as of 11/23/48. His last known address and that of his company in Fort Dix are listed below.

If there is some other way I may be of service, please feel free to ask.

Jimmy felt confused. This didn't make any sense to him at all. He wondered, did he get sick and get a medical discharge? Did he get kicked out? Just slugging a sergeant shouldn't be enough to get kicked out for. Did something else happen? Maybe I could drive to Fort Dix and talk with somebody. Maybe my dad would come with me.

The boy carried the letter into the other room and held it up to his father. "Dad, what do you make of this?"

Buck put down his guitar and read the letter. He didn't look up immediately. Jimmy watched him pinch his lips together as though he was thinking deeply. "Do you mind if I show this to Alice? Maybe she can think of some way to pursue it further."

"What do you think it means? He's been out of the army for a whole month, and he hasn't come home or written. That's not like him."

"It's hard to say, but he's been hurt by the way his life turned out. He's been hurt pretty bad. I don't think he's gotten over it. It might help if he were to come see his mother's grave and realize that it wasn't entirely her fault. Maybe he still resents me. Life plays some tricks on all of us so we better enjoy the good things while we still can. Nobody knows what tomorrow will bring."

"I guess I don't feel like practicing now. I'm going to bed."

"I'm sorry about Philip, Jim, but you don't know that anything bad has happened. He could suddenly come walking in here any day now."

"I sure hope so. I don't like not knowing things and having to worry about him."

"Sleep tight, son. I'll just play a few songs while you're getting ready for bed. Then I'll let you sleep."

"Good night, Dad."

Jimmy's mind raced through all the possible explanations. He even wondered if it was his friendly relationship with Buck that caused Phil's strange reaction. He slept fitfully, twisting in bed and awakening several times perspiring freely and feeling confused by dreams that kept building toward impending calamities. Just as he was about to be sucked into a whirlpool or fall from a precipice, his mind would alert him of the danger and jar him awake.

Well after midnight he got up and went into the kitchen. He ate several cookies, washing them down with milk. He reread the letter again and returned to bed. Falling asleep, he dreamt about singing in the front of a church where everyone was nicely dressed. Then he noticed that he was naked. His mother was seated in the front pew and kept rubbing the forefinger of her right hand over the forefinger of her left hand in order to shame him. Soldiers carrying rifles with fixed bayonets guarded the exits so that he could not escape. Phillip came in wearing his uniform and sat silently alongside his mother. Buck played 'Rock of Ages' on a huge organ while Father Orgebin, resplendent in gold and white vestments, faced the congregation. He spread his hands widely, intoning "Oremus!"

Chapter 52

Because of her close association with county Red Cross officials, resulting from her social work, Alice Wehrmann happily agreed to pursue Jimmy's search for his soldier brother. Just before the Christmas holiday, a rural mail carrier delivered a letter written on Red Cross stationary.

Jimmy usually preceded Buck home since the man had a longer way to drive. When the boy stopped his car to retrieve the mail from the box, he realized that snow, pushed up by the county plow, was crowding the mailbox. He removed the mail and tossed it into the front seat of the car. He nosed the car into the driveway and left the vehicle idling while he got out to extract a short-handled snow shovel from the trunk. He widened the parking area near the mail box and drove the Pontiac under the shed.

Remembering that Buck had made a new batch of molasses cookies the previous evening, the boy reached into the cookie tin and withdrew a half dozen of the dark brown disks. He inhaled the sweet aroma and sank his teeth into the top victim on the pile. He placed the rest of them on the table and walked to the refrigerator to look for milk. The glass container was nearly empty, and since he was uncertain whether or not his father would remember to bring more milk home that evening, he left what was there untouched. Instead he poured himself a tumbler full of water.

He didn't really care very much for the milk from the dairy because it seemed so much thinner than that he was used to. Moreover, it was homogenized so that there was no cream to skim off the top for use on desserts. Then he thought about the cow and wondered if, perhaps, they should have sold her when the cattle buyer came around last time.

He ate the cookies, washing them down with water. He had noticed that the water pressure seemed weak and wondered if something was clogging the pipes or if the pump was failing again. He decided he should hike down to the springhouse to examine the pump before the sun slipped any further below the horizon.

The shortest day of the year, he thought. At least, now the days will start getting a little longer. He wished that winter didn't last so long. He remembered the last time that he and Phil had skated all around Echo Lake. That was just about this time of year. It had been a dry fall and, even by late December, there was practically no snow on the ground and none at all on the ice-covered lake, the wind having whipped it bare.

That fall their father, David, had purchased new racing skates for the boys, and, on years like this, it was exciting to soar across the shiny surface as though propelled by a whirlwind. That day, after circling the entire lake in a little more than an hour, they decided to try ice fishing over near Deep Inlet. They replaced their skates with snowpacs while they gathered their fishing gear and loaded it onto a hand sled. Jimmy tipped over the worm box inside a corner of the basement and found enough angleworms for one last attempt at catching fish before spring.

They joked as they hauled the sled across the bare, frozen ground, past the barn and down the road leading to the boathouse that their grandfather had built. That fall the lake level had lowered considerably so they had to work their way around rocks and rotting logs that normally would be submerged.

"You know, Jimmy, if the lake level were to sink any farther, we could find the metal boat that sank when those fishermen drowned."

"Maybe, but I don't want to think about that anymore. At least the water won't drop enough to expose that monster rock anchor we hauled out with the rowboat that time you tried to get rid of me."

"Ha! I couldn't even do that right."

"Better luck next time, brother Cain."

"Cain wasn't able – or was it Abel?"

"Whatever. Do you think we can find the channel of the stream this time? What with the low water, it'll be farther from the treeline."

"We may have to chop several holes before we find it. We'll have to be careful, though, because it hasn't been very cold yet, and where the current is, the ice may be weak."

When the boys reached the ice, they switched once again to their skates and stashed their boots in the wooden box fastened to the sled. They checked to make sure the long steel ice chisel was tied securely and, each taking hold of the rope, sped across the lake.

They found the stream channel on the second try and rigged up their short poles for fishing. The perch were hungry, and soon two dozen of them were flopping around on the ice or already stiffened by the cold. Phil hauled in one small brook trout but released it uninjured since that season was closed. Perch, however, were considered a trash fish, and there was no closed season or catch limit.

By three o'clock the temperature began to plummet and the boys had difficulty keeping their holes open because of freezing over. What had been a day of moderate temperature with a crystal clear sun was rapidly deteriorating. Long tongues of cirrus clouds invaded the sky depriving it of its ability to produce warmth. They packed up their equipment and fish and skated home to fillet their catch.

Jimmy had mixed feelings about reveries such as this had been. Although it was pleasant to remember past events, it interfered with his current plans. Now, he would have to use a flashlight to examine the water pump, and he hadn't changed clothes yet. Buck would be home soon, and he hadn't yet started the evening meal.

The boy changed clothes, grabbed a flashlight, and walked through the snow to the springhouse. Earlier he had covered the little building with snow to help insulate it from freezing. Now the area in front of the door needed to be shoveled open.

He crouched beneath the four-foot doorway, stepped inside, and closed the door to keep out the cold. A mist formed above the water in the spring. "Cold Spring," he thought. When Grandpa was alive, he called his farm 'Cold Spring Farm.' Right now, during winter though, the spring water is warmer than the air.

The spring lay close to the state highway and had almost been covered over when the new highway was constructed. Fortunately, it had been spared. Over the years the pool, fed by the bubbling water, had gradually been increased in size by the removal of rocks and sand so that now it was six feet in circumference and nearly as deep. It produced an even flow of clear water year round. Other people in the area had to contend with shallow hand-dug wells that frequently went dry during dry weather.

Jimmy shone his light on the pressure gauge and noted that it was down to a mere five pounds, hardly enough to force water up the hill to the house. With his bare hand he felt the electric motor to see if it had been overheating but found it cold. He turned his attention to the fuse box close to the doorway and noticed that the mica window had blackened and that the lead ribbon inside had melted. He replaced the fuse with the spare one he had seen David place above the doorway and was happy to hear the motor start running. He watched as the needle of the pressure gauge rose to forty before shutting off.

"Okay, Mr. Pump," he said out loud, "now you're working again. So what's your big problem? Aren't you getting enough you know what? I wish that all I needed was a new fuse once in a while to keep me happy."

He couldn't understand what caused the fuse to blow. The system had been wired by David's cousin, a certified electrician, and the fuse was the correct amperage.

Maybe, he thought, it has something to do with the high humidity in here. Maybe something shorts out. Look at all the frost on everything. Maybe it's the cold. Well, for now, I better make sure I keep a supply of fuses.

The boy recovered the spring house with snow, leaving the shovel stuck near the doorway and walked the hundred and fifty feet up the hill toward the house. As he reached the crest, he saw the headlight glow from Buck's Buick. He opened the overhead garage door for his father and greeted him as he was closing the car door.

Buck was feeling happy and pretended to wrestle with his son. They rolled together on the snowy driveway as though they were both young kids, and then sat down to toss handfuls of snow toward one another. Finally, Buck stood up and wrapped his arm around his son's shoulders, and they walked into the house still clinging and jostling one another.

Inside the house, Buck noticed the boy's work clothes and asked, "Oh, have you been doing your chores already?"

"No, Dad, I've been working on the water pump. It quit again. It was just a blown fuse."

"That's too bad. Well, if you want to take care of the animals, I'll start supper. Can you survive pork chops and potatoes again?"

"Fine with me, old master chef, but only if I get to do the dishes this time."

The evening farm chores did not take long. Jimmy kept the animal feed grain in a wooden bin in the basement. He loaded one pail partly full of hog chow and middlings. Then added some food scraps from the kitchen. Since it was a cold night he decided to give the pigs a treat by mixing the food with hot water instead of scooping up cold water from the creek. Daisy, too, still received her ration of chow plus a pail of water. He had hauled this down the hill on a home-made bobsled, splashing some of the water along the way.

Jimmy always thought of the inside of the barn as a friendly place even if the pigs each tried to gobble up most of the food for themselves. Other than that they got along well enough. He had watched the boar servicing the young sow some time earlier so he knew that she would produce a litter in the spring. He didn't find the odor of animal excrement particularly unpleasant nor the task of cleaning after them onerous. It was just a job that had to be done.

As soon as the boy entered the barn with the kerosene lantern already glowing, the cow stood up unsteadily and turned her head in the stanchion. As usual, the two pigs were already shoving one another for best position at the trough so he hung the lantern on a nail and carried the pail of warm mash to their pen. Before he could dump it, however, they got overly zealous and rooted the vee-shaped wooden trough so that it upended.

"Okay, you two gluttons, just for that you're going to have to wait until after I feed Daisy."

He placed the mash outside the pen while the pigs squealed their disappointment at not being fed immediately. He poured a measure of ground grain into the feeding box next to the cow's stanchion and added a shovelful of chopped corn ensilage into it. The cow sniffed at this but did not eat. He brought her a bucketful of water which she drank completely without raising her head once. Then he climbed the ladder into the hay mow to throw down some loose hay for both feed and bedding. Enough moonlight shone through the open window of the hay mow and through the vertical slats in the boards that he could see without a lantern. This was just as well because he knew that an accident with the lantern could cause disaster.

As he grasped the handle of the hay fork, he sat down, suddenly remembering the summer night he and his brother had slept there and how that day changed his life forever. He moved over to the open window and peered out, marveling at the blueness of the snow when it was bathed in moonlight. Glancing toward the separate log chicken coop he thought he perceived a motion, such as might be made by a small animal. He dismissed it as the playing of moon shadows from the maples' branches acting on the snow drifts.

He forked down the hay, and, closing the trap door behind him, descended the ladder. The cow watched him, still not eating the grain.

He wondered if she might have a tooth ache or a belly ache or whatever ails old cows. He observed that there wasn't much dung behind her in the gutter. Still, he cleaned her sleeping area and spread new hay for bedding.

The sow and the boar were still acting up so he used a hoe to upright their trough and poked them with it into the far corner so he could spread their mash. They ate side by side mouthing huge gulps of the feed. He entered the pen to clean it carrying the five-tined dung fork. He appreciated the fact that pigs do possess a certain sense of cleanliness, always doing their business in one back corner of the pen. This way he didn't have to clean the entire pen each day. He spread more hay for them. By now they had thoroughly consumed the mash, and the boar sniffed at his trouser leg to see if it might be edible. He poked one of his hams with the butt end of the cleaning fork to show him who was the boss. Both animals now grunted contentedly. Jimmy sloshed some water into their trough and they consumed that also.

The boy knew that he could save the cleaning chores until morning but then he would have to get up earlier and would have to take a complete bath before going to school. As it was he had to change clothes before going to school and also had to wash thoroughly in the sink. A few of the farm boys were not particular about this and risked derogatory comments from the town students.

There was no sense feeding the chickens. He knew they would be roosting in the skinny poles arranged in ascending order on a wide shelf to the rear of the coop, each with its head tucked under one of its wings. He would feed and water them in the morning when he gathered the eggs. In winter they laid far fewer eggs than in summer time, perhaps because of the shorter daylight or of the absence of live forage.

The chickens were a mixture of all-purpose types, mainly Barred Rocks and Rhode Island Reds. They produced bigger brown-colored eggs while the White Leghorns were known for higher production of standard-sized white eggs. He remembered that the egg shells were beginning to get thinner and realized that he would have to purchase some crushed oyster shell at the feed store.

He recalled the time when he was about ten years old, and his mother sent him out into the yard to fetch a nice, plump old hen for Sunday dinner. He had started to name all of the chickens although many of them were look-alikes. It was always a difficult moral task for him to decide the life-and-death fate of an animal. None of them deserved to die; yet it was his duty to man the guillotine so that everyone in his family could eat.

Unable to select by assigning guilt, he grabbed one red chicken and carried her to the chopping block. She struggled by beating her wings in his face and he was forced to drop her to protect himself. He was slightly angered by having been shown up by a chicken. He wanted to recapture the same old biddy but, by now, she was alerted and avoided him.

Suddenly, his mother bellowed out the window, "Jimmy, for Christ' sake, where's the Goddam chicken?"

Frightened by her outburst, the boy grabbed a black and white Barred Rock and held her in both hands, pinning he wings against her sides. He had watched Phil perform the beheading process several times but had never before done it all alone. His brother was out cutting firewood so completion of the task was his responsibility.

With his left hand, he held the chicken's legs securely. Then he laid the chicken's head and neck against the elm block. He stretched out its neck and stroked it gently to calm her. As he was raising the double-bitted axe with his right hand, he noticed the rooster coming his way. Little Jimmy knew this rooster was one to keep your eyes on when he was roaming the yard. He took great delight in sneaking up behind the children and trying to sink his inch-long spurs into their legs. There was no more time to waste nor to reconsider moral values. He raised the axe and struck. Spurts of blood squirted from the severed neck of the victim, but when the boy let go of her, she wasn't yet ready to give up. Headless or not, she ran in a straight line with the rooster in hot pursuit.

Jimmy grabbed a long skinny stick and chased the rooster away before retrieving the chicken which had finally fallen. He carried it to the back porch where his mother had set up a steaming canner of hot water. He immersed the chicken in the water several times and stripped off the feathers. His mother came out to watch and criticize. Finding everything in order, she handed him a knife and said, "Alright, now. Take the guts out and go bury them in the woods."

He had observed the evisceration process several times before and had even helped so that now he found it a rather easy task. He presented the plucked and drawn animal to his mother and disposed of the feathers and innards.

After he had cleaned up, his mother put him to work setting the table and completing other household tasks. These he performed gladly, chatting from time to time with her. When everyone was seated around for the meal, Jimmy's mother praised him highly for being such a good helper. Then she went upstairs and went to bed without eating. David checked on her, then went down to finish the meal with the boys. The next day she went on one of her mysterious trips.

Chapter 53

The beginning of Christmas vacation was always awaited at Rock Mountain High School with anticipation. Jimmy sat in the auditorium with other students as the members of the band and glee club assembled on stage to perform their daytime Christmas program. All of the children from the elementary school attended also, even though they had already put on their own traditional pageant the previous evening for the benefit of the parents.

Jimmy had planned to sit with two of his male friends, and he was saving spaces for them when Vera and Margie approached from opposite directions and suddenly occupied the two seats which flanked him. The boy was embarrassed because he hadn't dared to talk with Vera since the get-together in her house. He knew that Vera must have talked to Margie about his inability to perform for her.

He felt both hemmed in and humiliated. He wondered what his friends would think and what gossip would result from the seating arrangement. He started to leave, but just then the principal walked to the microphone.

He tapped on the mike with his fingers and, as usual, no sound came out. He yelled something off stage and a loud playback squeal erupted. Someone reduced the volume, and he tapped again. This time the students heard the familiar 'pupp, pupp, pupp.'

"I have a few announcements before the program begins," he said. "First of all, be sure to invite all your parents and friends to come this evening at eight o'clock to enjoy the Christmas concert. Of course, all of you are welcome to enjoy it again if you so choose.

"Another bit of good news is that when school reconvenes after New Years, we will have a new teacher on the staff. Miss Faye Morgan from Albany will be our French and English teacher to replace Mrs. Wilson.

"The other bit of good news is that school will be dismissed early today as soon as the Christmas program is concluded. The buses will be here ready to load. I wish everyone a happy and safe holiday."

The students applauded and Mr. Wagner left the podium. Jimmy looked around for his friends but could not see them at first. Then, Vince and Charlie each gave him a friendly jab in the back so he knew they had taken seats directly behind him and would be teasing him about sitting down with the girls.

As soon as the lights went down the girls started in on him.

"Hi, Jimmy," said Vera, her voice oozing with raw sex.

"Hello, you handsome hunk of man," said Margie.

Jimmy cleared his throat and was glad the darkness concealed his blush. He was in the habit of resting his hands on the arms of the seats and, as soon as he did this, Vera took a hold of one hand while Margie held onto the other. Vera turned his hand over and seductively stroked the palm of his left hand while Margie did the same to his right one.

The program began with a series of numbers by the glee club. The two girls completely ignored the music and started a conversation with one another as if Jimmy were not there.

Vera began by whispering, "You know, Margie, I've met the most handsome boy in the whole school."

"Oh, really," said Margie in mock surprise, "what does he look like?"

"Well, he's not too tall, about average, but he's built like that statue of David you have hidden in your French book."

"How do you know he looks like that?"

"Don't ask, but, believe me, I know. In fact, he makes the statue look like it should take some vitamin P."

"What does the 'P' stand for, Vera?"

"It's not petunias, Honey."

Jimmy squirmed in his seat, trying to think of a way to escape without attracting the attention of the ever-watchful faculty. The girls continued stroking his palms. Slowly, and unintentionally his manhood began to make itself apparent. With his hands occupied there was little he could do to reduce what was becoming obvious even in the dim light.

"What else can you tell me about this marvelous hunk of meat?"

"He's the spitting image of Errol Flynn."

"You mean he's got a moustache? I just love handsome men with moustaches. It makes them look so, so…"

"So what, Margie? You can tell me."

"So irresistible! I simply want to rub my hands all over his gorgeous body."

"Well, why don't you?"

"He's got a little problem to overcome."

"What's that, as if I didn't know?"

"I hear that he's awfully innocent, incredibly shy."

"It sounds to me that he needs a real woman doctor to cure his problem."

"I think you're right, Doctor. Would you like me to assist you in this operation?"

Before Vera could answer, one of the female faculty members who had been irritated by the students' talking sidled up to the talkers and hushed them by threatening a punishment.

Jimmy took the opportunity to pull his hands away from the girls and rearrange the binding in his crotch. He joined his hands together in his lap and stared straight ahead at the performance.

As soon as the program had finished, the two girls prepared to leave but not before saying in unison, "Bye, Jimmy, be seeing you around."

Vince and Charlie razzed him in a friendly way as they went to their lockers together.

"They both want your body, Kiddo. If you can't handle both of them, send one to me. I'm not particular," said Vince.

"Hell, I'll even take seconds," added Charlie.

"Make it sloppy thirds," kidded Vince.

"Hey, relax, you guys. I'll pick my own women. Give me a break. Take a look at every girl in the junior class. Think for a minute. Now tell me what you see."

"Pukesville," erupted Charlie.

"Trash Valley," sneered Vince.

"You see what I mean, you guys? Some of these girls might look all right if they knew how to fix their hair and stop smearing so much make-up on their faces. They don't know how to dress. They don't know how to act or anything."

"From what I've heard from the senior boys, there is one thing that both Vera and Margie know how to do."

"I suspect you are right," said Jimmy, "but I'm looking for a girl with more class."

"You're too fussy, Jim. Why don't you settle for ass instead of class?"

"Hell," said Vince, "I'm so hard up I'll take whatever I can get."

"Okay, you guys," said Jimmy, "you go after whatever you want, and I'll go after whatever I want but, so far, I don't see it. Is that fair enough?"

Vince continued, "Marcie will probably be pretty as soon as she cures that mess of cold sores around her mouth."

"And I hear," said Charlie, "that Lorenna will be getting a new wig soon. She outgrew that one of her sister's."

"All cats are gray in the dark," said Vince.

"If it's not dark enough, put a paper bag over their head," said Charlie.

"Listen, you guys, I'm not trying to put these girls down. It's just that none of them really turn me on. In a few years some of them might be knock outs."

"Knock out, knock up, what's the difference?" said Vince. "Take what you can get."

Jimmy told them "so long" and drove home. He had been surprised by the early dismissal from school and wasn't sure what he wanted to do with the extra time. It was too early to do any farm chores. He and Buck had cleaned the house the day before and done all the laundry. There was still nearly two hours of daylight left.

He got out his guitar and played a couple of gospel songs including "It Is No Secret" and "Abide with Me", but his heart wasn't in it. He changed clothes, dressing warmly, and put on his skis. Starting from the basement door, Jimmy skied down the trail to the barn. This went easily because the trail was packed, but, once past the barn, he had to push his way through unbroken snow and pole his way toward the lake.

The water level had fallen drastically during the dry fall weather so that now he could tell where the old shoreline was. Years ago, an electric company had bought up all of the land surrounding the lake, had the trees cut, and constructed a dam at the outlet. A spillway controlled the water flow from the lake to accommodate a hydro-electric plant.

The distance between the new shoreline and the old one varied according to the contour of the land. It was about two hundred feet to the front of the Coulbron property. Jimmy skied out to the site of the old sand beach and removed his skis so he could hike along it. Normally, as much as ten feet of water covered the former beach; now it was bare.

Strong winds had whipped the snow away from the hundred-yard arc of sand and left it exposed. Jimmy had never seen the old sand beach like this before, and he went to examine it. The fine, yellow sand lay in tiny windrows and dunes. Here and there a rock was exposed. For the youth, it was almost like reliving history. He thought that maybe this was the first time anyone had walked on this sand beach in many years. He admired the clear quartz pebbles, worn smooth by wave action, and the orange and pink ones that reminded him of jewels.

A cylindrical, grayish-white object caught his attention. The drifting wind obviously had uncovered it. He reached over and picked it up. There was no doubt in his mind that it was the lead of a bullet, but it was one such as he had never seen before. It was of a rounded, conical shape and much larger in diameter than a modern deer-hunting cartridge. He guessed it was about sixty calibre. That would place it close to the size of those used in the Civil War or shortly thereafter.

He remembered a picture of his Great-grandfather Guillaume. He was a short, wiry man with a full beard. Jimmy pictured him shooting a deer with the big-bore carbine on this very spot, or maybe he had target practice on a stump at the lake's edge. He marked the discovery spot with a small pylon of stones so that he could return later to investigate some more. Then he continued his search.

He picked up a brown-colored shard and examined it closely. It was immediately obvious to the youth that it had been decorated by someone. Then he recognized it as a fragment of pottery with an incised cross-hatch pattern. His finding was no more than an inch in size, yet it excited him. He had never once heard of anyone finding evidence that Indians had once lived here, but now he knew that they had. This was no recent piece from a shattered dish because it was unglazed and the clay contained grains of sand and bits of fiber.

He was on his hands and knees now, examining closely. He picked up another fragment and compared the pattern. It did not match. Then there was another. A shiny gray flake of stone caught his attention. He placed it in his pocket with the pieces of pottery. Soon he noticed several of the same kind of flakes, all about the same size. They seemed to extend along the beach in a line as though spread by strong waves. He picked them up. Then, suddenly, there it was! A nearly perfect arrowhead made out of the same kind of rock as the flakes. He surmised that there had once been a campsite here or a village where people lived and cooked food and chipped projectile points from flint. Maybe the things he just found had lain there for a thousand years.

Jimmy stood on the sand beach and looked up toward the barn. The area in between was essentially level, only rising slightly. If ever there was a natural site for a village in this hilly country, this was it. He imagined bark canoes pulled up on the beach with children playing and smoke rising from cooking fires.

He felt so elated he was nearly euphoric as he continued to scan the beach, heading toward the channel where a brook entered the lake. Here, he knelt down and found a tiny black arrowhead, different in design than the first one but perfectly formed. He wondered why such a tiny arrowhead was needed. Then he considered the possibility of a bird point to shoot at ducks or a fish point to aim at spawning trout or suckers. He tried to picture, in his mind's eye, a youth just his age spearing a large trout and carrying it home to his mother.

The revelation suddenly overwhelmed him. My ancestors could have chipped those arrowheads and molded that pottery. This valley surrounding Echo Lake really is my world and has been for a thousand years. It's more my world than Phil's or David's or even old Guillaume's. This is Buck's world and my world. If anyone in the whole world belongs here, it's us. And, I intend to stay.

One more ancient fragment revealed itself. Jimmy reverently picked up a four-inch section of bone. From its shape and size, he thought it might be part of a human leg bone or, perhaps, that of a deer. He wrapped it in his handkerchief and hurried home with his treasures to show everything to Buck.

Chapter 54

It was a Saturday, and Buck decided to do the morning chores so that Jimmy could sleep late. He remembered himself at that age and knew young men, regardless of their strength and seemingly boundless energy, do need extended sleep time occasionally in order to repair their bodies after overdoing.

He put on his son's chore boots and coat and headed out to the chicken coop carrying water and feed. He kicked some new snow away from the door and, as soon as he opened it, he saw a scene of disaster. Dead chickens lay strewn in awkward positions on the raised platform beneath the roosts. Buck picked up one of the Rhode Island Reds and examined it closely. He could discern no sign of trauma on it. He checked several others and was baffled as to the cause of their death. He considered that they might have been poisoned but realized that the live ones scratching around on the dirt floor seemed healthy. In all, twelve laying hens were dead as well as the rooster. Only five birds remained alive. He fed and watered those few and went on to the barn.

Inside the barn, he didn't have to examine the cow whose body was stretched out in her stall. She was stiff-legged and her tongue stuck out grotesquely. Poor kid, Buck thought about his son. He gets hit with a double whammy – dead cow and dead chickens. Of course, he knew the cow wasn't long for this world, and the boy had seen death before – David's death. I may as well let him sleep for as long as his body needs it.

Buck slopped the remaining sow and the boar. He scraped their pen clean, spread bedding, and returned to the house trying to think of a way to ease the bad news to Jimmy.

The father had come in late the previous evening after a double-feature movie date with Alice in Plattsburg. Jimmy, therefore, hadn't had the opportunity to show Buck the Indian artifacts he had discovered. The youth had placed the items he found in a shoe box and arranged them on a bed of cotton batting on the kitchen table with a note intended for his father.

After changing clothes and washing, Buck started to prepare breakfast by stirring some pancake batter and slicing fresh sowbelly from the refrigerator. While setting the table he noticed the box and note. He read, then smiled broadly:

Dad,

Remember when I said that I didn't belong around here? I thought that Echo Lake wasn't my home because David wasn't my real father. Well, I was wrong. Take a look in the shoe box. I just found everything that's in there on the old beach straight out from the barn. My guess is that the pottery and arrowheads are very old. They may not be Mohawk, but they certainly are Indian. What should I do with the piece of bone that's wrapped in the handkerchief? It might be human.

Jimmy

When he came into the kitchen, rubbing his sleep-filled eyes, all the youth was wearing were his pajama bottoms.

Buck looked at his son's strong chest and arms. He noted the short chest hairs sprouting in a hollow between his pectoral muscles. He was proud of his son.

Jimmy spoke excitedly, "Did you look at what I found, Dad? What do you think?"

Buck said nothing, but simply walked over to the lad and hugged him. Jimmy returned the hug and blurted, "Look at this big one! It's almost perfect."

The man examined the arrowhead closely and felt its sharp edge. He pressed it against his chest while saying, "I'd hate to have that slicing through my lungs."

"Do you think they could be Mohawk, Dad?"

"It's hard to say. There are anthropologists who study these things closely. They can date pottery and arrowheads, too. Maybe you can find a book about it in the public library in Plattsburg."

"Yeah! Good idea, but what do you think?"

"First of all, not everything is necessarily from the same period. That campsite or village may have lasted a long time or it might have been a hunting camp that was used every summer. Different tribes may have rediscovered it over and over again for several thousand years. Another problem is that the site had been disturbed by the waves and ice."

"Could Mohawks have used it?"

"Certainly. The Mohawks were one of the members of the Iroquois or Haudinoshone Confederacy. At first there were Five Fires, and the Mohawk were one of these. They lived in what is now New York State and parts of Ontario. Two hundred years ago, this northern part of New York was held by the bark eaters or Algonquian people. They were often at war with the Iroquois."

"But, then this stuff couldn't be Mohawk."

"Why not? Raiding parties and hunting parties frequently penetrated one another's territory. Oftentimes they brought back captives and made them members of their tribe. So the people are really mixed. The other possibility is that some of your findings may go back to a time before either Iroquois or Algonquians existed. Those ancient ones could be our ancestors."

"Dad, how do you know stuff like that? Sometimes you sound just like a professor."

"Well, I'm no professor, but I was a reader. I never finished telling you my life story."

"Oh, yeah. You were starting to tell me about Mrs. Pierce teaching you how to read better."

"We'll be getting back to that, Jim."

"I can't wait to see what I can find in the library."

Buck knew he would have to wait at least until after breakfast to give the boy the bad news about the animal losses. He wanted him to savor this moment more thoroughly. He simply said, “Don’t worry about the chores. I did them already.”

“Thanks for doing the chores. Did you look at the bone? Do you think it could be human?”

“I can’t tell because it’s so old. According to the Indian way, if it’s a bone, it should be returned to its resting place. There used to be a medicine man who still knew the Mohawk burial rituals, but I’m sure he’s dead by now.”

“I guess I shouldn’t have touched it. Maybe I should just put it back where I found it.”

“I’m sure that would be fine, son. There’s no rush.”

“But, Dad, if I wait too long the snow will be so deep I won’t be able to locate the exact spot, and if I wait until next spring, the old beach will be covered by water.”

“The exact spot isn’t important, Jim, because the waves have probably washed everything around. Even in the summertime you can locate the old beach, can’t you?”

“Sure, it’s easy because the water gets shallower there, and I know that I was lined up with the boathouse and the barn.”

“Well, then, if you find out that it really is a human bone, you can just tie a metal spike to it for weight and allow it to sink to where you found it.”

“Sounds like a good idea to me, Dad.”

“Hey, Jim, how about if you show me how to make maple syrup next spring?”

“Terrific! We still have all the stuff David used right in the shed and there certainly are enough maple trees around here. Maybe Phil will be home by then, and he can help, too.”

“Since we’re going to be making more syrup, I’m going to drench my flapjacks some more. You want some, Jim?”

"Sure, why not? Pour it on."

After eating they worked together to finish the dishes, and were going over to pick up their guitars in the living room when Buck announced the bad news concerning the cow and the chickens.

Jimmy didn't act surprised. "Weasel. I saw one just the other night lurking around. That has happened before. I think they just suck the blood out of one of them and kill the other for the fun of it. How many hens did you say were left?"

"Only five."

"Oh, well. None of them were laying much anymore. I think we should just eat the rest of them one at a time. How about if I chop the heads off one of them this afternoon, and you invite the lady of your life to come have Sunday dinner with us tomorrow?"

"Sounds good to me. I'll give her a buzz. I never thought that my own kid would be my matchmaker. Tell me the truth, now. What do you think of Alice?"

"If you don't grab here, I will. She's really very pretty and awfully nice."

"Does it bother you, Jim, that she will be taking your mother's place in my life?"

"No, Dad, Mom's been dead for some time now, and it's pretty obvious to me that Alice is good for you."

Buck was relieved to hear Jimmy's response because it meant that the boy realized that life must go on. Not wanting to dwell on Lillian's death, he changed the subject.

"What should we do about the dead animals?" Buck asked.

"In the old days they would simply haul a dead cow out in the woods with a team of horses and let the crows have a feast, but we don't have any horses or a tractor either. Now, there's a disposal company that will pick up dead critters. I'm not exactly sure what they do with them – glue, maybe, or bone meal for fertilizer. That idea doesn't bother me – hamburger would."

"You liked the cow, didn't you?"

"I remember when she was young. She used to come to me when she saw me in the pasture, and I'd pet her. When I was really little, I'd ride on her back. I think I'll go look around in the barn and chicken coop now. I'll just dump the dead chickens outside so they freeze. Later, I can toss them in the woods."

"Okay, Jim."

"Yeah, and I'll get the twenty-two from the barn in case the weasel comes back."

"When I was a boy on the rez," said Buck, "I did a lot of mink and muskrat trapping. Sometimes, when I used fish as bait to trap mink, I might catch a weasel instead. You have any traps around?"

"David didn't have any. I'll ask some of the guys I know. I think Clarence's dad has some."

"This time of the year, they're all white except the tip of their tail. They're very pretty, but often they're full of lice so don't cuddle one in bed if you trap it."

"Do you know how to skin and tan them, Dad?"

"Skin them, sure, but I never tanned any. Ask that guy with the taxidermy sign in Rock Mountain. He might know how."

"Maybe I'll have it stuffed instead and make a lamp or something."

"Don't count your ermine before you trap them, Jim."

Chapter 55

Buck LeTarte sat behind the steering wheel of his new Buick Roadmaster waiting for Alice who was in the drug store. He thought of the recent changes in his life. Not many months ago he was trying vainly to hold together his tiny congregation in Malone, New York, a congregation consisting mainly of the poorest people in the small city and some from impoverished farms. He had tried various ways to attract some of the wealthier city inhabitants to his service, but in an area consisting primarily of Catholics and Presbyterians, he made few inroads.

One thing that held the group together was his plan, vague at first, to seek a kingdom where the down-and-out could create a new life, one free from alcoholism and despair, somewhere far away in Montana. The other thing was his vibrant style of evangelism which he punctuated with gospel songs as he accompanied himself on the guitar. For many members of the congregation, it was the free meal that followed the service that attracted them. Buck never claimed to be an ordained minister, but he did claim to be doing God's work and he knew that in his own way, he was. No one else was reaching them. No one else wanted them.

He had travelled widely in the U.S., starting when he was fourteen, living with the Pierces after he walked away from the reservation. He learned the art of evangelism from them, the man having graduated from a small southern Bible school, the woman being the daughter of a country preacher. He thought of their daughter, who was slightly retarded and hot to hop in bed, as he remembered being seduced by her the same day he showed up at their door begging for food.

The family, along with Buck, travelled from New York to Texas once each year, playing their musical instruments, singing gospel tunes, and preaching the word in any church that would accept them. If the crowd seemed in the mood, the Reverend Pierce would perform a few pre-arranged cures along with moral conversions, and made the Apocalypse abundantly vivid to them…"Repent or perish!"

Buck ran this slowly through his mind now as he waited for his lady friend, Alice, who was in the drugstore purchasing some Dr. Scholl's corn patches. Their relationship had grown quickly, and already they were planning their nuptials.

When Harry Spencer, a duly ordained young minister, offered to assist him, Buck listened intently to the man and was impressed with his zeal to help the poor. He also thought about his son, Jimmy, and what kind of life he wanted to help him have.

Versed in both testaments, although in a spotty way that suited his brand of preaching, Buck suddenly recalled the day he stepped into Mrs. Pierce's life, and 1 Peter 5, verse 9, popped into his mind, "Cheerfully share your home with those who need a meal or a place to stay for the night." This certainly applied to her. What a wonderful woman she was!

This immediately was followed by his recollection of verse 11, "Are you called to preach? Then preach as though God himself were speaking through you."

He pondered this, thinking – well, God certainly didn't call me. I fell into the racket by chance. I'm not doing much good anymore. The drunks and sinners have changed me more than I've changed them. They still drink and sin and, more and more, so do I.

Speaking to the minister, Harry Spencer, Buck (still known in Malone as Reverend Dodgson) suddenly asked, "Are you called to help others? Do it with all the strength and energy God supplies." With Jimmy and Alice in mind, Buck suddenly offered the surprised minister the whole congregation. The man was overwhelmed, and when Buck offered to help him get started, the deal was arranged.

The self-styled preacher, using the name Cecil Dodgson, had first met the woman, Lillian Coulbron, in a bar. She claimed to be single, was somewhat inebriated, and wanted a man right now. He brought her to his rented room and, there, on the sagging mattress of his iron bed with a long skinny headboard, his son was conceived. It was sixteen years later that this fact was revealed to the father and son, only a few days apart.

There were several incidents when the relationship between man and boy might have blown up, but luckily this eruption had been averted.

Buck knew intensely that the agent that caused his present happiness and good fortune was his own son, Jimmy. He knew, likewise, that after a short traumatic period of time, the two of them were now good friends. All of this seemed too good to be true.

The fact that Alice, in her role as social worker, had appeared on the scene with an order to bring the boy to the county home made everything that much more incongruous. The Children's Home was a horrid place from all aspects. Even staff members were at a loss to tell if it resembled a scene from Charles Dickens more than it did one from Charles Addams. It was this woman, headed for spinsterhood, who was now his fiancée. It was she who had helped him get a steady job and had insisted on loaning him the money for a new car.

He watched Alice exit the store and head for his Buick. She smiled and snuggled next to him, and they drove off to see "Snow White" for the second time. Even as he drove, Buck continued his recollection of how he had been extremely careful not to rush her into an erotic encounter before he was certain she was ready for it. She needed to be romanced, and he was willing to bide his time. Love was growing and the rewards for his efforts seemed great.

Alice felt happy as she soaked warmth from Buck's body this cold evening on their way to the Strand Theatre in Plattsburg. She had never slept with a man. She had never cuddled with another man. Until she met Buck, she had been afraid of having a serious romantic encounter.

Because of her overly strict upbringing, she was frightened about this aspect of life, but with him she felt both safe and strangely aroused, excited. For some time, life had been passing her by. Now she felt ready to savor it and accept all that it might offer. Her new mission in life was to please Buck as well as herself and that marvelous teenage son of his.

Her family life had been severe, non-supportive to the needs of an adolescent. In her social work, she met many disadvantaged families and not a few dysfunctional ones. Some, however, exuded joy in spite of adversity. And joy, in all its aspects, is what she now sought and was beginning to experience.

As they drove down Main Street, past Kresge's and the Montgomery Ward department store, Buck squeezed her arm gently. She hummed in pleasure, almost purring like a kitten on his lap.

"Alice, sweetheart, Jimmy would like you to come for Sunday dinner. He's been busy for two days getting everything ready. Will you come?"

She reached over and kissed his cheek. "Of course, my darling man."

Sometimes, Jimmy and Perchy Garew took turns doing the farm chores for Yvette Papineau. Other times, they worked side by side splitting wood, hauling water, and completing the myriad of farm tasks. Most importantly for her, one or the other drove her to Sunday Mass, although often Jimmy merely dropped her off and picked her up later. She, in turn, flooded them with cookies and conversation. When the three of them were together, a constant, rapid chatter in mixed Quebecois French and English filled the kitchen, interrupted only by howls of laughter and still more cookies.

Gradually, Jimmy realized that this happy regimen seemed to be doing wonders for Mrs. Papineau's arthritis. Only on rare occasions did he notice her limping. He loved the sparkle in Perchy's eyes as they spoke, even though the youth did not completely comprehend all of the speedy French conversation. Sometimes, one or the other of the adults would explain a joke or a particularly rapid exchange to him. She cried easily but only tears of happiness. Perchy was a little man, bald except for a fringe of frizzy hair. Jimmy thought he resembled a banty rooster, hopping around to take charge of the jobs instead of the hens.

Earlier, Jimmy had promised to go ice fishing with Perchy in Crystal Lake where the man usually fished most of the year but, now that Perchy was coming frequently to Echo Lake to work for Mrs. Papineau, the lad decided to bring him to the lake he knew so well. Not only would this give the old timer the experience of fishing in a different lake, Jimmy didn't know any hot spots to try in Crystal. In Echo he was almost certain of success. Barring a blizzard or extreme cold spell, a date was set during Christmas vacation.

Yvette Papineau lay on her daybed in a small room off the kitchen. Earlier, Perchy Garew had cared for the farm animals, kindled her fires, and informed her that he had to go to Roswell's store to buy some chew. Although most of the chewers he knew preferred either the sweet-flavored string tobacco or the compressed plug, he favored Copenhagen snuff. His wife (God bless her) had discouraged him from continuing his messy tobacco chewing but, in time, she did compromise by allowing her husband his pinch of snuff. He missed her after she died.

Mrs. Papineau's husband Cletus, had chewed and, since he was toothless, the brown stain, which dribbled down the sides of his chin, was unappealing to her. She considered Perchy's habit of placing a pinch of powdered Copenhagen in his cheek much more acceptable – especially indoors.

Seated in the movie balcony with the teen-age smoochers, Buck and Alice held hands during the "Movietone News". Alice's bag of popcorn was discarded and fell to the floor during the "Porky Pig" cartoon as soon as he began nibbling on her fingers. Just as the wicked stepmother in "Snow White" asked, "Who is the fairest of them all?" his lips tentatively brushed her cheek. She knew, beyond any doubt, that she was in heaven.

By the time the Seven Dwarfs began singing, "Hi, ho, hi, ho", a casual observer would not have been able to distinguish the adolescents from the adults.

Chapter 56

Jimmy lay in his bed reminiscing about the school year that had come to a close that day. Gradually, however, his thoughts were interrupted as he discerned more and more sounds of intimacy coming from the adjacent room – giggles and ecstatic moans. He didn't try to drive this out of his mind; rather, he felt pleased that Buck and Alice had discovered one another and got along so well. He was relieved that, this time, he wasn't being adversely affected by it like that time last August when he overheard his mother and Buck. He accepted this as normal behavior for married adults and realized that their blissful union was what a marriage was supposed to offer. They deserve happiness, he thought. They are good people. Someday, maybe, I'll find the right woman, too.

Three sudden, loud moans erupted. This was followed by a shushing sound from his father and then more giggles. Jimmy smiled and wanted to say, "You lucky dog!", but he knew that he would never even hint, let alone acknowledge, having overheard anything so intimate.

He mulled over the recent week of testing at school. This was the first time he had been in the math room while Bascomb was present since that day in December when he had knocked the incompetent pedagogue on his big, fat fanny. He chuckled about the event as the thought of it flashed through his mind.

According to state regulations, only the principal, Mr. Wagner, could handle the testing materials prior to the precise moment when a test would be handed to each student. No one was more of a stickler for this type of rule-following than he. Bascomb was there as a proctor as well as Miss Morgan.

Mr. Wagner held the packet of testing materials firmly in his hands as he watched the seconds tick by on the clock. When only a few minutes remained, he glanced at his wrist watch to verify the time. Bascomb mimicked the principal by checking his own watch. Miss Morgan stood at the rear of the room overseeing the whole operation.

Every students' eyes focused on the hands of the clock. Immediately, when the second hand reached twelve, they glanced toward Mr. Wagner and watched as he ripped open the envelope containing the intermediate algebra tests. The proctors placed the test booklets face down on each desk. Mr. Wagner informed the students that the tests would be collected in exactly two hours and that if anyone was obliged to leave the room, they would be accompanied by a teacher.

After being given the signal to begin, Jimmy turned over his test and examined each page briefly. Immediately he noticed several test items that were identical to those he had solved while going over previous years' tests. He was glad, now, that he had asked several of his friends to join him in the library one period each day to study together by going over the old tests, an approved study method at the time. He knew that without this, his friends would not have been able to pass. This way they had a good chance and he, having been tutored by Miss Morgan, had no fears. Because of her, he thought, they will pass too, because I've tried to pass along to them what she taught me. He wished he could have involved more of the students in this, but many were disinterested.

A few minutes after the testing was underway, Bascomb pretended to be watching for any student infractions such as sneaking looks at other students' papers or using crib cards. When he reached a position next to Jimmy, he hovered close to the youth. Too close, Miss Morgan thought.

The man folded his arms tightly against his chest and stared at the youth's paper. Miss Morgan began to feel a sense of irritation. The longer the man stayed there, the more her emotion turned to anger. What is the matter with Mr. Wagner, she thought? Doesn't he see that Bascomb is trying to intimidate Jimmy? The youth did not notice her pick up a ruler and conceal it in one sleeve of her blouse. She approached the man slowly, and, standing directly behind him, jabbed the point of the ruler forcefully into his ribs. He yelped and glanced menacingly at her. She looked up at Mr. Wagner and felt relieved when she saw him wink in approval of her action.

Jimmy completed the test with forty minutes to spare. He glanced around the room and noticed the other students hunched over in obvious attention to the task. He used this time to run through each calculation and response he wrote in the test booklet to assure himself of its accuracy. Then he waited for the dismissal bell.

The students were obliged to remain seated until all the test booklets had been collected and accounted for. Those who had studied with Jimmy huddled around him on the way down the corridor.

"Thanks, old buddy," said Vince, punching his shoulder. "You sure saved my ass."

"Me, too," added Charlie, "I walked right through that test. I think I'm gonna get at least a 'B'."

"Stop counting your chickens, Charles. They may not all hatch," warned Jimmy.

"Well, I bet that most of mine will," said Booger. "Hey, Jimmy, you're coming to Vera's party tonight, aren't you?"

"Nah. Not this time. I'm still trying to get over her last party. But I want you guys to make sure you come to my place this summer. We've got a swell beach – and bring some girls, if you want to."

"Yeah," said Charlie, "they can bring the sandwiches."

"That's the only way you'll ever get bred," kidded Vince as he poked Charlie. "You get it, you bunghole?"

Outside in the bright June sun, Jimmy waved good-bye to his friends and drove off toward home.

State regulations required that Regent's examinations be corrected and graded by independent examiners in the state capital. This was supposed to avoid any possible collusion between teachers and students and, in general, assure the validity of test scores. Because of this, the official notification of grade scores was postponed until late in the summer. Since grading and graduation could not be delayed that long, teachers were permitted to unofficially correct the test and assign provisional scores.

Inside the math classroom, Miss Morgan, Mr. Bascomb, and Mr. Wagner stood discussing the testing session. "You know, George, since we've got to have all these tests graded by tomorrow, suppose I take them all home and work on them tonight?"

The principal noticed Miss Morgan shaking her head. "You know we can't do that, Alvin. I'm locking them up in the safe. You and Miss Morgan will have to correct them in the morning. He noticed a sneer of disdain spread across the math teacher's face. He knew, also, that Bascomb had received his notice of dismissal only a week ago.

"In that case, Wagner, I'm not coming in tomorrow. I plan on being sick. Let little old Miss Do-Good correct them."

Bascomb strode out of the room. Miss Morgan and Mr. Wagner looked at each other knowingly. The principal shook his head in disgust.

"Mr. Wagner, just so there is no question about it, would you please take the time right now to correct James Coulbron's paper with me? I know he is going to score very high, and I don't want someone like Alvin Bascomb raising doubts."

"I will be glad to. Here is the answer key."They sat side by side, examining each item. There were no errors at all on the first page. The two examiners paused and looked at one another, then continued. On the second page they noticed a misplaced decimal point which caused Jimmy to lose two points.

"Whew!" whistled the principal when they were finished. "Ninety-eight percent! It's too bad he wasn't teaching the class instead of Bascomb. You did a remarkable job with him, and I thank you for it."

"There are several other boys who will pass because of James. He has held a class for them in the library every school day since January."

"That's remarkable! It really is. I'm glad I didn't have him canned when he and Bascomb had that blow up."

"So am I, Mr. Wagner."

"Say, Miss Morgan, is there some way I can change your mind about leaving us? We certainly could use you next year."

"No, that is impossible. I love the students, but I am leaving for personal reasons."

"Well, one thing is for sure. I'm writing a bang-up recommendation. You will have no trouble getting another job anywhere in the state."

At the sound of the word, 'bang-up', Faye's face grew somber. She dropped her eyes and tears formed.

The principal noticed the sudden change in her expression. "Is anything wrong, Faye? Aren't you feeling well?"

"No, no. Everything is fine. I was just thinking how much I am going to miss my students."

"Well, all I can say if this. They are certainly going to miss you. All of us will miss you. If you are ever in town, be sure to stop in."

Miss Morgan walked home and headed up the outside staircase to her apartment. Halfway up she became aware of being tired. She stopped to breathe deeply and continued. Inside her bedroom she removed her dress and slip, then, stared in the mirror. She removed the band of cloth she had used to bind her abdomen. She looked at her figure and started to whimper. The sounds grew. They became harsh and angry. She grabbed a framed photograph from the wall and threw it against the floor.

She heard someone coming up the inside stairs. The person knocked timidly on her bedroom door. "Faye? Faye, is anything wrong, dear? It's Edith. May I come in?"

"Oh, Edith, yes, please come in!"

Mrs. Manvel pushed open the door and observed the young woman lying face down on her bed.

"Faye, my dear, what in heaven's name is wrong?"

Faye rolled over and sat up on the edge of the bed. Mrs. Manvel rushed to comfort her. Wisely, the older woman said nothing but allowed the young woman to cling to her.

Finally, the younger woman's sobbing diminished and Mrs. Manvel handed her a handkerchief.

"My dear, you must let this flow out of you."

"Edith, look at me." Faye placed one hand on each side of her abdomen.

"Well, dear, I can see that you have put on a bit of excess weight, but, surely, you can get that problem under control."

"No, Edith. Not fat – baby! There is a baby in there!"

Mrs. Manvel suddenly felt flustered. "Oh my! Oh dear! I see. Oh, yes, yes. Ummm – what shall we do?"

"I don't know, Edith. I was so stupid. I didn't even enjoy it. I just did it for him. He kept begging me and begging me."

The sobbing returned and Edith Manvel comforted her. When the young woman was once again in control, Mrs. Manvel continued, "Well, now, you know there are alternatives you may wish to consider. Arvin has been called upon to interrupt pregnancies a number of times. It is really quite easy if it has not progressed too far. The condition is barely noticeable on you. What would you say? Less than four months?"

"I know exactly when it happened. It was Easter Sunday. Oh, Edith! I was so stupid!"

"Now, now, things will work out. Do you want me to talk to Arvin about it? It has to be very hush-hush, of course."

There was a long silence. "No. I couldn't ask your husband to jeopardize his career by violating the law. Besides, I don't think I could live with myself – knowing that I took a life. I made a mistake, and I will make the best of it."

"It must be your decision, dear. Please remember that I will help you in any way that I can. I am very sorry but I can't be here with you tomorrow. I promised Arvin that I would accompany him to a medical convention down state. Men are so helpless, you know. They can't get along without us."

"How long will you be gone, Edith?"

"Only three days, dear. You can hold on until I get back, can't you?"

Darkness began to fall down on the flats across from the school as Mr. Wagner was reading his newspaper. A growing urge had been building inside him. He called to his wife and told her he was going out for a walk.

He placed his set of school keys and a flashlight in his pocket. He stuffed a baseball bat under his belt parallel to his spine and exited by the back door of his house. He walked across several back yards until he reached a spot where he knew the street light was out. He hurried across the street and then stepped off the edge of it into a ditch leading toward the rear of the school yard. He skirted the playing field by passing through a brushy grove and entered the schoolhouse through the boiler room door. He recalled the lessons in escape and avoidance of capture he had learned in the Marine Corps. He felt elated at re-enacting the old days.

Unlocking the door, he entered the building and remained silent for several minutes, listening. Hearing nothing, he covered the lens of the flashlight so that it scarcely emitted a single ray. He attuned his senses to the spirit of the structure. He knew precisely where each strip of maple flooring creaked when stepped upon, and he avoided them. He recognized each hissing heating element. He felt as though he were a ghost on the prowl, and he loved it.

He forced himself to count to ten before taking one more step up the basement stairs. With his flashlight extinguished, he stopped at the summit of the stairs and waited. He listened for several minutes, then hugged the walls and proceeded toward the office. Several times he paused to listen.

Finally, when he reached the door to his office, he felt elated at finding it unlocked because he knew for certain that he had locked and double-checked it before leaving.

"God", he thought, "I hope he's still in there! That bastard!"

Silently, he eased open the door and, at the same time, freed the baseball bat that had been secured behind him. He turned his eyes toward the school safe and watched.

A thin smile spread his lips wide, and he waited for the explosion he knew was about to happen. A shadowy shape was crouched in front of the safe. The shape turned on a tiny penlight and rifled through some files. Wagner had no doubt concerning the identity of the other phantom.

The ex-marine principal eased into the room and crouched next to the wall. Soon the specter doused his light and turned, carrying a sheaf of papers with him. He headed toward the door.

The blow from Wagner's baseball bat connected with Bascomb's left knee.

Chapter 57

Jimmy felt strangely happy as he carried a cardboard box filled with Miss Morgan's books up the outside stairs to her apartment. Yesterday had been the last day of school and, already, he wanted to see her. He kept telling himself that he needed to thank her for the tutoring help she had given him that year. And, of course, he had to return the books she had loaned him. Yet, deep inside, there was something else, something not fully recognized, that drove him at that moment.

He knocked at the door. She opened it and, upon seeing him, smiled. In class he had always been casual but respectful toward her. Now, for the first time, he felt awed by her presence. After all, this was her private residence – not a school classroom.

She opened the door wide and invited him to come in with the books. This seemed wrong for him to do, as though he were trespassing, violating her living space. He felt flustered and suddenly embarrassed. Searing heat rose in his cheeks. He thrust the books at her.

"Uh, here, Miss Morgan. Thanks. Thanks a lot."

He turned suddenly and left her standing there. His ears buzzed from the pressure building up inside his head. He rushed down the stairs two at a time and stumbled when he hit the landing. He didn't dare look up at her for fear she might have seen him in an awkward position and be aware of his incompetence. He felt like a bumpkin – naïve and unworthy.

Earlier, as he was leaving Echo Lake, he had noticed the storm clouds building up over the mountain peak. He hoped he could deliver the books and return home before the storm started.

Still smarting because of his immature departure from Miss

Morgan's presence, he was unaware of the thunder rumbling over the peaks. He stood next to his car and stared in awe as a wave of churning water surged down the stream that separated this part of town from the rest. He watched as a great wave struck the bridge and sprayed over it. Water rose and overflowed the structure.

Leaving the car there, Jimmy sprinted toward the bridge to see if it was safe to cross. Two or three at a time, the loose wooden planks floated downstream. The framework of the bridge bowed against the burden of the water. He knew it was unsafe to cross either by walking or in a vehicle.

The youth decided to check upstream. He knew that mining trucks sometimes forded the brook at a shallow spot close to the dam. The rain came slowly at first, then settled into a solid downpour. Jimmy continued upstream for three-quarters of a mile until he could see the dam. The earthen structure had not burst completely. Rather, there seemed to be an eight-foot rift in it like a burst levee. Jimmy reasoned that heavy rainfall farther upstream had caused the dam to overflow and partially wash out.

He watched as a huge truck carrying a load of boulders backed toward the breach in the dam in an attempt to plug it. The rear wheels lost footing in the current, and the vehicle was stranded. The driver crawled onto the cab and yelled to other workmen.

Jimmy stood alone on his side of the stream. When he approached the water to see if he could wade across, workmen frantically waved him back. He continued to watch as a bulldozer crept toward the truck, nosed its blade close by the vehicle's front bumper, and slowly spun around so that its winch could be reached by the driver. Jimmy wanted to be there helping, but all he could do was watch.

The bulldozer pulled the truck and the driver to safety. Jimmy waved to the men hoping that they would cross the flooded stream in the yellow crawling machine and give him a ride, but once again they waved him back toward safety. After the workmen left, Jimmy returned downstream toward his car. The rain continued, and darkness began to fall.

Faye Morgan had also been watching the swollen stream. She had watched the youth walk upstream and return. The street lights flicked on and she noticed a girl, wrapped up in a raincoat, frantically waving from the other side of the bridge. From this distance she was unable to identify the girl but thought she might be one of her students.

She watched in horror as Jimmy walked tentatively out onto the falling bridge. My God, she thought, it is going to collapse any second. What in the world is he doing?

Miss Morgan grabbed her umbrella and a raincoat. She rushed toward the bridge. The youth, meanwhile had noticed the girl. Because of her screams, he could not help but see her puppy cringing in the middle of the bridge. Planks on each side having been washed away, the animal was trapped.

Jimmy sized up the situation and gingerly he stepped out onto the bridge even though water rushed and tugged at his feet. The puppy rushed back and forth in the narrow middle section that remained intact. The girl held her hand to her mouth. The youth was aware of the first section which was unsupported by planks. At this spot the water churned and gurgled with foam and debris. He leapt across a three-foot chasm and, landing unsteadily, grasped the twisted guardrailing.

One more washed out section separated him from the animal, but it was wider than the first. He hesitated a moment, then lay down, allowing the water to lap against his body. Slowly, he stretched himself forward, holding on to the side with one hand.

"C'mon, Pup," he called, arching his neck and encouraging the pet with lip sounds. He stretched out one hand in supplication.

"C'mon, Pup, come right now or I've got to leave you."

"The girl called, "Jimmy, be careful! For God's sake, be careful! Go with him, Silky. Go, now!"

The puppy leaped toward the youth, who grabbed it with one

hand. Still holding on to the side of the structure, he worked his way forward while remaining prone and sloshing through the water. Jimmy brought the puppy to the far side of the bridge and waved to the girl.

Faye Morgan met him just as he reached the safety of land and threw a raincoat over his shoulders. Her umbrella fluttered in a sudden gust of wind. She pushed him and the puppy toward her stairway without a word. He paused long enough to wave toward the girl once again.

Inside, Jimmy removed his soaked shoes and placed them on a rubber mat next to the door, still grasping the dog.

"Good Heavens! You are drenched to the skin, Jimmy. Let's get you dried off. You are spending the night right here." She said this emphatically like a teacher's command.

He smiled slightly so that his dimple showed. Miss Morgan observed him closely – so closely that his face began to redden.

"You must be exhausted, Jimmy. After you take a hot shower to warm up, leave your clothes by the door, and I'll hang them to dry for you."

"Uh, okay, thanks, Miss Morgan. I've got to dry the poor little pooch first. He's so frightened he's quivering. Do you have an old towel or something?"

"Of course. I'll dry the puppy and give it something to eat, but you must get yourself warmed up right away."

"I'm worried, Miss Morgan. I'm sure Buck is wondering where I am. Maybe if I had walked upstream farther, I could have waded across the brook and come down on the other side. Maybe I could have found a house with a telephone that was still working."

"Perhaps, Jimmy, but that's unlikely. Telephone service in the whole town often goes out whenever there is a storm like this. Write down your father's number, and I'll keep trying to contact him for you. You get warmed up in that shower and get some sleep before you come down with pneumonia."

"Okay, thanks, Miss Morgan." He handed her the dog.

The youth checked to see that he was alone. He stripped off his sodden clothing and piled them in the hallway. He glanced around sheepishly and ducked into the bathroom. He was still feeling chilled from his outside excursion and was glad to feel the hot water pounding on his body. He dried himself with the Turkish towel Miss Morgan had laid out for him, then searched the medicine cabinet for some hair oil to control his hair. There was none. He considered using some petroleum jelly but settled for cold cream instead. He wrinkled his nose at the aroma. He appreciated that the woman had supplied him with a new toothbrush and loaned him her safety razor.

He used a corner of his towel to wipe condensation off the window pane. Out in the yard, the street light highlighted rain spitting so hard it formed bubbles in the driveway. A rivulet rushed by on each side of the street. In between, sheets of rainwater surged on the asphalt. The electric lights, both inside and out, flickered twice before resuming a steady illumination. Once again, an eerie brightness lit the area, and Jimmy jumped at the snap of a lightning bolt that made the house shudder. This was followed by a long roll of thunder.

He craned his neck far to the right so he could see the metal bridge which separated this section of town from the rest of Rock Mountain. The bridge lay like a discarded toy, fallen and twisted in the streambed, its concrete abutments having been undermined by the flood.

Instead of the usual foot of water trickling its way down Dead Mule Brook, a raging torrent was loosening boulders and tumbling them downstream. As he watched, a large tree tottered on the current's edge, then slowly pitched itself into the current. Gathering momentum, it was sucked away, the root system in the lead.

Again, the lights of the town hesitated, resumed momentarily, then remained unlit. Having nearly finished shaving, Jimmy wiped the soap off his face with a towel and draped it over his neck. Still nude, he opened the bathroom door and stepped out into the darkened hallway. He stood there a second groping for the door to his bedroom.

At that moment, Miss Morgan stepped into the hall to see if any of the house lights were still working. She saw his firm body silhouetted against the window when lightning flashed once more. She raised her hand to her mouth, and her heart seemed to skip several beats. She hoped he had not seen her because she didn't want to embarrass him.

Up the hill, inside the power plant, the technicians switched the town's electrical power over to local production as soon as the workers realized the outside line was down. When Jimmy turned to enter his room, the hall lights flashed back on, and Miss Morgan savored a rear view of him. He turned suddenly, remembering his wallet in the bathroom. They stood facing one another six feet apart.

"I'm sorry!" stammered the youth. He rushed into his bedroom and closed the door.

Miss Morgan smiled involuntarily and mouthed some words almost silently, "A Greek god! He's just like a Greek god."

An erotic sensation flushed through her body. Suddenly she felt pleased, realizing now that subconsciously she had been waiting for this moment for months but had been unable to allow the thought to penetrate the conscious regions of her brain.

You are shameless, Miss Faye Morgan, she thought. Here you are lusting after a boy – one of your own students, and you are enjoying it. You are glad this happened, and now he is thoroughly embarrassed. You know how bashful he is.

"But, God help me," she thought, "he is no longer a boy!"

Chapter 58

Inwardly Faye was still smiling when she picked up Jimmy's soggy clothing and carefully arranged everything on a wooden rack to dry. She adjusted the air flow from an electric fan so that the drying would be hastened. She scraped the mud from his shoes, wiped them with a cloth, and placed them to dry.

She had already dried the puppy with a towel and fed it. Now she made a warm bed for it in a cardboard box, hugged it, and put it to bed. Then she approached the youth's door and tapped gently.

"What is it?" he quavered.

"Don't feel embarrassed, Jimmy. I didn't see anything. The glare of the lights made me blink."

"Yeah, sure. Let's just forget about it."

"Ha!" he thought, "blink my dink!" He knew she was lying because both her eyes and mouth were opened wide, and she had scanned him from top to bottom.

"Try to go right to sleep. I'll see you in the morning, Jimmy."

"Good night, Miss Morgan."

Gradually, as he continued to think about it, the feeling of embarrassment diminished, and he was glad she had seen him in his entirety. He had no deformities to be ashamed of, no deficiencies of manhood. He was delighted, now, that she had finally seen him for what he was – a man. And that thought excited him.

In the safety of what used to be the Manvel son's bedroom, he tried on a pair of the doctor's pajamas that Miss Morgan had brought to him. The waist was several sizes too large, but he wore the bottom anyway. He tossed the top on a chair and dozed off quickly.

Miss Morgan, however, was wide awake. She leafed through her diary and smiled as she reread several pages. It surprised her that she had mentioned Jimmy in the journal on the first school day at Rock Mountain. She had met him in the hallway when the principal called him over and introduced him as the person she was asked to tutor. That afternoon she was impressed by the total attention he gave in class.

As she read, she recalled the many incidents that had inspired her to mention him. She sat back on her chair, shook her head, and tried to understand this infatuation for a student. She realized that she was scarcely three years older than Jimmy was, although it was a crucial three years. She wanted to be near him. She longed for him and she wanted the feeling to last forever.

Lightning snapped once again on the hill above the house. The lights flickered and went out. She waited for them to return. When they did not, she located a candle and lit it, then placed it on her dressing table.

Faye Morgan tiptoed toward Jimmy's bedroom and pressed her ear against the door. She heard no sounds. No light came through the crack in the door. She felt light-headed. Her heart thudded, and a hand seemed to be clutching her throat.

Slowly, so very slowly, she turned the doorknob. She waited a moment, then eased open the door, stepped inside, and closed it behind her. She waited for her eyes to grow accustomed to the darkness. She knelt next to the youth's bed and caressed his face with her eyes. She longed to lie next to him.

He had kicked the covers off when his body, overheated from the shower, made him uncomfortable. She marveled at his physique as his chest expanded and relaxed. He moaned slightly and scratched his groin. Vaguely, from the light of the window, she could see a bulge forming inside his pajamas bottom and she desired him.

She laid her hand on his bedsheet and extended it toward him until she could feel the warmth and the smoothness of his body. She hesitated when he muttered some sounds in a dream. Then he rolled away from her, and the spell was broken. She slipped out of his room and, trembling, returned to her own.

Jimmy's dream mind was a jumble of incoherent images except for the one of her. This was clear, sparklingly clear, and he continued to live it for a few moments after he awoke perspiring. His pajamas were sticky with seminal fluid. Low, far-away rumbles echoed through the mountains.

Silently, the youth arose and headed for the bathroom to release the pressure of his bladder. Turgid, his flesh resisted the commencement of any flow. He turned the water on in the lavatory, remembering that sometimes this sound helped relax him. When it did start, the sound reminded him of the flow of a stallion, and he was afraid she might hear him. He aimed his stream to one side of the bowl and resumed.

She did hear him, however, and smiled.

While heading back to bed, the youth thought, I shouldn't have been so bashful. What I really wanted to do was let it roar just like that flood, just like Niagara Falls. Then, he felt embarrassed for his thoughts. He was startled by her voice.

"Jimmy, please come here. I'm so frightened."

He stood outside her open doorway and noticed the soft glow of the candle. "It's okay, Miss Morgan. The storm is almost over."

"It's not the storm that frightens me, Jimmy. It's what is happening to my life. I need someone strong to talk to – someone who cares – someone who will listen. Please, Jimmy, don't be afraid. Come in and hold me."

He swallowed involuntarily and stepped slowly into her bedroom. He could see her sitting on the edge of her bed wearing a red silk robe. In the light of the candle, silver tears glistened in her eyes.

She held out her hands, and he touched them. She held on to his hands tightly and drew him to her.

"Hold me, Jimmy. Please hold me. I need your strength."

Awkwardly, he wrapped his arm around her shoulders. His mind was a blank, but he sensed the warmth of her body and its sweet smell. She buried her face into his chest and sobbed. He held her more tightly. He felt confused and embarrassed. He wondered what to do. His face prickled with excitement and his heart pounded.

Faye faced him now, and the sobbing stopped. "Kiss me, Jimmy."

He brushed his lips against her cheek and tasted the salty tears. Then he kissed her fully on the mouth and closed his eyes. They sat clinging to one another for several minutes. When Jimmy opened his eyes, they darted into the crevice of her breasts. The fabric drooped forward, and he could see a nipple. He bent low and kissed it. She moaned and took his face in both of her hands, then kissed his lips sensuously.

"If you want me, Jimmy, take me now. I owe you that much."

"I – uh – don't understand, Miss Morgan."

"Do you really want to make love to me?"

"Uh – golly, yes, more than anything else in the world, but, I – uh – I don't have any rubbers. I might get you pregnant."

She began to caress his genitals with her hands, and he shivered. "No need to worry about that now, Jimmy."

Everything was happening too fast for him. He wanted to slow things down.

"You said you were afraid, Miss Morgan. What of?"

She recognized his reluctance and respected it. She released her hands slowly and gripped his biceps. "I need to talk to someone I can trust – someone I love."

"You can tell me your problem, Miss Morgan. I won't tell anyone else. I promise."

"You know that I'm not coming back to Rock Mountain next year. I told that to the class last week."

"Yes, we all wondered why. Is it something one of us did?"

"No, no, Jimmy, I couldn't have asked for better students. It's something I did."

"Something here in Rock Mountain?"

"No, Jimmy, it happened during Easter vacation, and now – I'm going to have a baby."

"But why? How? I don't understand." Slowly, imperceptibly, as the school year progressed, she had become the ideal woman to him. Now, the realization that she had erred confounded him. He felt it a betrayal on her part, but he was not ready to blame her. He reserved his anger for the person who had defiled her.

"Jimmy, sweet lovable Jimmy. Please try to understand that I'm not a saint. I'm a flesh and blood woman. I have feelings. Just now I offered my body and soul to you because I've fallen in love with you. Now, I'm afraid you hate me because I was weak and human."

He wondered how many others she had offered her body to and if she might become just like his mother. "I don't hate you. I want to help you. Why is it that sex always causes so much trouble?"

"It doesn't have to cause trouble, Jimmy. It can be beautiful."

"I'm not so sure, but I do know it would be beautiful with you because you're different. I've never felt this way about a girl before."

"Don't give up on other girls, and don't give up on sex."

"I'm mad at sex. It's nothing but trouble. Can I tell you a secret?"

"Of course, but you don't have to."

"You remember Tadpole and Helen? Well, they died making love for the first time. Buck and I found their naked bodies in the car and we dressed them so no one would know."

"That was very, very kind of you, Jimmy. Noble, in fact, but their death was a freak accident."

"How about my mother? She was a tramp. She loaned her body to anybody who would give her a drink of booze, and she got herself killed because of it."

"I'm sorry, Jimmy, but you know she was sick." Faye hugged him, and it was his turn to sob on her breast.

"Miss Morgan...," he began to speak, but she interrupted him.

"Please call me Faye, Jimmy. I'm not your teacher anymore."

"Faye," his voice quivered. "Faye, - she did things to me – terrible things."

"Your mother?"

"Yes," he spoke through sobs.

"What kind of things?"

"Sex things. Dirty sex things."

Faye kissed his cheek. "Don't worry, my darling. That won't change anything for you."

He cried openly and clung to her.

"It's good that you told me, Jimmy. Now, be strong – stronger than you have ever been in your life. Forgive your mother for her sickness, and please forgive me because I was weak."

He faced her now. "I forgive you, Faye, and – Mom, I forgive you too."

The youth wiped his eyes and cleared his throat. He forced a smile. He wanted to take control of the situation – to find a solution. "Okay, okay, enough of that kid stuff." He coughed nervously, "Let's think. What are your plans?"

"I'm going to Albany to have the baby. It won't come until December. My poor father will be shocked, but I think my mother will understand."

"When are you leaving Rock Mountain?"

"As soon as I can catch a train out of town."

"When will I see you again, Faye?"

"That depends. Maybe never."

"No! I won't let you."

The woman lowered her eyes but said nothing. There was a long pause before the youth continued almost arrogantly, "Who's the father?"

"My college boyfriend, Ronald." Her eyes misted over and she could not face Jimmy.

"Are you going to marry him?"

"I will for the baby's sake, if he will take me."

"Do you love him?"

"Jimmy, I didn't know what love was until I met you."

"Did you tell him? Did he agree to marry you?"

"I told him, but he's got to get permission from his father, and that is far from certain. His father doesn't want him to marry until he is ready to take over the family business."

"I suppose they have a shoe factory or something."

"No. Underwear and stockings."

"Underwear? You want to marry somebody who makes underwear?"

"I don't want to marry him. I want a father for my child. Is that so wrong? Don't condemn me, Jimmy."

"Forget that creep, Faye. I'll marry you." Jimmy rattled the words off. "I'll take real good care of you and your baby. I'll get a job. We can live at Echo Lake. It's beautiful there. I love you so much, Faye."

She kissed his hand and pressed it against her cheek. "I wish it could work out that way, but it wouldn't be fair for you, Jimmy."

"Why not?" His voice trembled as he pleaded with her. "We could make it work. Buck and Alice will understand. It'll be okay with them. They'll help us. I know they will."

"No, it wouldn't be fair at all. You have a great future. You are going to a good college and make something out of your life. I would be a millstone around your neck. I would hold you back. The lucky girl who finds you will make you a good wife. You will have lots of babies together, and you will be a great father."

"I want you, just you. I don't want any other girls. They're so dumb."

"Do you want me right now, Jimmy?" She bared her breast to him and stood up. She released the cloth belt that held her robe. She wriggled her shoulders, and the red material shimmered in the candlelight as it fell in a mound around her knees. Jimmy's mouth opened and he sucked in his breath as he stood to face her.

It surprised him that now, when both were bare-footed, he was taller than she was. He kissed her forehead tenderly, and her breasts pressed against his chest. She bent down and skinned off his pajamas before kissing his virile member. They no longer needed words to communicate. Their thoughts went numb as their bodies merged on the sheets.

Hours later, they still lay side by side, savoring the love they had shared. Her head lay on his chest while his arm cradled her neck. The candle flickered once before extinguishing itself in a pool of liquid wax. Hidden in the darkness, their faces glowed.

Inside, Jimmy burst with happiness. He knew that he had finally escaped from childhood and the haunts of the past. Faye raised her head and kissed his cheek.

Chapter 59

Jimmy's dream mind reformed itself with the sight of a yellow bulldozer battling the surging flow of water which had burst from the dam. Floating debris grasped at his legs as the water rose ominously. He called frantically to the operator of the huge machine and flailed his arms to get attention. Slowly he regained consciousness as Faye gently stroked his face.

"You have been having a nightmare, Jimmy. You were yelling and flinging your arms."

"I'm sorry, but it seemed so real." He was embarrassed upon finding himself nude in Faye's bed. The events of the evening relived themselves briefly. He blushed.

Jimmy could hear an engine roaring and metal scraping sounds outside. The youth rushed to the window and looked out. Using a crane and the winch of a dozer, workmen were removing the mangled metal bridge which separated this section of homes from all the rest. There were only eleven houses in this area, but one of them was Doctor Manvel's. That, in itself, made a rapid repair a priority. He noticed that there was a large pile of squared timbers next to the bridge waiting to be made into a temporary structure. Jimmy blushed again, covered himself with a towel, and rushed into the bathroom.

While watching Jimmy, Faye smiled outwardly but was sad inside. She had already ironed his now-dried clothing and piled the items neatly on a chair. While ironing, she had started humming a persistent melody, but now tears were forming. She dried her eyes with a tissue and started preparing breakfast.

The familiar aroma of frying bacon enveloped the room. Dressed now, he stood in the doorway admiring what he saw. Sheepishly, he approached and sat at the table. Faye noticed him and placed a golden-brown pancake on his plate.

"Help yourself to the bacon, Jimmy. I suppose that you recognize that syrup container."

He did recognize it immediately. It was the one that he had secretly placed on her desk at school a week after Christmas vacation. The maple syrup it contained was some that he and Phil had made months earlier.

Jimmy thought of the beauty of this scene. He fantasized that they were married and that Faye was preparing their very first honeymoon breakfast. Then it was his turn to get weepy. They consumed the meal silently. Jimmy averted her gaze but could not help glancing up frequently.

Suddenly Jimmy called out, "My car! People will see my car, and they will know."

"Don't worry, my darling. I found your keys and parked your car in the doctor's garage. You are safe for now."

The rescued puppy tugged playfully at the fabric of Jimmy's pant leg. Then the boy remembered. "That was Hazel on the bridge with her little dog. She recognized me. Stories will go around about us."

"I wouldn't worry too much because I'll be gone, and you have graduated. Each of the students will go his or her own way, and everything will be forgotten. Oh, and Doctor Manvel will be talking to you when he returns from his meeting. He says that he will sponsor you if you want to go to McGill and become a physician. I think that he is hoping that you will take over his practice. He plans to retire about that time."

"Gosh! I never thought that something like that could ever happen to me."

"I'm sure that he means it. It is a great opportunity, Jimmy."

"I want to see you again someday, even if you are pushing some guy's baby in the carriage. I think destiny brought us together and, then, suddenly snatched us apart."

"Yes, Jimmy, you are right. And I'll always treasure every moment we were together. We had something special. Like a rare flower it grew and it flowered. Now you have to think about your future, and it will be a fine one. Don't worry about me. I'll get along."

Jimmy continued to watch the removal and reconstruction of the bridge. "At this rate they won't be finished for a week," he complained. "I've got to notify Buck and Alice. I'm sure they're worried."

The phone call that came just then was not expected. Repeatedly, Faye had tested the line without success. This call was from Hazel wondering about her dog. Jimmy spoke with her and reassured her that he would bring it to her as soon as possible. She asked if he had stayed at Miss Morgan's house that night. He could hear the tongues wagging. "Yes, of course, Hazel, and don't you worry about your puppy. Faye, uh, Miss Morgan is taking good care of it."

Jimmy phoned Buck next and told him about the missing bridge. Buck sounded relieved and asked the boy to return home as soon as possible because there was some serious water and flash flood damage to attend to.

"I have to go home," Jimmy said. "We have problems there. The water has gone down enough that I can wade across the stream and hitch-hike home. I'll get the car later."

"I understand," she said. "I can wait for the bridge to be completed and then take the train. Good-bye, Jimmy. Remember our time together. It was precious, and I know that I'll love you forever."

"Oh, God, Faye, I can't leave you."

"You must. Now go."

"I'll, uh, I'll take the pup to Hazel."

Faye could see the glistening of tears in Jimmy's eyes and feel the welling up in her own.

Well after dark Jimmy borrowed Buck's car and returned to Rock

Mountain. Once again he waded across the stream. He climbed the outside staircase to Miss Morgan's apartment. Hesitating for a few seconds he breathed deeply and knocked on the door.

"Who is it?" Faye asked.

"It's Jimmy. Let me in."

"No, Jimmy. I can't. I'm sorry. It is over. Now, go home."

"No! I'm staying."

She did not respond anymore. An hour later she opened the door to check. She saw him curled up and asleep. She covered him with a warm blanket and locked the door. In the morning he was gone. It was over.

Chapter 60

Father Adam Labarre was feeling increasingly apprehensive. He rode luxuriously in the back seat of Bishop Ryan's Cadillac which was being driven by John, a seminarian acting as a chauffeur. Just last week the bishop had called him into his office and assigned him an important position for which he felt ill-prepared. Only recently he had pledged his vows and had been duly ordained as a Catholic priest. He had not yet served as an assistant to an experienced clergyman. The bishop announced summarily that the newly ordained priest had been chosen by God to serve as the interim pastor of the Rock Mountain Catholic parish called Saint Matthew's. He was charged with the complete responsibility of providing the pastoral services to the faithful in this remote mining town. He had grown up in Albany, N.Y., and was very much a city boy.

The apprehension continued as they motored up the foothills. "Why don't you sit up front with me?" the seminarian asked.

"It is by the order of His Eminence, Bishop Ryan", the young priest replied a bit jokingly. "It is to impress the faithful and make my presence known. I suppose that soon tongues will be wagging. Do you know exactly where Saint Matthew's Church and the priest's residence are located?"

"Yes, Father. We can't miss it. I'll give you a complete tour of the town first of all, if that is okay."

"Yes, John, I'd appreciate that. There is supposed to be a housekeeper and cook there part time to help me out. There is no car for me yet, and I certainly can't afford to buy one."

"I don't think that you have to worry, Father. The bishop usually provides a junker at first for the young guys."

The tour took a little over an hour. This included looking at modest homes, the management's nicer homes, a few stores, the concentrator on the surface of the mine, the tall headframe with its pulleys, the office, the maintenance buildings, and several enormous piles of ore tailings. Father Labarre was amazed that the piles were so huge, realizing that all of this material was discarded substance that once had existed within the bowels of the Earth. When he commented on this to John, the seminarian responded, "Of course, that is not all of it because the real ore itself has been separated and made into sinter before being sent out by rail to Troy. Before that there was a blast furnace nearby. And before that, who knows. It's a very old mine. Then, too, a lot of the tailings are sold for road construction, for the railroad, and whatever else it is needed for."

"How do you know all of this stuff about the mine?"

"Ha! I worked here for one summer on the rock job. Do you see that string of rail cars headed toward that conveyor? That is where I worked."

"Yes, I see. There are men on top of some of them. What's going on?"

"The cars are loaded with slush coal. It's like coal sand. The loaded cars are stored on a siding which is at a little higher elevation. The men are dropping those cars down by gravity, and they are manning the brakes."

"It looks dangerous. Did you ever do that?"

"Oh, yes, Father, until I had an accident and knocked a loaded rail car off the tracks. I almost got killed. I know very well that someone important was on my side that day. That's when I started to think about the seminary. After that they gave me another job weighing trucks and their loads of sand or crushed rock. We made one kind of really fine sand which the steam locomotives used when the rails were slippery. There were hoppers near the drive wheels for traction."

"Maybe you should be the priest here instead of me. What are the people like?"

"Gosh, I don't know. They are like anywhere else, some good, some bad, I suppose."

"Can't you be more specific, John?"

"Well, some of the men drink a lot, a few of the women, too. Father Orgebin used to encourage them to take the pledge during Lent. Maybe it helped some. There is a lot of coarse language at the mine. There is usually at least one woman around who will offer her feminine charms to men for a fee."

"And how do you know about that, my young seminarian?" the priest asked jokingly.

"Remember, Father, I worked with these guys. Word gets around."

"Yes, I expect so. There were some allegations about Father Orgebin's relationship with boys. Was there any substance to that?"

"Uh, well, I think so."

"Think so? Open up."

"It wasn't just the boys. He liked young men as well. He would make sly suggestions to some of the guys, and later they would joke about it with one another. They called him Horny Orny. They knew that I was going to go to the seminary, and they tried to sic him on me."

"Is there any reason I should hear your confession, eh?" again speaking jokingly.

"Thank you, no. It didn't happen to me, thank God."

"'Thank God' indeed. The whole thing is incredible. It will make my job harder. Some people will suspect me. I hate being under suspicion."

"I don't think that will be a problem for you, Father. Of course, some folks with time on their hands may keep tabs on you for a while."

"What else should I know about Rock Mountain?"

"Well, most people are Catholic, and most are very good people. Many of them are second generation Poles and lots of other nationalities. I'm sure that many of them will be helpful to you and make you feel at home. You will be invited to Sunday dinner, kids' weddings, and all kinds of things. They will deliver cakes and pies to your house. You may gain some weight. There is Bingo, of course, but the men run that. The ladies put on a big ham dinner in late October. It is kind of a harvest supper. Some Sisters come to hold summer religious instruction for two weeks. Also, on Friday afternoon the kids walk over to the church for religious instruction and preparation for confirmation. I suppose that will be your responsibility for a while. Perchy Garew used to live nearby. He digs the graves for burials and looks after the cemetery. Before you know it, he will be inviting you to go fishing with him. I hear that he got married recently and moved to a farm close to Echo Lake. He still works at the cemetery as he is needed."

"It sounds like my work is cut out for me. I don't know how long I'll be here. Bishop Ryan said he is going to appoint a permanent priest later, and I'd become an assistant somewhere. If it is his wish, I believe I could stay here."

"Well, good luck and God be with you. Here's the priest's residence. Perchy always used to call it *"ze oblate"* or something like that. I'll help you bring in your luggage."

An hour later, Father Labarre was strolling down a path to the cemetery. He was reading his breviary and occasionally glancing at headstones. He noticed a young man bent over next to a grave. As the priest approached the spot he noticed that the man was actually an older teen-ager who was planting some flowers near a headstone. He watched a few minutes and then spoke, "Hello, I'm Father Labarre, the new priest. Is this a beloved relative of yours?"

"Hello, Father, I'm glad to meet you. Yes, this is the grave of David Coulbron. For sixteen years I thought he was my father, but actually, he wasn't. I finally found my real father a while back. Wait, I can't say it that way. David was a real father, too. I love them both. How can I explain this?"

"How about if you call one your biological father?"

"Maybe, but you see what I mean?"

"Don't worry, God knows that David was a saintly man."

"My mom's sister helped me buy this stone after our not-so-saintly man, Orgebin, had my wooden cross ripped down and chopped up."

Jimmy brushed the soil from his hands, and they shook hands firmly.

"What is your name, Son?"

"It is Jimmy LeTarte now, but it used to be Coulbron."

"That is very interesting. As soon as I get unpacked and settled in I would appreciate it if you could stop over at the parish house so we can become better acquainted. You are the very first person that I have met here. Do you belong to this parish, Son?"

"Well, sort of. You won't believe how mixed up my life has been the last two years."

"It is my job to listen, Son. Sorry, Jimmy, I shouldn't say 'Son'; you're almost as old as I am. They teach us to say that in the seminary. I was just ordained last week."

"Congratulations, Father, and, yes, I'd enjoy stopping by for a visit whenever you are available."

"I'm available right now, Jim. Anything special on your mind?"

"Yes, there are a lot of things bothering me. I'd like you to hear my confession. I stopped going to church when Father Orgebin was there. I didn't trust him."

"Of course. Let's go to the confessional in the church, and we can do that now."

"If it is okay with you, I'd like to do it right here. Nobody is around, and I'd like my old dad, David, to hear it." Tears formed on Jimmy's cheeks and began to flow. He wiped them away without embarrassment. "I'm sorry, Father, it's just that I loved him so much. Sometimes the sorrow is more than I can stand even though I know he is in Heaven."

Jimmy got on his knees and pressed the palms of his hands together the way the sisters had taught him to do during religious instruction. "Bless me Father, for I have sinned."

"You don't have to do that, Jimmy. Stand up. God wants you to let it all out and be cleansed."

The priest laid out his right hand and Jimmy stood up and grasped it with both of his. He trembled. "I've been holding too many things inside me for too long, and more things keep happening faster than I can control them."

Like a burst dam, the fears tumbled forth. "I killed a man. I had sex with a woman. I hit a teacher. I haven't been to mass in a long time. I'm a rotten, dirty bastard and a sinner." He squeezed harder on the priest's hand.

Father Labarre felt unprepared and unsure how to sooth the boy's torment. "Let's go sit down inside, Jim. David will hear us wherever we are." Jimmy followed the priest toward the residence. At that moment the priest's housekeeper came hurrying over from across the street. She lived in a concrete duplex which was owned by the mining company. She came close to the priest and curtsied.

"Father, I'm Hazel Manley, your housekeeper and cook. Would you like me to brew you some coffee or tea right now?" She ignored Jimmy.

"I am delighted to meet you Mrs. Manley. This is James LeTarte."

Father Labarre noted that her eyes suddenly opened wide and her lips parted slightly although she said nothing. "And, yes, I would really enjoy a good cup of coffee in about a half an hour, and make it strong. Later we can all get acquainted."

"Jim, do you think you could give me a tour of St. Matthew's right now?"

"Sure thing, Father, just follow me. Uh, it was nice seeing you again, Ma'am."

After Mrs. Manley entered the house and closed the door, Jimmy said, "I'll bet she's on the phone already."

"Why do you say that?"

"Well, she's a widow. Her husband was killed in a rock slide in the mines. The company gave her a place to live. She runs the teacherage right over there across from the school. And, of course, you know that she is your housekeeper. Anyhow, she thrives on all of the local gossip, especially about school and church matters. One teacher caught her snooping in the teacher's grade book. You will get to know her well. It's not my job to say anything, but it might be a good idea for you to keep personal letters and things safe."

"Why did she seem unhappy to see you?"

"Oh, it's partly because I'm a half-breed. Buck, my, uh, biological dad, was born on the Mohawk reservation. It's not far from here. Some 'good' people are quite prejudiced against us. She would have heard lots of versions of how and why I slugged Mr. Bascomb."

"You've graduated, right?"

"Yes, just this year. I'm eighteen now. I liked most of my teachers, but some voted against me when the school board had an expulsion hearing. I survived that though."

"Is this Mr. Bascomb still here?"

"No way! He got canned and spent time in the hospital."

"You sent him to the hospital?" asked the priest incredulously.

"No, not me. The school principal bashed the guy's knee with a baseball bat when he caught him stealing stuff in the school offices at night. It would be awfully hard for me to say that I'm sorry for Bascomb's problems."

"How did your problem with Mr. Bascomb start?"

"Oh, well. He was the most incompetent teacher I ever met. I disagreed with something he said, and he slapped me very hard in the side of my head. It made my teeth rattle. I didn't say a word to him right then. I don't know why, but I actually turned my other cheek to him, and he smacked that one even harder. That's when I got up and floored him. Then I got kicked out. After that he started telling lies about me. The principal and lots of teachers were on my side. They knew what a disaster of a teacher he was, and the school board wasn't going to re-hire him anyway.

"I see. Let's check out the church. Lead the way."

"The front door is rarely locked. Some of the old grandmas come in to pray."

The boy opened the right side of the huge door and held it open for the priest. Father Labarre blessed himself with holy water from the baptismal font and Jimmy did the same. The priest removed a quarter from inside his cassock and dropped it into the poor box. The priest's eyes glanced left toward the Stations of the Cross, then straight ahead at the altar. He noted a plaster statue of the Blessed Virgin to the right of the altar. She was wearing a pale blue cloak. Joseph, the carpenter, stood on the opposite side holding a tool. High above the altar one could see a religious saying inscribed in Latin. The boy knew how to read it but said nothing because he didn't want the priest to think that he was showing off. The confessional was built into the wall toward their right. Jimmy raised his eyebrows and pointed to it quizzically.

"No, Jim, we are friends already. Let's forget formalities. I would like you to just relax, and you can unload your burdens. We can sit in the front pew facing the Holy Sacraments."

"That's fine with me, Father."

They each genuflected at the altar and sat side by side in a pew.

"Jim, tell me why you think you killed someone."

"Oh, I killed him all right. It's a long story. I still say prayers for him and his family even though he was a bad man. I'm not sure how I should feel about it."

"Just give me the short version for now. You can explain all of it later."

"Okay, Father. Here goes. I was driving the car because three men beat up my father, and I fought with one of them to help my dad when we were in Dannemora. They followed us in their car and sideswiped us so we crashed into the river. Buck was knocked out and bleeding a lot. I dragged him to the far bank. The men came back and started shooting at us. It was dark and we hid. They left when someone else was coming on the highway. I stopped a truck, and the driver helped me bring Buck to Doctor Manvel's office here in Rock Mountain. Buck awakened then, and the doctor checked him over. Doctor Manvel had to set Buck's broken arm, and he plastered it and patched him all up. Doc Manvel thought at first that Buck should go to the hospital, but that's quite a ways away, and anyway he took care of everything. I brought my dad home and put him to bed. I was afraid the men might return so I stayed up all night and hid in the barn with my rifle. The men did come. They were carrying a can of gasoline. I knew that they were going to burn us to death. I fired some shots to scare them away. I didn't want to hit any of them. Somehow a bullet hit the can or close to it. Some sparks flew and soon flames were spreading all over the man."

"Did you see it happen?"

"Yes, it's something I'll never, ever, forget."

"Then what happened?"

"Buck and I were afraid that the police would arrest us, and we were afraid that the other men might come back so we hid out on the reservation where Buck was born. Finally a couple of months later the police did find us, but they knew the whole story by then, and they knew those guys were no good to begin with. They sort of covered for us, and we were never charged."

"What happened to the other men?"

"Prison."

"And how about your sex adventure? You don't have to go too deeply into that. It might embarrass me."

"Her name is Faye. I really, truly, still love her and probably always will. She is older than I am. She is pregnant right now with another guy's baby, and she is going back to marry him and raise their kid. I told her that I'd take care of her and the baby, but she wanted me to get a good education and marry a fine woman. She said she loved me, too, but she said that marriage now wouldn't be fair for me. Please don't think badly of her. Maybe someday I will meet her again."

"You know, Jim, sex is something that is going to happen to most men sooner or later. The time isn't important. What counts is love and commitment. And, also, the desire to do what is right. The reason God created sex was to insure the survival of the human species. It shouldn't be a game. I chose to forego that so I could better serve God."

"Gosh! You almost sound like my dad, Buck."

"How long have you known Buck?"

"Almost two years now. I'm embarrassed because I used to hate him, but I got over it. He really has helped me to grow up a lot."

"How about your mother?"

"She's dead. I'd rather not talk about that now, Father. Maybe later."

"So now, what are your plans?"

"I've been accepted in the medical school at McGill in Montreal. Dr. Manvel is helping me. I'll be much too busy to be chasing girls. I know what sex is like now. I also know that it has to be with love."

"I'm sure that you will be a fine doctor, Jimmy. It truly is a noble profession. I really don't think that you made too many bad decisions. When you get home say an Act of Contrition. Then say five 'Our Fathers' and five 'Hail Marys'. Now, I will give you my blessing. Then, you are absolved. Your sins are forgiven. That wasn't too bad, was it?"

"No, Father. Thank you. Oh, maybe when Perchy wants to go fishing with me again, do you want to join us?"

"Absolutely, Jim. Just give me a call. I don't know much about fishing, but I'm willing to learn. Do you drink coffee?"

"Uh, not much, but, like someone else I know, I'm willing to learn."

"Then it's settled. Let's go shake up Mrs. Whatshername so she can earn her keep, and, besides, we'll give her something to gossip about."

"I hope she doesn't poison my coffee."

"Don't worry. I'll switch cups with you."

All that summer a sense of camaraderie grew between the two young men. They did go fishing with Perchy at Echo Lake. Jimmy introduced him to Yvette, who plied both of them with molasses cookies and cheerful chatter. Father Labarre became a frequent visitor at the little farm of Buck, Alice, and Jimmy. On one occasion, the two friends drove to the reservation to visit with Cora and Bert where Father Labarre was happily introduced to venison.

Jimmy was driving Buck's old convertible now since Buck had the gift of the Roadmaster. On several occasions, Jimmy managed to return to the reservation. Then he would drive Aunt Cora to the movies and hunt with Uncle Bert. It pleased him to see that the Lincoln-Ford still ran well.

Eventually Bishop Ryan decided to replace Father Labarre with an older priest, and Jimmy's new friend was transferred to Saranac. They did continue their correspondence, however, and occasionally got together for old time's sake.

Chapter 61

When the pomp and circumstance was over, James C. LeTarte, M.D., mingled with the rest of the happy group of graduates who met with their family members and friends. He watched as fathers and mothers hugged their offspring and, with cameras flashing, immortalize those wearing black gowns and mortar boards. He savored his classmates' joy. He shook hands with his closest friends, those with whom he had shared seemingly endless hours of study at McGill University in Montreal.

One friend, Cedric Flynn, rushed over to him, beaming, "That was a great speech, James, my friend. Great speech. Don't forget my offer to join me in father's clinic. We could use a good doctor like you."

Professor Osgood, from whom James had taken a course in cardiology, tapped his shoulder and drew him to one side.

"Doctor LeTarte," he asked, "where are you doing your internship?"

"Oh, hello, Professor. I'm interning in Plattsburg and also with a family doctor at Rock Mountain in upstate New York."

"I wish you would change your mind about that. You are wasting your time becoming a G.P. The field of cardiology is growing by leaps and bounds. We are making fabulous new discoveries every year. You could be in on that."

"Yes, I know, and I would like to, but I have made promises. I have obligations."

"I understand. Do keep us in mind when you are ready."

"Thank you, Professor, and thank you for having me in your class."

"Some thanks also goes to you because I learn a great deal from my students, just as you will learn from your patients."

James smiled and told him he would give the offer thorough consideration. In truth, he envisioned his own small clinic with just his name on the shingle – either that or a white house with his office to one side of Dr. Manvel's in Rock Mountain.

These decisions would have to wait, though, because his internship as a general practitioner with the old doctor must be completed first. Doctor and Mrs. Manvel had told him they would attend his graduation and bring his little sister Sarah along as well. He searched for them among the crowd and was disappointed they had not arrived.

The young doctor wished his little sister could have come. She was eight years old and adored Jimmy. Unknown to him, Edith had tried unsuccessfully to get through by telephone to inform him that her husband had been suddenly called away for a meeting.

Mrs. Papineau was unable to travel very far any more, and, even so, Perchy Garew would have found the trip too difficult. He seldom drove his pick-up truck any distance greater than twenty miles. James wondered why he still sometimes referred to her as Mrs. Papineau, even though she and Perchy had been married for several years.

Most of all, he wished that Buck and Alice could have been there. They were so proud of him and so supportive. He recalled Buck's insistent way of challenging him when he was still a youth by saying, "You're as good as anyone else, Jim, better than most."

His brother Phil probably would have come if he hadn't been stationed so far away. Phil was a marine now – a drill instructor at Camp Lejeune. James felt happy that his brother had finally found a niche in life that suited him.

Suddenly the long repressed image of one other person that the young man longed to hold tightly flashed into his conscious mind. "Faye!" he whispered hoarsely. "If only Faye were here."

"What did you say?' demanded a matron next to him.

Doctor James LeTarte blushed and announced that he had to leave immediately.

"Strange young man," the woman said to her husband, wrinkling her nose.

He had already packed his belongings in the trunk of the Roadmaster – Buck's car but now his since the plane crash last year in Mexico. He had felt responsible at first – responsible for their death. After all, he was the one who encouraged them to take the vacation, and the memory of the Oedipus curse still lingered, although muted.

Buck's heart attacks had left him weakened and unable to work at a steady job. As a medical student, James had monitored his father's decline closely. When Alice suggested a winter vacation on the Mexican beaches, the young man knew that it was a now-or-never chance for them. Still, the sudden loss of his parents so far from home had been a shock that continued to pain him deeply, and it gave him the added responsibility for his half-sister.

When Buck and Alice's charred remains were being interred in a Plattsburg cemetery, James held Sarah's hand and helped her place a floral spray on each casket before they were lowered into the grave.

Both the Manvels and the Garews volunteered to care for the girl while Jimmy was away in college. He knew his sister would be safe and well-cared for in either house. They ended up sharing the girl during the school year, but she remained with her big brother in the summertime, much to their mutual delight.

The young doctor hastened as he departed the building and headed for his automobile. He exited the campus of McGill University and headed toward Sherbrooke Street. At the intersection he noticed a directional sign for Papineau Boulevard. He smiled because it reminded him that he would soon be seeing his old friend who made molasses cookies and wore flour-sack dresses.

He glanced toward the great lighted cross on Mont Royal, then turned left and headed across the Mercier Bridge which spanned the St Lawrence River before pointing him in the direction of home.

The engine of the automobile hummed monotonously as the young man thought of the homestead at Echo Lake. He recalled how he almost lost it to strangers during his senior year of high school. After months of not hearing from him, his brother Phil had appeared at the house. It was a Saturday, and Jimmy was home alone, Buck and Alice having decided to go for a drive.

The youth hadn't seen the car stop along the road next to the driveway that late September day, allowing his brother to exit before it drove off. Nor had he observed his brother hiking toward the house through the grove of maples resplendent as the sun shone through the orange and red foliage.

Jimmy was completely absorbed as he played his guitar in the living room. He hadn't heard the kitchen door open and close. Phil sneaked up close behind him, grabbed his shoulders, and shouted, "Gotcha!"

It had been over a year since the brothers had seen one another and nearly as long since Phil had written. Startled, Jimmy snapped his neck around, then jumped to his feet. He placed the guitar on the chair and grabbed Phil in a bear hug.

"Easy, little brother," said Phil. "You'll crush my ribs."

Jimmy's face was animated with happiness. He hugged his brother again before standing back to admire him. "Gosh! Phil, you look so much older. I can hardly believe it."

"You too, Jimmy. When I left you were a kid. Now you're a man."

"I don't know about that. I just finished high school."

"You're too smart already. When we were kids, I envied you. You got all the A's while I got C's and D's."

"I'm going to college soon, Phil. I want to become a doctor."

"Hey! That's great. But how are you going to afford it?"

"I'll have to work, of course, but Buck had offered to help. And you know what? Doc Manvel is helping, too. I've gotten to know him and his wife really well. They're the ones who encouraged me to go into medicine in the first place. How about you, Phil? What are your plans?"

"That's what I've come to talk to you about, Jimmy – serious talk. I need money."

"I can loan you some."

"No, I mean lots of money. I ran up some debts. If I don't pay these goons back soon, you may not have a brother."

"Can you tell me about it, Phil?"

"It's best if you don't know the particulars. Let's just say that after I got busted out of the service, I started working for some pretty tough customers. They trusted me with some of their dough, and I blew it gambling. Now, I'm on the run."

Jimmy looked worried. "You can't hide forever."

"That's for damn sure. They've got connections all over. It's only a matter of time before they come looking for me here. You may be in danger, too."

"I know a state police lieutenant who's a real nice guy. He helped us when Mom got hurt and Buck and I were in trouble."

"No way! No cops for me. I got trouble enough."

"If you pay the money back, will they leave you alone?"

"If I pay them back with enough interest, they will, but I've got to really make it worth their while."

"Where can you get that much money?"

"The only thing I've got is my half of this farm. If we could sell the farm in a hurry and split the money, I'd be in the clear."

"Gosh! I've never thought of selling the farm, but it is half yours. I think Buck and Alice will understand if I decide to sell it. I know they like living here, but they work in Plattsburg and commuting in the winter is no fun for them. Maybe they only stay because they know I like it here."

"They've been pretty good to you, haven't they?"

"I like them both a lot."

"I'm sorry I raised hell with you for living with this Buck character in our house. It's just that I was so damned mad at him and our mother for shacking up together."

"I know, Phil. I understand. I really do because I felt the same way at first until I began to know Mom's problems better. Buck really is my father, though, and he's been awfully good to me."

"I'm glad for you, Jimmy."

"Let's go visit Mom's grave tomorrow, then we can talk to a real estate agent."

"I'm living on borrowed time, Jimmy. I can't wait around."

"Well, then, we'll see her grave later."

"I haven't seen her since she threw me out of the house. How bad was it at the end?"

"Pretty bad. You wouldn't have recognized her."

"It's sad, isn't it? It's been hard for you because you were here all the time to watch it happen. I ran away."

"You had no choice. C'mon, Phil. I've got something to show you."

Jimmy led the way toward the shed which was attached to the barn. "Close your eyes," he said as they rounded the corner.

The brothers stood facing two old cars – Phil's Pontiac and Buck's convertible.

"I polished both cars this morning, Phil. What do you think?"

"Cripes! The Pontiac looks better than when I left."

"I don't run it any more except to charge the battery. I told you I'd take good care of it. It's all gassed up and ready to go." Jimmy reached his hand above a wooden beam, retrieved the car keys, and tossed them to his brother.

"No, I can't take them. I gave the car to you. I meant it."

"You'll need it Phil. Besides, I've got this one. It's Buck's old car. We had it repaired after we banged it up. He's got a big new Buick now. C'mon, start your car up and listen to her purr."

"O.K. And – don't worry about selling the farm."

Where will you go?"

"Canada. I remember some of that frog talk. I'll get a job as a chore boy in a dairy farm."

Jimmy fed his brother a good meal, gave him what cash he had, and hugged him good-bye.

Chapter 62

The young man had made the automobile trip between Echo Lake and Montreal so frequently since he began his university studies that he no longer had to think about route selection. He was able to anticipate each turn well in advance. He had his choice of several border crossings and often varied his route to avoid boredom. Even so, many of the border guards on both sides recognized the big Buick as it approached and frequently waved him through without inspection. This time he headed toward the town of Hemmingford, Quebec, with the intention of crossing the international boundary just north of Mooers, New York.

He was glad that traffic was light so that he could try to make good time. The misty rain that was falling, however, made the asphalt roads blacker than usual. With his headlights struggling to pierce the darkness, he activated the windshield wipers then, immediately, wished that he had not because the disintegrating collection of splattered night insects smeared the glass nearly to the point of obliterating his vision.

Rounding the curve, his right front tire veered from the safety of the pavement and ripped gravel from the shoulder of the road. Slow down, Jimmy Boy, he thought. Slow down or you'll be needing a doctor yourself.

A temperature inversion caused ground fog to form wherever the driver encountered a low spot. "Slow down some more, damn it! You're not using good sense." His eyes burned from the glare of the road and from the strain of too little sleep.

James opened the front windows of the Buick to admit a flow of fresh air. He rotated the radio knob and punched the first button. The speaker filled the car with music from the Glenn Miller orchestra. "Long ago and far away, I dreamed a dream one day..."

Immediately, the memory of the night he spent with Faye welled up inside him. "Thrills run up and down my spine..."

He felt a swelling in his throat. A long time ago, he thought. So very long ago. I wonder how she is..."and then I knew that all I longed for was you."

Knock it off, Stupid. She's a married woman with a kid. I wonder if she even remembers me. Maybe I was just one more little interlude for her. Maybe she's just like my mom, and I'm a fool for thinking otherwise.

One year ago and nearly two hundred miles farther south, Faye Morgan sat uneasily on the sofa of the apartment she shared with her husband Ronald and their daughter. She didn't like the way he stared at the girl while she was in the bathtub, nor the way he insisted on being the one to dry her body with a towel afterward. It worried her.

There were other things that worried her – his excessive drinking, for instance, and the way he forced her to comply with his demands by twisting her arm. Equally unfortunate, he had not permitted her to return to teaching.

Faye did remember the evening she spent with Jimmy. She remembered it with stark clarity. She thought of him often and wondered why she could not have found some way to erase their age difference, although it was small. She worried about him and often inquired about him in her letters to Edith Manvel.

The young doctor's left leg cramped from driving. He was glad that Buck's old car had an automatic transmission.

As he drove steadily along, young Dr. LeTarte recalled an incident that happened during his senior year in high school. When he had been in school Jimmy had often relived old memories in detail. As an adult this still persisted. Something he thought he had forgotten reappeared quite vividly.

His illness had started out simply enough – rather like a bad cold. Jimmy's stomach started to feel queasy right after lunch at school, and he wondered if he had eaten something spoiled. Then the headache came and the need to vomit. He excused himself from class and headed for the boys' lavatory. Inside, three sophomores were puffing alternately on the same cigarette. They listened as Jimmy retched violently in one of the stools. They smirked at one another.

"What's the matter, LeTarte? You been smelling too much senior cunt lately?"

Jimmy didn't respond. His face was bathed in perspiration, and he felt the need to evacuate his bowels.

"Jeez, now he's blasting the can loose. I can't stand the smell. I'm getting outta here."

"Getting so you can't enjoy a smoke no more around here. Let's go."

Jimmy was relieved to hear them start to leave. One of them kicked the metal door of the toilet with his boot on the way out.

Sophomores, he thought, *sophos moros* from the Greek. Well, the name fits these three 'wise fools'.

In the corridor he noticed the same three boys leaned up against the wall with Mr. Wagner, the principal, yelling at them. "Get down there and give me fifty push-ups."

Jimmy walked over and touched the man's shoulder. "I think I should go home, Mr. Wagner."

The principal stared at the beads of perspiration on his face and his blanched appearance.

"Okay, LeTarte. No, wait. Go see Doc Manvel first. There's some really bad stuff going around. You got your car, or do you want me to take you?"

"I can make it alone and thanks."

"Take care of yourself, LeTarte. You, Petarsky! Who told you to slough off? Keep that body pumping or I'll have you start over from scratch."

Sometimes Mrs. Manvel served as her husband's nurse. Such was the case when Jimmy pressed the doorbell. "Oh, James," she said. "Is this a social call, Dear?"

"No, Ma'am. I'm not feeling very good."

"Um, yes, I see. Come in and lie on this cot. The doctor is with a patient. I'll take your temperature."

"I'll be okay, Mrs. Manvel. It's probably something I ate. You don't have to fuss."

"Young man, it is my job to fuss, as you call it. The doctor will be with you in a few minutes. Now take off your shirt." She snapped a thermometer to rejoin the streaks of quicksilver and placed the instrument under the lad's tongue.

Jimmy watched as an ample woman in a black dress knotted a babushka under her chin and pulled on her coat. When Dr. Manvel stepped out of his office, the patient spoke to him in broken English, then said something that sounded like *"Dubja, Dubja"* and left.

The youth started to rise.

"No, no. Just lay yourself back, James. I'm still capable of bending."

He slid a wooden stool next to the cot, sat down, and checked Jimmy's pulse and blood pressure. He retracted an eyelid and observed it. He scoped each of his ears. Mrs. Manvel handed her husband a tongue depressor.

"His temperature is 103, doctor."

"James, I want to watch this closely, and I don't want you driving home alone. When can your father come to pick you up?"

"Not until five-thirty."

'Edith, you keep the boy comfortable here until then and call his father when he gets home. Take his temperature every half hour and have him drink plenty of water – no food."

"Yes, Doctor."

In one way Jimmy felt he was imposing on them, yet waves of nausea that struck him made him glad that someone was there who cared about him and was willing to help.

"Doctor, there will be patients coming and going through this room all afternoon. Perhaps the boy would be more comfortable on our living room sofa."

"That's fine, Edith."

The woman held Jimmy's arm snuggly as she helped him through the doorway and into the living quarters of the house. She fluffed a pillow for him and bade him to stretch out, then removed his shoes. She bathed his face with a cool cloth and handed him a glass of water. She arranged a small commode and a basin next to the sofa, then darkened the room by pulling shut the drapes. Dr. Manvel appeared shortly, examined him thoroughly, and diagnosed Jimmy as having influenza.

Within moments the boy dozed off but fitfully as though his mind was churning through the past. Mrs. Manvel checked on him frequently and twice overheard him whisper, "Faye, where are you Faye?"

When the woman bathed his face again, his eyelids fluttered and he smiled blissfully.

Edith Manvel hummed an old melody as she left Jimmy's side and tip-toed up the stairs toward a telephone. She reached the long-distance operator and gave her a number to call. She continued to hum as she listened to the ring on the other end of the line.

A woman's voice answered, "Hello?"

"Faye, dear, is that you?"

"Yes, Edith. How are you?"

"Oh, I'm fine, but there is a young friend of yours downstairs who is not well. He's asleep now and calling out for you."

"It's Jimmy! What's wrong with him?"

"The doctor believes it's influenza. We will have to wait and see."

"Oh, good Lord, Edith. What have I done? I've probably ruined his life."

"Now, you just relax, Dear. Let's take care of the physical problems first, and if I know this young man, there will be no lasting psychological problems. I will keep you informed of his progress."

"Edith, I'm coming to see him."

"No, Dear, not yet, and certainly not here in Rock Mountain, especially in your condition."

"Of course, you're right. Edith, I love him so much. What am I going to do?"

"Nothing for the moment, Dear. These things take time. Now, trust me. And one more thing – you never told me the whole story. Is James the father of your child?"

"No, Edith, but God, how I wish he were!"

At Hemmingford the fog thickened, and James was forced to slow down even more. He crept past the Canadian customs and eased up to the window on the American side. The agent recognized him and was about to wave him through, but the young man pulled over to one side to stretch his legs and rest his eyes.

He recognized Al Roussy and walked over to his booth to visit, knowing that there would be few travelers this evening.

"Hi, Al, I see you've pulled the night shift."

"Yeah, and it's deader than hell. You want some coffee, Jim?"

"I'd love some. I can hardly stay awake."

"What brings you south tonight?"

"Well, I graduated today, and there are people I want to see."

"So, you're a full-fledged doctor now, eh?"

"Not quite. I have to intern for a while before I'm on my own."

"You gonna practice here in the North Country?"

"I think so – at least for a few years, anyway. We'll see what happens."

"Where is it you studied, I forget?"

"McGill. In Montreal."

"Oh, yeah. I think there's a couple other docs around here who went there. Must be a good place."

"Sure is! Good and close by."

"I was sorry to hear about your old man's accident. That's too bad."

"Thanks, Al."

"He had a little girl, didn't he? Who takes care of her?"

"I do in the summertime – Mrs. Manvel and Mrs. Papineau do when I'm not around."

"When you getting yourself a wife? A young, good-looking doctor like you will always have women beatin' his door down day and night." The man laughed and slapped his knee. "I'd sure like a problem like that. My old woman's pretty good in bed, though. One's supposed to be enough, but who am I to say? I think you're smart to wait until all of your schoolin' was finished. Now, you can take your pick. And you can take it from somebody who knows that looks ain't everything."

"Thanks for the advice and the coffee. Now I've got to make tracks for home. You won't be seeing the Buick through here so much anymore."

"Good luck to you, Doc."

The young man flicked on the car lights and headed for Echo Lake, and for home.

Chapter 63

When he reached the village of Mooers, Doctor LeTarte turned east along the valley of the Chusy River. At Ellendale Corners he took a left turn onto Plank Road. He recalled that once Perchy Garew had told him that the road actually used to be covered with wooden planks part of the way and that when he was a young man, he had a job as a teamster hauling wagon loads of charcoal from the kilns near Echo Lake to forges and blacksmith shops in Ellendale and beyond.

He turned again and headed into the mountains. He could sense the mixed feelings of joy and sadness the closer he came to Echo Lake – joy to be back to his roots and sadness that many of those closest to him could no longer be found there. Tomorrow he would visit with the Garews and say some silent words over the grave of David, but tonight he would spend alone with the spirits of the house.

Just as James approached the lake from the east, the gray skies began to clear and, although it hid from time to time, a three-quarter moon mirrored itself in the water before breaking up into a thousand stars that created a sparkling path pointing directly home. He slowed the automobile and eased it onto the shoulder of the highway, then stopped. With the headlights extinguished, he surveyed the world of his youth. Rock Mountain still rose up straight ahead. To the south-east, near Deep Inlet, there was a low pass, and in that pass the tip of Whiteface Mountain showed itself. Chateau Mountain stretched to the south like the rounded back of a gigantic boar.

The young doctor got out of the car to relieve the pressure on his bladder. Feeling as though he had been transported backward in time, he felt himself a boy again and, as boys are wont to do, decided to leave his mark. With a smirk on his face and with deliberate aim, he wrote the letters 'JC' in the sand on the shoulder of the road. Then with ammunition remaining, added a capital 'L' and dotted all three.

He glanced up at Coulbron's Mountain – his mountain – and relived for a few moments the day that marked his march toward adulthood. Vaguely, when the light of the moon was brightest, he could see the cliff he had descended naked and shook his head at the naiveté of youth.

Hurrying home, he drove past the shallow river where he and Buck had been forced off the highway by his mother's attackers years earlier. When the low, scudding clouds permitted, the moon continued to wink at him as though sending a coded message.

He drove past the house where his school friend Clarence used to live. Clarence was married now and worked as a prison guard in Dannemora. James remembered the old stories of guard brutality toward prisoners and knew as a result of his friend's letters that now, with new administration, things were changing.

The hill where he and Phil had wrecked David's car rose into view and, involuntarily, James' tongue rubbed his upper molars whose cusps had been chipped off in the roll-over. Driving past the one-room school house, he wondered if it might still be used by students and if there were still bullies like Billy Ducharme who needed to be set straight. He thought of the dime he had lost in the sand of the pitcher's mound in the school yard and hoped that a student had found it and spent it.

I'll have to paint the house this summer, he thought. It looked rather shabby last year. David would never let it go that long without repainting. I wonder if I should change the color this time. I'll ask Sarah what color she would like.

When the Coulbron house came into view, James was surprised to see the porch light on, but then remembered that he had written to the Garews and told them of his pending arrival. Then he knew that

Perchy would have volunteered to prepare things for him by switching on the water pump and completing other tasks. He remembered, too, that the old French-Canadian preferred to be called by his given name, Medor.

The young man backed the trunk of the car close to the porch to facilitate unloading and switched off the ignition. He walked across the porch and attempted to unlock the door but found it unsecured. The familiar odor of food cooking surprised him. In the darkness of the kitchen he felt along the wall for a switch but, before he could reach it, the lights flashed on.

He squinted from the sudden brightness and opened his mouth in astonishment as several loud voices shouted, "Surprise!"

Yvette squealed, "Jimme-e-e!" and enveloped him in a hug. Medor and Clarence each pumped his hand and squeezed his shoulders. Clarence's wife, Mae, smiled as she greeted him. Looking splendid in full uniform, Sergeant Philip Coulbron spoke in mock brashness, "Straighten those shoulders! Suck in that gut, Doc! You look worse than a civilian."

James hugged each of them in turn and wiped a tear from his cheek.

"*Venons!* Come, right now," shouted Mrs. Garew. "We go to eat in *zee salle à manger*. Me and Medor, us, we 'ave ever'ting all ready."

He stared incredulously at the roasted turkey and the mounds of other food.

"*Asseyons!* Ever'body sit. Jimmee, you sit 'ere by me so I fatten you up. You a pretty man, all right, but you much too skinny. Women, zem, zey like a man wit' some fat on his *fesse*. I fix zat for you."

Jimmy stared at Medor and knew that she was right. Since his marriage to the former Mrs. Papineau, his old friend had rounded out considerably. The man winked and passed him the potatoes.

Eyes turned as a small, dark-haired girl padded barefoot into the room. She wore a long nightgown and James immediately recognized the floral print pattern of the garment as being the same as that worn by Mrs. Garew that evening. So, she is still sewing with feed sacks. Well, good for her, he thought.

The daughter of Buck and Alice, James' half-sister, rubbed her eyes and squinted at the group of people surrounding the table. Suddenly, she focused on her brother and rushed to him. She climbed onto his lap and snuggled into his shoulder. James kissed her cheek and whispered soothing words into her ear.

"Ah, *ma mignonette*," said Mrs. Garew, "she love her *grand frère* so much, she talk of him ever'day. She call me her 'Grand'mere' and Medor, him, is 'Gran'pere'. We love her *beaucoup*.

"Well, Jimmy, it's just like you've already got a daughter, so you better start looking around for a wife."

"Don't rush me, Phil. One of these days I'll find what I'm looking for. What about you, Gyrene?"

"No women for me, Jim. I'm married to the Marines, and that suits me fine."

The little girl, Sarah, dozed off almost immediately. James carried her to a day bed, covered her with a blanket and brushed his lips against her forehead before returning to the table. "Don't worry ever'body, she sleep sound like ever'ting. We eat now. Jimmee, you have more turkey and gravy. I fatten you up good. Soon, you look just like Medor."

"You tell me, Jimmee," announced Medor, "when you want to take the *fille* for a 'orseback ride. Me, I 'ave the 'orse all readee for you. Zey gettin' too lazee, dem 'orses. Zey need to be ridden, zem."

"That's great, really great, Medor. Maybe Phil would like to ride also."

"No can do, Jimmy. I'm heading back in the morning. We've got a new bunch of green recruits coming in this week, and it's my job to scare the pants off 'em."

"I'll bet you are good at that 'Hup, two, three, four' jazz, Phil."

"Yeah, it's pretty easy, though. A lot of it is a big act. We keep 'em scared and keep 'em hopping. Most of these young guys actually like discipline, and they know it's good for them and good for the Corps."

"I've always felt guilty about never serving in the military, Phil."

"It's not your fault. You couldn't because you had a little girl to look after. Besides, there's lots of ways a guy can serve his country. Being a doctor is one of them."

"I wouldn't feel bad about it," said Clarence. "I was stationed in Korea during the conflict and darn near got my head shot off. I never did figure out what in heck we were supposed to be doing there. Some of my best buddies never made it home."

"Maybe you come to fish wit me pretty soon, Jimmee. Ze trout, zem, zey bite good now and *zee barbotte, aussi*," said Medor.

"Yes, sure, but what's a barbotte?"

"Ah, zee barbotte, him. He is zee black one wiz zee whisker. You and me, we catch lots of zem at night. *Ben ouais,* zey taste real good."

"Oui, oui, oui, Jimmee, you go wiz Medor and catch *beaucoup de poissons.* I fry zem for you wit' lot of grease."

"Uh, thanks, Mrs. Garew."

"Jimmee after me and Medor wash all the dish, you want I bring *la petite fille* home wit' us so you get zee good sleep in *zee matin*?"

"No, thank you, Mrs. Garew. I can manage alright. Phil, you're spending the night, aren't you?"

"You betcha, but I've got to get up fairly early."

"Clarence and I will help clean up," said Mae. "Jimmy, you can check on Sarah."

"Hold on everybody," said Phil. "this Marine knows all about K.P. duty. I'm helping, too."

James gently lifted his sister and carried her to a bedroom. She awakened as he lay her down. She hugged his neck and kissed him. "I'm so glad you're home again, Jimmy. I love you."

"I love you, too, sweetheart. Go to sleep now because we have a big day ahead of us tomorrow."

She dozed off almost immediately. James walked to the window and gazed out toward the barn and chicken coop. These structures were no longer inhabited except for the ghosts of the creatures he once knew so well.

He thought of his two fathers, David and Buck, and wondered how he could have been so lucky. He thought, too, of the moral transformation that Buck had achieved. A whisper, barely discernible, escaped from his lips, "If not for them, where would I be now?" Then, he thought about the other significant people in his life and knew he owed them a great deal.

The moon rose higher in the sky, but stray scraps of ragged clouds whipped by it, brightening and darkening the landscape alternately.

Chapter 64

The marriage between Faye Morgan and Ronald had become increasingly rocky, and a separation was imminent. Ronald's new girlfriend made it perfectly clear that she had no intention of raising another woman's brat. When her divorce became final, Faye petitioned to have her legal name returned to Morgan. Her daughter, Cara, was now almost nine and was the image of her mother. The girl slept now curled up in the rear seat of Edith Manvel's automobile. The doctor's wife, having consented to have cataract surgery, felt more competent while driving and her husband worried less.

The Manvels had maintained a close relationship with Jimmy LeTarte as he pursued his studies at McGill. Edith had kept up her correspondence with Faye and had invited her to join them in welcoming Jimmy home following his graduation from medical school. Perchy Garew had made a special trip in his pick-up to inform the Manvels of the party they had planned. Faye could not help but feel apprehension as well as sensing a tingling of joy. Edith was well aware of the attraction between Faye and her former student. Now she sensed the emotion building in the younger woman.

"Suppose he doesn't remember me?" Suppose he hates me?" Faye asked, her mouth dry and trembling.

"I wouldn't be concerned about that, Dear."

"Stop the car and turn around, I can't face him."

"Don't be silly. You sound like a schoolgirl. I'm not trying to be a matchmaker, Faye. Besides, you owe it to him."

"What if he has a girlfriend?"

"He doesn't. Now just relax. We are almost there." Having been a nurse, Edith knew how to be insistent as well as being able to calm fears.

The house came into view and Edith slowed down. Faye shivered involuntarily and then tensed up. “I’m afraid, Edith.”

“Just hope that you don’t give him a heart attack when he sees you.”

The two women approached the porch. At the steps, Faye slowed and then stopped and remained out of sight. Edith urged her forward by gesturing with her whole head. Edith knocked on the door. They could hear the sounds of merriment.

Jimmy opened the door. Edith moved closer and stood in the opening. They hugged. Edith whispered in Jimmy’s ear, “I brought someone to see you.” Then she stepped back so he could see.

Faye stepped forward, and the two stood face to face.

“My God!” Jimmy said hoarsely as he closed the door behind him. “Faye,” he cried.

“Excuse me,” said Edith, speaking with pretend irritation. “I’d like to meet the people inside if I may. Heavenly days, Jimmy, have you no manners?”

Jimmy took Faye’s hand and led her to a bench on the deck of the porch. Silently, they clung to one another. Finally Faye spoke, “Come with me to the car. I need your help.”

Jimmy looked inside the car window. “What’s her name?” he asked.

“This is my Cara. She is almost nine. I’ve left Ronald for good. I should never have gone back to him.”

“Come on. We’ll carry her to bed,” Jimmy whispered as he led the way into his old home. He held the young girl tightly to his chest but said nothing. Faye followed closely behind him. Each person in the room diverted his or her eyes toward the couple and the child. The room was hushed.

People whispered and wondered. “I knew it,” one said.

“No,” another one said incredulously.

“Is zat *zee femme* and *zee bebe* of Jimmee? Yvette asked.

Her husband whispered, *“Peut-être,* but I don’t know, me. He did not tell me anyzing about zat.”

Hearing the quizzical mumbling from those gathered, Faye and Jimmy looked at one another with a wink and a smirk on their faces and continued up the stairs.

They entered Sarah's room. She was sound asleep. Jimmy noted a veil of perspiration on her brow and pulled back one of her blankets. Inwardly he smiled at the rhyming of their names. "We'll see what Sarah and Cara think about each other when they awaken in the morning together in bed."

Faye selected one of Sarah's flour sack nighties and placed her daughter in bed next to Sarah. She and Jimmy stood side by side admiring the scene. They interlocked their arms.

"They are like angels," Jimmy whispered.

Faye broke the trance by asking, "Jimmy?"

"Yes, Faye?"

"I'm so proud of you now, but after each time I spoke to Mrs. Manvel about you by phone, I cried for hours. I wanted so badly to come to your side, but Edith said that I should wait for you. It seemed like an eternity before she invited me here for your graduation party. Much earlier Ronald sensed that something was wrong, and he pushed me around a lot."

"I'm in pretty good shape now. You want me to break his arm for you?"

"Not a bad idea, but he is not worth it."

Slowly Jimmy asked, "Do you have any plans now?"

"I thought that you would never ask. I've taken a teaching job in Plattsburg."

"That's only twenty miles away!" He squeezed her arm, and she retaliated lovingly.

"Do you believe in destiny?" Jimmy asked.

"Every day of my life, my darling."

THE END

CPSIA information can be obtained at www.ICGtesting.com
Printed in the USA
BVOW08s1040161013

333881BV00001B/3/P